The Hangings

By
Jarosław Marek Rymkiewicz

Translated by:
Mateusz Julecki

The Hangings
by Jarosław Marek Rymkiewicz
Translated by Mateusz Julecki
Cover from Jan Piotr Norblin
This edition published in 2022
The map of Warsaw is based on the 1820 map of the city

Winged Hussar is an imprint of:

Winged Hussar Publishing, LLC
1525 Hulse Rd, Unit 1
Point Pleasant, NJ 08742

Copyright © Winged Hussar Publishing
ISBN 978-1-950423-82-8 HC
ISBN 978-1-950423-83-5 Ebk
LCN 2022932290

Bibliographical References and Index
1. History. 2. Poland. 3. Kosciuszko Revolt

Winged Hussar Publishing, LLC All rights reserved
For more information
visit us at www.wingedhussarpublishing.com

Twitter: WingHusPubLLC
Facebook: Winged Hussar Publishing LLC

This publiction has been supported by the © POLAND translation Program

THE TABLE OF CONTENTS

THE HANGINGS – A HISTORICAL NOTE

The Hangings takes place in Warsaw in 1794 at a pivotal time in Polish history. Mr. Rymkiewicz presents a series of essays about what was happening (primarily in Warsaw) during this critical period of history, recreating parts of the city for the reader. This was at a time when the Reign of Terror was heating up in the French Revolution and both Russia and Prussia were concerned about radicals on their doorstep. Some historians have even argued that the events in Poland helped save the French Revolution by diverting reactionary armies to Poland-Lithuania,

Prussia, Russia and Austria had reasons to keep the politics of the Commonwealth in chaos. None of them wanted a strong Poland on their borders and each had taken the opportunity to make use of Polish-Lithuanian resources for their own good, but were not prepared at first to start carving it up. Eventually in 1772 Poland-Lithuania was partitioned for the first time by Austria, Russia and Prussia.

From 1772 to 1791 the Polish-Lithuanian Commonwealth attempted to reform itself. In the late 1780's the Commonwealth started to reform the army in the hope of joining the Russians in fighting the Turks to renew their national spirit. When that didn't materialize, the Reformist took the opportunity with Russia's involvement in wars with the Turks and the Swedes allowing them to reform the state through a series of measures that resulted in the 3 May Constitution in 1791 – the first written constitution in Europe, creating the "Commonwealth of Two Nations".

The reformers, known as "The Patriotic Party", came from different sections of society and touched on all aspects of the nation. The primary movers were the King Stanisław Poniatowski, Hugo Kołłątaj, Count Stanisław Małachowski, Count Roman Potocki, Stanisław Staszic and Scipione Piattoli. They represented a cross-section of society from the Conservative King to the radical reformers under Kołłątaj (Kołłątaj's Forge). To ensure the sejm was allowed to vote on it the King's nephew, Prince Józef Poniatowski made sure the city guard was in place to stop any disruptions.

They were opposed by the more conservative "Hetman's Party" who were against reform and pro-Russian in their outlook. The

Hetman refers to the commanding generals of the Polish and Lithuanian armies and their leaders included the Hetmans Franciszek Ksawery Branicki and Seweryn Rzewuski as well as Stanisław Szczęsny Potocki and Kazimierz Nestor Sapieha. They opposed the reforms on different levels, especially as it would affect their "Golden Freedoms".

The Constitution increased the size of the army, expanded the enfranchisement of the populace, streamlined the government, and created a modern constitutional monarchy. Upon the cessation of the Wars with the Swedes and the Turks, Russia was invited to invade the Commonwealth to overthrow the Constitution and restore the old order. This was facilitated by the Confederation of Targowica made up of members of the Hetman's Party.

The resulting invasion became the *War to Protect the Constitution* from May to July 1792. While the Commonwealth's forces were outnumbered, they were able to fight the Russian forces to a stand-still, until the king lost heart and threw his support to the Hetman Party's Targowicia Confederation which sought to undo the reforms. The army was halted in the southeastern part of the country as an armistice was declared, resulting in the second partition with both Russia and Prussia taking huge parts of the country. The execution of Louis XVI in September 1792 further reinforced the position of the reactionary governments, led by Catherine in Russia to stamp out, "revolutions".

In the spirit of Polish resistance, the reformers planned a national uprising against this new partition, but while the army was being demobilized, some units were incorporated into the occupying forces. General Antoni Madaliński refused to demobilize his command and marched on Kraków, taking the leaders of the uprising by surprise and forced Tadeusz Kościuszko to rush back from Paris. This led to uprisings against Russian troops garrisoned around the country.

On 4 April, Polish troops under Kościuszko which included scythe bearing peasants defeated a Russian force at Racławice. On 17 April the Russian troops attempted to arrest conspirators and disarm the Polish garrison in Warsaw. On Holy Thursday when Russian troops were unarmed on their way to church, many were overwhelmed. Troops and the citizens not only attacked the occupying Russians, but also sought vengeance against traitors – especially the leaders of Targowice. After two days of fighting the Russian troops were forced to leave the city. On 23 April a similar uprising was started in Vilnius by Jakub Jasinski.

This was the closest to a Jacobin uprising outside of Paris and aside from attacking occupying forces the following action was taken against these high profile individuals:

Stanisław Szczęsny Potocki was the Marshal of the Targowice Confederation. He was sentenced to death, but never apprehended. Instead, on September 29, 1794, his portrait was hanged. In 1795 he was rewarded by Catherine the Great with the Russian Order of Alexander Nevsky and the rank of Général en chef.

Józef Ankwicz a diplomat in the pay of Austria was convicted of treason and sentenced to hanging on 9 May 1794.

Karol Boscamp-Lasopolski who was the Chamberlin of the King and in the service of Russian diplomats. He was active behind the scenes of the Confederation and hanged June 28, 1794.

Franciszek Ksawery Branicki, was the Crown Grand Hetman. Sentenced to death during the Kościuszko Uprising, but never apprehended. Having emigrated to Russia, he died at Belaya Tserkov, 1819.

Szymon Marcin Kossakowski was the Grand Hetman of Lithuania. Hanged in Wilno on April 25, 1794, during the Kościuszko Uprising.

Józef Kazimierz Kossakowski, Bishop of Livonia and on the Russian payroll. Hanged May 9, 1794, in Warsaw during the Kościuszko Uprising.

Ignacy Jakub Massalski, Bishop of Vilnius. Hanged June 28, 1794, in Warsaw during the Kościuszko Uprising.

Piotr Ożarowski, Crown Grand Hetman, convicted of treason and sentenced to hanging on 9 May 1794.

Feliks Potocki was never apprehended; his portrait was hoisted on the gallows instead.

Seweryn Rzewuski, Field Hetman of the Crown. Sentenced in absentia by the Supreme Criminal Court to death and the confiscation of his estates. Executed in effigy on 29 September 1794.

Józef Zabiełło, Field Hetman of Lithuania. Convicted of treason and sentenced to hanging on 9 May 1794.

In May 1794, Kościuszko issued the "Proclamation of Polaniec" which partially abolished serfdom and granted civil liberties to the peasants. Throughout the summer Polish-Lithuanian troops had mixed results in battle and eventually the Prussian and Russian forces began to pour troops into the country. At the battle of Maciejowice in October, Kościuszko was defeated, wounded and captured.

On 4 November Russian forces broke through the defenses of Praga, outside of Warsaw, and carried out a massive sack of the city resulting in approximately 20,000 deaths. On 16 November, Warsaw surrendered.

We have use a map of Warsaw from the 1820's to headline the appropriate chapters to show where the actions described there in took place.

ABOUT JAROSŁAW MAREK RYMKIEWICZ'S *THE HANGINGS* by *Maciej Urbanowski*

1.

The Hangings (*Wieszanie*) by Jarosław Marek Rymkiewicz is one of the most important Polish books of the 21st century. Published in 2007, it immediately aroused heated discussions and disputes. They involved not only literary critics and readers of belles-lettres, but also historians, sociologists, philosophers, political scientists, and finally – which does not happen often - politicians. In one of the debates on Rymkiewicz's book, even the then Marshal of the Sejm of the Republic of Poland spoke out! In the Warsaw magazine *44* it was noted: "*Hangings* and *The Hangings* are talked about today in the media and at university, in the pub and at the family dinner table. Throughout all cases and with the most diverse intentions, people are constantly conjugating: 'I am hanging', 'are you hanging?', 'hang!'".

A kind of crowning achievement for the extraordinary career of Rymkiewicz's book was honoring it in 2008 with the Józef Mackiewicz Literary Award, one of the most important in Poland. Its patron was a great Polish emigrant prose writer who was famous for his non-conformism, also in the way in which he saw the history of Poland and the world in the 20th century. Mackiewicz's words - "Only the truth is interesting" - are the justification given by the jury in awarding the award which carries his name. Including the one awarded to *The Hangings*.

2.

The significance of Rymkiewicz's book was to some extent determined by an important and at the same time separate position that its author occupied in Polish literature from the mid-1950s.

At the time *The Hangings* were published, its author was already 72 years old. He was born in 1935 in Warsaw. His father, Władysław, was the author of historical novels, which he published under the pseudonym Rymkiewicz. He changed his surname Szulc, inherited from his German ancestors, in 1947, not wanting to associate himself with a nation that had committed terrible crimes during the recent war. This, of course, also changed the surname of his only son.

"I belong to the first generation that this [communist - MU] system could influence in its educational efforts," said Jarosław Marek Rymkiewicz years later. Brought up in the milieu of the liberal intelligentsia, the author of *The Hangings* thus attended a model Marxist school, was a member of the communist *Union of Polish Youth* and walked with red flags during the May 1st processions. However, he quickly lost the illusion as to the nature of the totalitarian system imposed on Poland by the Soviet Union. The reading of books by emigrant writers, especially Czesław Miłosz, which were banned in the country, contributed to this. The year 1956 was also important, when after the recent death of Joseph Stalin there was a short moment of freedom, then called *The Thaw*. During this time – to be precise: in 1957 - the first collection of Rymkiewicz's poems, *Conventions* (*Konwencje*), was also published.

The title was not accidental, because in the next volumes of poems and in the accompanying essays, the young poet will defend conventions in literature, i.e. patterns and symbols inherited from tradition. He rejected the avant-garde, but also Marxist, mythology of progress that "everything humanity has gone through is to be discarded as a horrible dustbin of history". He was also alien to the vision of beauty gained at the cost of rejecting, ridiculing, and even invalidating dead writers. "When I started writing - he recalled years later - basically everything that I did [...] came from resistance to the liquidation of the past".

As a result, Rymkiewicz was quickly recognized as the leading representative of modern classicism in Polish poetry. Critics wrote about a changed classicism, tragic, permeated with death and the Baroque, which toughens up its faith in the order in the "furnace of doubt". Rymkiewicz himself will not polemize with this. He will publish a volume-manifesto *What is Classicism* (*Czym jest klasycyzm*), the first sentence of which was: "The poet writes down that which is ancient and constantly returning". He then included Thomas Stearns Eliot, Carl Gustav Jung, Osip Mandelstam, Ezra Pound, and Miłosz among his mentors. In his poems he maintained a constant dialogue with old poets and philosophers. He reached out to Plato, Spinoza, and Heidegger, and updated the poems of Polish Baroque poets.

In the following decades, Rymkiewicz's output grew significantly. The writer published not only subsequent collections of poetry, but also comedies, essays, translations, and even novels. His biographical books, the heroes of which were great Polish writers, were a surprise. The first volume of the series devoted to Adam Mickiewicz was called *Żmut*, which in the old Polish meant a "tangle" of hair which is difficult to comb. The biographies mentioned above were such tangles - ostentatiously "unkempt" because they avoid chronology, were subjective, destroying "combed" legends, revising and demythologizing them by revealing dark, poorly researched, or shamefully hidden fragments of the biographies of great artists.

From a specific aestheticism in the 1960s, Rymkiewicz also evolved towards political involvement. During the "Solidarity" period, he was already one of the leading anti-communist writers. This was related to the writer's increasingly clear fascination with Romanticism and the history of Poland and Russia. The results were excellent, extremely important books published in the country outside the reach of the censors or in exile. I have in mind the collection of poems *Mandelstam Street* (*Ulica Mandelsztama*), or the novel *Polish Conversations during Summer 1983* (*Rozmowy Polskie latem 1983*), which were published in the 1980s, i.e. during martial law. These books were hits of the underground publishing movement, they were distinguished, among others, by the award of "Solidarity". At the same time, the writer was under surveillance by the communist political police, and in 1985 he was dismissed from work at the Polish Academy of Sciences.

After the breakthrough of 1989, related to the so-called Autumn of Nations, Rymkiewicz retained his position as a moral and literary authority whose opinion was valued by the public. He was still publishing great books. The collection of poems *Sunset in Milanówek* (*Zachód słońca w Milanówku*) won the prestigious Nike Literary Award, given by the liberal-leftist *Gazeta Wyborcza,* in 2000. At the same time, the writer was increasingly in conflict with the political and literary *mainstream.* As one of the relatively few Polish writers, he criticized the direction of changes in Poland after 1989. He did so especially in loudly commented on interviews. In one of them, published in 2004 in Krakow's conservative bimonthly *Arcana*, he said: "The founding act of the free Polish state in 1989 should be hangings on Krakowskie Przedmieście in Warsaw, in front of St. Anne's and in front of the Staszic Palace - this is precisely what our enemies deserve from us".

Three years later *The Hangings* were published.

3.

The above-mentioned dispute over *The Hangings* was largely due to the context cited here. Here is an outstanding writer, who cannot be denied great merits and achievements, expressing a firm opinion on how communism and communists were (not) held to account in Poland, while his book should be treated as a kind of literary and historical disguise by means of which the artist comments on current and socially sensitive issues.

These included the problem of the attitude towards the heritage of the People's Republic of Poland existing in the years 1944-1989, a puppet, non-sovereign, totalitarian state subordinate to Soviet Russia. However, the first non-communist prime minister, Tadeusz Mazowiecki, announced a "thick line" policy, which many Poles considered as a sign of reluctance to account for the crimes of communism. In reaction to the "thick line" policy, also referred to by historians as "rationed revolution", some parties originating from the former "Solidarity" announced the necessity of de-communization and lustration in Poland. It was supposed to purge the state apparatus of communist functionaries as well as their secret agents, and to give Poles the feeling that they had regained political sovereignty. The government of Prime Minister Jan Olszewski attempted to carry out these demands in 1992, which ended with its overthrow by the opposition, in which there were ex-communists and their not-so-old opponents. Of course, this did not end the dispute over whether or not and how to settle accounts with the legacy of Bolshevism in Poland.

The Hangings seemed to form part of these disputes and at the same time provide a radical answer to the aforementioned questions. Though this was an indirect response, dressed in the costume of a story about the dramatic events in Poland between March and November 1794, when during the anti-Russian uprising, the Warsaw mob lynched over a dozen representatives of the then Polish elite, hanging them as alleged traitors to the national cause. This uprising did not really produce any results, King Stanisław Poniatowski, the main - according to Rymkiewicz - traitor, escaped punishment. Poland soon lost its independence, was divided between

Russia, Prussia, and Austria, and disappeared from the map of Europe for one hundred and fifty years.

Rymkiewicz again reached for events scarcely written about by historians and overlooked in its social memory as irrelevant, and at the same time embarrassing and irrational. From the writer's perspective, of course, it was completely different. The titular hangings turned out to be a key moment in Polish history. It was an Event, somewhat in the sense in which it was understood by the French philosopher Alain Badiou: it could have influenced a different, more auspicious course of Polish history: "The Poles could then have become a different nation, their history could have then been directed in a different direction, they themselves could have also (pushed by a wild, volcanic force hidden inside of them) taken a different direction - unimaginable and beautiful like everything unimaginable".

That is why his book was not only a meticulous reconstruction of the titular *The Hangings*, but also their specific praise. Specific, because many readers had - and probably still have - trouble reading Rymkiewicz's intentions. In his interviews, he himself most often avoided an unambiguous interpretation of his book. He said, "I only wanted to know what had happened because it was unclear to me". Or: "I am carried away by the aesthetic qualities of this spectacle". The same was true when he was receiving the Mackiewicz Award: "*The Hangings* do not encourage anything, it does not call for anything, I do not want to have an influence on anything".

However, some readers became indignant, seeing in Rymkiewicz's book a call to street riots and lynchings. Others pointed to the irony characteristic of Rymkiewicz's book's, with which he reconstructs the dramatic events of 1794. This irony is largely the result of the very understanding of history in *The Hangings*, but also of our, human, existence. One journalist did not agree to describe Rymkiewicz's book as a historical one, because, as he claimed, it is rather "a story about the horror of our nonsensical existence". However, the pessimism of such a vision of history and existence does not exclude humor. This is the kind of humor that in Poland is called - *nomen omen* – gallows humor. It is about laughing at macabre, painful things, but also about laughing at a borderline, final situation, such as that of a condemned man just before his execution. The description of the executioner Stefanek, which ends with a children's rhyme, is colored with such humor. This is how

Rymkiewicz sees the efforts of the enlightened - and implicitly also of today's - modernizers. A manifestation of gallows humor is also the recognition of street executions as a sign of the Europeanization of Poles in the 18th century. Since revolutionary terror was invented in Paris itself ...

The aforementioned nonsense of history, of course not only of Polish history, is also the impossibility of establishing their internal order, drawing a line that would connect certain causes with their effects. We do not know what influences the course of history, so everything in it is potentially important, the author of *The Hangings* seems to claim. Even the smallest, seemingly amusing little detail, on the periphery, like the color of a condemned man's hat, or Marysia in a green corset, who went missing during the Warsaw riots. While at the same time, in these details one can see banal life that goes on despite the historical Events and - perhaps - sometimes influences them. It is not surprising then that *The Hangings* have been linked to postmodern micro-stories like *The Great Cat Massacre on Rue Saint-Séverin* by Robert Darnton.

Though it is worth remembering that in Poland at the beginning of the 21st century, the memory of the alleged "end of history" announced by Francis Fukuyama was still alive. Already in the 1960s Rymkiewicz claimed that "the past is not a thing to be lost, it is not a lost address, or a page torn out of a book", and that "the past is the present". Now he repeated it, adding that history is, or must be: bloody, wild, and cruel. With this the thought of contemporaries, that history, and precisely this kind of history, will not return, is an illusion. "It seems to us that history is something that can be taken care of with white gloves, at a diplomatic dinner or during political negotiations, and then suddenly monsters appear, and we see that blood is pouring", which Rymkiewicz warned in one of the interviews about *The Hangings*. While in the book itself, he wrote that history is "something which resembles the eruption of Vesuvius, something like the flow of lava, which seethes and hisses, but soon cools down, will soon cool down, and after this eruption and cooling down, there will be another eruption, equally accidental and equally nonsensical...". From this perspective, history is a series of cataclysms, it is elements and destruction. In this there can be seen a distant echo of cultural catastrophism, known, for example, from the poetry of the aforementioned Miłosz.

The unusual composition of this book resonates very well

with this. It consists of 33 parts/chapters, quite short, admittedly arranged chronologically, though loosely connected with each other. They are a bit of a mosaic and a bit of a puzzle. Each part is an autonomous entity. Questions rather than answers dominate here. The latter often have the nature of speculations, hypotheses, guesses, or digressions. The word "maybe" returns in Rymkiewicz's work, but also "today". The narrator does not hide his presence and the fact that he talks about the hangings from a specific, current perspective of time. He resembles a pedantic detective, omnipresent, a bit nosy, looking through every detail, suspicious, trying to build a picture of the whole out of scattered fragments and traces of the past. He uses books and documents, but also his imagination, which allows him to fill in the historical blank spots.

It is on this structural level that we are dealing with the manifestation of seeing history as "pieces" that, after many years, we can arrange at will. At the same time, a manifestation of faith in the power of poetic imagination, without which it is impossible to discover, or rather to arrange, the past.

The Hangings can therefore be read (arranged) in a variety of ways. As a micro-historic study, a philosophical tale, a morality play, an essay, a guide around old Warsaw, a historical story or a modern hybrid combining all these genres. Though also as a political treatise. Refined, and from the perspective of the Polish reader in 2007: current. In the simplest, journalistic work Rymkiewicz justified the thesis, with the help of historical allusions, that the exemplary punishment of communists should have taken place in Poland after 1989 and that the abandonment of this was the cause of a failure of the state which was being constructed at that time. Just like the failure of the hangings in 1794 decided about the fall of Poland. In a more in-depth reading, *The Hangings* provoked questions about the political nature of Poles. Whether they are really, as they often said about themselves, a gentle nation, avoiding violence and terror. If it really is so though, is it a virtue or flaw? Is the fact that there were no regicides among Poles a title to glory? Does reluctance to political violence doom nations to the peripheral in a modernity which affirms power? Is the inability to conduct a successful revolution proof of the political weakness of the elite? Should "enlightened" elites pursue policies counter to the "dark" masses? If so, is it a good and effective policy? Also, what is a nation? Rymkiewicz unequivocally defended the right of the "dark masses" to speak out about Poland's matters, and more broadly the state, casually warning against that which is the result of ignoring this "wild" force. On many points, however, he provoked his readers to respond even more.

After *The Hangings* were published, an appeal to return to seriousness in politics was also seen in it. "Political subjectivity, sovereignty, if it is to mean anything, must be taken with gravitas, seriously; when it is necessary - seriously even to the limit of consequences" - this was the message of Rymkiewicz's book, according to the editor of the conservative *Political Theology* (*Teologia Polityczna*). This seriousness is also the belief expressed in *The Hangings* that whoever causes a revolution, or an uprising must take into account that they must be bloody and cruel if they are to be victorious.

The paradox, but also the beauty of this book, lies in the fact that this appeal for seriousness is made in a form that is at times extremely witty, at times ironic, literally brilliant.

It might be worth mentioning that the reactions of critics in Poland to *The Hangings* did not coincide with political divisions. The Left did not like the patriotism of this book, conservatives were furious at Rymkiewicz's "Jacobinism", Catholics were offended by the absence of God in Rymkiewicz's vision of history, liberals were offended by suggestions that they were following in the footsteps of former collaborators. *The Hangings* did not and does not have party colors. Rymkiewicz was first and foremost an artist. His politically incorrect revolutionary conservatism and anti-modernity must have irritated many. Though it also delighted many.

4.

The Hangings is important also because it initiated a whole series of Rymkiewicz's books on Polish history. In 2008, *Kinderszenen* about the Warsaw Uprising in 1944 was published, two years later *Samuel Zborowski* about a Polish nobleman beheaded in 1584 for a rebellion against the king, and nine years ago - *Reytan. The Fall of Poland* (*Reytan. Upadek Polski*), about the only deputy protesting against the partition of Poland in 1773. Each of these books was equally hotly debated, each engaged in a more or less explicit dialogue with *The Hangings*.

Jarosław Marek Rymkiewicz died on February 3, 2022 in Milanówek near Warsaw.

Maciej Urbanowski

FROM THE AUTHOR

This book is intended for lovers of Polish history – for those who like to read about what Polish life looked like long ago and about how our ancestors lived, what kind of adventures they had and their customs. It tells about events that took place in Warsaw over two hundred years ago, between mid-April and the beginning of November 1794. It also mentions several events which took place slightly later and slightly earlier, as well as (for example and comparisons) events that took place at the same time in Vilnius and Kraków. This does not mean that my story tells about all the important events that took place in Warsaw in 1794. This matter is made sufficiently clear by the title of the book - the subject is events related to hanging on the gallows, that is, to put it in another way, the legal or illegal execution of death sentences - sometimes judicial ones, and sometimes carried out spontaneously by the people of Warsaw.

A history book - even if its author, while researching and describing the events which took place in the past, also has ambitions of a slightly different kind, and would like to research and describe something else - should have footnotes or bibliographic notes - such that would allow one to accurately locate (and eventually check) the citations and would also indicate all the sources from which the information is derived. In compiling the bibliographies to be given at the end of each chapter, however, I came to the conclusion that there were too many of these notes and that they take up a great deal of space, perhaps too much space - in some cases such precise bibliographic notes almost equaled the size of the chapters which they referred to. So, I decided not to publish them - a book so burdened with footnotes would become difficult to read, and for a reader who does not intend to check the author (whether he cited something accurately and faithfully), the value of such footnotes would be rather small. Instead of footnotes and notes, there is a bibliography at the end of the book - those would like to learn more about the hangings in 1794, can access the works listed there, most of them quite easily available (in professional libraries). This bibliography is complete - in the sense that it includes all the works that I used at the time I wrote this.

As the rules of Polish orthography when it comes to naming various municipal objects, buildings, streets, squares, gardens, as well as the names of various institutions, authorities, organizations, are inconsistent, and in general vague, unsuccessful, and what is worse - often refer to the ambiguity of the writer, I had to come up with my own rules for the purposes of this book (in which the precise terminology of this time takes an important place). I will not explain them exhaustively here, because the matter is not worth it. To put it generally, in all the names of places and objects I use capital letters (though not necessarily consistently) wherever possible - so that there are as many of them as possible.

When only the dates of days are given in the text, it is always referring to the year 1794. Therefore, May 9 or June 28 is always June 28 or May 9 in 1794. If I give the date of a day referring to another year, I also add the year to it.

Like my previous encyclopedic books, published by *Sic! Publishing*, this endless story can also be read in fragments or in order, for pleasure or benefit, for education or for fun, and one can start reading anywhere - at the beginning or at the end, and also in the middle – in other words however one wants and however one likes to read. I would recommend one to start reading from the middle or the end, because that's precisely how I wrote this book - a little from the middle and a little from the end.

Chapter 1.

THE DECAPITATION OF PRINCE GAGARIN

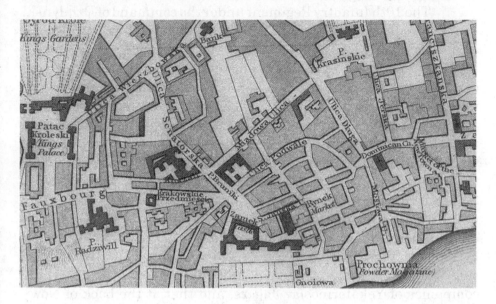

In the place, on the corner of Królewska Street and Krakowskie Przedmieście Street, where the *House without Corners* now stands, there was at that time a complex of buildings called the Saxon Forges or the Saxon Forge. The forges, built in 1726 for King Augustus II the Strong, occupied almost exactly the space that the *House without Corners* has occupied since 1934 - from the side of Krakowskie Przedmieście there was then a one-story building, it was probably residential, there were stables in the ground floor wings from Królewska Street and from the courtyard of the Saxon Palace, and in the middle, in the inner courtyard, there was the building of the Saxon Forge, where (as it can be assumed) horses of the royal guardsmen were shod. What this Forge, standing in the inner courtyard, looked like, I cannot say - I have not managed to find any engravings that show it; it may be that no such engraving exists. So, one has to imagine the Saxon Forge as looking like any other forge – with a sloping roof covered with red tiles or gray wood shingles, with a wide-open gate underneath it, darkness inside, and in the darkness a hearth, bellows and anvils, as well as blacksmiths in long leather aprons. Anyone who remembers what forges looked like (I saw them in my early childhood) is in a privileged position here.

One can hear the clatter of hammers and the neighing of horses, those in the stables on Królewska Street, and those that are tied up in the inner courtyard, waiting for their turn.

The 10th Infantry Regiment under the command of Działyński - in short called in Warsaw the Działyński Regiment, or, even shorter, the Działyńczyk's - left the Ujazdów barracks on April 17, according to the testimony of the regiment's staff doctor, Jan Drozdowski (his *Memoirs* were published in 1883), at eight o'clock in the morning. "Eight rang out, we moved out across the square towards the avenue". Col. Filip Hauman, commanding the regiment, intended to reach the Royal Castle, where Stanisław August Poniatowski was waiting for the arrival of Działyńczyk's, through Ujazdów Avenue, the place called *Crosses* or *Three Crosses* (the current Three Crosses Square), Nowy Świat, and Krakowskie Przedmieście. On the way to the Castle, Hauman's regiment had to pass by the Russian units quartered near Nowy Świat. The description of the march, prepared by Wacław Tokarz in his *Insurekcja warszawska* (*The Warsaw Insurrection*), says that at the exit of Mokotów Street there were three companies of Yekaterinoslav Jägers, and that at the back of Nowy Świat, in the vicinity of the Cabrit Aprtment House and the Vauxhall Garden outside of it, there were two squadrons of Akhtyrsky Chevau-légers. The Yekaterinoslav Jägers and the Akhtyrsky Chevau-légers did not try to stop the Działyńczyk's, apparently even military honors were given, and the regiment reached the place where Nowy Świat joined Krakowskie Przedmieście almost without problems. There, at the intersection with Świętokrzyska Street, they had to stop, because on Nowy Świat, closing access to Krakowskie Przedmieście, between the Holy Cross Church and the Dominican Observant Church (now the Staszic Palace stands where the Observant Church was), there were three rotas from a battalion of Siberian grenadiers.

They had orders to stop any Polish unit that would head towards Igelström's headquarters, i.e. the Russian embassy on Miodowa Street. According to the *Pamiętniki o rewolucji polskiej* (*Recollections of the Polish Revolution)* of the Russian general Johann Jakob Pistor, quartermaster of the Russian troops stationed in Warsaw, the grenadiers standing near the Observant Church had three cannons. According to the *Diariusz* (*Journal*) of Stanisław August, there were five Russian cannons "hauled onto Krakowskie Przedmieście", and according to Jan Kiliński, there were ten. Kiliński also claimed that they stood a little further back, in the depths of Krakowskie Przedmieście - more or less on the line that we could now connect the gate of the University of Warsaw with the gate of the Academy of Fine Arts. The Działyński Regiment had, as Antoni Trębicki claimed in his diary, "four small field cannons", Tokarz's description says that there were only three Polish cannons. Tokarz, which this great historian rarely did, probably made a mistake at this point in his description, because there is also a mention of four Polish cannons in Drozdowski's *Pamiętniki* (*Memoirs*) - they were "four 6-pound cannons".

The Siberian grenadiers were commanded by Colonel Fyodor Gagarin, an officer that was well-known and respected, perhaps even liked in Warsaw. He came from a well-known princely family and was then thirty-seven years old. The commander of the entire section was General Miłaszewicz, also allegedly liked by the Poles. Colonel Hauman tried to negotiate with the Russian commanders, he twice sent his adjutant to them with the assurance that the regiment did not want to fight the Russians or take part in the Polish uprising, that it was only going to the Castle to defend the king. General Stanisław Mokronowski, sent by Stanisław August, came to the Holy Cross Church with a similar mission – to convince Miłaszewicz and Gagarin to let the Działyńczyk's pass.

According to the version of events in Antoni Trębicki's diary, Prince Gagarin considered Mokronowski as one of Kościuszko's generals and said: "Return from where you came. I only listen to the orders of Igelström, my monarch's general". Then there was a verbal skirmish between Gagarin and Mokronowski, and when the Polish general got on his horse by the Holy Cross Church and rode off with his entourage towards the Castle, the Siberian grenadiers, on the prince's order, fired a volley in his direction. Mokronowski escaped with his life and returned to the Castle, but two uhlans from the unit accompanying the general were killed. This volley, according to Trębicki's description, became something like a signal, because the Działyńczyk's, hearing it, started firing canister shot at the Russians from their three or four small field cannons which were set up at the crossroads of Nowy Świat and Świętokrzyska Streets. The Siberian grenadiers responded with fire from their three, five or ten cannons, and thus began the bloodiest battle of the Warsaw Insurrection. It occurred between the Dominican Observants and the Kazimierz Palace, while lasting about an hour and a half, from ten to eleven thirty, maybe half an hour longer. When it ended, where there is now the gate of the University, the entrance to the Department of Philosophy, the exit of Traugutt Street, and a little further the gate of the Academy of Fine Arts, stairs leading to an underground passage and the Prus Bookshop, there was not a single piece of free space on the road - as Tokarz wrote, "Krakows-kie Przedmieście was covered with dead and wounded". The victory of the Działyńczyk's, who, probably after eleven o'clock, carried out a bayonet attack (the regiment, as we read in Stanisław August's *Journal*, "having launched a bayonet attack, broke up and dispersed Gagarin's unit"), was decided not so much by this attack but by the fact that a bit earlier a dozen or so soldiers, the regiment's best shooters, managed to get, after breaking the door to the Dominican Observant Monastery, to the tower of the Dominican church, while a dozen or so others reached the upper floors of the Karaś Palace.

These sharpshooters of the Działyński Regiment were called Kurpik's - they had green uniforms and round green hats, and were armed, as Drozdowski wrote, with "carbines, which were called threaders. [...] These carbines had such range and accuracy that at 400 paces one could not miss". The fire from the church tower and from Oboźna, and then also from houses on Krakowskie (from where civilians were shooting at the Russians) completely eliminat-ed the Russian artillerymen from the fight. Around half past elev-en, General Miłaszewicz ordered his grenadiers to take the useless cannons (there were no more horses) and ordered a retreat towards Królewska Street and the Visitationist Church. "Struck by the fire from the windows of the soldiers of the Działyński regiment," Pis-tor wrote in *Recollections of the Polish Revolution*, "onto Nowy Świ-at and Aleksandryjska Streets, having already used the cannon's ammunition, they had to retreat to Saxon Square". Aleksandryjska Street, or rather Alexandria, is the section of the present Kopernik Street, which now connects (and then connected) Nowy Świat with Ordynacka Street. The Russians were retreating, dragging their five or ten cannons over the corpses, and coming after them, over the corpses, were the Działyńczyk's. This was one of the most more beautiful bayonet attacks in the entirety of Polish history. I bring up this wonderful scene here, because it seems that hardly anyone remembers it now - the Działyński Regiment carried out the bayo-net attack along the entire width of Krakowskie Przedmieście, from the Staszic Palace (that is from the Dominican Observant Church) and further, between the gate of the Corps of Cadets and the Holy Cross Church. Their navy-blue uniforms, yellow shoulder marks and collars, pink turnback's, bayonets and pałasz's shining in the April Warsaw sun between the gate of the University and the bus stop in front of the Prus Bookshop "When the whole regiment moved forward - wrote Drozdowski - we walked over the corpses of our enemies all the way to King Zygmunt". Probably right after ordering the retreat, General Miłaszewicz was seriously wounded while still in front of the Holy Cross Church and perhaps thanks to this he survived - all the gates on Krakowskie Przedmieście were blocked, but the retreating Russians broke through one of them and hid the wounded commander in one of the houses. Prince Fyodor Gagarin, who took over command from Miłaszewicz, died several minutes, maybe half an hour later.

The story of his death is known in two versions. According to the first version, the prince, also wounded in front of the Holy Cross Church, was riding a horse which was being led by his Siberian grenadiers, who at the same time were protecting their commander from fire from the direction of the Karaś Palace and from the direction of Saxon Square. There were probably not many of these grenadiers left, retreating towards Miodowa Street and the Castle, as the Saxon diplomat Johann Jakob Patz wrote in a letter to Dresden two days later, "that battalion [Siberian grenadiers] was almost entirely massacred next to the Holy Cross Church". The prince was wounded a second time somewhere near the Visitationist Church and at the intersection of Krakowskie Przedmieście and Królewska Streets he slipped off his horse, perhaps he lost consciousness. The grenadiers took him in their arms and carried him to the Saxon Forge – to the inner courtyard mentioned above. He was placed on a table there and - according to Drozdowski's account - someone, some doctor (it is not known whether Polish or Russian), started treating his wounds. "I saw the prince there - wrote Drozdowski - and with him a doctor with surgical instruments in his hand". This lasted for a few minutes, then a dozen or so people who (it seems) were fighting the Russians on Saxon Square, entered the Saxon Forge, and the one who was treating Gagarin's wounds was pushed away. Karol Wojda's diary (*O rewolucji polskiej w roku 1794*, *On the Polish Revolution in 1794*) mentions that they demanded that the prince surrender, but this demand was rejected by him. "He was - Wojda wrote - a young and dignified officer, respected by the Poles, but called upon to demand to be spared, when he would not demand it, he was killed". One of the accounts says that the first blow dealt to the prince was by a coachman he knew well, one who drove him around Warsaw for several years. Prince Gagarin was nailed to the table on which he lay with pałasz's, cutlasses, and butcher's spits. The second version, which is probably closer to the truth (in the sense that it appears more often in accounts; Wacław Tokarz, however, accepted the first version in *The Warsaw Insurrection*) says that the prince did not reach the Saxon Forge and was not brought there by his soldiers, but was killed when, wounded, he found himself on the corner of Krakowskie Przedmieście and Królewska Streets, right next to the *House without Corners*. "The un-fortuitus and truly worthy of respect Gagarin - wrote Antoni Trębicki - [...] wishing to dress his wound at the Saxon Forge, some blacksmith, having run out of the Forge, took his life with an ax or other iron implement". According to another version, the wounded prince rode up on his horse to the *House without Corners*, and then a boy in a leather apron, a blacksmith's apprentice, almost a child, came out of the Saxon Forge with a large, red-hot iron bar, and striking with this bar (he must have jumped if the prince was sitting on a horse) to Gagarin's neck. The bar struck the neck, cut it, maybe burned through it, Fyodor Gagarin's head fell off of his body and onto to the road, the headless rider staggered in the saddle, but he pulled the reins and kept his balance, and his head fell where now, vis-à-vis the Visitationist Church, at the exit of Królewska Street, cars, coming from the direction of the Hotel Victoria and intending to turn right onto Krakowskie Przedmieście, stop at the red light there - and it rolled under the wheels of the cars.

Chapter 2
THE DISPOSAL OF WASTE

Waste - house waste and street waste, usually mixed with the autumn and winter mud - was one of the biggest problems of 18th-century Warsaw. Although Warsaw stood out among other European cities with its cleanliness, it was much cleaner than Vienna, London, and the terribly dirty Paris, waste remained a problem that was dealt with great difficulty. In order to understand what this problem was, one first needs to understand what the cesspits at that time looked like. They were holes that were dug in the ground - in courtyards or in gardens, but also inside houses, in halls or under stairs; much less often in some storage areas - and in such cases one could talk about elegant restrooms. As for Warsaw, a great number of these internal, domestic holes were in the Old Town, which was densely built-up and densely populated. There was, of course, no possibility of cleaning them - no effective methods seemed to have been known, so it all stank terribly.

The city was a great reservoir of animal and human stench, and in order to get rid of it, the waste had to be removed somehow, that is, the owners of the houses had to be forced to take appropriate action - and that was precisely the problem. As a nice story goes, which can be found in a booklet by Franciszek Giedroyć, published in 1912 (*Warunki higieniczne Warszawy w wieku XVIII. Ulice i domy, Hygienic Conditions in Warsaw in the 18th Century. Streets and Houses*; it is a work devoted not only to the history of the fight against waste, one can also learn many other interesting things from it), the first attempts to remedy this problem occurred in the 1740s. Earlier, in the first half of the 18th century, in the 1720s and 1730s, cleaning the streets of waste consisted of sweeping it into one place. How the waste from houses was dealt with back then, I have no idea - people probably couldn't manage it at all. Whereas in the streets there were, or rather piled high, in the fall and winter months, great heaps of waste. One could see them, because that's where they had their privileged place, in front of the magnate palaces on Senatorska, Miodowa, Długa, and Krakowskie Przedmieście. Admittedly, there were regulations ordering street waste to be cleaned, maybe even hauled out, but they were issued by the municipal council and the magnates did not have to subordinate themselves to them. The removal of waste was also made difficult or even impossible due to the fact that at that time in Warsaw there were a dozen or so jurydyka's, i.e. separate towns, and each such small town was somebody's private property - their owners could clean their waste, but they also could, if they wanted to, not clean it. The Warsaw jurydyka's were not liquidated until the Law on the Cities, passed by the Four-Year Sejm in April 1791. So, the waste piles lay in the streets until spring, even summer, and the waste decayed and of course stank. This also made it difficult to move around the city - when King Augustus III established the *Street Commission*, which happened in 1740, it stated that vehicles and pedestrians had difficulties getting to Krakowskie Przedmieście, because there are heaps of waste and mud that are difficult to avoid on the streets (there were no sidewalks at that time) that connect to this important artery. The situation improved only in early summer, when the waste mixed with mud dried up and thus could be disposed of. Towers were then built from it (they supposedly reached the height of the first or even the second floor), and then the towers were set on

fire and something along the lines powerful torches of waste illuminated Warsaw at night. Later, in the nineties, these towers were no
longer on the streets of Warsaw, the memory of them was even lost
(as is usually the case with such devices), and for me there is a lack
of them in precisely this time - several-story waste towers, burning
in May and June in front of the Dominican Observant Church on
Nowy Świat and in front of the Brühl Palace on Wierzbowa Street,
and illuminating the gallows and those being hanged swaying on
ropes, it would be a wonderful sight; this would be one of the greatest and wildest landscapes in Polish history.

The burning towers disappeared thanks to the aforementioned *Street Commission*, created by Augustus III. It must be said
here that although the Saxon kings harmed us in many areas of
our lives, their civilization activities had good results - the Saxon
civilization undoubtedly changed the appearance of Warsaw for the
better. The Street Commission undertook several initiatives that in
truth did not eliminate the waste problem (the final elimination of
this problem would mean a complete Vernichtung – the end of our
species), but slightly improved the unpleasant situation. The Grand
Marshal of the Crown, Franciszek Bieliński, who for many years
chaired the *Street Commission*, introduced, first of all, a tax intended for keeping the streets and squares clean. This tax, collected from
1743, was called the *ell tax* - the façade of a house was measured,
and the owner had to pay for each ell of its length. Secondly, also in
1743, Marshal Bieliński's Street Commission issued a decree that
forbid throwing rubbish and mud on the streets, and that property owners have the responsibility to form piles from them on their
yards, while the city undertook to take care of their removal. In connection with this idea, thirdly, a Kara Warehouse was established
in Warsaw in 1743, i.e. a depot for the wagons used for garbage and
waste removal. This name comes from the fact that waste wagons
were then called karas. There were only a dozen or so karas around
1750, but it was probably a sufficient number, as Warsaw was then
a relatively small city, at least in terms of population - it had around
30,000 inhabitants. The Kara Warehouse was located on Nalewki
Street number 2235 - behind the Krasiński Garden, where Nalewki was then connected with Nowolipki Street. Now there are tram
tracks in this place on Władysław Anders Street (connecting Żoli-
borz with Śródmieście), and a few dozen meters further (towards
the west) there are apartment blocks at the corner of Anders and

Nowolipki Street. Fourth and finally, on the initiative of the *Street Commission*, street sewage systems began to be built in Warsaw in 1745. The channels, placed in the middle of the street, were lined with oak logs and covered with boards. This device also worked at the end of the century, though not very efficiently, because although it was forbidden to throw rubbish and waste into the channels, this prohibition was not respected and the sewers were often clogged, and then the sewage flooded the streets and passersby's waded in liquid feces. The work of Marshal Bieliński, who died in 1766, was continued by his successors. In the mid-seventies, behind the Gunpowder Depot, the one at the intersection of Boleść Street and Mostowa Street, a pier intended for waste wagons was built on the Vistula River, from which waste and feces could be poured directly into the river. A regulation of the *Street Commission* from 1775 stated that entrepreneurs, who were called night people (they were seen only at night), were to pour the waste from the karas "straight into the water and at a great depth". In the same year, the *Street Commission* set out the routes that the karas carrying feces were to take to Mostowa Street. Out of care for the comfort of the inhabitants, who could be awakened by the smelly carts of the cesspit cleaners, it was decided that their routes were to be changed from time to time. "So that the inconvenience to the inhabitants would not be great, the cesspit cleaners are to use different roads, so that they would not always ride one road, but in equal proportions of the time, change their route".

The second place, apart from the pier over the Vistula, to empty the waste wagons was Góra Gnojowa (Waste Hill). This impressive structure (if you can call something like that a structure) began to be raised in the last decades of the 17th century. It was located - and grew from year to year - behind the Poznań Episcopal Palace on Jezuicka Street, between that street and the bank of the Vistula, more or less where Bugaj Street turned towards the castle garden called the Terrace. If one (then) looked at the Vistula from the side of the Old Town, then on the right they would see this garden descending towards the Vistula, from the left (i.e. from the north) the Butcher Shops of the Old Town, called Herring Shops, and in the center, between the Herring Shops and the royal garden, Góra Gnojowa. Now, more or less at this point, there is an observation deck and stairs leading down from it to the Vistula River. The karas carrying waste and rubbish reached the Hill through the Old

Town Square and the street called Gnojna. Later, for the sake of decency, the street descending towards the Vistula was called Celna; that is what it is called today. It seems to me that it was also possible to reach the foot of the Hill from the direction of Bugaj Street. I have not come across any document that would give even an approximation of the Hill's height, but it was enormous, and was becoming ever higher. Everything that could be poured out and thrown away was poured out and thrown away there: the contents of the cesspits, horse and cattle manure, also all street waste, rubbish, as well as mud. When the Hill reached a certain height that made it impossible to unload waste and feces on its top, the structure was leveled, dropping its top into the Vistula River. Although the material used to build it was rather fluid, the Hill slowly hardened, which allowed (it happened sometime in the seventies) homesteads to be placed at its feet, and then on its slopes – servants probably lived in them, who bustled around the Hill and made sure that it had the right shape and height.

There is also some vague evidence that something was produced and sold in the wooden huts on the slopes of the Hill - from Antoni Magier, the author of *Estetyki miasta stołecznego Warszawy* (*The Aesthetics of the Capital City of Warsaw*), we learn that someone called Feter was selling gunpowder "in a wooden shack on Gnojowa Góra". Since this Feter was also involved in publishing broadsheets, perhaps it was also created on the slopes of the Hill. The work by Magier also mentions that the hill was useful in yet another way - patients suffering from venereal diseases were buried in the waste there. This was a radical treatment for such diseases known throughout Europe; I don't know whether it was for everything or only syphilis (then called the French disease or the Frank disease). "Such unfortunate people, receiving little help from the doctors of that time, were destined to be buried up to their ears in the waste. It was quite easy to see such patients on Gnojowa Góra next to the Castle, behind the Jesuit schools". As the stinky structure stood near the Castle and the stench (especially in summer, when windows were opened) filled the royal rooms, Stanisław August, who had dizziness and vomiting (not necessarily because of the Hill, rather it was due to some mysterious disease), demanded that the city authorities fix the problem of the stinking neighborhood. As Magier wrote, in 1774 the Hill, "by the king's will", was covered with grass. I do not know what that could mean: whether

grass seeds were planted on the waste, or that ready turf was laid
- as it is done now on soccer fields. A more pleasant name was also
thought of - the waste structure was to be called Green Hill.

All of these procedures did not make the slightest impression on the Hill and its servants, the cleaners of the cesspits. Even
though there was already a pier on the Vistula at the extension of
Boleść Street, the cesspits were still poured out by the Castle, and
the Hill, with disregard for the king's will, was still called Gnojowa.
The hill, which was to function for another several dozen years (its
slow leveling lasted somewhere until the mid-nineteenth century),
stopped growing dangerously at the turn of the eighties and nineties, and so even before the insurrection. Karas with waste and rubbish were still going through Jezuicka and Bugaj, but a significant
part of the waste began to be discharged (as is done today) directly into the Vistula. This was the result of an order of the Grand
Marshal of the Crown, Michał Mniszech, issued in 1784. It forbade
pouring onto roadways and sidewalks (the first sidewalks appeared
in Warsaw that year): "slop, soapsuds, dregs, grounds, and other
things, mud multipliers and stench causers". All these impurities
were to be poured into the gutters - so that they could flow freely
through the street's gutters into the river. Mniszech's regulation
also significantly reduced the amount of mud on the streets, because
it imposed on homeowners the obligation to send people who, when
it rained, "thinning the mud, raked it into the street gutters and
into the sewers". After the fall of the Insurrection, the first garbage
cans appeared in Warsaw in 1795. Their local inventor can be considered the then Russian commander of the city, General Fyodor
Buxhóvden - he issued, along with other repressive orders (putting
guns and pałasz's in police stations, walking at dusk with flashlights, closing taverns at eight in the evening, and kaffen-hauses at
nine), an order saying that rubbish can only be thrown into garbage
cans and that a garbage can must be in every yard.

Chapter 3.

SIX THOUSAND RED ZŁOTYS

The magnificent six vo-
lumes by Tadeusz Korzon
- *Wewnętrzne dzieje Polski
za Stanislawa Augusta.
Badania historyczne ze
stanowiska ekonomicznego
i administracyjnego* (The
*Internal History of Poland
under Stanisław August.
Historical Research from
an Economic and Admin-
istrative Standpoint*) – is
probably only read today
by specialists dealing with
the 18th-century history
of Poland, so I am extract-
ing from this (somewhat
forgotten) work what I
learned about the Russian
money of King Stanisław
August - that is, the money

Jacob Sievers by Joseph Grassi

that the ruler of the Poles received (in the form of gratuities) from
his Russian protectors. The king's domestic income from the econ-
omy, i.e. the so-called *dobra stołowe*, as well as from royal duties,
royal post offices, salt mines, as well as from various other sources, was quite good - according to Korzon, who analyzed the entries
from the royal treasury books, amounted to, in the sixties and seventies, an average of six to seven million Polish złotys a year - but
the monarch, mindlessly wasteful and fond of expensive pleasures,
ballerinas, and poets, was constantly in financial trouble – and so
the money he received from the Russians was certainly very useful
to him. *The Internal History of Poland* appeared in the years 1882-
1885, the king's money (as well as the Russian money) is the topic of
the eighth chapter in the third volume, entitled *Stosunki pieniężne
Stanisława Augusta* (*The Monetary Relations of Stanisław August*).

It must be said at the beginning that our great historian hated the king, considered him a traitor, even more so, a criminal - so he may be suspected of partiality. "Stanisław August - he wrote - carried in the depths of his soul a moral decay, the disgustingness and incurability of which will only be shown in its full horrendousness when all the pages of his private and public life are brought together". Though numbers are numbers - someone who copies them from accounting books cannot be accused of bias. Some of the king's financial operations (especially those involving borrowing money) could, in our modern language, be called scandals. The king took bribes - and he was not ashamed of it, because he wrote them down in the books.

From the 88th book of the royal chambers, Korzon wrote out the royal loans from the sixties, including two loans that were granted to the king at the end of those years by some Genoese people - probably Genoese bankers. One loan was for 1,693,776 Polish złotys, the other for 418,750 Polish złotys. Both loans had quite low interest rates - the first at 5 ½%, the other at 5%. There would be nothing wrong with borrowing from the Genoese at a low percentage (the King borrowed from the Carmelite Maidens at 7%, from the largest of Warsaw's bankers, Piotr Tepper, also for 7%) - but by some strange coincidence in 1769 the Genoese received a lease from the Crown Treasury Commission to introduce their Genoese number lottery throughout the Crown, known as the Lotto di Genova; and even stranger, they were released from paying the lease. After the Genoese, the number lottery (public drawing took place twice a month at the Krasiński Palace) was leased by Piotr Tepper, who paid 180,000 Polish złotys annually for the lease. As for the Russian money - as Korzon called them, "disgraceful donations" as well as "beggars' charity" - they were obviously not entered into any accounting books. Information on this subject - certainly incomplete - comes from the reports of subsequent Russian ambassadors, that is (because they should be defined this way) of the Polish king's successive superiors. Stanisław August received his first large Russian largess almost immediately after his coronation.

After the death of Keyserling (Keiserling), Repnin became the Russian ambassador in Warsaw and the Petersburg Tsarina ordered him to pay the king 100,000 ducats "for primary needs". According to the exchange rate at that time, 100,000 ducats was 1,800,000 Polish złotys. For this gift, as the furious Korzon wrote, "the paid servant [...] sent his guardian a box of truffles". The next Russian payments to the king are included in the accounts, which - after the capture of the Załuski Palace on April 18 - was found in papers left at the embassy by General Igelström (all these sums are given in red złotys, i.e. in ducats).

The King received:

In 1764, September 17	12,000
November 19	24,000
In 1765, 20 February	6,000
In 1766, August 21	20,000
October 15. In addition to 11,000 ducats that were received	9,000
In 1768, September 27	40,000
In 1769, September 19	10,000
In 1770 and 1771	18,000
For maintenance of Branicki's corps	<u>15,000</u>
	154,000[1]

It cannot be said, of course, that all of these gifts of the Tsarina were only for the king's private entertainment and pleasures, for his ballerinas and his poets - some of these sums (especially those paid after 1768), as the last item testifies, could have also been used to pay the royal troops waging a civil war with the troops of the Bar Confederation. 154,000 ducats equals 2,772,000 Polish złotys. This was a huge sum, but it can also be said that - in comparison with Stanisław August's national income of several million - it was actually not very much. Korzon even believed - given that the calculation covers six or even seven years - that the Petersburg Tsarina "made a good deal", because the services of Stanisław August were "at a low price". The author of *The Internal History of Poland* had some other accounts in his hand, probably from those papers that Igelström did not manage to take with him when he retreated from Warsaw, and which on April 18 were found, partially burned, in the

---

[1]Originally in French under the tile *Le Roi a Reçu*.

Russian embassy - but his description here is a bit unclear and we only learn that one of these accounts, for the "total sum of 291,928 ducats, or 5,254,704 Polish złotys", included "election bribes, supplying the fortress in Kremenets, and financial support against the Bar Confederation", and that the king - even before the election, as a Lithuanian pantler: "to pantler Count Poniatowski" – received from the Tsarina a kind of allowance in the amount of 65,994 ducats, or 1,186,992 Polish zlotys. This whole matter is difficult to ultimately clarify, because Igelström's papers - after 1815 - again fell into the hands of the Russians, and Korzon, writing *The Internal History of Poland*, was using copies (probably from the collection of Leon Dembowski).

The receipts and bills found in the Russian embassy concern - as far as it concerns the king - only the sixties and seventies, about how it went on, that is, what the payouts looked like in the eighties (when the relations between the Petersburg Tsarina and her Polish king broken down a little), not much is known. On the other hand, the amount of the gratuities and allowances that Stanisław August received from the Russian embassy during the Grodno Sejm - the one which decided on the second partition of Poland in 1793 is quite well known. Before leaving for Grodno, the embassy paid 20,000 ducats to the king in Warsaw, then it added another 10,000 ducats (to pay for travel expenses). This was only an advance, the real money, the king's income from the second partition of Poland, appeared in Grodno. Catherine allowed her ambassador at the time, Jakob Johann Sievers, to spend a small amount in Grodno to pay for the costs of the partition, because it was only 200,000 silver rubles, or 1,200,000 Polish złotys – that makes it barely 67,000 red złotys. According to Korzon's calculations, a significant part of this sum, even almost all of it, was at that time collected by Stanisław August. In May 1793 he received 400,000 Polish złotys from Sievers in Grodno, 30,000 red złotys in June of that year, and 6,000 red złotys in November. In September and October, he received 14,000 red złotys each month, but these two payments did not come from the Russian coffers - on the order of the ambassador, the money was paid to the king from the crown treasury.

If we count only what the king then took from the money that Catherine allowed Sievers to spend on the second partition, that is, from those 200,000 silver rubles (1,200,000 Polish złotys), then it will turn out that it was at least (because the Russian ambassador probably paid the king something else in November) - some 58,000 red złotys, or 1,044,000 Polish złotys. 1,044,000 out of 1,200,000. If we look at it precisely in this way - that is, from the point of view of money - we will have to say that the one who made the most money from the second partition of Poland, benefited the most from it, was the king of Poles. Perhaps, however, the Tsarina - because the deliberations of the Grodno Sejm were prolonged and Sievers failed, as he initially intended, to have the partition approved in two weeks - turned out to be a bit more generous and the Russian ambassador got more money. To the money we are talking about here, we must also add the bit unclear - that is: being of unclear origin – the sum of 6,000 red złotys, which was paid to Stanisław August from the common coffers of three courts - St. Petersburg, Berlin, and Vienna. When this happened, it is not known, Korzon assumed that the king took the money right after the first partition - "it was paid out at the end of 1772 and at the beginning of 1773". It was precisely these 6,000 red złotys or 108,000 Polish złotys - that was the cause of a great scandal which broke out in Warsaw at the end of August 1794.

The scandal began with the fact that the *Gazeta Rządowa* (*Government Gazette*) (followed by other newspapers of that time, the *Korrespondent Narodowy i Zagraniczny* [*The National and Foreign Correspondent*] and the *Gazeta Wolna Warszawska* [*The Free Warsaw Gazette*]) published in issue 52 of August 23, a small part of the Igelström archive - that is, a part of those burned Russian papers that fell into the hands of those that captured the embassy on April 18 and whose reading and analysis was then dealt with by the Investigation Department and the Audit Department (also known as the Deputation for Paper Revision). Both of these Deputations were organs of the Supreme National Council, that is, of the insurrectionary government - something like its ministries. The publication of *The Government Gazette* (edited by Franciszek Ksawery Dmochowski, who had the opinion at that time in Warsaw of a Jacobin) was entitled "Extrakt z dowodów autentycznych i z regestrów moskiewskich na pensje brane od Moskwy, przez Deputacje rewizyjną roztrząsanych i spisanych" ("Extract from Authentic Evidence and Muscovite Registers on Salaries Taken from Moscow, Discussed and Written by the Audit Department"). "We will put here - *The Gazette* wrote - excerpts from these papers, so that the public would know who sold the country and for how much. That the living receive an appropriate punishment, and that the names of the dead, over whose graves some of us, not knowing about their bad nature, may weep, be cursed today and by the next generations".

Among those whom Dmochowski gave to "be cursed [...] by the next generations" were, among others, Adam Poniński, Prince Antoni Czetwertyński, Prince August Sułkowski, Bishop (and Primate) Antoni Ostrowski - from the receipts and lists printed in *The Gazette* it was quite clear that they were taking money from the Russian ambassadors. This, however, would not have caused a great sensation, as the receipts only confirmed what everyone back then knew well - that Poniński, Czetwertyński, Sułkowski, and Ostrowski were traitors and jurgieltniks[2]. The sensation was caused by one item, one short sentence from the list titled *Wydatki kassy wspólnej trzech dworów w czasie sejmu delegacyjnego* (*The Expenses of the Common Coffers of Three Courts during the Delegation Sejm*). The sentence went like this - "His Royal Highness, 6,000 red zł". If at that time the terrible bill titled *Le Roi a Reçu* (*The King Received*) was known, then the 6,000 red złotys - ultimately a small amount, in the face of hundreds of thousands of ducats, only 108,000 Polish złotys - would not have caused much surprise. The fact that someone who took hundreds of thousands took 6,000 more - what's so strange about it? Although nobody knew about those hundreds of thousands at that time, and the king knew that nobody knew. Therefore, he could calmly play a wonderful comedy, act the role of an offended and hurt virgin-topielica - at the same time preventing further publications, which were announced by *The Gazeta Rządowa*. The great political skill of the Polish king was revealed then in that he asked the Supreme National Council for a correction, but he also immediately turned (knowing that he could not count on the favor of the Council), neither with a request nor a demand ("I have the right to insist on a solemn explanation") to Kosciuszko.

In a long letter (of August 26), full of complaints and lamentations, he assured the Chief that he had never signed any chirograph ("nor was it dared to demand it from me"), had not taken even a penny from anyone ("I have never taken a salary from any foreign court") and that he had always opposed the partition of the country ("I was strongly against it"). He also tried to convince Kościuszko that the first partition made him a pauper king, so he had to accept

---

[2]Jurgieltnik: From the German "jahrgeld" (Polish: jurgielt) which means an annual payment. These were high ranking Polish officials who received annual payments from Russian ambassadors as bribes.

6,000 red złotys as a kind of compensation for the royal economies lost due to the partition – "the occupation without exception of all the royal salt mines and my incomes by all three powers brought me to and kept me in such a complete deprivation that I truly did not have a livelihood, and therefore it was necessary that I should be given the same things for life by those that stripped me of everything". The next letter on this matter from the king to Kościuszko on August 27 is also very interesting, Stanisław August justified his conviction that the Russian papers (receipts) should not be disclosed. "In my opinion, whoever does not sin now, whoever now wants to serve the country, should not be deterred by the threat of past sins, if there were any. [...] after all, there are not many of us, let us not reduce our number even more". We do not know whether Kościuszko agreed with the king's arguments and believed his explanations, but he reacted immediately, and with strange agitation. In a letter to Stanisław August (dated August 26), sent from a camp near Mokotów, he called the mention of his name in *The Government Gazette* "indecent by all means" and assured the monarch that he had learned about it "with the greatest worry" and that he has nothing to do with this matter - "on my honor I can guarantee Your Royal Highness that it happened without my knowledge".

The letter to the Supreme National Council, written that day, is something like a military order. Calling, also in this letter, the mentioning of the king's name in *The Government Gazette* "indecent by all means", Kościuszko ordered the Council to impose censorship on this matter - "that the edition of the newspaper in which it is found should not be issued and that the post should not send it to the provinces". We also have a post scriptum there - "I order the royal explication to be published in *The Gazette*". On this - that is, on virtually nothing - ends the scandal of the 6,000 red złotys. What happens next is not really particularly interesting – *The Government Gazette* included two corrections or rather two statements from the king in subsequent editions (Stanisław August was not satisfied with the first statement, as the editors added their own comment to it, which showed that the king had his opinion on this matter, and *The Gazette* their own), Dmochowski, trying to continue the publication of the papers, corresponded on this matter with the Supreme National Council, the Council, undoubtedly taking into account Kościuszko's clear order, assured that the "seized extracts from the Muscovite papers" would with all certainty still be disclosed to the public, but it did not disclose anything, while its Security Department stated that if there were any interesting papers found, and the Council passed an appropriate resolution, they would give them to the editorial office. *The Government Gazette* also announced that it would continue its publications - "we will continue to publish a list of paid Muscovite servants when the relevant papers, which are now in the Security Department, will be granted to us" - and that was the end of the current lustration.

The most interesting thing in all of this is Kościuszko's decisive decision, which saved the king at that time - one could even say that it saved his life. The Supreme National Council, in which different views clashed, would have probably finally given way and allowed the publication of the account *Le Roi a Reçu*, Kościuszko did not. This could possibly be explained by the social position of the Chief and what this position imposed on the person who held it - Kościuszko, being the Chief of the National Armed Forces, that is, in fact, the Chief of the Nation, was still a moderately wealthy Polish nobleman - and when he met the king, privately or in public, he kissed his hand. Although such an explanation seems insufficient - the then letters of Kościuszko to Stanisław August, their laconic nature, their cold and openly unfavorable tone, clearly show that the Chief, although he kissed the king's hand, simply did not like him, was probably even disgusted by him. So why did he save him after that sentence, which referred to the 6,000 red złotys, was published in *The Government Gazette*? The only answer can be this - Kościuszko knew that if Dmochowski's *Gazette*, which would be followed by other Warsaw newspapers, continued to publish papers from Igelström's archives, then it would end with another hanging. He also knew that it would not be such hanging as on May 9 or June 28, because the masses would capture the Royal Castle and the king would be hanged on Bernardine Square, beneath St. Anne's Church. Kościuszko probably did not want to agree to this - maybe for some higher, that is ethical reasons, or maybe because it could (in his opinion) harm some military undertakings he was preparing. The decision to save the king - made in the camp at Królikarnia on August 26 - was also the decision that decided the fate of the insurrection. After that day, it must have ended just as it ended - fatally, that is. If the Poles, in the last days of August 1794, had hanged the king who had betrayed them in front of the Bernardine Church (or a little further, on Wide Krakowskie Przedmieście, beneath the windows of the royal brothel – the Sophie Lhullier tenement house) would the events of the insurrection have gone somewhat differently? Of course, we cannot know that - all this could have still ended with Maciejowice and the Massacre of Praga. Though the risk could have been taken - and it must be said that the leaders of the insurrection, Kościuszko, also Ignacy Potocki and Hugo Kołłątaj, as well as two generals, Jakub Jasiński and Józef Zajączek, then missed this extraordinary moment, one of those moments that appear unusually rarely in the history of nations; the moment when some completely different future (other than the one that followed) was opening up for the Poles - a future of regicides. The Poles could then have become a different nation, their history could have then been directed in a different direction, they themselves could have also (pushed by a wild, volcanic force hidden inside of them) taken a different direction - unimaginable and beautiful like everything unimaginable.

Chapter 4.
IGELSTRÖM'S GOUT

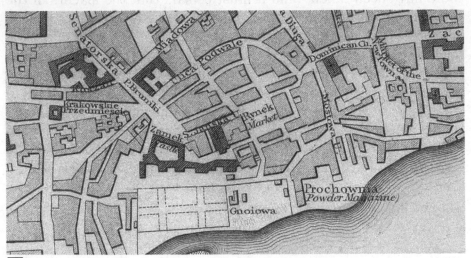

The circumstances of the death (real or alleged) of the Grand Chancellor of the Crown, Prince Antoni Sułkowski, are not clear, they are even very mysterious, and it does not seem that this case, one of the darkest episodes preceding the outbreak of the Warsaw Insurrection, could now, after so many years, be sufficiently explained. One thing is beyond doubt in this matter – Sułkowski's place in the hierarchy of the authorities at the time, that is, in the hierarchy of Muscovite jurgieltniks, or, in other words, in the hierarchy of traitors, was such that he would not have avoided the gallows. Antoni Trębicki, in his work *O rewolucji roku 1794 (On the Revolution of 1794)*, wrote that the grand chancellor, "although belonging to the Muscovite party through his politics", was nevertheless "noble and impeccable in his conduct as an official and man". However, one does not necessarily have to believe Trębicki, and Sułkowski, although he may have been noble, was hated by the masses of Warsaw to an equal extent, perhaps even more than Marshal Ankwicz, General Ożarowski, or Bishop Kossakowski. That is those who were hanged?

So if Sułkowski, after the outbreak of the insurrection, precisely like those later hanged, was arrested and locked up in the Brühl Palace or in the Gunpowder Depot, then, on May 9, we would have not four but five gallows in Warsaw. Then on the 5th - maybe this would have been the fourth gallows in the Old Town Market Place, or maybe the second one beneath St. Anne's Church - would hang the Grand Chancellor of the Crown. It would not be a pleasant spectacle, because Prince Sułkowski, as Trębicki wrote in his diary, was "an old man already decrepit and weakened with age" - born in 1735, he was three years older than Bishop Kossakowski and fifteen years older than Marshal Ankwicz. General Ożarowski, who was six years younger than the chancellor, was considered a great old man and was carried to the gallows due to his age. Then if he was hanged, Prince Sułkowski would have been the oldest of those hanged - I do not have to convince anyone here that old men should not be hanged; better let them die, as God commanded, slowly. After reflection, I would say that I have no definite opinion on this matter - maybe it is better to die quickly on a noose than die slowly and inevitably of an incurable and painful disease which is called the life of an old man. The miraculous rescue from the second gallows, which would have stood beneath the Bernardine Church, Chancellor Sułkowski owed, as it was later said, to a great uproar that broke out literally on the eve of the insurrection - probably on April 15th or 16th. The argument had its cause, at least one of its causes, in the podagra that afflicted the Russian governor, the Tsarina's plenipotentiary minister, Osip Igelström. Before I tell you about this brawl - and about the participation of the Grand Chancellor of the Crown in it - I must briefly tell you about podagra. Podagra (as was often said then) or gout, now long recognized (but I don't know if curable) as an arthritic disease of the joints of the big toe on the left or right foot, was then a mysterious suffering about which little was known and no treatment was known.

The level of knowledge about podagra at the time is well illustrated by a sentence from Julian Ursyn Niemcewicz's *Pamiętniki czasów moich* (*Memoirs of My Times*). We learn from it that Stanisław August's trusted general, Stanisław Mokronowski, precisely during the insurrection, "was attacked by terrible podagra; in order to free himself from it, he ordered that bloodletting be performed on him, hence he soon got a great disease that did not leave him until his death". Whether bloodletting was performed on Igelström when he had an attack of podagra, and whether (similarly to Mokronowski) it ended with epilepsy, I don't know. Though the Russian general suffered terribly - his sufferings were widely known in Warsaw and the people were also very afraid of them, because the attacks of podagra were associated, which is hardly surprising, with attacks of rage, even of mindless madness. Some information about Igelström's podagra can be found in the letters of Ludwig Buchholtz, a Prussian envoy in Warsaw, to King Frederick William II. In early January 1794, Buchholtz wrote that the general "has been very badly affected by podagra for three weeks - so much so that he is on crutches and cannot yet hold audiences". Later letters also mention that Igelström "wants the wounds to heal hastily" and that "he only moves on crutches". It must have been a very serious disease - maybe not only one of the toes, but the entire feet of the Russian ambassador were cracked and covered with ulcers. Immediately after the outbreak of the insurrection, Buchholtz informed his king that the military successes of the Poles were caused by disorder in the Russian army - and this disorder resulted from the fact that Igelström "did not leave his room due to his illness". In Buchholtz's letters we have one more noteworthy piece of information - he wrote that Igelström, unable to walk, received Polish dignitaries in his bedroom. "He gathers the Permanent Council at his bedside every evening". The Permanent Council, which, by its nature, was to rule the country (the king was part of it), had to appear every day at the Russian embassy on Miodowa Street - because the big toe of the tsarina's plenipotentiary minister was in pain. This council, restored in 1793 by the Grodno Sejm (it had previously been abolished by the Four-Year Sejm), then consisted of eighteen people.

One can imagine them there, Polish dignitaries - their order sashes, uniforms, cassocks, court swords, and wigs - around the bed, on which, in lace sheets, lies an angry (because his toe hurts) Igelström. They're in uniforms and cassocks, he in a nightgown - and pulling his leg out from under the covers, shows them his smelly sores and dirty bandages. Whether Stanisław August attended the meetings at the ambassador's bedside is not mentioned, perhaps because even talking about it would be terribly humiliating. The fact that dignified and wealthy Polish gentlemen would come to the bed of a Russian officer and look at his ulcerated leg there could only be explained in one way, they were terribly afraid of him. The assumption that they were also afraid of his podagra, that is, of the moods of his swollen toe, will probably not be far from the truth. A few weeks before the outbreak of the insurrection, Igelström's police arrested two conspirators - Klemens Węgierski and Stanisław Potocki (later a general, known as Staś).

Initially, they allegedly held up well, but after a dozen or so days of interrogations in the basements of the embassy on Miodowa Street, they turned out to be willing to negotiate - and, as Antoni Trębicki wrote in his memoirs, "unable to withstand the severity of how they were dealt with, they revealed their partners". On the basis of these testimonies, Igelström compiled a list of conspirators, and then, after summoning Prince Sułkowski to the embassy, gave him a note addressed to the Permanent Council, in which, reportedly quite brutally, he demanded the prompt arrest and trial of all those whom he had placed on his list - giving the Council twenty-four hours to do this. "Having a list of - wrote Trębicki - several dozen people belonging [to the conspiracy], he gave a threatening diplomatic note to the king and the Permanent Council, that all those conspirators be immediately tried and punished with death". Trębicki may have exaggerated a bit - according to the description in Karol Wojda's work *O rewolucji polskiej* (*On the Polish Revolution*), the note contained the names of "Twenty most eminent people"; according to the Russian general Pistor, Igelström "demanded the imprisonment of the twenty-six suspected persons". Among those whose imprisonment (and perhaps sentencing to death) was demanded by the ambassador, there were several people well known in Warsaw at that time - as Wacław Tokarz claimed, the list included the names of Józef Pawlikowski, Eliasz Aloe, and Father Józef Meier. The brutal tone of the note is evidenced by the description in General Pistor 's *Pamiętniki* (*Recollections*) - it was, in his opinion, "a memorial [...] written with sharp words", which, in the general's opinion, "undoubtedly contributed to the inflaming of minds and accelerating the beginning of the uprising". Why was it that Prince Sułkowski was called to the embassy is not entirely clear to me. Igelström should have summoned Ankwicz to Miodowa Street, because it was he who, as the Marshal, chaired the Permanent Council.

Though perhaps Sułkowski had to come to the ambassador's call because he presided over the Council's Department of Foreign Interests, which made him something like a minister of foreign affairs, and so receiving and conveying diplomatic notes was his responsibility. Having received Igelström's note, which probably happened on April 15 - if everything went on as it should (that is, according to the order of things that is currently available to us), then three or four days later, Prince Sułkowski would have been arrested by the insurgents, and after more or less three weeks he would have hanged on the second gallows near the Bernardine Church - therefore, having received this note, the Grand Chancellor presented it the next day (April 16 - on the eve of the insurrection) to the Permanent Council, which was then deliberating at the Royal Castle. According to Trębicki, the Council, having found itself in such a troublesome situation (here a Russian governor, and here, also not far away, conspirators), called on Sułkowski to speak about the ambassador's demands - "he gave his opinion as a defender of the law in such an important matter". The Grand Chancellor, perhaps taking a small risk, spoke in the sense that the matter of punishing the conspirators was not within the competence of the Permanent Council, because it "is not a judiciary". The council was very pleased with this opinion (probably because it already knew who Igelström's anger would be turned against) and sent Sułkowski to Miodowa with the order that he should give such an answer to the Russian governor. What happened next, as all accounts say, was dramatic. Igelström, when he heard that his Polish subordinates did not want to imprison and convict the conspirators, fell into a rage. "He received him [Sułkowski] with a deputation - wrote Trębicki - in the most insulting manner, reproaching him for having offended his monarch in a decisive circumstance, and surrounding him with expressions of contempt and shame, sends him back to the king and the Council".

It is easy to imagine what these expressions of contempt and shame looked like - Igelström, leaning on his crutch, jumped on one leg around Sułkowski, maybe even, with one hand holding the rail of his bed (he is wearing a nightgown), slamming the old chancellor on the head and on the back with that crutch, and only repeated this famous Russian word: - Svoloch, svoloch, svoloch (bastard, bastard, bastard)! - Returning to the Castle, where a session of the Permanent Council was taking place, Sułkowski, "smeared and mixed with mud," stood in front of his colleagues and began to tell them how he was received at Miodowa. He did not manage to finish his story. "When he was finishing his report - we read in Trębicki – he was struck by apoplexy, falling unconscious. [...] everyone rushed to the rescue of the dying chancellor". The death of the Grand Chancellor - maybe not death, but, as we shall see in a moment, some half-death, something like a quarter-death - anyway, whatever it was, the stroke that Sułkowski undoubtedly suffered did not allow the session to continue – it was no longer possible to deliberate, because, as Trębicki wrote, "by this accident the members required for the deliberations was broken". Thus, the Permanent Council asked Igelström how to proceed in this situation - "what is left for it to do". The ambassador found the answer to this question easily - he ordered the Council to acknowledge that Sułkowski was alive and to continue the session. "This mindless despot - I quote Trębicki – ordered Sułkowski to be set up, almost dead, on a chair and to decide". Whether this, according to Igelström's will, really happened, that is, whether the Grand Chancellor, dead, half-dead, or quarter-dead, sat in his chancellor's chair and listened to the further deliberations with a half-dead ear – it is not certain. Trębicki stated that Stanisław August did not agree to Igelström's proposal and interrupted the meeting, declaring that the Council would not meet "until there was a full complement". Another version of the continuation of the event was presented by Wacław Tokarz in his book *Warszawa przed wybuchem powstania 17 kwietnia* (*Warsaw Before the Outbreak of the Uprising on April 17*) - based on the testimony of members of the Permanent Council, arrested during the insurrection and questioned at the time by the Investigation Department, he claimed that after returning from the embassy, Sułkowski was "struck by apoplexy" and "fell dead", the meeting at the Castle was not interrupted. The body of the Grand Chancellor was left in the council room - it seems to have been placed there on a kind of hastily improvised catafalque; but I don't know if a catafalque could be improvised, so maybe he was simply put on a table or placed in an armchair - and the Council, along with the king, moved "to the royal reception hall" and continued deliberating there. What happened next?

That is, what happened next with the dead or half-dead chancellor, seated in an armchair and left in an empty hall through which, from time to time, a footman ran with a dish in his raised hand; into which, from time to time, a lady would come there for a moment to adjust her garter and pull up a stocking, which had slipped a little. People were certainly not very interested in the corpse (if it was a corpse), because there was no time for it, they were at that time interested in something else - shooting began on Miodowa and Podwale before dawn; in such a situation, it is rather difficult to assume that there would be someone in the Castle who would have the head to look after an old man after a stroke – especially an old man who was then not needed by anyone for anything.

Forgotten, in an empty castle hall, an old, paralyzed traitor. There is also, a young lady who hides behind the door there and fastens her garter. Or alternatively. Forgotten, in an empty hall, the corpse of an old traitor. The same young person who puts her hand over her mouth to avoid screaming when she realizes the someone who is lying on the table is looking at her garter. Was the Chancellor - if he was not a corpse - led out of the Castle by an old butler who took pity on the half-paralyzed old man? We'll never know that. Sułkowski was presumed dead - probably also because there was no such thing as resuscitation at the time, there were no intensive care rooms in hospitals and no such thing as ventilators were known, so whoever had a heart attack or stroke (was affected by apoplexy) died quickly. "He was touched by apoplexy - wrote Karol Wojda in his book *On the Polish Revolution* - and it was a favor to him as he was not hanged on May 9th; because the common people were very prejudiced against him". The verb used by Wojda seems a little nonsensical, but only at first glance - Igelström and his podagra, and the result of this podagra, his rage, and the result of this rage, apoplexy, and finally the result of this apoplexy, all this actually served the Chancellor, but in the end, it is not very clear what for. Teodor Żychliński, the author of the *Złota księga szlachty polskiej* (*The Golden Book of the Polish Nobility*), claimed in the fourth volume of this work (published in 1882) that the death of Prince Antoni Sułkowski did not take place on April 16, 1794, in Warsaw - this event took place over a year and a half later, on January 26, 1796, in Rydzyna.

That Rydzyna, the capital of the Sułkowski Estate, was the prince's hometown. Żychliński even had some grudges against nineteenth-century researchers that they considered an attack of apoplexy tantamount to death. The authors of such genealogical compendiums usually know exactly what they are writing about and are rarely wrong. Though it can also be assumed that the author of *The Golden Book*, to whom the papers from the Rydzyna archive were made available, transferred the death of the Grand Chancellor of the Crown to Rydzyna at the request of his grandson or great-grandson. What really happened, we will never find out. What does this tale of podagra and apoplexy reveal? Here's what it reveals. On April 16, a metaphysical scandal took place in the triangle between St. Anne's Church, the Royal Castle, and the Załuski Palace on Miodowa Street. For arthritic pain in someone's big toe, right or left, to decide whether someone will hang or not, that is -

from some transcendent point of view – completely nonsensical and unacceptable. It can also be concluded from such a point of view (which, moreover, is inaccessible and unimaginable to us) that our entire history is also nonsensical and unacceptable - that the right to make decisions, about what happens in the world, about someone's life and someone's death, could be held by some ulcerated and sore toe.

Chapter 5.

THE HANGING IN KRAKÓW (OR BEHEADING WITH A SCYTHE)

The news that hangings had started in Kraków reached Warsaw almost immediately, on the fourth or fifth day after Kościuszko had initiated the insurrection. By March 29, the Prussian envoy in Warsaw, Ludwig Buchholtz, reported to his king (Frederick William II), that in Kraków "a gallows was erected - in the absence of a guillotine - a tribunal was established

Scythmen of the Kosciuszko Uprising

and a trial was immediately initiated against Poles who are supporters of Russia". We can find similar information in the diplomatic correspondence of Johann Jakob Patz, the Warsaw charge d'affaires of the Saxon court. On April 2, he informed Dresden that "a gallows has already been erected in the Market Square in Kraków, on which the traitors of the fatherland and those who would not obey Kościuszko's orders would receive punishment". We also learn from Buchholtz that Kościuszko was the initiator of hanging in the Market Square in Kraków: it was precisely he who got involved in the "various madness's and cruelty modeled on France" - or at least gave permission for such madness and cruelty - and, following the example of Robespierre, "ordered people to be judged and hanged". This information looks very exaggerated, because Kościuszko, as it was quickly discovered, was not a supporter of hanging at all, on the contrary, he openly condemned the Jacobin methods of action, and maybe the inhabitants of Kraków even wanted to hang someone at that time but went about doing this (as is typical of the inhabitants of Kraków) a bit sluggishly - and as far as I know, no gallows were ultimately erected on the Kraków Market Square. As for Kościuszko, I must also say that if he were not so gentle (as he was) and began with French madness, i.e. hanging, then maybe later, on the battlefield on Maciejowice, he would not have had to put a pistol barrel in his mouth. As you can see, I am speaking in a radical, even Jacobin spirit - playing a bit of a Kołłątaj or Father Meier. Kosciuszko's pistol, as it is known, did not fire, because the gunpowder was damp. The diary of the then president of this city, whose name was Filip Nereusz Lichocki, tells about the fact that it was intended to hang and behead people in Kraków (but it was just intentions, and somehow the people did not know how to or did not really want to do it). We have a very interesting description in his diary of what happened in Kraków on March 24 - that is, on the very day when Kościuszko swore to the nation on Kraków's Market Square. When the said Lichocki, after a conversation (which was a bit unpleasant for him) with Kościuszko and General Wodzicki, entered the seat of the municipal authorities, he found "crowds and constriction [...] of citizens, young people, even ladies standing in front of windows".

The youth (as Lichocki wrote: "wearing sashes with various inscriptions" - "Freedom or Death!" And "Vivat Kościuszko!"), seeing the president, actually the deposed president, decided that it would be good to start the insurrection by bringing him to justice. "As if - said Lichocki (a cunning collaborator, but a keen observer and a brilliant stylist) – ready to fight over something with someone [...] they were rubbing against me, hitting me, looking into my eyes, ears: a guillotine for the president! They whispered". When Lichocki found out that they wanted to behead him with a guillotine, he recognized (rightly, though perhaps a bit prematurely) that the most terrible thing had come - revolution. "I found young people who were not from Kraków, but Paris, French people, I suffered a lot by their hands, and I could not push myself through to the presidential seat which was mine". The president heard for the second time that the revolution demanded his head the next day, March 25, when Kościuszko summoned him, along with the entire magistrate, to the Szara Town House at the corner of the Market Square and Sienna Street. The Chief's headquarters and his military chancellery, headed by Aleksander Linowski, were then located in the Szara Town House. There, Lichocki met a certain merchant from Kraków, whose name was Alojzy Krauz (as we read in his *Pamiętnik* [*Diary*]: "a Kraków merchant, and once a counselor for the Constitution of May 3"). The merchant, seeing Lichocki, became very happy - "and whispered in my ear: 'Oh the guillotine for the president! To the lantern and the gallows with him!'". These whispers into his ear quickly became loud and the Kraków commissioners of order (appointed at that time by Kościuszko) were supposed to confer (at least this is what Lichocki himself claimed) whether the president should be hanged, preferably in the Market Square, somewhere near the Cloth Hall or St. Mary's Basilica - and they even voted on it. "As a noble person told me, they consulted about me and voted with each other, if it would be proper to hang me, a man guilty of nothing". The President of Kraków was to be hanged or beheaded (at least according to his version), to set an example - "especially to instill fear into the populace". The voting, about which the author of the *Diary* wrote, most likely turned out to be somewhat favorable for him, because the whole thing ended in nothing - Lichocki still had some small unpleasantness', but he was not hanged, and then he was probably forgotten, because a month later when the Criminal Court of the Kraków Voivodeship was established by Kościuszko's order (issued on April 28 in the camp near Stary Brzesko), no attempt was made to bring him before it.

Of course, a question arises here as to why no one was executed at that time in insurrectionary Kraków (apart from a certain priest, whose story I might tell later), while in insurrectionary Warsaw, the executed could be counted in the dozens (along with the hanged, who were hanged because they hanged others). I do not know if a good answer can be given on this point, mine would be this. Back then, Kraków was a small city, with less (probably even much less) than 10,000 inhabitants. "When Stanisław August stayed there after his return from Kaniów in 1787 - wrote the publisher of Lichocki's *Diary* - the magistrate gave him a statistical view of the city, which shows that the total population did not exceed 9,449 male and female souls". Six years later, the population was probably even smaller, even much smaller. The presumed population of Warsaw at the beginning of 1792 was (according to various twentieth-century calculations made on the basis of partial results of the census conducted in January and February of that year) from 98,000 to 116,000 people. Warsaw was therefore - in terms of population - at least ten times larger than Kraków. So maybe hangings were not carried out in Kraków precisely because it was then a small town, in addition desperately depopulated, and in small towns, hanging usually fails - in order to hang effectively, at least for political or national reasons (it is different in the case of exclusively personal reasons), you need a large crowd, preferably thousands of people, one that is able to forget that it is made up of individuals, that it is divisible and divided into persons, and admits that it is precisely - a crowd. The point is that it is not only the hangmen who hang - that is, those who are right next to the gallows. Everyone hangs, precisely the whole undivided crowd, those who hang and those who look at it, and even those who don't want to look, but are present. The hanging crowd becomes one person who hangs. It becomes one big, terrible monster - overwhelmed by the desire to kill. I speak about a great monster, but I would caution against saying that a hanging crowd is something inhuman, that this monster is inhuman, and that a hanging crowd is inhuman. On the contrary. The hanging crowd is one person (all the hands that are there do the hanging), and the hanging is deeply, most deeply human. One could even say that it is fundamentally human - human in its essence. Hanging is one of the few human activities that have absolutely nothing to do with the activities of the animal and plant world - and thus one of such activities that effectively separates people from plants and animals, excludes them from vegetation and animality, it sets a border and beyond this border creates their own human world, thus making them - precisely human.

It is good to be aware of it and draw conclusions without being hysterical. Hanging (this also applies to guillotining, anyway, all technical methods of murder) is deeply humanistic and exclusively humanistic - it is, in the animal and plant universe, something completely unique. One could even say that it is some kind of humanistic miracle, one of such miracles. Hedgehogs do not hang hedgehogs, neither has it been heard of cats that would hang other cats. On the other hand, there are cases of people hanging cats. People would hang hedgehogs too if they didn't prick their fingers. As for Kraków's ideas regarding the use of the guillotine, which are mentioned in the *Diary* of Filip Nereusz Lichocki ("the guillotine for the President"), it is worth adding here that - as the historian of the that insurrection, Tadeusz Kupczyński, tells us - on March 24, when Kościuszko took the oath in the Market Square, and the gathered people disturbed the elevated ceremony, demanding the immediate punishment of the traitors of the fatherland (i.e. their immediate decapitation), voices were heard there, proposing the use of a familiar and easily accessible tool to carry out the death sentences - namely a scythe with its blade put upright. This idea, as can easily be assumed, was caused by the fact that at that time there was no one in Kraków who knew how to construct a guillotine - and then there was no one who knew how to operate it. Specialists would have had to have been brought in from Paris or Warsaw (there were a few French people who knew their stuff and offered their services in the capital at that time), and that was impossible - it was too far to Paris, and the Muscovites still ruled in Warsaw. Beheading with a scythe would probably not be easy, but it was a feasible thing - some technique would just need to be developed. The fact that this Krakowian invention - a scythe instead of a guillotine - was not applied, may also be attributed to the stiffness and helplessness (also inborn goodness) of the Krakowians. Beheading President Lichocki with an upright scythe - the president is kneeling, folding his hands in prayer, in front of St Mary's Basilica, and then the executioner, leaning on the scythe (blood is dripping down the blade, and the executioner is wearing a Kraków sukmana), lifts his head by the hair and shows it to the people – that would have been a great scene that would be told by generations later. The Krakowians could have been proud - that they also have such a beautiful memento.

Chapter 6.

A CIRCUS AT THE CORNER OF BRACKA AND CHMIELNA STREETS

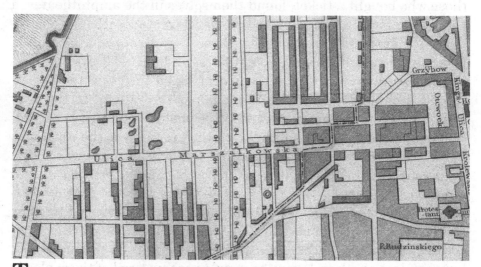

The circus was located more or less where, years later, a home was built, which housed the Jabłkowski Brothers' big shop. Perhaps the placement of the circus - I'm not sure - should be located a little closer to the current intersection of Chmielna, Bracka, Szpitalna, and Zgoda. Maybe it even stood in the middle of this intersection. I often walk that way, and every time I stand at the crossroads with a slanting view of the Palace of Culture and Science, I hope to hear the roar of wild animals. Or their cries - when they are dying. Though somehow one can't hear anything like that there now, and this intersection has also been civilized. Maybe someone will put up a circus there again (or put it in the basement of the Jabłkowski Brothers' home) and we will hear the roars again. The circus, which a jeweler named Ingermann (or Ingerman) had put up at (or near) the intersection in 1776, was a round wooden structure in the shape of an amphitheater. The entrance was through the gate of a ground floor house, the frontage of which faced (probably) Bracka Street, and just behind this front building, in the depth of the back yard or courtyard, between two annexes, the circular amphitheater was situated. Further there was a kind of park or garden, which occupied (this is how I imagine it) the area between the present Bracka and the present Marszałkowska. Italian poplars grew in the park. Those who entered the amphitheater (there were three entrances there, two, I suppose, intended for viewers, and the third for wild animals, which were kept, also according to my guess, in the annexes of the front building or somewhere in this garden behind Bracka), and those who bought a ticket, found themselves in the amphitheater, a three-tiered arena, around which box seats were located.

Or perhaps it was that the box seats were only on the ground floor, and there were benches on the first and second floors - or maybe there were no benches, and whoever had a ticket for the first or second floor had to stand leaning against the railing. In the very center, opposite the main entrance - the one through which, according to my guess, the animals entered the arena - was the royal box, intended for Stanisław August and his lovers. The circus was a kind of animal theater - as Antoni Magier wrote in his *Estetyki miasta stołecznego Warszawy* (*The Aesthetics of the Capital City of Warsaw*), "ferocious animals stumbling against each other or hunting those animals was supposed to amuse the masses of Warsaw". According to Magier, the animal theater was initially very successful, but then less and less: "soon the people became tired of these bloody performances and there were few fans for them". As for the animals that appeared at the corner of Bracka and Chmielna Streets, it can be assumed that the Warsaw viewers visiting the circus must have been a bit disappointed with them. In one of the illustrations, which shows the amphitheater, we see, in the middle of the arena, an elephant - it seems, fighting with animal tamers attacking it (such tamers and hound valets were then called circus masters) - but it seems that this elephant must have been some unusual exception on Bracka. Perhaps the elephant was just the author's idea, and in reality, there was no elephant there. The description by Antoni Magier states that there were fights of "wild oxen, bears, buffaloes, wild boars, as well as various species of dogs". Friedrich Schulz, who was most likely at the circus in 1793 (and later described this spectacle in his *Podróże Inflantczyka z Rygi do Warszawy* [*Travels of a Livonian from Riga to Warsaw*]), saw a bear torn apart by dogs, a lion devouring a sheep, as well as a bull fighting against wolves on Bracka Street. The Livonian assessed these performances as bloody and cruel, but he probably did not like them very much - he wrote, comparing the Warsaw circus with a similar (and then famous) spectacle he watched in Vienna, that the masses in Warsaw "applauded warmly, but those more demanding like us experts only moved their arms with pity".

An opinion that completely rejects the Warsaw animal theater can be found in the account of an anonymous German who was on Bracka Street in June 1791 - and described his trip around Poland in a report published that year in the journal *Berlinische Monatsschrift (Berlin Monthly Bulletin)*. According to this German, the spectacle that was shown to him in the amphitheater on Bracka Street was something indescribably disgusting. "There is nothing more disgusting and miserable - he wrote - than to watch when weakened, frightened, howling beasts crawl out of the openings of their cages into an open place and soon try to escape back. Such were all the animals and wolves that were released. Not a single animal was merry and agile, except for the circus masters and their dogs. [..-] It was disgusting to see a mannequin representing a human being placed on an ox with a rocket tied to its tail; when the tired ox started jumping around, the mannequin fell to its side and was dragged along the ground. The audience laughed terribly loudly, while I was ashamed for the people before these animals that were looking at us". According to the Livonian Schulz, the circus was one of the favorite pastimes of the people of Warsaw - the amphitheater on the corner of Bracka Street was visited almost exclusively by the common people: shoemakers, butchers, blacksmiths, cart drivers, soldiers, monks, and street girls. A similar claim was made by an anonymous German traveler who "with the exception of a few strangers" (i.e. foreigners) did not see anyone "from the exquisite and beautiful world" there. If only the Warsaw masses enjoyed the entertainment on Bracka Street, then the royal box on the ground floor and the royal presence there may be a bit surprising - why did Stanisław August go to the amphitheater and what was he looking for, what entertainment? However, it seems that he went there quite rarely, although almost all the accounts mention his visits to the animal theater. "The king was asked - wrote Antoni Magier - that he grace such a spectacle with his presence, but his soft heart could not find any enjoyment in these murderous battles, and so, he ordered the animals to be changed immediately". Magier must have mixed something up - the demand to change the animals didn't mean a dislike of such fights, after all. There are many good and bad things to be said about Stanisław August, but it certainly cannot be said that he had a "soft heart" - he was a man of a hard and insensitive heart.

From another place in Magier's work we learn that the last king of the Poles "had short eyesight and used binoculars to look into the distance", and his royal pockets were filled with many different objects - the king carried with him, apart from the binoculars, also a compass, a pencil, a box for sweets, wood for picking in his teeth, a thermometer, a calendar, a pocketknife, and some other small items. He also always had "*sal volatile*" in his pocket (as he had convulsions). So we can now imagine what can be seen through the royal binoculars, when the king is sitting in the ground-floor box of the theater on Bracka Street - first howling dogs crawl out of the cages, and then an ox approaches the box, dragging a mannequin dropped onto the arena. The rocket tied to the ox tail explodes and the king convulses; the candy box, compass, toothpicks, thermometer, calendar, and the *sal volatile* fly out of the royal pockets and end up under the hooves of the raging animal. It is then that the animals are swapped and, in the arena, instead of an ox, dogs and sly foxes appear. How long did the circus on Bracka exist? The *Opis wszystkich pałaców, domów, kościołów, szpitalów i ich posesorów miasta Warszawy* (*The Account of all the Palaces, Houses, Churches, Hospitals, and their Property Owners of the City of Warsaw*) from 1797 (published by Władysław Smoleński as one of the addendums to his *Mieszczaństwo warszawskie* [*The Warsaw Middle Class*]) the circus is not mentioned at all, which could vaguely mean that in the place where the circus should have been, there was already some other house this year - and that the circus, a little earlier, was demolished or (being a wooden building it must have been flammable) it burned down along with its animals. Burning bears, wolves, and foxes running along Chmielna, Szpitalna, and Bracka Streets, venturing even to Nowy Świat and Marszałkowska, hunting for passers-byers as they escaped from the beasts of fire to Świętokrzyska and Krakowskie Przedmieście - is a beautiful sight, a beautiful vision of Warsaw at that time. In *The Account of Houses, Palaces*, we have the name of the jeweler Ingerman - with an indication that he was the owner of a wooden building at 1576 Bracka Street at that time. Whether it was still the wooden, two-story amphitheater, or some completely different building, it cannot be established. There are reports which indicate that the circus was liquidated even before the insurrection broke out, maybe even earlier, right after the adoption of the May 3rd Constitution.

According to Antoni Magier, things happened differently. The circus (also called, according to this author, the Hound House [szczwalnia]) still existed in the first years of the nineteenth century but shows of a different kind were shown in the wooden amphitheater then. In 1808, the building belonged to an Italian named Padavani who showed his wife in the arena to the masses of Warsaw. These were, as Magier wrote, "spectacles of an unburned woman." It is not clear what that would mean - perhaps Padavani set his wife on fire, who, although she was burning, could not be burned precisely because she was non-flammable - that is in other words, fireproof. Later this Padavani divorced his not-quite-burnt *madame*, and the latter, after the divorce, became the owner of the building at the intersection of Bracka and Chmielna, finally civilized the circus - then it became a venue for performances by vaulters and gymnasts visiting Warsaw. If that was the case, then the flaming fur as well as hooves, fangs and claws were replaced with colorful striped costumes, and instead of torn guts, torn intestines and blood oozing from torn maws, viewers could admire the skillful jumps of acrobats. Anyone in the audience who tasted the spectacle of torn intestines would probably not be interested by these jumps, the not-quite-burnt *madame* also did not seem too fun for them.

Chapter 7.

THE SUNDERING OF MAJOR IGELSTRÖM

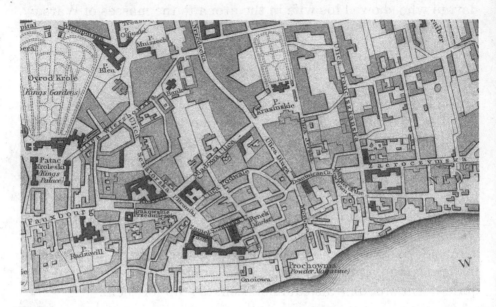

Major Igelström was one of the first, perhaps even the first, victim of the rage that engulfed the people of Warsaw at dawn on April 17. Warsaw woke up - it was still dark, three or four in the morning - and went into some astonishing and inexplicable frenzy. What happened then cannot be explained in any way which would make sense. The Russians were the occupiers, and therefore, as occupiers, they pushed around those they occupied. This, of course, could arouse the anger, even rage of the Poles. In Warsaw, however, there were some miserable remnants of Polish power, there was the king and his Permanent Council, there were also Polish officials, there was a Polish army, and there was a Polish self-government in the city. All this was controlled by the Russians, but Polish money was circulating, people were allowed to speak in Polish, trade in Polish, and pray in Polish. Thus, Poland somehow, though miserably, still existed, and there were even chances that - by deft politics - it would be possible to extend this miserable existence a little longer.

So why did Poles then become overwhelmed with something that could be called the madness of death or the madness of dying?

Why did they prefer to die than live under the rule of the Russian ambassador from Miodowa Street? This is precisely what cannot be explained. The outbreak of the insurrection itself does not explain anything here - it was prepared by conspirators, and may or may not have succeeded, but the fact that it broke out did not mean that those who joined it would fall into a frenzy of murdering and dying. It would be nice to assume that, speaking of the fury that engulfed the people of Warsaw on April 17 and 18, we are dealing with a particular and indigenous tendency of this people, something that is peculiar to this people, and only to them - it is capable of falling into historical madness, to succumb to such madness, precisely because (and only because) that they are the people of Warsaw. Though there is no good evidence for this thesis. It must also be said here (which also does not explain anything, it just complicates the whole matter) that what I called the madness of death happened to both of the belligerent parties at that time - on April 17 and 18, the Muscovites murdered with the same fury on the streets of Warsaw (and died with the same fury, in the same frenzy) as the Poles. Which speaks very well for them - that while defending themselves against the Poles, they fell into a Polish murdering frenzy, and they murdered with equal enthusiasm, even with equal joy. They had no other choice, because when they were surrounded and locked in the center of Warsaw, somewhere on Miodowa or on Krakowskie Przedmieście or in front of the Krasiński Palace, there was virtually no chance for them to be saved, they could only die - and maybe they fell into a frenzy of death just then when they realized this. As for the young Igelström, the circumstances of his death were as follows. Soon after the fighting broke out, probably around half past four in the morning, the old Igelström decided to contact Stanisław August and sent one of his officers from the Załuski Palace to the Royal Castle. This first deputation was intended to clarify the situation - as General Johann Jakob Pistor later wrote in his *Pamiętniki o rewolucji* (*Recollections of the Revolution*), Igelström "sent to the king, demanding an explanation of what had happened".

It was the beginning of negotiations that lasted an hour or two and concerned the possibility of Russian troops leaving Warsaw. It is not entirely clear, but probably a few more envoys from the ambassador appeared in the Castle between four and five or even six - it remains a mystery how the Russian officers managed to get through the crowd that gathered at Miodowa, Senatorska, and Podwale Streets, which was certainly not sympathetic to any possible negotiations between the king and the Russians. "Several messages between His Royal Majesty and General Igelström", mentioned in Pistor's report (under the title *Pamiętniki o rewolucji polskiej z roku 1794* [*Recollections of the Polish Revolution of 1794*], there is a report that this general, when he arrived in St. Petersburg, prepared for Tsarina Catherine), were not successful and Stanisław August finally sent to Miodowa his brother Kazimierz, called the ex-chamberlain prince. From Stanisław August's *Diariusz* (*Journal*), we learn that the king "sent his older brother to Igelström, to persuade him to leave [...] the city, so that the king could calm the city down with this, because the people with the army shouted loudly that until this would happen, they would not stop fighting". According to the *Journal*, Igelström replied to Kazimierz Poniatowski that he would "follow this advice", that is, he would withdraw from Warsaw, "but he did not do it" and "the fire did not stop". After the ex-chamberlain prince, two trusted generals of the king, Stanisław Mokronowski and Arnold Byszewski, went to the Załuski Palace on Miodowa - they were also supposed to persuade Igelström to leave Warsaw. If we are to believe the king's *Journal*, the ambassador reacted quite unexpectedly to their arrival - he stated mainly, that he wanted to "go to the king himself". When the generals heard this, they must have been quite scared, because there was no doubt that if the old Igelström showed up on the street, he would be immediately murdered - he probably would not even have been able to reach the intersection of Miodowa and Senatorska Streets. Mokronowski and Byszewski managed to persuade Igelström from carrying out his unfortunate idea and the ambassador finally decided to send his nephew to the Castle (as Stanisław August's *Journal* puts it, "on Byszewski's advice", which means this was probably the idea of this general), a young major, who had the same surname as him.

According to the *Journal*, the young Igelström was to go to the king, "it is unknown with what mission", according to Pistor's report, he received some authorizations regarding the negotiations on the withdrawal of Russian troops from the city: "in order to reach an agreement with the king in this respect, the main commander recognized the need to send his nephew Major Igelström with General Byszewski". Little is known about the young major, his first name is unknown, and even his functions in the Russian embassy are unknown. We only know that he was (Pistor mentioned this) "an officer full of the most beautiful hopes" as well the favorite and adjutant of the ambassador. Most reports call him the nephew of old Igelström, but there are also those which state that he was related to the ambassador in some other, more distant, way. According to Father Jędrzej Kitowicz, the young Igelström was the son of the Russian governor, but this seems unlikely. At that time, there were three Igelström's in Warsaw and the ambassador's nephew should not be confused with the third of the Igelström's, Lieutenant Colonel Count Igelström, who on April 17 commanded two squadrons of Akhtyrsky Chevau-légers - when the young Igelström left the embassy on Miodowa in the company of two Polish generals, Mokronowski and Byszewski, the Akhtyrsky Chevau-légers were standing, ready to attack, near the Cabrit tenement house on Nowy Świat, and it was precisely about this time that the Działyński Regiment, walking along Nowy Świat in the direction of the Holy Cross Church, passed them. After leaving the embassy, Mokronowski and Byszewski took the young Igelström between them and walked along Miodowa towards Senatorska Street. Once at the crossroads of Senatorska and Miodowa Streets, they turned left (I would like to remind you that they were going to the Castle) and came more or less to the place where there is now an entrance to a paid parking lot between Podwale and Miodowa. They were perhaps a little closer to Podwale than Miodowa, perhaps they were already on Podwale. It was there, at the entrance to the parking lot, that they were surrounded by a crowd - a crowd armed with cutlasses, pikes, and pałasz's. At that time stood there, between Miodowa and Podwale (and still stands, but after a few reconstructions slightly moved), the Branicki Palace, where the king's sister, Izabela Branicka, known as the Lady of Kraków, lived.

The shoemaker Jan Kiliński, in his *Drugi pamiętnik* (*Second Diary*), also described the place from which the young Igelström could not go any further as a little closer to Podwale than Miodowa: "the nephew was killed in front of the Palace of Mrs. Kraków from the direction of Podwale". The place of the death of the young Igelström was situated a little differently by Father Kitowicz, who claimed in *Historia Polska* (*Polish History*) that the major had been driven from the parking lot to or dragged to Zygmunt's column: "while his son [Igelström's], a colonel, was driven in another direction in the tumult, before the column of king Zygmunt [...] and was killed". General Mokronowski, who was liked in Warsaw, was driven away, General Byszewski, who was disliked, was beaten with the flat side of pałasz's. At least, this is what Kiliński maintained in his *Second Diary*: "General Byszewski was horribly beaten with pałasz's". Stanisław August put it differently in his *Journal*, according to which Mokronowski was pushed away, while "old Byszewski [...] was badly wounded in the head". Kitowicz, on the other hand, believed that Byszewski had received a blow with a kord: "the general was hit by a kord in the hand, after receiving this strike, having abandoned the Muscovite [...] he fled to the king"[1]. When Byszewski (with his face covered in blood or beaten) escaped to the Castle, the people went after the young Igelström. None of the accounts give in depth details of the death of the nephew and favorite of the last governor of the First Republic. We learn something more only from Father Kitowicz, who devoted one sentence to this matter: "it was not enough that he was killed, but also torn to pieces by the enraged mob". Kitowicz also claimed - but this is obviously a fabrication - that the scene of being torn to shreds (or pieces) was watched from the Castle window by Stanisław August, "this hypocrite". He was to be, "overcome with fear", shouting: "I hold with the nation, beat, kill our tyrants" - and then, in great fear and madness, he ran along the corridors and castle stairs, still shouting: "Beat, kill!" A fabrication, but a great one, worthy of the great writer that was Kitowicz. As it seems to me, it was impossible to see what was happening beneath Zygmunt's Column from the Castle windows, even more so what was happening in front of the Branicki Palace - the view was obscured by the tenement houses in front of the Castle, their frontage, which connected with the Kraków Gate.

When the crowd finished their work and from the parking lot, they went towards Miodowa and towards Podwale, in the place where the young Igelström was last seen, there was nothing: no body, no corpse, not even shreds of clothing, not even shreds of a hat, even one golden thread of officers' braiding. It was all gone - as if those who tore the young man to pieces put his remains into their pockets.

---

[1]Kord: A short sword or long knife, stiletto, or dagger.

Chapter 8.
A GALLOWS IN VILNIUS

Pac Palace Vilnius, Wikipedia

Hetman Szymon Kossakowski, anticipating the imminent outbreak of the uprising, perhaps even being informed of it by his officers, returned to Vilnius quickly on the night of April 21-22. An anecdote – though not necessarily being true - says that as he was crossing the Green Bridge (Lit: Žaliasis tiltas, Pol: Zielony Most) his horse stumbled, and the rider painfully banged himself up as he fell. However, he did not fall into the Neris, and when his adjutants put him on his feet, he was supposed to laugh and say: - *What is supposed to hang, will not drown.* - Another version of this anecdote, written down by the Russian general Engelhardt, places this event in a slightly different time of the year. According to this version, the hetman "during his last trip to Vilnius" was riding across some "small river" and fell into the water when the thin ice broke under his horse. "From this - Engelhardt claimed – an inscription was made on his gallows: What is supposed to hang, will not drown".

The second version is highly unlikely, as no other source mentions the inscription on the gallows, and the event took place at the end of April, when the rivers were not frozen anymore. After returning to Vilnius, Kossakowski went to General Nikolay Arsenyev, the commander of the Russian troops stationed in Lithuania, striving to persuade him to withdraw from the city. He believed that Vilnius could not be defended, and the Russians would only be able to fight the insurgents effectively if they concentrated their troops in a camp outside the city.

Had Arsenyev heeded the prudent advice of the hetman, events would have turned out differently - and Kossakowski would probably have enjoyed his somewhat fictional hetman title for many more years. The title was a bit fictional, as Kossakowski received it from himself - he named himself Lithuanian Field Hetman in June 1792, when Russian troops and the troops of the Targowica Confederation that supported them entered Vilnius. There were also those who claimed that the title of Lithuanian Field Hetman had been given to Kossakowski by order of General Mikhail Krechetnikov, who was commander of the Russian army entering the eastern territories of the Republic at that time (that is, in June 1792). Julian Ursyn Niemcewicz spoke about the first version – that Kossakowski gave the title to himself - in *Pamiętniki czasów moich* (*Memoirs of My Times*); the second version - that the title was given by Krechetnikov, that is in fact by Tsarina Catherine – is mentioned by Michał Kleofas Ogiński in his *Pamiętniki o Polsce i Polakach* (*Memoirs about Poland and Poles*). It is all the same - when Arsenyev, having deemed that there would be no insurrection, disregarded the prudent warnings of the hetman and went to sleep, Kossakowski was left with nothing more to do but go to sleep himself; when they both woke up it was all over.

The insurrection began on the night of April 22-23. The Polish units, which the conspirators managed to win-over to their cause, encountered almost no resistance in Vilnius. Arsenyev, who lived in the Pac Palace on Didžioji Street (Wielka Street), woke up with his legs tied; his officers, too, had been tied up before they could do anything. As for Hetman Kossakowski, there are several slightly different stories about his arrest. One thing is certain - Kossakowski, of all those who were hanged by the Insurrection of 1794, was the only one who tried to defend himself. The others (those hanged later in Warsaw) begged for mercy and kissed the feet of those hanging them. The self-proclaimed hetman, surprised in bed by the insurgents, pulled a pistol out from under his pillow. Whether this was because he was a brave man by nature, or because he had no illusions and knew what awaited him, if he let himself be tied up - we cannot establish; moreover, there is no reason to establish this. This happened in Miller's House on Vokiečių Street (Niemiecka Street). One of the stories says that Kossakowski, hearing the firefight and screams in the street, ordered his bodyguards to defend the house, and he himself, pistol in hand, climbed the back stairs to the attic and hid behind the chimney. When four officers who had come to arrest him appeared in the attic and summoned him to surrender, he started shooting at them from behind the chimney. General Engelhardt even claimed in his *Pamiętniki (Diaries)* that the hetman was incapacitated "after a desperate defense", that he fired "as long as he had loaded weapons" and that "he killed or injured several of the attackers". Though this might be an exaggeration.

According to another story, Kossakowski did not manage to get out to the attic and four of Jasiński's officers (their names are known: Michałowski, Achmatowicz, Gawlasiński, Kleczkowski) surrounded him on the back stairs of Miller's House. When the hetman called them insurgents or rebels, one of them (it was Michałowski) insulted him in some unknown way – he probably spit on his face or hit him in the head with a pistol butt. Yet another version of the arrest was presented by the Warsaw *Gazeta Powstania Polski (Gazette of the Polish Uprising)* in the issue of May 8. "Hetman Kossakowski - we read there – hated by his own guard as well as by the entire army was not defended. Though when the officers came to take him from his bed to detain him, his adjutant Rudziński, was the only one grabbing a pistol in the Hetman's defense, and was shot in the head, while the Hetman was arrested and taken to the Cekauz". What happened to that adjutant - whether he survived or not – it is not known.

The overpowered Kossakowski had his hands tied behind his back, a hemp rope was placed around his neck and, as he stood - in a yellow nankeen banyan and in morning slippers - was dragged by a rope through Vokiečių, Didžioji, and Pilies Streets (Zamkowa Street) to the Arsenal - as in Warsaw, it was called the Cekhauz and was located behind the Castle Gate. Kossakowski spent two days in the Cekhauz - where Arsenyev and several senior Russian officers were also imprisoned. Other Russian officers and soldiers were kept in St. Casimir's Church on Aušros Vartų Street (Ostrobramska Street) - previously (just in case) the Blessed Sacrament was taken out of there. The leaders of the Vilnius Uprising clearly wanted things to transpire quickly. As it can be assumed, for the sake of the success of the uprising, they wanted what they were doing to be final and irreversible. This policy of fait accompli decided the fate of the Hetman.

Two days after the outbreak of the insurrection, on April 24, the Supreme National Council was established in Vilnius, the next day a Criminal Court was established to sentence the traitors. In the universal of the Supreme Council issued that day, it was stated that the Criminal Court was to act quickly and effectively: "if a sudden need requires it within 24 hours, the accusation, evidence, and the decree should be finished, and the decree will either be the dismissal of the accused's reprimand, or the death of the guilty by the gallows". The Criminal Court complied with the order of the Supreme Council and on the same day, April 25, issued its first sentence and ordered its immediate execution. The whole matter was successfully completed within two days - this undoubtedly proves both the organizational talent and the determination of Jakub Jasiński. The fact that Kossakowski would be hanged on April 25 must have been known even before the sentence was passed and announced, maybe even on the evening of the previous day, because the first viewers appeared near the gallows, which was erected in front of the City Hall, at dawn. Jasiński chose the place in front of the Vilnius City Hall probably not by accident. As King Stanisław August wrote in his *Diariusz* (*Journal*): "Kossakowski was hanged in the same place where he had appropriated the hetman's dignity two years ago". From the *Gazeta Narodowa Wileńska* (*The Vilnius National Gazette*), which was just then starting to appear, one can learn that the execution began at two in the afternoon. It was a spectacle carefully planned (undoubtedly by Jakub Jasiński) and perfectly carried out. The hetman was brought to the gallows in a multi-horse blue carriage that was allegedly owned by Jasiński. The carriage, going towards the Gates of Dawn (Lit: Aušros vartai, Pol: Ostra Brama) along Pilies Street was surrounded, as *The National Gazette* wrote, by an infantry unit in "square formation" and by "officers on horses with pistols pointed at each other" - it must probably be understood that the officers were holding pistols in their hands that were aimed at Kossakowski, who was riding in the carriage. The hetman was dressed in the same outfit in which he was arrested - that is, in that yellow nankeen banyan (a robe that was very well made, as it was supposedly lined with lambskin), and in slippers of unknown appearance. Of course, the question arises why this domestic outfit was chosen, and not something more appropriate for such an occasion, i.e. something more solemn.

There is no doubt for me that Jasiński must have thought through this matter. He could have decided to hang Kossakowski in the outfit of a Lithuanian Field Hetman - but something like this would probably be an insult to the Republic, its attire, and customs; it could also be understood by the public as acceptance of the appropriation done by the self-proclaimed hetman. Another option, risky but worthy of consideration, could have been to hang Kossakowski in the uniform of a lieutenant general of the Russian army - he was said to wear this uniform every day, and the rank of lieutenant general was awarded to him by Tsarina Catherine right after the establishment of the Targowica Confederation. However, this would have been very risky on the part of Jasiński, because it would in fact mean something like a challenge (even a brazen one) towards the Tsarina. Kind of like saying to this nasty woman – here, have your beloved general, but on a noose. Perhaps that is why the insurgents (a bit afraid of Chatherine's fury) decided not to dress Kossakowski in his favorite uniform. By the way, it is worth adding here that the Hetman was a great admirer of the Petersburg empress - and he had great ideas on this matter, such that that none of the members of the Targowica had the nerve to come up with.

On June 26, 1792, the day after the establishment in Vilnius of the General Confederation of the Grand Duchy of Lithuania (this was the Lithuanian equivalent of the Targowica), Kossakowski, now as Field Hetman of that duchy, issued a universal which contained the best of his ideas - the Russian tsarina was presented in it as a miracle of nature. "I cannot see and no one can perceive the general happiness of our country, unless it is in regards to this enormous neighborly power, which has in its own self-interest, to see us capable of governing ourselves and happy; as in the person whom the next centuries will lay between miracles of nature and greatness - the Brightest Empress of all Russia".

On the other hand, those who do not love and adore this miracle of nature, Kossakowski presented in his universal (in a somewhat poetic manner) as "lizards jerking their mother's guts; slow-worms devouring their own fetus'". I am a bit sorry now that Jasiński had not decided to dress this scoundrel in his Russian lieutenant general's uniform before the execution – he was ultimately

(I speak about Jasiński) killed on the ramparts of Praga, so the fury of the Russian tsarina would not hurt him in any way. Though I return to the City Hall, or rather - because this is where the gallows were situated by *The Vilnius National Gazette* – to the main guard house near the City Hall. There stood, as described in *The Gazette*, "the army arranged in several lines", as well as "all the magistracy and an innumerable crowd of people". As the description of the events prepared by Henryk Mościcki (in his book about the life and death of Jasiński) state, when the blue carriage stopped under the hauptwache, Jasiński, without getting off his horse, delivered a short, one-sentence speech to the army and the people. That one great sentence went like this. "Gentlemen! an action will be completed here about which no one is allowed to echo, and whether they like it or not, everyone should remain silent, and whoever raises their voice will immediately be hanged on these gallows". Right after Jasiński, the Vilnius lawyer Gaspar Elsner, who was also from horseback, took the floor, acting as a public counsel (or, in other words, prosecutor) of the Criminal Court. He read out a short decree which included five charges brought against Kossakowski by the Criminal Court. He was accused, firstly, of invading "in the ninety-second year [...] the countries of the Republic" (Poland and Lithuania) "with the Russian army" and "in the spirit of the Targowica conspiracy"; secondly, the insolent appropriation of the title of Lithuanian Field Hetman (abolished by the Constitution of May 3) and the unification of "the field buława with Russian army generals"; thirdly, for the persecution of those "hated only by him [Kossakowski]" and otherwise innocent citizens; fourth, for the seizure of power over the Lithuanian army; and finally fifth, for the appropriation of money from the public treasury and military coffers. The decree, signed by eight judges, ended with the statement that the Criminal Court found Kossakowski "unworthy of honor, good fame, and life" and, consequently, sentenced him "as guilty of betraying the Fatherland, to death by the gallows".

After the speech of the instigator, confession followed - it took place in the blue carriage, and since it happened in Lithuania, Kossakowski, probably according to some Lithuanian custom, confessed to and was prepared for death not by a Capuchin priest, but by a Bernardine priest (those who were later hung in Warsaw, Capuchin priests heard confessions). After his confession, "having prepared himself for death", Kossakowski, as the continuation of the report in *The National Gazette* says, "got out of the carriage and stood under the gallows", tried to say something, "began a few words" - maybe it was supposed to be a speech arguing the decree read by Elsner, or Jasiński's speech. From the small article in *The National Gazette* one can vaguely conclude that the hetman, when the noose had already been put on him, decided in any case to say something unpleasant to the people gathered under the gallows, perhaps even a little threatening - from what he said, the only thing understood was that he "gave an order to Baranowski's regiment against the uprising of the nation".

That Baranowski, a colonel named Mustafa, was the commander of a Polish light cavalry regiment stationed at that time in Vilkaviškis. He refused, in the first days of the Lithuanian insurrection (maybe even before its outbreak), to sign the act of uprising and to take an appropriate oath, telling the officers who were members of the insurrection conspiracy and were trying to persuade him to join (as we learn from Mościcki's book about Jasiński) that "not only will he not join the uprising, but he felt it was his responsibility to suppress it wherever it breaks out". As one can see, Mustafa sided, openly and brazenly, with the self-proclaimed field hetman as well as with the Russian occupiers. His further fate, is a very interesting thing for me personally (he was some relative on my mother's side, maybe even my great-great-great-great-grandfather), are unknown - whether he joined the Russian service after the insurrection, and his son (my great-great-great-grandfather) was educated in the Petersburg cadet corps, or he was earlier, in Vilkaviškis, without embarrassment and without noise, hanged on some pine by officers of the light cavalry regiment, disgusted (as they say now) by his treacherous tendencies. If that Colonel Mustafa had been carelessly hanged in Vilkaviškis, the further history of the Baranowski Tatar family might have had a completely different course, it might even have stopped or turned in some unknown direction, it might have been completely twisted, also in such a way that I would not be here in the world now, I would have never even come into it – a slight sadness if anything, but it should be admitted that it would be a bit inconvenient and embarrassing eventuality for me (and for the continuation of this book that I am writing right now). This book would not be here, and you, my dear reader, would not be reading this book now - such would be the result of hanging Colonel Mustafa on a pine in Vilkaviškis. The effect for Mustafa would have been completely fatal - not only because he would be hanging, but also because in 2006 he would not have been recovered by me from complete oblivion. So, I hope that Mustafa was not hanged – the evidence (which is somewhat unclear), is this book's existence. Once again, I have gone on some tangent, so I am returning to the Vilnius hauptwache and the gallows.

The last words of the hetman, warning those gathered against the revenge of the Tatar (or rather Russian) Mustafa, were drowned out by the beating of drums and shouts, as *The National Gazette* put it, of "liberated people" who shouted: "Long live the Republic!" This great shout "filled the whole square and streets". During the hanging, the bells in St. Casimir's Church were rung, and the crowd also shouted: "Vivat!", which did not fit the situation, at least for the situation of the person being hanged. Though perhaps the shout was for General Jasiński and the army standing beneath the City Hall. When the hetman was finally hanged (the technical details of the execution are unknown and we only learn from *The National Gazette* that "the executioner had done his duty"), a kind of parade took place beneath the gallows - the people of Vilnius paraded beneath it, "letting it be known that even to a dead corpse, barely any heart had anything to say". This wording, quite crude, probably says that the hanged man was spit on and cursed at. Kossakowski hung until seven in the evening, and then the "removed body" was "taken away by the servants of the executioners from the gallows to outside the city on waste wagons" - the removal was openly disgraceful, because these two-wheeled wagons were intended for the removal of municipal waste. *The National Gazette* mentioned the gallows outside the city, which seems to indicate that Kossakowski was buried somewhere near the Vilnius execution site. Where it was then I cannot say. However, this was not the end of the Hetman's post-death adventures. Before the First World War, collecting materials to his book about Jakub Jasiński, Henryk Mościcki found the records of the expenses of the city of Vilnius from 1794 in the Vilnius archives, where, on August 16, there was such a record. "For the excavation of Serene Lord Kossakowski, hetm. Of the G.D.L. for people – Polish złoty 3; for garrison soldiers carrying S.L. Kossakowski - Polish złoty 11; for the coffin of S.L. Kossakowski - Polish złoty 80". This amounts to 94 złotys in total. The Russians had captured Vilnius five days earlier - their troops under the command of General Knorring entered the city on August 11. A note in the expense report states that the admirer of the St. Petersburg miracle of nature was found and honored by his protectors for the price of 94 złotys, almost immediately after the Russians restored their order in Vilnius. This speaks, of course, very well of the Russians - that they care so much for their agents, even after their death. We also learn from the Vilnius expense records that in this month of August the city paid 900 rubles to the widow of Szymon Kossakowski as "emergency aid". Where the traitor's corpse lies now, I could not find out - I looked through the lists of those buried on Rasos, but I did not find Kossakowski there. It is not known whether he was buried there in August 1794 either. It should also be added that soon after the Vilnius execution, sometime at the end of April or at the beginning of May, Jakub Jasiński's adjutant and friend, the otherwise famous adventurer Chaćkiewicz aka Chodźkiewicz came from Vilnius to Warsaw (later the owner of many European brothels and gaming houses, appearing in French and Turkish service as General Lodoisco). As Franciszek Karpiński claimed in *Historia mego wieku* (*The History of My Era*), the news he brought about the hanging of Kossakowski made a considerable impression in Warsaw, where hangings had not yet begun. According to Karpiński, Chaćkiewicz was sent "intentionally from there" - that is, Jasiński sent him to Warsaw. The heroic defender of Praga and the author of the famous poem *Jaś i Zosia* (*Jaś and Zosia; Chciało się Zosi jagódek* [*Zosia Wanted some Blueberries*]) can therefore rightly be considered the person behind the idea of hangings in Warsaw. Even if he didn't cause them, he was the first to think of the possibility - and he also thought it would be good to do something about it. At that time, in Warsaw, a sentence was quoted that the adventurer sent by Jasiński was said to be repeating, encouraging to hang people. The sentence was derisive, even a bit offensive, because it accused the Warsawians of laziness or cowardice. "Do you not have hemp, then Lithuania will provide it for you".

Chapter 9.
INK, SHOE POLISH, RAT POISON

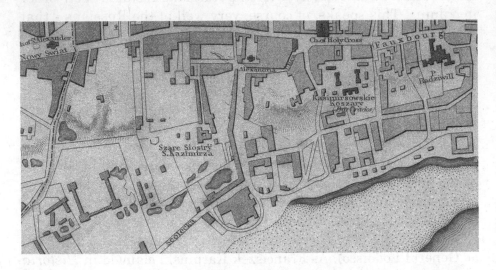

The *Dziennik Handlowy Zawierający w Sobie Wszystkie Oko-liczności, czyli Ogniwa Całego Łańcucha Handlu Polskiego* (*The Journal of Commerce Containing All Circumstances, That is, the Links of the Whole Chain of Polish Trade*), began to be published in Warsaw in 1786. At first it was published once a month, then, in 1792, twice a month, and finally, in 1793, once a week - always with a circulation of about 500 copies. The name of the *Journal* changed a bit from year to year, in 1787 it was the *Dziennik Handlowy Zaw-ierający w Sobie Wszystkie Okoliczności, Pisma, Uwagi i Myśli Pa-triotyczne, do Handlu Ściągające się* (*The Journal of Commerce Con-taining All Circumstances, Letters, Thoughts and Patriotic Comments, Dealing with Trade*; I turn your attention to these "pa-triotic thoughts" – this probably testified to the change of moods in Warsaw at that time), in 1791 it was the *Dziennik Ekonomiczno-Han-dlowy Zajmujący w Sobie Wiadomości Ekonomiczne, Targowe, Fab-ryczne, Transportu Spławnego i Lądowego, Opisanie Miast i Ich Jarmarków, Kontraktowe na Dobra, Summy i Różne Produkta Kra-jowe, a za tym Zajmujący Wiadomości Całego Handlu* (*The Econom-ic and Trade Journal dealing with Economic, Trade Fair, Factory, Naval and Land Transport News, Description of Towns and their Markets, Contracts for Goods, Summas, and Various Domestic Prod-ucts, and therefore Dealing with News of All Trade*). The *Journal* was printed in the Du Pont apartment house on Krakowskie Przedmieście (as a note in one of the yearly's says, "at the 9th Printing House [...] near the Royal Castle, under No 454"). It had two editors - its publisher and editor-in-chief was Tadeusz Podlecki, later ritt-meister of the national cavalry, while Podlecki was probably helped by Father Józef Meier as co-editor (and author of most articles). The articles in *The Journal of Commerce* were not signed, so what Podlecki wrote and what Meier wrote, cannot be precisely deter-mined now. From *The Journal* one can learn many interesting things about contemporary Polish life - first off, but not limited to, economic life. The "Regestr materii" ("Register of Materials"), dis-cussed in *The Journal* in the second half of 1791, lists (among oth-ers) the following topics: "O Kontraktach Krajowych na Dobra, Summy i Różne Produkta"; "Sposób uniknienia opłaty Cła Pruskiego, rodzony niedawno od jednego Senatora"; "Gabinet Krakowski do czytania, warty naśladowania po wszystkich Miastach, przynajm-niej wydziałowych"; "Projekt Generalnej Kompanii Krajowej Eko-nomicznej pod znakiem Orderu Śgo Izydora Oracza"; "Urządzenie Diecezji Poznańskiej względem opłaty Chrztów, Szłubów, Pogrze-bów"; "Kontrakt Xcia Stanisława Poniatowskiego Ex-Podskarbiego Lit. zabezpieczający własność Poddanych swoich, Służyć mogący w czym za wzór innym Dziedzicom"; "Jak są potrzebni Kommisanci po Miastach Portowych, gdzie Handel Polska prowadzi, zamiast uży-wanych dotąd Szyprów"; "Doniesienie JP Monety Doktora JKMci o niezawodnym i łatwym sposobie leczenia ukąszonych od Psa wściekłego, Witka, Węża, Gadziny, Żmii" ("On National Contracts for Goods, Summas and Various Products"; "Method of avoiding the Prussian Duty fee, suggested recently by one Senator"; "Kraków Cabinet for reading, worth following in all cities, at least in depart-ments"; "Project of the General National Economic Company under the sign of the Order of St. Isidore the Laborer"; "Arrangement of the Poznań Diocese with regard to the payment of Baptisms, Mar-riages, Funerals"; "Contract of Prince Stanisław Poniatowski Lithu-anian Ex-Podskarbi, securing the property of his Subjects, serving as an example to other Heirs"; "How are the Commissioners needed in the Port Cities, where Poland trades, instead of the Skippers used so far"; "Report of JP Moneta, doctor of HRH, on a reliable and easy method of treating those bitten by rabid dog, wolf, snake, vermin, and serpents") - to these *Reports* Fr. Meier added "Zaświadczenie autentyczne o skuteczności tego sposobu łeczenia" ("An Authentic Attestation of the Effectiveness of this Method of Treatment") as well as "Uwaga Dziennika o potrzebie rozszerzenia wiadomości tego lekarstwa" ("The Journal's Comment on the Need to Expand the Knowledge of this Medicine"). Also noteworthy is the "Specyfikacja jak wiele Piwa Angielskiego w Londynie wyrabiają? i jak go wiele w Polszczę wypijają?" ("Specifications of How Much English Beer They Make in London. and how much of it do they drink in Poland") as well as "Sposób wieczystego tarowania Chleba w Gdańsku, warty w całej Polszczę naśladowania" ("The Method of Perpetual Taring of Bread in Gdańsk, Worth Following Throughout Poland"). As can be seen from this short list, the ambition of the editors of *The Journal* was primarily to inform about what was happening in various spheres of Polish life, but they also implemented a certain project, as we would say today, modernization - Poland, thanks to the introduction and dissemination of various ideas by the editors of *The Journal*, was to become a modern country, that is, one in which those bitten by a rabid dog or a viper would be treated not with prayers in churches, but with reliable medicines. The "Register of Materials" also indicates that Podlecki's and Meier's modernization ideas were not particularly radical at that time, they urged the replacement of ship pilots with commission agents and the standardization of church fees for baptisms and funerals, but they did not intend to infringe on property and oppose the authorities. It is curious as to why at a certain point Father Meier got bored with such modernization - that is, painstakingly persuading newspaper readers that they should definitely modernize and Europeanize - and started hanging people. Promoting domestic contracts and bringing ministers to read was a tedious job, which could bring about some changes (Europeanizing Polish customs and Polish mentality) after many years, so maybe Meier, seeing that nothing was changing (and those bitten by a rabid wolf, still run away to prayer), wanted to speed things up. Though I don't have a good answer to that question. In May 1787 (precisely when *The Journal* contained *Thoughts and Patriotic Comments, Dealing with Trade*) Podlecki and Meier printed a short article in their paper, entitled "O fabryce atramentu i szuwaksu w Warszawie" ("About the Ink and Shoe Polish Factory in Warsaw"). As I guess, this was something written to order - a kind of extensive advertisement aimed at advertising the earlier mentioned factory or rather its interesting products. It can also be guessed that the owner of the factory, a Warsawian producer of ink and shoe polish, paid the editors for writing and publishing the text advertising his products. The worth of the article about ink and shoe polish is not limited to advertising these products. Even if the editors of *The Journal of Commerce* took money from the owner of a Warsaw factory, they also remained faithful to their modern principles - firstly, they decently informed their readers about a small fragment of Polish economic life; secondly, as part of their modernization project, they reminded the readers of *The Journal of Commerce* that there are certain modern ways of life worth knowing and learning about, including the use of ink and shoe cleaning. The information that there existed (and advertised itself) in Warsaw at the end of the 1780's a factory of ink and shoe polish has, of course, quite a significance for us as well. On the basis of such information, one can guess that there must have been a certain demand for these goods in the capital at that time, and this guess allows us to formulate another one - the demand for various types of ink indicates that writing was done very often and variously (with various inks) in Warsaw at that time; the demand for shoe polish - that in Warsaw shoes were cleaned and it was done in a sophisticated way, with the use of various strange types of shoe polish. For this reason alone, the report on ink and shoe polish is noteworthy. We will see in a moment that it is noteworthy for other reasons as well. Reprinting this short article here, I shortened it a bit, but without damaging its substance; I also modernized punctuation and spelling, but I did so carefully, trying not to spoil the peculiarities of Father Meier's style (if he was the author).

"About the Ink and Shoe Polish Factory in Warsaw"

It is the duty of citizens to report, not only about domestic trades and factories in general, but also to inform the populace about all necessary inventions, especially in a capital city, where fair profit and earnings are not reprehensible in a society of a multitude of burdensome and harmful sluggards. For these reasons, it is announced that the noble Jan Kiszel Zaporowski lives on Bednarska Street in the Obuszyński apartment house at number 2687, who makes and sells the following good quality items: Chancellery ink, a bottle for zł 3. Half-mass ink, bottle for zł. 5. Whole-mass ink, bottle for zł. 8. Dry English ink, a tablet two inches across and lengthwise for zł. 4. All of these inks are of such virtue that they do not mold and last unspoiled for future times. As for the blackness of them, the blacker the more expen-

sive it is. The aforementioned noble Zaporowski in the Obuszyński apartment house also makes and sells: hard Viennese shoe
polish made with varnish, excellent for polishing and does not
allow smudging of clothing, a stick for zł. 4. General English tal-
low shoe polish for shining all hides, which, when it dries up, can
be mixed up with beer of any kind, and does not spoil leather,
as long as liczkowa leather is blackened as little as possible, and
should be wiped with a brush for a clean shine. A quarter jar for
zł. 2. Prussian jar-type olive shoe polish, especially for the shining of soft leather, which is not for mixing up, but beer should be
poured on the top of it in the jar for preservation, so that it does
not dry out, can be used to shine all leathers. Half-quarter jar
for zł. 3. High quality bottled Viennese shoe polish with varnish,
bottle for zł. 12. With such shoe polish, treated shoes do not lose
their shine and it does not melt in the presence of fire, shiny and
beautiful, but is not suitable for mud. This shoe polish in a tablet
is also of the same virtue, except that it is not used for liczkowa
leather, but for overturned ones. Standard bottle of shoe polish
for goat, calf, and Turkish liczkowa leather. A ready bottle of
runny polish for zł. 4. The mentioned Zaporowski also makes rat
and mice poison, that is, sympathetic pills which, when a rat or a
mouse eats them, does not kill them quickly, but it walks around
for a day or night, and bites and chokes others until it dies. A
quarter-jar for zł. 4. He also knows how to do many other things
that he will gladly do, as long as he is informed ahead of time.

Behind the Obuszyński (or Obusiński) apartment house at
number 2687, located at the corner of Bednarska and Sowia Streets,
there was a large courtyard, in which - as it appears from the plans
of Warsaw - there were some huts and outbuildings. I assume that
it was in these huts that the noble and ingenious Zaporowski produced his shoe polish, inks, poisons, and many other things that
could be commissioned for him to make. There were two entrances
to the courtyard, from Sowia and Mariensztat - this news may be of
use to those interested in the history of Warsaw as well as of sympathetic pills for rats (rat poison). When *The Journal of Commerce*
ceased to be published (this happened in 1793), Father Meier did
not give up his modernization ambitions and at the beginning of
the following year he began publishing a new commercial newspaper - it was published under the title *Dziennik Uniwersalny* (*The
Universal Journal*) and was intended as a continuation *The Jour-*

nal of Commerce. Meier's new newspaper was to provide its readers - as its subtitle says – with "various moral, historical, political, economic, and agricultural news, all the skills of inventions, recipes, some for comfort and health". *The Universal Journal*, however, was not a success though (maybe Rittmeister Podlecki's journalistic talent was missing?) and probably collapsed quickly. The matter is not entirely clear - according to the *Bibliografia prasy polskiej* (*The Bibliography of the Polish Press*) by Jerzy Łojek, four issues of *The Universal Journal* were published in January 1794, according to the fifteenth volume of *Bibliografia Polska* (*The Polish Bibliography*) by Karol Estreicher, only fifty-nine pages of this journal are known, and it seems that this is the number Meier managed to release. What has survived to this day (and what I had in my hand) are these fifty-nine pages that are filled with information about the fields of morals, agriculture, botany, the judiciary, and medicine. As always with Meier - they advise readers to imitate European ways of life, suggesting (this is not stated directly anywhere) that whoever becomes civilized and Europeanized will be happy.

Just before the outbreak of the insurrection, the name of Father Meier was reportedly on the list of conspirators whose arrests and convictions were ordered (from the Permanent Council) by General Igelström - this would indicate that the priest-editor's modernization projects took on a slightly different shape, which the Russian authorities did not like. Meier managed to hide and was not found, thus avoiding unpleasant interrogations in the basement of the embassy on Miodowa. Soon after the outbreak of the insurrection, Father Józef started publishing the *Gazeta Warszawska Patriotyczna* (*The Warsaw Patriotic Gazette*). It was published from 22 April to 16 July, twice a week, similarly to *The Journal of Commerce* - under various titles: *Gazeta Warszawska Patriotyczna od Czasu Powstania Siły Zbrojnej Narodu Polskiego* (*The Warsaw Patriotic Gazette from the Time of the Armed Uprising of the Polish Nation*); *Gazeta Obywatelska i Patriotyczna Warszawska z Wiadomości Krajowych i Zagranicznych* (*The Warsaw Citizen and Patriotic Gazette with Domestic and Foreign News*); *Gazeta Obywatelska z Wiadomości Krajowych i Zagranicznych* (*The Citizen Gazette with Domestic and Foreign News*). Łojek's *Bibliography* records its twenty-five issues. In the Library of the Institute of Literary Research, seventeen issues with addendums are available: from No. 4 of May 3 to No. 20 of June 28. According to Estreicher, an issue from July 16 is also known. In

addition to editing *The Patriotic Gazette*, Father Meier had other re-
sponsibilities at that time - he was seen on the streets of Warsaw in
a cassock tightened with a leather belt; he wore a saber or cutlass at
his belt. Can it be said that the moderate modernizer had fallen into
a modernization frenzy after the outbreak of the insurrection? This
is not so simple. Father Meier - the archetype of the Polish modernizer and the Polish Jacobin - is one of the most mysterious figures of
Polish eighteenth-century history. Though ultimately Robespierre
- that is also a mystery. In issue 4 (from May 3), the readers of *The
Warsaw Patriotic Gazette* could read (for 12 groszy - that was the
cost of the copy) the "Dalszy opis sprawy spiskowej w Paryżu" ("The
Further Description of the Conspiracy Matter in Paris") prepared
by Father Meier. The end of "The Further Description" stated: "The
Diedrichten patron was the first beheaded; the heads of de Lacroix
and Danton fell last. Only Danton's head was shown to the people
amid prolonged cries of - Vive la Republique, Long Live the Republic". In number 8, which was issued after the first four executions
in Warsaw (on May 17), Father Meier published an article on the
treacherous activities of the Permanent Council before April 17. "As
it clearly seems - we read there - there was no government or magistracy in our country at all, but servants and Muscovite jurgieltniks".
Further, Father Józef asked: "four have been hanged, and where are
more of them? These vile creatures must be destroyed from the free
earth, lest they with their poisonous breath infect the healthy and
clean air with a wind of harmful treachery and intrigue".

Chapter 10.
THE NUMBER OF GALLOWS

The place as well as number of gallows that were erected in Warsaw on the days of hangings are easy to determine - though only when it concerns May 9. At that time, four gallows were erected. Three of them were erected on the Old Warsaw Market Square in front of the City Hall building, and the fourth on Krakowskie Przedmieście in front of St. Anne's Church, then more commonly called the Bernardine Church. The three Old

Hanging the Traitiors in Warsaw,1794.
Jean Pierre Norblin

Town gallows are known from ink drawings made by Jean Pierre Norblin. They were massive constructions - two vertical beams supported the third, horizontal one, on which the hanging was done and against which the ladder used by the executioner and the executioner's servants rested. As Antoni Trębicki wrote in his diary *O rewolucji roku 1794 (On the Revolution of 1794)*, all four of the May gallows were very solidly built - they were "four mighty gallows". An image of the fourth gallows, the one from in front of the Bernardine Church, on which Bishop Kossakowski was hanged, is unknown to me – I looked for it without success. Though this does not mean that there is no lithograph or drawing that represents this mighty machine. As for the second day of hanging, June 28, the matter is much more complicated, because the reports differ among themselves in this respect - and they establish the place and number of gallows in various ways.

It is usually accepted that a dozen or so gallows were erected in June, more than ten in any case, and this is precisely how Karol Wojda put it in his booklet (somewhat misleading at times) *O rewolucji polskiej w roku 1794* (*On the Polish Revolution in 1794*): "on the evening of the same day [June 27] more than ten gallows were erected, which were dismantled on the recommendation of the president; but the people still decided to do it the next day". Similar information – that there were more than ten gallows - can be found in the first volume of *Pamiętniki o Polsce i Polakach* (*Memoirs about Poland and Poles*) by Michał Kleofas Ogiński (the one who composed polonaises). "On the same evening, 12 gallows were set up in different parts of the city. The president ordered them to be overturned, but the darkness of the night was used to set them back up". A slightly smaller number of gallows - and I think this could be a bit closer to the truth - is mentioned in a letter that Stanisław August (quite terrified at the time) wrote on the morning of June 28 to the President of Warsaw, Ignacy Wyssogota Zakrzewski. "Though when I hear that already 10 gallows are *actu* erected in Warsaw by the people, I also see my fears from yesterday are confirmed". Johann Jakob Patz, in his diplomatic reports sent to Dresden, also reported that ten (or less than ten) gallows were erected on the night of 27/28 June.

In a letter of June 28, he informed the Dresden elector that the masses "stubbornly demanding the death of a few prisoners, erected 8 to 10 gallows in front of the City Hall of the Old Town and on Krakowskie Przedmieście, near the Brühl and ex-hetman Branicki palaces. At 8 o'clock in the morning, the authorities ordered the demolition of the last two and for them to be thrown into the corner of the street". Patz's next letter, of July 2, mentions even fewer gallows. "On Friday night, 6 gallows were erected, including 3 in the Old Town Market Square". The letter goes on to detail exactly who was hanging on which of the six gallows - this seems to increase the credibility of Patz's account; while it is reduced by the fact that not all of those hanged were mentioned by him. Now let's talk about places that are landmarks of the people's anger. They remind us (maybe not, but should, whoever needs to remember, and remind preferably all of us) that not only educated and enlightened elites, but also uneducated, dark, wild, and enraged people have the right to rule Poland. They have at least the right to express their opinion on what Poland, in their opinion, should look like – as long as they want to express their opinion on this matter. As for the places where the June gallows were placed, it would be best to refer to someone who personally took part in setting them up. Such a person was Father Józef Meier, who bustled around the gallows all night from the 27th to the 28th and helped the Warsaw craftsmen, carpenters, and blacksmiths in their work, and even directed their work a little. We will soon see, however, that even Father Meier, although a specialist in constructing death machines, spoke at that time a little enigmatically about their contemporary locations.

In the *Gazeta Warszawska Patriotyczna* (*The Warsaw Patriotic Gazette*) which he published (for some time it was published under the title *Gazeta Obywatelska z Wiadomości Krajowych i Zagranicznych* [*The Citizen Gazette with Domestic and Foreign News*]) Meier included on June 28 this piece of information, which I am fully rewriting here. "From Warsaw on June 28. For the first time yesterday, the people went out in districts with small arms, scythes, and pikes to the trenches to drill, having returned from the trenches, declared their desires and wishes to the President to speed up the punishment for traitors, who cost so much of their work and hardships in keeping to the laws; while wishing to render their last service to the traitors, in the greatest calmness during the night they erected ten gallows, three of them in the Old Town; 4th and 5th in the Commissions Courtyard; 6th in front of the Brylowski Palace; 7th in front of the Branicki Palace; 8th on Krakowskie Przedmieście; 9th on Senatorska Street; 10th on Miodowa Street". As can be seen, Father Meier counted ten gallows - perhaps he even oversaw the building of all ten. This number looks very probable, especially since it is confirmed by Stanisław August's letter to President Zakrzewski - the king was surely thoroughly and regularly informed by his people about what was happening in the city. A note from *The Patriotic Gazette*, if we analyze it topographically, may, however, raise serious doubts. The three gallows in the Old Warsaw Town Square are well confirmed, as Johann Jakob Patz wrote about them, and they are also mentioned in other accounts. This also applies to the gallows in front of the Brylowski Palace, i.e. the Brühl Palace, where prisoners were kept, and the gallows in front of the Branicki Palace.

The first of these two gallows, the one in front of the Brühl Palace (now non-existent), stood either on Wierzbowa Street, or (more likely) somewhere between the Saxon Garden and Saxon Square, maybe in the northwest corner of Saxon Square, maybe a little closer to the guardhouse located there. The second is mentioned in *Historia Polska* (*Polish History*) by Father Kitowicz - it was placed "in front of the Hetman Branicki Palace, right across the Dominican Observant Church on Nowy Świat". The Branicki Palace on Nowy Świat (at the time number 1245) should not be confused with another Branicki Palace, the one near Zygmunt's Column, at the junction of Podwale, Miodowa, and Senatorska Streets. The Dominican Observant Church and the adjacent tavern of these Observants stood where the Staszic Palace now stands, while the Branicki Palace was on the other side of Nowy Świat. Later, after a radical reconstruction, a building was erected in this place, which in the 19th century was called (and is now also called) the Andrzej Zamoyski Palace or the Zamoyski Palace. Currently, in this place, at the intersection of Nowy Świat and Świętokrzyska Streets, there are two houses that imitate the Zamoyski Palace, and they are located exactly opposite the ground-floor windows of the Library of the Institute of Literary Research in the Staszic Palace. Putting it a bit differently: for forty-five years I had the gallows almost under my nose, or at least right in front of my eyes - it was standing across the street and when I looked up from a book while working in the reading room or left a book order form in the Library office, I had to look at it. The lady librarians, who sit in the office (for years located in such a way that whoever sits in it has the other side of Nowy Świat before their eyes), see these gallows every day at every hour. It's just that they don't know anything about it, and neither did I - that the sidewalk across the street is its place. The eighth gallows mentioned in Father Meier's note - "8th on Krakowskie Przedmieście" is also easy to locate and is well confirmed. It stood in front of the Bernardine Church (i.e. Saint Anne's), probably in the exact same place where the May gallows was erected - right in front of the church doors.

Unlike the mighty May contraption, the June gallows was of somewhat poor quality, made amateurishly, even ineptly, and therefore it wobbled a little. Father Kitowicz, precisely referring to the Bernardine one, wrote about "gallows badly dug in, wobbling, and therefore supported by pikes and sabers". The problem is with the ninth and tenth gallows from Meier's note - the one "on Senatorska Street" and the one "on Miodowa Street". The gallows on Miodowa Street is mentioned in the *Obrona Stanisława Augusta* (*The Defense*

of Stanisław August), a work which was probably authored by the
king himself, and which appeared (in 1868) under the authorship
of the royal chamberlain, Mikołaj Wolski. "It would not have taken
much - wrote Stanisław August (or Wolski) – for Węgierski to be
hanged, who even before the insurrection was imprisoned by General Igelström, who was a member of the Council [Supreme Nation-
al] and who, on the Council's order, ordered the gallows erected on
Miodowa Street to be torn down. Harassed and wounded, he barely
escaped with his life by taking refuge in a house where the Imperial
coats of arms were still affixed". There is a lack of clarity in this sentence - the Załuski Palace (the house with the tsarist coats of arms)
was burned out and partially demolished (as shown by contemporary lithographs), so it seems that it would not be a good shelter
from the wrath of the people - but either way, wherever Węgierski
hid, in the ruins of the Russian embassy or elsewhere, it allows us
to somewhat establish the location of the gallows on Miodowa Street
- it must have stood either in front of the Capuchin Church or in
front of the Tepper Palace (where the entrance to the W-Z Route
tunnel is now, or rather above it) or on the other side of Miodowa
Street - in front of the burnt-out residence of General Igelström,
maybe on the small lawn, which is now just in front of the entrance
to the PWN Publishing House. As for Senatorska Street, the matter
is more complicated. One might think that Meier's note refers to the
gallows erected in order to hang or rather to scare the Primate of
Poland, Michał Poniatowski. As it seems to me, in the end no one
was hanged on this gallows, but it was put up - or rather it was intended to be erected in the courtyard of the Primate's Palace, right
under the windows of the king's brother, and then, when it failed (I
do not know for what reason), it was placed nearby, somewhere on
Senatorska Street. There is a mention of this matter in the work of
Father Kitowicz - "but despite this relieving, the people were able
to erect a gallows next to the outbuildings of the prince primate's
palace, the sight of which caused this gentleman to become agitated
and die".

A similar opinion is also found in the report of the Saxon
charge d'affaires, who informed Dresden that the primate had died
as a result of worries that befell him "on 28 June, when it was desired to erect a gallows in the courtyard of his palace, which as a
result stood near his premises". These claims seem a bit misleading, since the primate poisoned himself or was poisoned only about

two months later, but anyway it allows us to locate the gallows on Senatorska Street. If the primate saw it from his windows, it can be placed with a high degree of probability on the other side of the street - somewhere between the exit of Miodowa and the exit of Daniłowiczowska (currently Daniłowiczowska runs a bit differently, and the street called Nowy Przejazd comes to Senatorska Street here). The point is, however, that some other gallows was probably erected on Senatorska Street on June 28 - but it was placed not near the Primate's Palace, but elsewhere, if one is to look at it from the king's brother's windows - beyond Bielańska Street and Wierzbowa Street, almost where Senatorska then slightly turned (and probably still turns) towards Elektoralna and Rymarska. The history of this gallows is almost unknown, all that is known is that it stood somewhere near the Reformist Church. As Józef Ignacy Kraszewski wrote in the third volume of *Polska w czasie trzech rozbiorów* (*Poland during the Three Partitions*), "opposite the Reformists" - but whether it was on the same side of the street as the church and monastery, and further on the Blue Palace, it is unknown. It is impossible to find out which of the two gallows on Senatorska Street Father Meier might have meant when he was writing his note for *The Patriotic Gazette* - and it is also impossible to understand how one of the two gallows could have escaped his attention, because he must have probably known about both. I do not completely know what to do with the two gallows, which Father Józef's note describes as the fourth and fifth - "4th and 5th in the Commissions Courtyard". Both of these gallows undoubtedly stood somewhere in front of the Krasiński Palace.

When it was bought by the Republic in 1764, it began to be called the Palace of the Republic, but because it housed various state institutions, called Commissions - the Military Commission, the Treasury Commission, the Marshal's Commission - the name Commissions Palace was also used then (and still in the 19th century). The area between the Commissions Palace, the building that housed the National Theater (built in 1779), as well as Długa Street (present-day Krasiński Square), was called the Commissions Courtyard, so precisely just as Father Meier called it. Sometimes, instead of Commissions Courtyard, it was called, a bit vaguely, the place near the Commissions or at the Commissions, and this is the form of the name that we find in Antoni Magier's *Estetyki miasta stołecznego Warszawy* (*The Aesthetics of the Capital City of Warsaw*) - when he wrote about the taking apart of city gates "to widen the passage", he mentioned the demolished (under the rule of the Prussians) gate "at the Commissions from Długa Street, next to the former main guard of the pontoniers". The fact that these two of Meier's gallows, the fourth and the fifth, are somewhat located (somewhere between the Commissions Palace and the National Theater; one should remember that the two empire-style cast-iron wells which are there currently, were not there at that time; and that from the side of Długa and the end of Miodowa, there was a gate and a piece of wall) does not settle the matter. The Commissions and the Courtyard before the Commission – as well as the two gallows standing there - have not been found by me in any other account of the events of June 28. What was certainly obvious to the readers of *The Patriotic Gazette* - where the gallows stood; whether in front of the entrance to the Commissions Palace, i.e. the Krasiński Palace, or closer to the entrance to the National Theater; or next to the gate leading to Długa and Miodowa; and who hanged on them - remains a mystery to us. Thus, the gallows in the Commissions Courtyard look a bit shaky - maybe, like the Bernardine one, they were also supported by sabers, maybe even Father Meier supported one of them with his own saber, but I mean not so much their shaky quality as their shaky existence. Perhaps I can find something else on this subject - some account of the events related to the gallows that took place in the Commissions Courtyard.

Chapter 11.
MAY 9ᵀᴴ – THE TRIAL

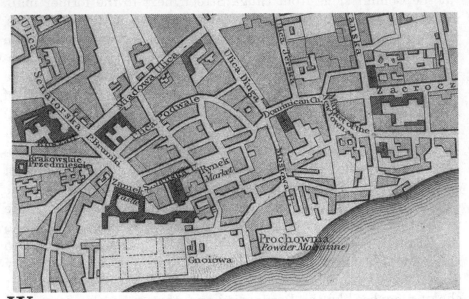

When, Józef Wybicki (the one who three years later wrote the lyrics to the anthem *Poland Has Not Yet Died*) woke up and stood at his window on the morning of May 9 – where he currently lived, having moved out of Wide Krakowskie Przedmieście, in the Old Warsaw Town Square, on its western side, the one which is now called Kołłątaj's side - so when Wybicki stood at the window at dawn that day, looking out along the front wall of the City Hall, he saw that there were gallows. "At sunrise - he wrote later in his diary entitled *Życie moje* (*My Life*) - I saw three gallows erected on the Market Square, one of which was dug into the ground before the very door of the City Hall, which we entered to attend proceedings, the fourth was erected in front of the Bernardine Church on Krakowskie Przedmieście". By dawn, perhaps even before dawn, those who, having placed the machines of death in front of the City Hall, waited around the gallows for the continuation of events. "Already several thousand armed inhabitants of the borough filled the Market Square". This observation of Wybicki's - that it was "several thousand...of the borough" - is confirmed by drawings by Jean Pierre Norblin, depicting the events of May 9.

We can see in them, around the City Hall and beneath the houses next to the Market Square, and on the roof of the stalls surrounding the City Hall, a huge, packed crowd, head next to head, at least a few thousand people, if not more. Antoni Trębicki, in his diary *O rewolucji roku 1794 (On the Revolution of 1794)*, even claimed (perhaps exaggerating a bit) that the crowd was much larger, not a few, but "a mob of tens of thousands, armed with scythes and pikes, irons, pałasz's, axes mounted on poles". Wybicki, who was a counselor of the Provisional Substitute Council (this allowed him to wear a crimson crepe handkerchief on his left forearm, which was a kind of a pass that allowed him to safely move around the city), seeing what was happening and what it would lead to, immediately went to the City Hall, where the Council, chaired by the President of Warsaw, Ignacy Wyssogota Zakrzewski, was gathering for its meeting. The Provisional Substitute Council was the predecessor of the slightly later insurrectionary government, which was called the Supreme National Council.

While walking through the Market Square, Wybicki might have witnessed a scene that was later described by several diarists - Kazimierz Konopka was standing on a large barrel called a hogshead in front of the City Hall and speaking to an armed crowd, calling for the traitors to be hanged. Konopka, who was then twenty-five years old, was in the employ of Father Hugo Kołłątaj - he first worked as a copyist for him, then he was something of a secretary for special orders. Perhaps because Kołłątaj used him (probably because he spoke aggressively and effectively) for propaganda activities, even during the Four Years' Sejm - Konopka was very popular in Warsaw. As he lived near the Market Square, in the Barssa apartment house (almost exactly opposite Wybicki, but on the other, eastern side, behind the City Hall), the inhabitants of the Old Town spoke of him fondly - "our patriot". "Having made a stand for himself out of hogshead - wrote Wybicki – he breaths murders and conflagrations to the intoxicated people in front of the City Hall: The Fatherland, he screams frothily, wants punishment for its traitors". We can see how, above the hogshead and a thousand axes on poles and pałasz's, a little green bow jumps, with which Konopka ties his red hair tucked into a black silk bag - this creates a kind of a tail, rather a squirrel's or cat's than a ponytail. Konopka's speech was probably quite long, but what was remembered from it was really only this - he demanded that the traitors be punished or (this would be a significant difference) called the people to punish them.

Konopka's speech, from atop a barrel in front of the City Hall, is also mentioned in Kiliński's *Drugi Pamiętnik* (*Second Diary*). It seems, however, that the brave shoemaker had only his own glory in mind when describing the scene, and that is precisely why the events of that day either got a little tangled up by him or he himself, wishing to appear in the best light, tangled them a little. Kiliński mainly claimed that Konopka read - not from a barrel, but from a stool - a four-point resolution that he, Kiliński, had previously drafted and that it was addressed to President Wyssogota Zakrzewski. "So I immediately drew the four points mentioned here from my sleeve, which I myself wrote at home, and having ordered a stool to be brought out onto the street, I ordered secretary Konopka to climb onto it and read it aloud, so that the people standing could hear it and understand it well". Kiliński's four-point resolution, the text of which can be found in the *Second Diary*, is most likely entirely made up (just like the stool in front of City Hall), but there is no doubt that President Wyssogota Zakrzewski, when he entered the City Hall at eight o'clock in the morning, was handed some piece of paper on which there were, written in five points, the demands of the crowd. This is stated in a letter from Zakrzewski to Kościuszko, in which the president - late in the evening of May 9, so when it was all over - reported to the Chief about the events of that day. "After eight o'clock in the morning - we read in this letter - I went to the City Hall. There, from countless people filling the streets and the market, I was greeted here with a shout, there with insistence that the traitors of the Fatherland be punished. Before entering the City Hall, during a speech, I was given 5 points from the people, of which 4, that I had facilitated with my instructions or with Council resolutions, were easy for me to answer".

What the content of these four demands was, it is not known, the fifth one said, as Zakrzewski wrote in his letter, "that Ożarowski, Zabiełło, Ankwicz, and Kossakowski be hanged". It is impossible to establish the author of these five points "from the people", but it was certainly not Kiliński - it can be assumed that the demands were written rather by one of Kołłątaj's people, maybe Konopka, or maybe someone else. The four accused (they can also be called condemned, because, considering the gallows waiting for them, it was obvious for everyone that they would be sentenced and executed) were brought from the Gunpowder Depot (i.e. from the Gunpowder Tower at the intersection of Mostowa Street and Rybaki

Street) to the Market Square, somewhere between eight o'clock and nine o'clock, maybe even ten o'clock. They were (in accordance with the demand received by Wyssogota Zakrzewski at the door of the City Hall, but undoubtedly also in accordance with some previous arrangements or agreements): Józef Kossakowski, Bishop of Livonia; Count Józef Ankwicz, Marshal of the Permanent Council (the highest state organ of the Republic); Józef Zabiełło, Marshal of the Lithuanian Generalization (Lithuanian equivalent of the Targowica Confederation) and Lithuanian Field Hetman; General Piotr Ożarowski, Counselor of the Targowica Confederation, Grand Hetman of the Crown, and also, before the outbreak of the insurrection, commander of Warsaw's garrison.

As I said, these four were driven into or brought to the Market Square between eight o'clock and ten o'clock, maybe a little earlier or a little later. A little more precise indication of the time at which the trial began seems impossible - and this uncertainty about time stems from the fact that none of the accounts present the sequence of events with sufficient clarity. The only clear (but at the same time not very specific) hint in this matter can be found in the *Raport o egzekucji Ożarowskiego i innych* (*Report on the Execution of Ożarowski and Others*), under the title of which the description of the executions, the trial, and other events on that day was included in the *Protokół czynności Rady Zastępczej Tymczasowej* (*Protocol of the Activities of the Provisional Substitute Council*) from May 9. "During the regular session of the Criminal Court - we read there - thousands of people filled the streets near the City Hall; the criminals were brought from their places of detention under civil guard and safely brought to the Court, to which the deliberations of their crimes were brought". If we even knew at what time regular sessions of the Criminal Court for the Duchy of Mazovia began at the City Hall, we could determine when Ankwicz, Ożarowski, Kossakowski, and Zabiełło arrived at the Market Square. What the procession going through Nowomiejska or through Brzozowa to the City Hall looked like - the ominous road that opened before it among sabers, scythes, pikes and axes on poles (sabers, even a huge number of sabers, we can also see in Norblin's drawings) - one can imagine based on what Karol Wojda wrote in his book *O rewolucji polskiej w roku 1794* (*On the Polish Revolution in 1794*). "Ożarowski, a seventy-year-old old man - says Wojda's story – was brought on a chair due to weakness. [...] Ankwicz and Zabiełło, holding their hats in their hands, were bowing to the people on all sides [...]. Bishop Kossakowski with eyes looking down and head tilted, passed through the ranks of people". As for the age of Hetman Ożarowski, Wojda exaggerated a bit, because the old man was then fifty-three years old. What seems interesting (even more interesting than the chair in which Ożarowski was sitting and in which he was later hanged) to me are the triangular hats of Ankwicz and Zabiełło - that they did not forget about them when they left the underground dungeons of the Gunpowder Depot (it was a warm, spring day, so they could do without them), probably indicates that headgear was something important at that time; maybe a *tricorne* or a *bicorne* with a frayed feather pinned to it was a kind of sign that said what place in the community belongs to those who wear such an expensive and glamorous hat.

A question arises here of how the decision was made that on May 9 Ożarowski, Ankwicz, Zabiełło, and Kossakowski would be judged and hanged – precisely them and no one else. That is - who decided about it and where. It can be concluded (considering Wyssogota Zakrzewski's letter to Kościuszko) that this decision was made by the people who gathered in front of City Hall. Or that it was taken there by Konopka, who may have previously consulted with someone on this matter. Though this seems very doubtful to me - everything from the moment when Wybicki, waking up at dawn, saw the gallows beneath his windows, and even earlier, from those night hours, hours before dawn, when the gallows were erected in front of the City Hall and on Krakowskie Przedmieście, looked precisely as if they were being prepared just for these four. Julian Ursyn Niemcewicz, moreover condemning (as a man of culture and belonging to the elite of the time) the spontaneous hanging, later claimed in *Pamiętniki czasów moich* (*Memoirs of My Times*) that Ankwicz, Ożarowski, Zabiełło, and Kossakowski were "the foremost traitors of the Fatherland". This is of course true, but there were at least over a hundred equally foremost or just a tad less foremost traitors in Warsaw prisons at that time, they were all either captured by the people in the first days of the insurrection, arrested a little later on Kościuszko's order, or (like Ożarowski and Ankwicz) handed over to the Provisional Substitute Council by the king, who - fearing that he himself would be considered the most foremost traitor - did not want to shelter in his Castle those who hid there on April 17 and 18. At that time in two of the Republic's Palaces, the Brühl and Krasiński, in the Gunpowder Tower, in the Arsenal, in the Marszałkowska Guardhouse, and in several monasteries turned into prisons, those eager to hang people had at their disposal various attractive collaborators, spies, and agents, and it was possible, with the same ease as with the four chosen, to prove that each of them had taken money and received gifts either from one of the successive Russian ambassadors or directly from St. Petersburg. Sooner or later, these four, Ankwicz, Ożarowski, Zabiełło, and Kossakowski, would of course be hanged anyway, so perhaps it is not worth wondering why they were chosen. Someone - on the night of May 8-9 - had to decide, however, that the people who demanded justice, that is execution, would be handed over these four - not some other four. This is precisely what is interesting - who was it? And where - as would we say today: at what level - was this decision made? This is a very difficult question, and an answer probably cannot be found.

Kościuszko could have made such a decision, but Kościuszko was not in Warsaw. It could have been undertaken - jointly or individually - by Hugo Kołłątaj and Ignacy Potocki, but they were also not in Warsaw yet. Apparently, in Warsaw there were some agents sent by Kołłątaj from Kościuszko's camp and they instigated, on the order of their patron, the events of May 9. However, these were only rumors that were circulating around Warsaw at that time and which were repeated later by Kołłątaj's enemies after the fall of the insurrection.

From the *List do przyjaciela odkrywającego wszystkie czynności Kołłątaja* (*A Letter to a Friend Discovering All of Kołłątaj's Activities*), written in 1795 by Aleksander Linowski (but published anonymously), we learn that it was actually Kołłątaj that "silently sent emissaries to Warsaw, who, by stirring the people, cooked the seeds of anarchy" and that these emissaries caused "the people's first movement in which the known four criminals were hanged". It even sounds quite probable, but if it was so, it is also obvious that those agents of Kołłątaj, sent by him to Warsaw to provoke some riot or (to put it a little more nicely) some popular tumult, could have led to the hanging, but they did not have any way of deciding who would be hanged. The main role in the events of that day - that is: the role of someone who tries to direct and even somehow manage such events that, by nature, cannot be guided - was played by President Wyssogota Zakrzewski. Was he the one who chose four that were suitable for hanging? As I said - there is probably no answer to this question. One can only say here that Zakrzewski was adored by the people of Warsaw not so much because of his political skills, but because he was generally considered a gentle man, even a man of great goodness and great nobility. If he really was such a man, then on May 8-9 he had a very hard night, because knowing that what was to happen was inevitable, he had to make a decision.

Behind the mask of gentleness, goodness, and nobility, there could of course be someone cold and ruthless who knew that a national insurrection must be bloody and cruel if it was to be victorious. Before the session of the Criminal Court began, an armed crowd broke into the interior of the City Hall. There must have been some sentries at the main entrance, but if there were, they of course fled. As I said, the sequence of events is difficult to determine, and also in this case, it is not known whether the crowd was in the City Hall before Ankwicz, Ożarowski, Zabiełło, and Kossakowski were brought to the Market Square, or if it went there with them. It seems to me that the latter is more likely. "Then he [Konopka] - wrote Wybicki - and another monster, a certain Father Meier with others like him, with bare pałasz's, loaded pistols, stormed the door of our room, which, when we were forced to open it, flooded us like a foamy spout". From the continuation of Wybicki's description it arises, though somewhat unclearly, that precisely then (and only then), when the crowd gathered in the Market Square entered the City Hall, the Provisional Substitute Council, forced to negotiate, decided to convene the Criminal Court and refer the case of the four accused to it. "Finally, the whole Council established that even though the arrested prisoners may be worthy of death as traitors, the criminal court should judge them and condemn them to it, should it deem that they deserve it. [...] Who could describe this scene! The ringleaders, astonished by our resolution, allowed for judgment. In a moment the criminal court gathered in front of our chamber and with a little formality we snatched from the hands of those greedy for blood arrestees whom the court had condemned to death". This sentence is somewhat vague - it is obviously not about the fact that Kossakowski, Ankwicz, Zabiełło, and Ożarowski were greedy for blood, but about the fact that the Provisional Council, by referring the case to the Criminal Court, extended their lives a bit.

Although the authorities managed to tame the people in this way, and law triumphed for a moment over lawlessness ("the first bloody scene was over with the seriousness of the government

saved somewhat"), Wybicki understood that the triumph of authority and law would be short-lived. In his opinion, not only he, but
all the members of the Provisional Substitute Council understood,
negotiating with the enraged crowd, that "soon our most beautifully
started revolution, brought together with the most sacred intention,
will take the form of the barbaric slaughter and inhuman horror
with which the French Revolution has disgraced itself forever". Although Wybicki was at City Hall and participated in the negotiations, he probably did not remember all of it too well, as it seems
that the events took place a bit differently than he presented in his
diary. The whole complicated (in a legal sense) procedure with the
appointment of the Criminal Court and commissioning it to conduct
the case of the four accused had probably come up with a little earlier - even on the night of May 8-9 or early in the morning of May
9 - by President Wyssogota Zakrzewski. If this was the case, it must
be said that he was not only a man of great goodness, but also a
foreseeable and skillful politician who (in this matter) had only one
goal – it was not about the lives of the four who had to be hanged
anyway, neither was it about the crowd that was raging in the Market Square, which had to disperse anyway, nor was it about that
Konopka with his bouncing green bow, who had to ultimately get off
the hogshead anyway – for him it was only about one thing and that
is what he wanted to achieve (and he achieved this), that the Polish
national insurrection would be legal and not become illegal.

The legal problem was that, according to the National Uprising Act announced by Kościuszko in Kraków (on the day insurrection began), "crimes of national treason" (committed in the past)
were to be tried, in an undefined future, by the Supreme Criminal
Court. Since the Supreme Criminal Court had not been established
by May 9, Ankwicz, Ożarowski, Zabiełło, and Kossakowski, as "persons guilty of the crime of national treason" (I am quoting here and
simplifying the reasoning presented by the Provisional Substitute
Council in an intricate letter of May 9), should be brought before
some other court. However, this was not possible, because the Criminal Court for the Duchy of Mazovia operating in Warsaw was in
turn competent "only as to crimes that could happen against the
National Uprising", and such crimes (as it was believed) were not
committed by any of the four defendants (and if they did, it was not
for sure). Thus, the Provisional Substitute Council made a decision
(it is difficult to say whether it had the right to do so) extending the

powers of the Court for the Duchy of Mazovia - "wanting to establish a dam against further intrigues, and finding their crimes visible and open, the Criminal Court of the Duchy of Mazovia authorizes, that the persons of Ankwicz, Ożarowski, Kossakowski, Zabiełło [...] be punished immediately with a sentence of the Court, appropriate to their crimes and offenses". This happened, of course, at the request of President Wyssogota Zakrzewski - in his evening letter to Kościuszko we read: "securing a trial for the accused and bringing them to court, I tried to make sure that the *supplicium* did not become *ante judicium*". The President of Warsaw also made sure that the Criminal Court for the Duchy of Mazovia received appropriate evidence that it could use when issuing the sentence. At that time, the Audit Department was already in operation – it was examining Igelström's archive, that is, reading the papers that the Russian ambassador failed to take with him when he retreated from Warsaw, and which, on April 18, a little burned, fell into the hands of the conquerors of the embassy on Miodowa Street. It was these papers (of course, whatever in them concerned the four defendants), that Wyssogota Zakrzewski ordered to be sent from the Deputation to the Criminal Court. This is mentioned in the evening letter to Kościuszko. "The receipt and lists of taken foreign salaries from the archives of the Deputation were sent to be part of the papers designated to be reviewed by this Court, which found a lot of confirmations in these papers, along with the voluntarily confessions of these rogues, to take their lives". All of this - and these efforts around the papers from Igelström's archive, and this extension of the Criminal Court's powers - testifies to the fact that Wyssogota must have worked on this matter before dawn. Maybe - anticipating or knowing what would happen - he had already been working on it the day before. It was impossible to settle all of this in a dozen or so minutes, in a City Hall conquered by armed people, because such actions simply required some time - even for reflection. They also probably had to be consulted with someone, as it seems unlikely that the president of Warsaw would act alone and without any support - it would be too risky.

The trial took place - as the *Diariusz króla Stanisława Augusta podczas powstania w Warszawie 1794 roku* (*The Journal of King Stanisław August during the Uprising in Warsaw in 1794*) informs - "in the lower room of the City Hall". As far as I know, no description of this room is known. Therefore, nothing can be said about this topic - neither on which side of the Market Square the windows faced, nor from which side the sun shone inside, nor where the accused sat, by the door or under the windows, nor whether there were people with axes on poles also present during the trial, apart from the accusers and judges. Since it was a room on the ground floor, those with axes could have stood (and certainly did stand) by the windows.

They looked into the windows, smiling at the accused and showing them their axes. Rather, this is how one should imagine it, because the king's *Journal* says that the trial took place "with closed doors" - the people who broke into the City Hall, were probably not allowed to enter the room. Or perhaps it was possible to persuade them to leave City Hall. According to Stanisław August, the whole trial lasted only an hour and a half, which, however, seems unlikely - "they were before the tribunal for an hour and a half". *The Protocol of the Activities of the Provisional Substitute Council* of May 9 mentions three and some hours - "three hours passed, the court was working on reviewing their crimes". Wyssogota Zakrzewski presented this in an even different way in the letter to Kościuszko. "Over the span of four hours - he wrote - these criminals were brought in, questioned, sentenced, and hanged". If, therefore, we adopted eight o'clock as the beginning of these events (when Wyssogota Zakrzewski entered the City Hall), then this all would have ended around twelve. Since (as we will see later) the hanging did not end until around four in the afternoon, maybe even after four, Zakrzewski, writing about four hours, their "span", must have meant the trial itself, maybe also later events - but if so, then only the ones by the City Hall. It can be assumed that the trial lasted from three to, at most, four hours. The four defendants were tried in turn. They were presented with papers provided by the Audit Department and each of them commented on what was in the papers - those, as we would say today, receipts. "Thus, the trial - states the report in *The Protocol of the Activities of the Provisional Substitute Council* - was initiated by the public prosecutors against the first of them Ożarowski, and then against the others. [...] Each of them summoned to the Court individually was not forbidden from defending themselves; everyone explained themselves extensively". There are many indications that the judgments were carried out hastily and superficially - which, moreover, considering the presence (at the door and window) of people with axes and pałasz's, was inevitable. "They were only asked - wrote Karol Wojda - whether the evidence that was read was their work [...] and the verdict was immediately announced". Wojda meant, the announcement of the verdict by being read in front of the City Hall, as those who were not present at the Market that day could become acquainted with it only after six weeks - at the end of June. It was then that the *Korrespondent Narodowy i Zagraniczny* [*The National and Foreign Correspondent*] announced in its Issue 49 (of June 21) the full text of the sentence under the title "Kopia Dekretu przez Sąd Kryminalny ferowanego Roku 1794, dnia 9 Maja i tegoż dnia do exekucyi na osobach Ożarowskim, Ankwiczu, Zabielle i Kossakowskim w Warszawie przywiedzionego" ("Copy of the Decree Passed by the Criminal Court in the year 1794, on May 9 and on the same day the execution of the persons of Ożarowski, Ankwicz, Zabiełło, and Kossakowski was carried out"). This delay (a bit strange) could be explained by the fact that on May 9, around noon, the sentence, written hastily and haphazardly, was not yet suitable for publication in the newspapers and it was necessary to work on it a bit. Though this is of course only my guess.

In the "Decree", printed in *The National and Foreign Correspondent*, we find the following allegations, that "public prosecutors of the Criminal Court of the Duchy of Mazovia from the Office working against Piotr Ożarowski, Józef Ankwicz, Józef Zabiełło, and Prince Kossakowski of the same name" presented to the "prisoners appearing in person". The first - and the most important – charge alleged that the accused "entirely and completely sold themselves to the services of the Russian foreign power", and that some of them received - "did not even shudder" to receive – "salaries from the St. Petersburg Court". The receipts, which the Audit Department found in Igelström's archive, were probably few in number and they were (as one can assume) incomplete, because of the four accused, the Criminal Court accused only two of taking Russian salaries - Ożarowski and Kossakowski, presenting them with "receipts signed by their own hand, and left in the enormous amount of papers in the apartment of Russian general Igelström, found by a fortunate event at the beginning of their audit". According to these receipts, the Grand Hetman of the Crown collected "first, on June 20, 1789, as salary (kindly, as he expressed it) calculated from January 1 to the last day of June red zł 1000, secondly on March 30, 1790, as salary from January 1, similarly to the last day of June also red zł 1000". The salaries of the Livonian bishop were, according to the receipts, a little lower, because he took from the embassy "first on June 28, 1789, for the last quarter red zł 750, and on January 5, 1790, for the current quarter similarly red zł 750". The fact that only the hetman and the bishop could be accused of taking money from a foreign power did not matter, because the next charges, equally serious, were brought against all the accused.

The second allegation concerned the Targowica Confederation - Ankwicz and Ożarowski were accused of "joining the Targowica Union", Kossakowski and Zabiełło for the fact that "they had created a similar union in the Lithuanian province from persons who were obliged to them and servants". The third allegation said that the four accused were "perpetrators of summoning the Grodno Sejm" and operating for money - "this is again confirmed by the register in the Russian language, found in the above-mentioned seizure of papers left by General Igelström" - "they became a tool and cause that the Polish country, already squeezed enough by the first partition [was] stripped of its vast provinces again". The fourth charge was related to the titles and functions that the accused had unlawfully appropriated and on the basis of which they robbed the treasury of the Republic - "considerable sums from the treasuries of the Republic under various invented appearances, such as: Ożarowski under the title Regimentarz, Zabiełło under the title Deputy Marshal, Ankwicz with the legation he held in Denmark ripped off and took away, and even helped others damage the treasury [...]". The fifth and last charge was virtually identical to the first one and was formulated only slightly differently. It said that the defendants "until they were captured, were favorable to the interests of the Court from which they were paid, and were hostile to the country's happiness", because "to many activities very harmful to the country [...] they applied themselves, to fully implement the will and orders of the mentioned Minister [Igelström], completely". The conclusion of the sentence was as follows. "The Criminal Court from such evidence [...] recognizes and declares as enemies of the Fatherland and traitors of the Republic, as well as denies all honor, fame, and Citizenship, and sentences to death as unworthy of human society and indeed harmful to it". The "Decree Passed by the Criminal Court" also determined the place and manner of the sentence's execution - "that these persons: Ożarowski, Ankwicz, Zabiełło, in the Old Warsaw Market Square, while Józef Kossakowski, after completing the usual degradation, on Krakowskie Przedmieście, are to be immediately hanged by the Master of Justice on the gallows erected there".

After the trial was over, the convicts were allowed to go to confession. It took place in the same room on the ground floor - as Stanisław August wrote in his *Journal*, "they confessed there before the Capuchin Fathers brought in for this purpose". We have interesting information on this subject in *The Protocol of the Activities of the Provisional Substitute Council*. It says that the people "were first to be inclined to allow the criminals to justify themselves before God" and "looked with respect at the confession completed by all". However, the condemned clearly abused the patience of the people, forcing them to assist at confession "even repeated twice by some". Why Ożarowski, Ankwicz, Zabiełło, and Kossakowski (two or three of them) confessed twice can be explained only by the fact that they were expecting something - that is, they hoped for some lucky event, something that would save their lives. Considering the crowd of several thousand that surrounded the City Hall, it is difficult to say what it could have been. The legal order - thanks to the ideas and efforts of Wyssogota Zakrzewski - was not violated, so there was no reason to intervene in its defense. Besides, there was no force in Warsaw at that time that could have taken the side of the four traitors. The intervention of the army - if the king had managed to persuade one of his devoted generals, Mokronowski or Cichocki, to such a risky move - would certainly lead to street fighting. Any intervention of the king, even in the form of a timid plea for grace, addressed to the Provisional Substitute Council, is also difficult to imagine - especially after the events of the previous day, when it looked like Stanisław August would be pulled out of a carriage and put to death (torn to pieces like a little earlier, young Igelström) on the square in front of the Castle. So the king preferred to remain silent. As Wybicki later stated, "not trusting the nation and terrified by the example of the French king Louis XVI", he was afraid that he would be the fifth to hang that day. The sentence - probably right after the confession of the condemned - was read in front of the City Hall.

In *The Journal of King Stanisław August* there is information that it was done by the court messenger of the Criminal Court for the Duchy of Mazovia - "and then the court messenger announced to the people that the sentence condemning them to death had been issued". We can also imagine Kazimierz Konopka, who, putting a pałasz blade to the messenger's throat (we can see a trickle of blood dripping down his Adam's apple), takes his papers, leaves the City Hall, jumps on the hogshead and reads the verdict, making long pauses between sentences - so that there is room for cheers, whistles, squeaks, and shouts. Again - above bare pałasz's and axes on poles – bounces a green bow and a red squirrel tail in a silk bag. The fact that the sentence was read out to the people gathered in the Market Square is also mentioned in *Protocol of the Activities of the Provisional Substitute Council* of May 9 - and this *Protocol of the Activities* shows the reaction of the people. "The people [...] approved the just verdict of the Court with general applause, looking with satisfaction at the punishment imposed on the offenders of the Fatherland". The real sentence was precisely that applause - and immediately after that, the hangings began. As for the frayed feather on the hat - I think about the hats with which, on their way to death, Field Hetman Zabiełło and Marshal Ankwicz bowed to the audience gathered in the Market Square – then interesting information on this subject can be found in the *Pamiętniki* (*Memoirs*) of Jan Drozdowski, the staff doctor of the Działyński regiment. Such feathers were hellishly expensive then, I do not know why, because Drozdowski does not explain this. The "white, trimmed feather, frayed at the top" for a military *tricorn* hat (in fact they were *bicorne* hats, customarily called tricorns) cost in 1794 one red złoty, so one had to give a whole gold ducat for it.

Chapter 12.
COFFINS IN THE CAPUCHIN MONASTERY

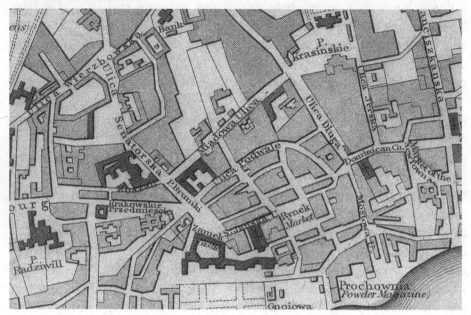

The vicinity of the Russian embassy in the Załuski Palace, which on April 17 and 18 became Igelström's fortress, looked a bit differently than it does today. On the other side of Miodowa, almost opposite the embassy, there was a Capuchin Church (in the same place as now), but between this church and the Capuchin Garden and monastery and the next building on Senatorska Street, the Tepper Palace (currently non-existent), there was no street. Now, above the W-Z Route earthworks, there is Kapucyńska Street, descending towards Solidarność Avenue, but in 1794, as the plans show, the wall surrounding the Capuchin Garden and monastery adjoined the garden (or courtyard) of the Tepper Palace. Kapitulna Street, which connects Podwale with Miodowa, ran exactly as it does now, but its eastern frontage was not fully developed and out of the entrances there, one lead to the premises of the Russian embassy. What also looked a bit different in this particular section, that is near Kapitulna and the Capuchin Church, was Miodowa – the Załuski Palace (i.e., the building where the PWN Publishing House is now located) was separated from the street by arcades where a Russian guardhouse was located, and which were burned down during the fighting. Now these arcades do not exist - there is a lawn more or less in this place. Miodowa was also called differently - in the contemporary, and even earlier, tariffs of real estate in Warsaw we find it under its current name, but then it was commonly called Kapucynów Street or Kapucyńska Street. This is the name used by Johann Jakob Patz when he related the events that took place on the second day of the fighting, April 18 in one of his letters to Dresden. "Yesterday - he wrote - was as bloody as the day before. Several Russian battalions went to Kapucynów Street to defend the house of General Igelström". We also learn from this letter that on April 18 Igelström, at a certain moment, found himself on the other side of Miodowa Street - "he took refuge in the Capuchin monastery, located opposite his residence".

It seems to me that Wacław Tokarz, who thoroughly investigated the events of April 17 and 18, must have overlooked this very interesting piece of news, which shows that the Russian governor, before he broke through from the embassy onto Krasiński Square, intended to get out of the trap in which he found himself on Miodowa, by some other route, maybe through Daniłowiczowska and then through Senatorska and Leszno. The buildings of the Russian embassy (its guardhouse, stables, and outbuildings) overlooked three streets. The Załuski Palace could be captured from Podwale, where there was the embassy courtyard, closed off from the direction of the street with a metal fence, it could also be captured from Miodowa, that is from the direction of the guardhouse in the arcades, as well as from Kapitulna - there, under Number 538, was another Russian guardhouse. If we now look at the plan of Warsaw - no matter whether its from that time or ours - we will immediately understand that the key position when it comes to the possibility of capturing the embassy was precisely the Capuchin Church. Whoever controlled the church could fire at the Załuski Palace and its arcades from up close, they also controlled the intersection of Miodowa and Senatorska Streets and - even more importantly - the exit of Kapitulna Street onto Miodowa. For the Russians, holding the Capuchin Church was tantamount to holding the Załuski Palace. While the Poles, when after several unsuccessful attempts it turned out that the embassy could not be seized from Podwale, had to get inside the church in order to capture it - only from there was an effective attack on the Russians defending themselves on the other side of the street possible. Now, opposite the church, there is a small bakery where one can drink coffee, next to it you can buy an educational book. It is very nice; I go there sometimes. You can also, while browsing an educational book over a cup of coffee, observe who is standing at the bus stop next to the church, who is getting off and who is getting on the bus. Anyone who enjoys city life has a good vantage point there. Back then, there were swollen corpses of horses on the road, next to them the corpses of Akhtyrsky Chevau-légers. In the evening of April 17, the Capuchin Church - and consequently other nearby buildings that were in the field of fire coming from the church - were in the hands of the Russians. "It was impossible to even know - we read in the *Diariusz króla Stanisława Augusta podczas powstania w Warszawie 1794 roku* (*The Journal of King Stanisław August during the Uprising in Warsaw in 1794*; this sentence speaks about the late afternoon hours) - whether Igelström was in his house or in one of the buildings still occupied by the Russians on Kapucyńska Street, from where they were constantly shooting from the windows, as well as along the street, from the very porch of the vestibule of the Capuchin Church". The attack on the monastery and church began on April 18, somewhere between one and two in the afternoon, with artillery fire from cannons that were set up in the garden surrounding the Załuski Library (now the so-called House under the Kings).

Wacław Tokarz's description in the *Insurekcja warszawska* (*The Warsaw Insurrection*) says that the cannonballs "destroyed the roofs of the monastery, smashed walls in the refectory and several rooms, smashed doors and windows". According to Jan Kiliński, who told about the capture of the monastery and the Capuchin Church in his *Drugi Pamiętnik* (*Second Diary*), after the capture of the Tepper Palace and the surrounding garden, cannons were brought there and the wall separating the palace yard from the monastery garden was destroyed, which made it possible to fire upon the monastery buildings at close range. "Since there was a very high and brick fence there, I ordered holes to be made in the fence and cannons to be put in, so that the Muscovites could be fired upon from there". When the Russians, shot at with canister shot from close range, withdrew from the garden to the monastery buildings, Kiliński's people burst in, breaking through the barricaded door that led to the choir loft, to the interior of the monastery, and hand-to-hand combat took place there - on the stairs, in the Capuchin's rooms, and in the refectory. According to calculations made by Wacław Tokarz, 75 Russians were killed in the monastery. A few, badly wounded, were saved as they were thrown into the rooms where the corpses were stored, and not found until the next day, when the fury of killing subsided a little. According to Tokarz, only a few Poles were killed during the fights for the church and monastery, while a few were injured. These calculations look very cautious, and the number killed could have been much higher, because Kiliński (admittedly, prone to exaggeration, and sometimes with great pleasure exaggerating in the description of atrocities which he and his people were to commit during the street fights) claimed that the losses on both sides were enormous - "they killed up to two hundred of us there, namely by the stairs, going to the first floor". As for the Russians, according to Kiliński, all of the defenders of the monastery and the church were killed during the fighting in the rooms and on the stairs - "Yes, my Muscovites started to call for pardon, but they did not get it, [...] when our people got to the first floor, they killed off every single one". Particularly fierce battles were fought in the rooms of the monastery - the insurgents seized them one by one, one after another, and after capturing them, they carefully searched them. This search of the rooms took place for two reasons - first, it was believed that Igelström was hiding in the monastery, which, as we know, was close to the truth; secondly, the conquerors of the monastery were convinced that the rooms contained treasures hidden there by the Russians - some money or some valuables. "Since it was known - wrote Antoni Trębicki in his diary *O rewolucji roku 1794 (On the Revolution of 1794)* - that the Muscovite coffer of the entire army was hidden within this monastery, nothing was respected until the object of much courage was found. The altars, sacristy, choir loft, rooms, cellars - were all ransacked, flipped upside down".

Later, Trębicki saw the Russian money with his own eyes, because his coachman, Piotr, who took part in the conquest of the monastery, brought him his prize for safekeeping - "on this occasion my Piotr obtained five hundred and sixty red złoty in gold, which he brought to my room and gave me for safekeeping, saying that thousands of people had filled their pockets with them next to him". Trębicki, probably exaggerating a bit, estimated the amount of money found in the monastery to be one million rubles. These were most likely not the coffers of the Russian army - according to Wacław Tokarz, who also relied on other accounts, Igelström's

coffer was located in the embassy on the other side of the street,
while private deposits were kept in the rooms, which were entrusted by wealthy residents of Warsaw to the Capuchins; the custom
of entrusting money to monasteries became common after the fatal bankruptcy of the great Warsaw banks, Tepper and Cabrit, in
February and March 1793. "The victors - wrote Tokarz - divided it
[the money] among themselves, they did the same with various religious trinkets". Since a few or a few dozen Russian soldiers (they
were probably Kiev grenadiers) took refuge in the cellars under the
church, Kiliński's men followed them there. They were also brought
to the crypts, which was a burial place, by the news that mysterious treasures - money and valuables - were hidden not only in the
rooms, but also in the coffins of the Capuchins. "At last - Antoni
Trębicki wrote - they got to the graves and no coffin was respected.
The calm corpses of dead men, their gloomy habitat turned into a
marketplace and as if it was the house of a money-changer [...] for
the coffers were supposedly hidden there". Trębicki's enterprising
coachman later assured him that "the coffers were hidden" in the
coffins. Kiliński presented a slightly different version of the events
in his *Second Diary*.

His story says that Russian grenadiers hid in the coffins,
having previously thrown out the bodies of the Capuchins. "The
Muscovites - we read in the *Second Diary* - threw the corpses out of
the coffins and laid themselves in them, but our people found them
there and they did not spare anyone's life [...]". The brave shoemaker, especially in the *Second Diary*, often indulged in various
wild fabulations (sometimes even very interesting ones), so it is not
known how justified the conclusion that can be drawn from the rest
of this sentence, in addition, a bit vague in terms of syntax, would
be - that there were also Capuchins in the coffins searched by the
conquerors of the church - but alive, those who hid there when the
cannons set up in the garden of the Załuski Library started firing
at the church and monastery - "[...] and the Capuchins lying prostrate, were found like that by us, for they, mortals, were in two fires
and terrors". Though if the living Capuchins who were hiding in the
crypts were lying prostrate there, then it would probably not be in
the coffins. Were the coffins, the "gloomy habitat" of the dead, really
the place where, as Trębicki's coachman claimed, chests or sacks of
ducats were hidden? This seems unlikely. Anyway, one can imagine what it looked like – this searching for the coffers and Russian

grenadiers in the monastery's cellar. Kiliński's people, systematically and without haste (after all it was not just about anything, but the coffer), opened coffin after coffin, putting aside the lids of the coffins. Then, disappointed (if there was no coffer), with the help of bayonets, cutlasses, sabers, and cleavers, they finished off those lying there, without inquiring who the lying were - whether they were Russian grenadiers or Capuchins, dead or alive.

General Igelström was no longer present in the Capuchin church (I remind of the information contained in the letter by Johann Jakob Patz) when the people broke into the crypts of the monastery, the Russian ambassador was probably in the Krasiński Palace and there, with his officers, he was preparing a plan to break through Świętojerska and Nalewki to the northwest, where Prussian outposts were located beyond the trenches. For the fact that he had left Warsaw and was unable to pacify the Polish rebellion, a terrible, most terrible thing was to meet him soon - a lifetime disfavor of the Petersburg Tsarina. So perhaps he should have stayed in the Capuchin Church and taken refuge, as his grenadiers did, in the monastery's crypt. If he had chosen such a thing, the tsarina would certainly have been delighted – for it would have meant that her general had given his life for her. In addition, there, in one of the Capuchin coffins, he would have had a beautiful death - nailed to the rotten boards with a butcher's cleaver, he would have become one of the heroes of our common Polish and Russian history.

Chapter 13.
THE SZARA APARTMENT HOUSE

Kościuszko taking the oath at Kraków's Market Square, 1794.

The name of the priest who stood before the Criminal Court of the Kraków Voivodeship and was sentenced to death was Maciej Dziewoński. He was accused of espionage - and it was he who ultimately became the only victim of the Kraków insurrection. The ninth paragraph of Kościuszko's order, issued on April 28 in the camp near Stary Brzesko, said that the task of the Criminal Court is to "indicate those who are guilty to death as assigned by the uprising act [...]" - "without any cruelty, however". One can imagine Kościuszko, who, on the margin of a draft prepared by advisers (Kołłątaj or Niemcewicz), adds these words, "without any cruelty, however" - because it is important for him that everyone know that the Polish revolution has a good heart and that he himself has a good heart, that he is a good Pole, not some French monster, a bloody Jacobin. Father Kołłątaj, also a good Pole, looks, there in the tent, at this note and winces a little, because he would prefer the Polish revolution to be cruel. The order did not specify the manner of executing the death penalty, the tenth paragraph stated only that the sentence be "immediately carried out" and that "the execution of each sentence should occur within twenty-four hours, in places designated by the court". The judges of the Criminal Court were selected from among the members of the Order Committee, established the day after Kosciuszko's famous oath. As we learn from a historian of the Kraków Insurrection, Tadeusz Kupczyński (from his book *Kraków w powstaniu kościuszkowskim* [*Kraków in the Kościuszko Uprising*]), there was a security section in this commission, then considered something along the lines of a Jacobin revolutionary tribunal. The Criminal Court established by Kościuszko was thought of the same way - the opinion was completely unjustified, because the Kraków Criminal Court, at least when compared to the Supreme Criminal Court for the Crown and Lithuania operating a little later in Warsaw, was an institution characterized by great restraint. The only fact that could testify to some Jacobin tendencies of the Kraków judges was the sentencing of Father Dziewoński. Historians later did not consider the priest's guilt proven, although the indications that he was engaged in espionage for the Russians were very clear.

In the *Pamiętnik* (*Diary*) of President Filip Nereusz Lichocki, it is mentioned that the priest was sentenced because Kołłątaj wished it - "it was Kołłątaj's doing, who deliberately established a criminal court for traitors, although they were not there". While the court, wanting to show that it was doing something, issued a "summary sentence, which it later regretted". Dziewoński was arrested on April 24, that is, before the creation of the Criminal Court, and was accused of having informed the Russians about what was happening in Kraków and in Bosutów, where Kościuszko was encamped. For almost a month, however, nothing happened in this matter and the priest remained quietly in prison, while the investigation was not initiated until May 22, when Kościuszko's units were leaving the camp in Bosutów. It was later believed - such a suggestion is found in Kupczyński's book - that this acceleration of the investigation was related to what had happened a little earlier in Warsaw, that is, with the hangings, on May 9 of Ankwicz, Zabiełło, Ożarowski, and Kossakowski. This is, of course, very likely – the Kraków judges could have been afraid that the inhabitants of Kraków, agitated by the slowness of the court procedures, would start building gallows, as was done in Warsaw. The evidence of betrayal, presented during the investigation of Father Dziewoński, were letters he wrote to a Russian officer named Parczewski, which (I do not know how) were taken and delivered to Kościuszko in Bosutów. That Parczewski, allegedly a lieutenant in the Smolensk Dragoons, was the fiancé of Dziewoński's sister. He was about to marry her, but he had to leave the city (because the insurrection broke out), and before leaving, he arranged with the priest, his future brother-in-law, that he would tell him about what was happening in Kraków through letters. As Kupczyński stated in his book, "the intercepted correspondence [...] contained mainly marriage negotiations", but the prosecutor demanded that Dziewoński be hanged. Other sources say that in one of the letters to Parczewski there was supposed to be a detailed plan of the Polish camp in Bosutów. We will, of course, never know what it really was - whether it was family correspondence or spy correspondence. We only know that another priest, named Marondel, who was supposed to work with Dziewoński, was also searched for. Marondel was not found, so the plot - if it was a plot - did not come to light. The first session of the Criminal Court was held on May 28.

During the trial it turned out (it could have had some impact on the sentence) that Father Dziewoński was a suspected person for other reasons as well. It was discovered that a year earlier he had embezzled a considerable amount of money (14,489 Polish złotys) from an institution called the Pious Bank of the Archconfraternity of Mercy. It must be added here that such financial crimes were then also subject to the death penalty. Although the prosecutor demanded the gallows for the priest, the Criminal Court did not agree to this request and sentenced the priest to be beheaded by the sword - thus giving proof that it is a conservative institution and faithful to old Polish traditions, and not, as it might seem, to Jacobin ones. The sentence was delivered after three days of trial, on May 30.

In accordance with Kościuszko's order, the Criminal Court ordered the priest to be beheaded within twenty-four hours and designated the place of execution. The place "designated by the court" was located in the Market Square in Kraków, in front of the Szara Apartment House. We learn from Kupczyński's book that the Szara Apartment House was then owned by the Castellan of Biecz, Franciszek Żeleński. Immediately after the insurrection began, Kościuszko's military office, headed by Aleksander Linowski, was located there - "from here dispatches, proclamations, and orders to the army were sent for several days". The execution took place on

May 31 at 10:30 before noon. Earlier, it was desired to deprive the priest (completely illegally) of ordination, for which, it was believed, at least some prelate was needed. As none of the Kraków prelates intended to do something like that, a small private ceremony took place in St. Mary's Church, the nature of which is not understandable to me. "This formality was fulfilled - wrote Kupczyński - privately in the chapel of St. Mary's Church". Although the inhabitants of Kraków are well-known and recognized masters in the field of anniversary celebrations, jubilees, and funerals, the execution of Father Dziewoński was not very successful - as if everyone was a bit ashamed of what had to be done. Military units were brought to the Market Square, but only those that were available in Kraków at that time - around the Szara Apartment House, on the Market Square and on Sienna Street, a cavalry squadron and a unit of the city's volunteer militia, called the City Hall Militia, were set up. Apparently, the cavalrymen did not present themselves the best, as they were just recruited and brought from the surrounding villages - some were wearing shoes, some were without shoes; some were shaved and some not; the horses were not matching either. Some insurrection officials whose presence was certainly obligatory, but not described, probably stood a little closer to the place of the execution. The execution began with the executioner burning Dziewoński's spy (or family) letters in front of the Szara Apartment House.

This is almost all of the information about this event, because this is where we have a gap - that is, we see a small fire near the Szara Apartment House and an executioner leaning over it with papers in his hand, and soon after the executioner lifts the beheaded head of the priest and in the revolutionary French custom he shows it to the cavalrymen, militia, officials, priests and the people. "The people - this is also a quote from Kupczyński's book - shouted three times: Long live the nation!". The militia called the City Hall Militia, barefoot cavalrymen, and Fowler rifles also shouted, but the shout was uneven, and the shout was not very successful. Priests, apparently gathered in large numbers near the Szara Apartment House, to the shouts of "Long live the nation!" were to answer with shouts of "Misericordia!" - Neither the executioner's sword, nor the head of Father Dziewoński lying on a stump, nor the stump itself - have, as far as I know, been described by anyone. This ceremony was a bit paltry - and we touch here on some important (for the Poles) difference between Kraków and Warsaw. The hanging in Warsaw was cruel, wild, terrifying, but also cheerful and full of panache, and the Kraków beheading was disgusting, unconvincing, and not noble, unsure and ashamed of itself. To put it a bit differently, one could also say that hangings in Warsaw had something in itself of Handel's great arias for mezzo sopranos, those from *Rodelinda* or *Rinaldo*, both happy and tragic, full of joy and despair - *"Lascia ch'io pianga mia cruda sorte"* - and the Kraków beheading was like the squeak of a mouse that jumped out from behind the scenes when the lights were turned off and Marylin Horne, mezzo soprano, had already left the stage.

When the events of the insurrection were coming to an end, attempts were made to behead in Kraków - perhaps also in front of the Szara Apartment House - one more priest, now unknown by name. Perhaps it was the mysterious Marondel, suspected of complicity in Dziewoński's matter. This priest was arrested on June 4 and sentenced to death on the eve of the occupation of Kraków by the Prussians. The charges against him were unclear; he reportedly had suspicious relationships with some Russian officers. On June 14 or 15 (the Prussians entered Kraków precisely on June 15), an anonymous convict was taken to the place of execution with the intention of beheading him, but the city was already in great chaos - the inhabitants of Kraków, anticipating that there might be a slaughter, were fleeing in panic to the Galician countryside. In the widespread turmoil, the execution was abandoned, and the unknown priest escaped with his life - nothing is known about what later happened to him. At present, in the Szara Apartment House - according to the information provided by my friend from Kraków, Professor Andrzej Nowak - various useful institutions are located. The letter I received from Andrzej says that "there is – from the direction of Market Square - a shop with Big Star jeans as well as the Szara Restaurant. From the direction of Sienna Street there is an entrance to the Faust Galeria and the Szara Bar. In the gate from the side of the Market Square there is information about the remaining tenants: they are the Penetrator Broker, the Under an Angel Advertisement Agency, Tishman Speyer Properties (a construction investor from New York, who was to build a second Kraków, but backed out) as well as AUSI Polska and EDS (I could not decipher the last two abbreviations)". The letter also informs that in the Gray Restaurant one can order marinated herring in three flavors as well as a cake made of finely chopped potatoes served with salmon caviar, sour cream, and red onion. Such a dish costs 28 złotys. As you can see, nobody remembers about the priest's head, which the executioner, aware of the Parisian custom, lifted by the hair and showed to the people. If you don't believe me, then ask those who eat caviar with cream there.

Chapter 14.
CORPSES

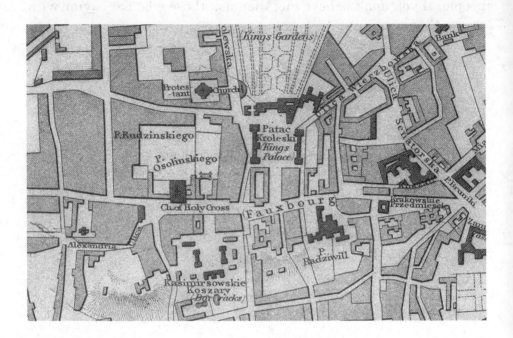

Some connection – a somewhat unclear one - with the hangings, which occurred in May and June, could be the large number of corpses that suddenly appeared on the streets of Warsaw on April 17 and 18. There were so many corpses - especially on Krakowskie Przedmieście, near the Holy Cross Church, in front of the Krasiński Palace, and in front of the Saxon Palace, as well as in the vicinity of the Russian embassy on Miodowa - that already on the first day of the insurrection, on April 17, around noon, they began to interfere with the fighting being conducted effectively. The cannons had to be rolled over the corpses, and in turning them - which was necessary in street fighting - the corpses had to be moved from place to place. On some streets - especially on Krakowskie, beneath the Holy Cross Church and by the Department of Philosophy (that is, by the building where this Department is now located) - there were apparently so many corpses that they hindered infantry maneuvers - because there was not a single piece of free space on the road between the hill on which stood the Holy

Cross Church (then more often called the Missionary Church), and the buildings of the Corps of Cadets, the infantry attacked walking over the corpses, and the soldiers, preparing to fire, kneeled on the corpses. There is word about the corpses that were lying in front of the Krasiński Palace on April 17 (and the importance - which they acquired during artillery skirmishes) in the *Pierwszy pamiętnik (First Diary)* of the shoemaker Jan Kiliński (written for Julian Ursyn Niemcewicz in the Peter and Paul Fortress and much more credible than the *Drugi pamiętnik [Second Diary]*): "so we only escaped with one cannon, and we had to leave the other, because there was no one to pull it, and it [the street]was still covered with corpses all around, so the corpses first had to be dragged away and then the cannon could be taken, but we did not have time for that at all".

Immediately in the next sentence, Kiliński wrote: "but since we encountered Muscovites when we went onto Kozia Street with these cannons, we thus luckily defeated them, because we covered the whole street with corpses". An interesting expression concerning the corpses (also in this case Russian ones) can be found in the *Diariusz króla Stanisława Augusta podczas powstania w Warszawie 1794 roku (The Journal of King Stanisław August during the Uprising in Warsaw in 1794)*. The king wrote in it about a message that reached the Castle on April 18 around 10 a.m. - it said that "Igelström wants to capitulate, and he is in the home of a butcher on Wołowa Street". This news caused the king to send General Mokronowski to the butcher's house on Wołowa - "he went there with a trumpeter and two or three people but found only a pile of Russian corpses". Upon learning that Igelström and his soldiers were retreating towards Wola, Mokronowski "followed in their footsteps marked with the corpses of Russian soldiers killed in this fight". The number of various (military and civilian) corpses that lay in the city center on April 17 and 18 (but also, as can be seen from the king's *Journal*, in the streets far away from the then center), allows us to thus conclude that the insurrection began with a great bloody slaughter that had never before been seen in Warsaw, and if it was to be seen later, then perhaps only many years later, in August and September of 1944. The difference between the slaughter of 1794 and the slaughter of 1944 is that in 1794 the city was not demolished (although it was badly damaged) and right after the fighting was over, passers-by appeared in the streets – they walked jumping over corpses or moved the corpses away. The word "slaughter" was probably first used by the poet Franciszek Karpiński when he was writing about the April Insurrection (who, by the way, knew these events only from stories, because he was not in Warsaw at the time).

"The bloody slaughter - he wrote in *Historia mego wieku* (*The History of My Era*) - began on all sides and lasted this whole day, that up to a few dozen thousand Muscovites were killed". The Russians also later portrayed the April events as a slaughter - and although they did it for a somewhat unsightly purpose (trying, for their propaganda purposes, to make the Poles a bloodthirsty tribe, murdering their innocent, perhaps even defenseless neighbors), they were of course right - what they encountered in April 1794, was precisely a slaughter. General Johann Jakob Pistor presented April 17 in his report for the tsarina, written in January 1796, as a day where there was no mercy for the Russians and the Poles who collaborated with them. "Every officer - we read there – every person recognized as a Muscovite, who only appeared on the streets, was killed". Elsewhere in the report, Pistor wrote: "wherever the Poles came across one of ours, they kidnapped, beat, or murdered them. Our officers, quartered in remote streets, were taken and abused, and their servants were for the most part murdered". The bloody slaughter is also mentioned in the memoirs of Johann Gottfried Seume, a Saxon officer in the Russian service, who watched the course of the fighting from some attic near the Saxon Palace, where he hid on Good Friday morning. According to Seume, on Good Friday morning the people of Warsaw went mad with rage. "It was only then that the furious and cruel slaughter began, as the Poles had already secured themselves a decisive advantage everywhere, and it is difficult to expect human feelings from armed masses". Seume also stated that if "order reigned" among the Poles, then all Russians in Warsaw would probably have been murdered - in any case "few [...] would have escaped". Naturally, the Russian officers blamed the Poles for the slaughter they saw on the streets of Warsaw and were right in the sense that it was the Poles who initiated the slaughter - trying to free themselves from Russian captivity. Though the Warsaw slaughter of 1794 cannot be called a Polish slaughter or a Russian slaughter, only Polish or only Russian, because it was a slaughter, so to speak, which was bilateral, i.e., a Polish-Russian slaughter, and whoever wants can also see in it something along the lines of a kind of archetype - the archetypal model of Polish-Russian friendship. The Poles murdered the Russians, and the Russians, with equal gusto and willingness, murdered the Poles. The Russians, although they were our enemies, must therefore be given justice (and this was done once, with great courage, by the most prominent Polish historian of the insurrection, Wacław Tokarz) - engulfed in the madness of murdering, Russian soldiers fought extremely bravely on the streets of Warsaw, and many of them (this applies especially to senior officers) proved then that there are also among the Muscovites those who feel contempt for death and die willingly - though only, if by dying, they could contribute to the deaths of Poles. "The [Russian] grenadiers - wrote Seume - dismissed with contempt every offer and call to surrender and said that they would clear a passage for themselves with bayonets".

The heroic retreat of Igelström, Apraksin and Zubov through Świętojerska, Koźla, and Inflancka, "marked with the corpses of Russian soldiers" (also with the corpses of Warsowians fighting on these streets), is undoubtedly a beautiful example of Russian bravery. The relationship between the number of corpses at that time on Krakowskie Przedmieście or Krasiński Square (Plac Krasińskich; sometimes also called Plac Krasiński) and the slightly later hangings in May and June could be this - seeing these hundreds or even thousands of corpses, which, moreover, were not cleaned up, it was easy to accept (without thinking about it at all), it was easy to admit the thought, that violent death is something obvious, daily, ordinary, something that does not disturb at all (and in no case does it destroy) the inherent divine order of the universe. Of course, the murdering and then hanging masses did not think about the divine order, nor did they (most certainly) consider the spiritual structure of the universe - whether killing is something that destroys it or something that supports it (and complicates it - makes it something more complex). Though the hundreds of corpses that were just lying on the cobblestones (and which were walked on, trampled on - because it was impossible to avoid them) and with which later there was a great problem, because they needed to be disposed of somehow, as these corpses were effectively eliminating, they could eliminate all of the so-called moral scruples, they created (it can also be put this way) a new (in those days) world order, one in which violent death fit well - it was, for the good functioning of this world or even universal divine factory, something indispensable. Whoever accepted (without even knowing, that they are accepting something like that) that these hacked up and stinking corpses were a necessary element of divine order and a divine plan, then this question must have seemed completely justified to them: if several hundred Russians and several hundred of ours were killed, even several thousand Russians and several thousand of ours, then why couldn't a few or a few dozen of those who betrayed also be killed? Why shouldn't these dozen or so also fit into some impossible to understand divine plan? It seems very likely to me that this was the reasoning then - or at least that was how it was felt at the time. What were these few against those several hundred or those several thousand lying in blood in the streets - these few or a dozen or so, in the face of this total carnage, were a small matter that had to be taken care of quickly, taking care of it did not have to be, even could not be, something especially troublesome.

Hence the laughter of the masses, when those who were hanged in May or June, had their pants fall off or wooden prostheses fell out of their mouths. Small matter, big laugh. It can also be expressed like this: all those murdered on April 17 and 18, Russians and Poles, all those stabbed, cut with pałasz's, and torn apart with canister shot, allowed the murdering to continue, they were effectively justifying further murder as obvious and belonging to the natural (i.e. divine) order of the universe, but they not only justified it, they even ordered it - the corpses lying on the streets in the first days of the insurrection were also something of a spiritual command, they said something like this: if you want to be victorious and you want to be free, if you want to be Poles, if you want to live in your Polish and at the same time God's way, this is precisely what you are supposed to do - murder. It was later attempted to calculate in various ways the number of corpses that were collected from the streets in Warsaw after two days of fighting, but the calculations were unsuccessful, and their little credibility was immediately obvious to those who carried them out. As the soldiers were counted separately (these losses, concerning the Polish side, included in regimental reports, were still somewhat reliable), civilians separately, Russians separately, Poles separately, men separately, women separately, the wounded who died in hospitals separately, and those who remained in the streets separately - and since this all mixed together, crossed over and excluded a little, never was there a figure reach that looked convincing and could be believed.

The first attempt to count the dead was made shortly after the fighting ended. We know the results of this count thanks to the *Gazeta Wolna Warszawska* (*The Free Warsaw Gazette*), which - edited by Antoni Lesznowolski - began to be published on April 24. In its 8th issue (or rather in a supplement to this issue) there was, in the form of a table, the "Raport wskazujący ilość trupów i pleyzerowanych" ("Report Showing the Number of Corpses and Those Wounded by White arms"). The person who made these calculations (perhaps the same Lesznowolski) was aware of their low credibility, as they included a note in the title saying that the report was "inaccurately done due to the difficulty of finding out the number of actions which occurred in many distant or side streets [...]".

In the table we have a "list of streets covered with corpses on April 17 and 18" as well as the number of dead and wounded found on these streets - with an additional division into men and women, as well as Poles and Muscovites. As for the wounded, it can be assumed (it is not explicitly stated) that the report only included those who were seriously injured and died of the wounds they received, and perhaps also those who were collected from the streets and transported to hospitals. There is also an additional division in the table - into districts. As the list of streets was drawn up according to districts, the number of dead and wounded was also presented as it appeared in each of the six districts of the city. On this basis, we can learn that on April 17 and 18, death took a particular liking to the third district of Warsaw - that is Krakowskie Przedmieście and its surroundings. The second district of death was the first district, the Old Town. The table is complicated and therefore a bit unclear, so I present Lesznowolski's report (it can be called that, although there were probably several authors) here in a short summary. In the first district, the Old Town (in the Market Square, Mariensztat, Podwale, Miodowa, Senatorska, Długa, Mostowa, and Piwna), 625 Russians were killed while 92 were wounded. Fifty-four Polish men were killed there, 88 were wounded. 2 women were also killed while 5 were injured. All of the women, killed and wounded during those two days in all the districts of the city, were Polish, no Russian woman was killed or wounded then - which undoubtedly testifies to the good manners (a certain innate elegance) of the people of Warsaw. In the second district (on the streets of Stara, Koźla, Świętojerska, Franciszkańska, Wołowa, Nalewki, Bonifraterska, Inflancka, Zielona, Zakroczymska, Pokorna, Wójtowska, Freta, Gwardii, and Rybacka), 583 Russians were killed, while none were wounded - one can conclude from this, that the wounded Russian soldiers were killed there. Twenty-two Polish men were killed, 32 were injured. One killed woman was also found there. In the third district, precisely the one which was the district of death (on Krakowskie Przedmieście, Tamka, Aleksandria, and the surrounding streets), 955 Russians were killed, 30 were wounded, 117 Poles (including one woman) were killed there, while 40 were wounded.

In the fourth district, on Leszno, Żelazna, and Nalewki Streets, 62 Russians and 6 Poles were killed, while one Pole was wounded. In the fifth district (on Marszałkowska, Zielna, Królewska, Elektoralna, Chłodna, and under the Iron Gate), 11 killed Russians and 3 killed Poles were found. Finally, in the sixth, farthest district, on Solec and Czerniakowska, 28 Russians were killed. Polish losses were also small in this district - 2 men and 2 women; 8 Poles were wounded there. If we summarize all of this - following the table in *The Free Warsaw Gazette* - we will have 2,265 killed and 122 wounded Russians, as well as 203 killed and 169 wounded Poles; in addition, there were 6 women killed and 5 wounded. At first glance, it is clear that these numbers - at least as far as the Poles are concerned - are definitely lowered. The account written by Seume says that 250 officers and soldiers were killed only from the Działyński Regiment during the fighting on Krakowskie Przedmieście near the Holy Cross Church and the Dominican Observants. If that was the case, then of course the number of 203 Poles killed (in all six districts) on April 17 and 18, given in the report, is completely fictional. The number of men and women (23 people in total) killed over two days in the second district of Warsaw, i.e. on Świętojerska, Freta, Stara, Koźla, Franciszkańska, Bonifraterska, Inflancka, Zielona, Wołowa, and Zakroczymska Streets also looks arbitrarily imagined – as it was precisely along these streets on April 18 that Igelström was withdrawing towards Wola with several of his generals and several hundred soldiers. The fighting on Koźla, Zakroczymska, and Franciszkańska Streets were terribly fierce and bloody, and at least several hundred Poles must have been killed in the streets as well as in the houses and manors that were captured by the Russians during the retreat. Seume in *Kilka wiadomości o wypadkach w Polsce* (*Some Information About the Incidents in Poland*) stated that about 2,500 Russians were killed in Warsaw over two days, whereas he presented the number of Poles killed in a completely different way than the report in *The Free Gazette*: "Polish losses - he wrote - amount to between 900 and 1,000 people". To the number of corpses from Lesznowolski's report there should also be added (the posthumous difference is ultimately small, maybe even nonexistent) the horse corpses lying on the streets of Warsaw - because cavalry also took part in the street fighting on April 17 and 18, there was a huge number of them and there was also a certain problem with them about which the *Diariusz* (*Journal*) of King Stanisław August speaks.

"The clearing up of the slain horses - we read there - of which there were over 600, is going slower because of a superstition common in the people that no one should touch the body of a dead animal except the executioner; and since several of the executioner's servants were killed during the fighting, this kind of service is delayed". The number of 600 killed horses seems quite probable, although it may be contradicted by a note precisely on horses, which was included in this supplement to the 8th issue of *The Free Warsaw Gazette*. This is what it contained. "Specification of killed horses transported outside the city - 93 horses on Szymanowski Field. 4 on Pokorna Street. 14 on Koźla Street. 33 horses behind Leszno. 18 on Włoka Piaskowskiego. 155 were thrown into the Vistula. 17 to various places. Overall, 334". As one can see, the title of the note is (probably) a bit confusing, and the information somewhat vaguely formulated - it is impossible to conclude on its basis whether the 155 horses thrown into the Vistula should be counted among those taken outside the city and whether the killed horses from Koźla and Leszno were also taken away somewhere, or something else was to be done with them. From *The History of My Era* by Franciszek Karpiński, we learn that the corpses from the streets of Warsaw were cleaned over two days and that straw was burned at the same time - the smoke from these fires was supposed to protect the city residents from plague, typhus, and cholera. "The corpses were taken away over two days and straw was burned everywhere in the streets". From the *Journal* of Stanisław August, it can be concluded that the great cleaning lasted at least two or three days longer - the phrase "the dead were buried" appears there under April 20, and so on the second day after the end of the fighting, but about the cleaning of the killed horses, also under April 20, the king wrote in the present tense, and so on Easter Sunday it was not finished yet: "the cleaning up of the horses [...] goes slower". Johann Gottfried Seume gave a brief description of the street cleaning on Easter Saturday in *Some Information About the Incidents in Poland*. "The corpses of the fallen - wrote the Saxon officer - were collected from the very morning and piled up in various districts of the city, where they were counted, then buried or thrown into the Vistula". Seume considered this lowering of the corpses into the current of the river as "evidence of barbarism" as well as "an insult to human feelings." He also claimed that the Poles did this for a specific purpose. "The throwing of the corpses into the river was to become, in accordance with the intentions of the Poles, a spectacle to scare the Prussians standing near Zakroczym".

According to the report by Lesznowolski, the corpses were thrown not only into the Vistula, but also into cesspits - and it was precisely this chaotic throwing "into cesspits and the Vistula" that, according to the author or authors of the report, was one of the reasons for the difficulties which later appeared in calculating the number of killed. According to Karol Wojda, the author of the book *O rewolucji polskiej* (*On the Polish Revolution*), where the number of corpses and those wounded by white arms is given according to Lesznowolski's report, on Easter Saturday and Easter Sunday, not only dead bodies were thrown into the Vistula, but also the badly wounded - "apart from this number, many that still alive were thrown into the Vistula".

Chapter 15.
MAY 9 – THE FOURTH GALLOWS

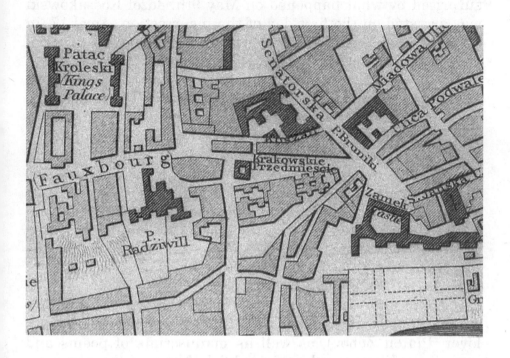

The fourth gallows, which was erected on the night of May 8-9, stood in front of St. Anne's Church. Now we would see it from the exit of Miodowa onto Krakowskie Przedmieście, but then Miodowa did not reach Krakowskie, it ended at the junction of Kozia and Senatorska Streets. If you were on Miodowa Street, to see the gallows at the Bernardines, you had to get through gates and backyards through Rösler's house (at number 451), which had a passage - from Senatorska Street to Krakowskie Przedmieście. According to some reports, two gallows were erected at the Bernardines on May 9 - and the latter, supposedly intended for Bishop Ignacy Massalski, remained unused. This was later stated by Józef Ignacy Kraszewski in his work *Polska w czasie trzech rozbiorów* (*Poland during the Three Partitions*), in his opinion the second gallows at the Bernardines were not used, because the bishop "remained in prison by promising to reveal other traitors and by the influ-

ence of the king". This version of events seems a bit questionable - if only because the king, firstly, had no influence at that
time on the course of events, and secondly, he was completely
surprised by what happened on May 9th. Józef Kossakowski
was arrested on the first day of the insurrection, April 17, in
the morning hours. The Livonian bishop lived at the corner of
Leszno and Przejazd in the royal jeweler Martin's tenement
house at number 653 - exactly where Leszno connected with
Tłomackie and Rymarska.

Now the Muranów Cinema is located more or less in
this place (or right next to it). Kossakowski could feel somewhat safe at Martin's, because the Russian general Khrushchov had his headquarters on the ground floor of that house.
There was also a kind of guardhouse in Martin's Apartment
house, Khrushchov was guarded by a dozen or so guards, and
after the outbreak of fighting, the house was manned by a battalion of Kiev grenadiers. The bishop, this speaks well of his
intelligence, did not believe that the Russians would defend
him - he burned his papers even before the insurrection broke
out. Apparently, among them were letters of his Russian protectors (ambassador Jakob Johann Sievers and the tsarina's
lover, Platon Zubov), as well as manuscripts of poems and
comedies - Kossakowski only published two or three stories,
and the rest of his works went up in smoke. The bishop may
not have been a famous writer, but on an intellectual level, he
undoubtedly had the highest of all those hanged in 1794, so
it's a pity we won't get to know the poems he burned, perhaps
a little hastily. The published stories of the bishop were didac-
tic in nature - using the language we currently use, he could
be called, on their basis, a supporter of modernizing Polish
customs and Polish ways of life; in them he persuaded Poles to
make their lives similar to those of other, more civilized Euro-
peans. One can also imagine the Livonian bishop reading his
new poem describing the heavenly beauty of the Petersburg
Tsarina to the Russian generals whom he invited to dinner
at Martin's Apartment house - after the reading the generals, with goblets in their hands, stand up and a standing ova-
tion follows; someone applauds, someone is crying, someone
is kissing someone. Around nine or ten in the morning, insurgents fighting on Leszno brought three or four cannons from

the nearby Arsenal, the Russian grenadiers escaped, some of them were captured, and Martin's corner apartment house was captured. Kossakowski was arrested by one of the conspirators - his name was Szydłowski and he was the Castellan of Żarnów. Later, in the *Drugi Pamiętnik* (*Second Diary*), the shoemaker Kiliński, who liked to emphasize his significant participation in such national events, credited the merit of arresting the bishop to himself.

In this shoemaker's work we have a detailed description of the arrest - first, the bishop takes the bell and calls the valet, then he demands a doctor ("he cannot make do without" because he has a disease called terno), then Kiliński or one of his men shouts: "Criminal, you have reached the end of your rope!", then the bishop is hit with the flat side of a pałasz ("when the soldier strikes him with a pałasz"), then an unpleasant event occurs ("it was impossible to look at the shirt and kecks") - and in this way the filthy bishop, "putting on a robe with fur and slippers on his feet", goes under the guard of Kiliński's people to the prison in the Gunpowder Depot. What the disease called terno is, I cannot say - terno is a term from the field of number lotteries and none of the Polish dictionaries known to me gives a meaning of this word that would have anything to do with medicine. It does not really matter, because Kiliński made it all up anyway - our national hero was a great scribbler, in addition a completely selfless one, because he wrote only for himself, without any hope that someone would publish it for him. Later, in 1899 when Aleksander Kraushar finally published the *Second Diary*, Tadeusz Korzon protested in the *Kwartalnik Historyczny* (*Historical Quarterly*) against its publication, claiming that the brave shoemaker deserved not to be made "a public laughingstock". Korzon was certainly right in different ways, because publishing the diaries of the megalomaniac who became a Polish hero could not do well for the national cause - but it can also be said that Kiliński wanted just such glory, that is, *"vous l'avez voulu, George Dandin"* ("'Tis your own fault, George Dandin"). Now I return to the arrest. Karol Wojda, in his book *O rewolucji polskiej* (*On the Polish Revolution*), later maintained that the arrest saved Kossakowski's life - those who were imprisoned on April 17 and 18, "did not succumb to the revenge of the people, but through strict confinement [were] removed from facing revenge". This is of course true, because if Kossakowski had remained free, the people, on Easter Saturday or, worse still, on Easter Sunday itself, would have torn him to pieces somewhere on Leszno or on Przejazd - anyhow, before the entrance to the Muranów Cinema. Though it can also be argued that in the case of the Livonian bishop it was not a significant difference - thanks to the fact that on April 17th it was thought about arresting him, he lived only three weeks longer. Castellan Szydłowski led Kossakowski to the nearby Arsenal - the conditions in the improvised prison there were almost luxurious and the bishop, it seems, could have, at least for the first days, his servants, valets, and secretaries.

Almost immediately after Kossakowski's arrest, on April 22, the Provisional Substitute Council, which had formed three days earlier, sequestered his estate. As a reason for the sequestration, the Substitute Council, commissioning the appropriate steps to be taken by its Order Committee, cited the "godless deeds" of the Livonian bishop of seeking "his private gain in the ruin of the country" – and all the while when "Muscovite violence [...] was tearing apart the public treasury, but also the private property of every citizen". The order issued by the Order Committee also said that "his highness Father Kossakowski, the bishop" was "among [...] servants of despotism" and as such a servant, "with the help of Muscovite violence, he appropriated national goods for himself, formerly belonging to the Bishopric of Kraków, in just inventories belonging to the treasury, of about 900,000 złotys, and by keeping the goods for almost a year and a half, he was the usurper of 700,000 złotys of annual income". The sequestration was therefore intended as a kind of retribution - the Republic was to recover what the bishop had stolen from it. The Provisional Council also indicated, in the order issued to the Order Committee, what could be recovered - these were state silver, sums in cash and in deposits as well as a warehouse of metal goods, which the bishop had in Warsaw. This operation turned out to be completely unsuccessful, because when the money was looked for, it became apparent that Kossakowski, although considered a wealthy man, did not have, at least in the capital, any significant movable property - neither cash nor valuables. Even the money that the Russian embassy paid Kossakowski on a regular basis disappeared (in a mysterious way; and as far as I know, they have never been found) - the Russians paid him a fixed salary from 1787; from January 1791 it amounted to 1,500 red złotys per year. Ultimately, the Provisional Council acquired several of the bishop's carriages, several of his horses, 6,200 Polish złotys (about 326 red złotys; rather ridiculous money, for such a rich man), as well as small jewelry boxes found in Martin's Apartment house. The second jewelry box that was supposed to be there – containing, according to Kossakowski's testimony, some papers regarding the collaboration of the Primate of Poland, Michał Poniatowski - mysteriously disappeared shortly after April 17. The bishop's stay in the Arsenal lasted several days - until May 6.

"Tomorrow" - the President of Warsaw, Ignacy Wyssogota Zakrzewski, wrote the day before to Tadeusz Kościuszko – "I will be sending the main arrestees to the prison called the Gunpowder Depot, they are: Kossakowski, Ożarowski, Zabiełło, and 20 others". I wrote earlier that on May 9 Kossakowski, Ankwicz, Ożarowskiego, and Zabiełło were brought to the Old Warsaw Town Square from the Gunpowder Depot, which was also called the Gunpowder Tower and which was located at the intersection of Mostowa Street and Rybaki Street. Later, however, I was overcome by doubts as to whether Wyssogota Zakrzewski, when writing to Kościuszko, meant this Gunpowder Depot at Rybaki Street under number 2564. At that time, there was another Gunpowder Depot in Warsaw, located much further from the center, beyond the trenches, alongside the road connecting the Powązki tollhouse with the Wolska tollhouse, so actually outside the city. Since, as it seems, the second Gunpowder Depot was also used as a prison at the time, those four who were to be tried on May 9 could have also been placed there at the behest of Wyssogota Zakrzewski. This is precisely what it is said in the 1969 edition of Johann Jakob Patz's letters - to the letter of May 7, which mentions that the four prisoners were transferred "last night to the prison in the Gunpowder Depot", a footnote is added, which explains that it is about the old tower between the tollhouses. If Kossakowski, Ożarowski, Ankwicz, and Zabiełło were kept in the distant

Gunpowder Depot beyond the trenches, they certainly could not have reached the Old Warsaw Town Square on foot and they must have been brought, probably somewhere near the Market Square, onto Jezuicka or Nowomiejska, on some wagon. It could have also been that Wyssogota Zakrzewski, who had a good heart, lent them his carriage for this purpose. Kossakowski, when he found himself in front of the City Hall door, might have asked himself why there were only three gallows there, if he was one of the four; he probably did not know then that the one intended for him is standing elsewhere, in front of the Bernardine Church. When the trial was over - it lasted, I remind you, according to the *Journal* of Stanisław August, an hour and a half, while according to the *Protokół czynności Rady Zastępczej Tymczasowej* (*Protocol of the Activities of the Provisional Substitute Council*) of May 9, "three hours passed"; therefore more or less twenty to forty-five minutes was spent on each of the accused —so when the trial was over and Ożarowski, Zabiełło, and Ankwicz were hanged in front of City Hall, the bishop must have had the certainty (although it is not known how he obtained it) that the gallows that had been erected for him was located elsewhere.

Why was it decided to hang Kossakowski separately, precisely in front of the Bernardine Church, and not in front of the City Hall, as well as who made the decision in this matter - whether it was forced by the people, decided by the Criminal Court for the Duchy of Mazovia, or whether the Provisional Substitute Council had something to say (and managed say something) in this case - it is now impossible to explain. It could be said that the decision was up to those who erected the gallows at night, but this in turn raises a question that cannot be answered - who, when the gallows were erected, decided about their placement and what did he have in mind placing them in one spot and not another one. There could be some symbolic intention in the fact that it was decided to hang the bishop separately and in front of the church, the singularity of the bishop's death could have symbolized something (in the conviction of those who participated in the hanging), but this symbolic meaning remains hidden from us and we cannot make sense of it. The *Protocol of the Activities of the Provisional Substitute Council* of May 9 explains, in the section devoted to Bishop Kossakowski, why he was hanged separately, but this explanation does not clarify much. "This difference in places - we read there - [...] seems to be justified that the criminal priest, guilty of treason of the fatherland was most respectably exposed to the public where everyone's rather lured eye was able to recognize the greatness of the betrayal combined with such a respectable character". As can be seen, we are dealing here with a very vague style, hiding an equally vague idea that some secretary of the Substitute Council was unable to formulate in a sufficiently comprehensible manner. The Bishop of Livonia, surely only when the hangings in front of the City Hall was finished, was led out or transported in a wagon from the Market Square to Krakowskie Przedmieście - the road (probably) led through Piwna, and then (for sure) under the Kraków Gate - this structure, currently non-exis-tent, but then separating Krakowskie Przedmieście from the Old Town, was at that time an important place in Warsaw. Accounts, as it regards this passage or transportation, differ from one another.

According to Julian Ursyn Niemcewicz's *Pamiętniki czasów moich* (*Memoirs of My Times*), the bishop was "taken to the Bernardines in order to first remove his priestly anoint-ings"; according to Wyssogota Zakrzewski (this sentence comes from his letter to Kościuszko) Kossakowski was on foot - "[he] was led out of the court room towards the gallows". Countless crowds took part in the march from the Market Square to St. Anne's Church – it was later said that there were thousands, even tens of thousands of people. Tens of thousands also gath-ered around the gallows. In the *Pamiętniki* (*Memoirs*) of Jan Duklan Ochocki, who at that time spent a few weeks in War-saw (precisely when the hangings were being done), we find a description of Warsaw churches - what they looked like during the insurrection. "The churches were open day and night; crowds of people, especially women and the elderly, broken by age, occupied them and filled the shrines - candles burned continually, masses and services were celebrated constantly". It can therefore be assumed that the hangers who were com-ing from the City Hall were also joined by those who were attending mass at the Bernardines when the hangers arrived at the gallows; perhaps also by those who were attending mass in the Augustinian Church on Piwna and mass in the Dominican Church on Freta; maybe those who were praying at the Visitationist Church on Krakowskie St. also made it for the execution. The *Protocol of the Activities of the Provisional Substitute Council* states that "thousands of residents assisted" in the execution of Kossakowski. Wyssogota Zakrzewski's letter to Kościuszko also mentions thousands - "thousands of people of both sexes [...] were giving these patriotic tragic scenes applause and shouts of joy". Antoni Trębicki, who compared the celebrating people of Warsaw to "the throngs of Parisian septemberists" (that is, those furious Parisians who hanged in September 1792), wrote in his diary *O rewolucji roku 1794* (*On the Revolution of 1794*) that this was "a band of drunks, which amounted to several dozens of thousands of people". This band, as Trębicki claimed, filled Wide Krakowskie Przedmieście from Wasilewski's tenement house (it was located at the corner of Bednarska, more or less where the square now begins and the statue of the Blessed Virgin Mary stands, as it stood at that time) to the Kraków Gate – there was such a crowd there that "it was impossible to pass through". Kiliński, who had no reason to be afraid of the people (because he himself was one of them), became terrified when he reached St. Anne's Church and saw what was happening there. "The crowd – describing the view from beneath the gallows – on the street was so large that they almost suffocated themselves [...]. Though it was then that it was possible to see this so terrifying sight of the people, that the hair on the heads of every person really stood up from fear".

Kossakowski behaved bravely while riding or walking to the gallows. He was spit on and yanked around, his clothes were torn off, he was probably beaten too, but he did not react to it. He only shouted – and this lasted, as it seems, all the way from the City Hall to Krakowskie Przedmieście - that others should also hang next to him. Among those, who are remembered, whom he wanted to see next to him were, the Bishop of Płock, Szembek, and the bishop of Poznań, Okęcki, as well as the Primate of Poland, Prince Michał Poniatowski. Several reports also mention that the bishop, on his way to the gallows, demanded the hanging of Stanisław August. Niemcewicz quoted a sentence in *Memoirs of My Times* that was remembered. Kossakowski, "as much as he had strength", shouted - "Hang the king too, for he is the cause of all bad events". It is worth quoting one more sentence by Niemcewicz, because it allows us to see the bishop transported to death (or dragged to death) a little better. He was a man of "an enormous, bony figure with a leopard face and the gaze of a fox". How he was dressed - during the trial at City Hall and later under the gallows - remains unclear. Kiliński stated that he was in a banyan and purple stockings. On this basis it could be argued that the banyan then became a kind of symbol of hanging, or perhaps the symbol of a hanged person - a little earlier, in Vilnius, the bishop's brother, Hetman Kossakowski, was hanged in a banyan; a few of those executed a little later in June were hanged in banyans; most interestingly, Stanisław August was at that time seen in a banyan in one of the Castle's windows. Trębicki maintained that the bishop was dressed differently - perhaps already in the Market Square or even earlier, during the trial, some of his clothing was stolen and "he was dragged barefoot in a vest and trousers". The accounts agree, however, that Kossakowski was, under the gallows, by the executioner - or by his henchmen; or by the people surrounding the gallows, as it is possible - stripped down to his underwear. Before this happened, in the church - or in front of the church - a rite was completed, which later, in memoirs, was called removing the episcopal anointment. There was some confusion on this matter afterwards (perhaps on that day as well) because, despite many efforts, it was not possible to ultimately establish who had performed the rite, being completely unlawful or even nonsensical from an institutional (that is, ecclesiastical) point of view.

It is only known that during the trial - maybe even at dawn on May 9, even before the trial - the Provisional Substitute Council asked the papal nuncio (then Monsignor Lorenzo Litta, titular archbishop of Thebes) to personally perform this act - that is, on the bishop, as it should be understood, to annul his episcopal ordination. "Without forgetting the respect for religious rites - in a letter of May 9, Wyssogota Zakrzewski states - we delegated to the nuncio that he remove the character of bishop from Kossakowski". The continuation of Zakrzewski's letter says that Litta refused (declaring that he "had not been given the power to do so from the See") and "gave the *facultatem* (ability)" to Canon Wodziński to hear the condemned man's confession and to do "what will be needed in such a case". Negotiations with the nuncio continued for some time - according to Zakrzewski, even when "the bishop was rising into the air" - and the rite, carrying out "ordinary degradation according to ceremonial", was finally carried out by the canon Wodziński and two other priests. Zakrzewski's version, which one could believe (if only because he was the President of Warsaw, and in addition one of the main actors of the events at that time, so he had to be well informed), was later questioned - it was stated that the removal or annulment of orders (if it could be called that) was made not by the canon delegated by the nuncio, but by Antoni Malinowski, the Bishop of Cinna, who was the parish priest of the Church of the Blessed Virgin Mary in the New Town (and a friend of Father Józef Meier), or by someone else - Father Onufry Kopczyński, author of the famous grammar textbook entitled *Gramatyka dla szkół narodowych* (*Grammar for National Schools*) and then known to all children who studied at the Piarists or the Dominicans. Father Kopczyński, a Jacobin and Voltairean, remained under the influence of the French Encyclopedists - according to him, language was a logical whole having its perfect source in the laws of logic. Antoni Trębicki, who accepted the version with Kopczyński, maintained that the grammarian had used a brick when annulling Kossakowski's ordination.

"He was jerked around like some kind of madman, they tore him among themselves and pushed him, while the Piarist Kopczyński [...] not in ceremonial dress, the wrong priest, was wiping off the holy oil from his crown and neck with a brick". Why Kopczyński was the wrong priest, Trębicki did not explain; the brick also seems unexplainable to me; I do not think that Kopczyński (although he was a Jacobin) used a brick to inflict pain on the Bishop of Livonia - there was after all no reason to additionally repress the poor man to be hanged or rather half-man to be hanged. Anyway, the procedure carried out by the grammarian-priest was completely fruitless (which in the revolutionary chaos was probably not realized), because, according to the provisions of the Council of Trent, each sacrament is (as it is called) an indelible mark, so it cannot be wiped off and invalidated. Not only are ordinations unable to be wiped away, baptism also cannot be annulled - and even the use of brick will not help here. Whether it was before this revolutionary removal of consecration, or after this event, Kossakowski tried to enter the Bernardine Church, desiring, as he claimed, to pray and receive communion. As Karol Wojda wrote, "he demanded that he be allowed to enter the church; he was denied this for fear that he might run away". This is described a bit differently in Kiliński's *Second Diary*, who probably understood Kossakowski's idea better than Wojda did - the bishop surely did not intend to escape somewhere after getting inside the church, because such an escape could not be successful in any way; whereas he would find himself, taking communion in the church, near the altar - and maybe that was what he wanted. "When the bishop gets hold of the monstrance - wrote Kiliński - that he does not want to let it go from his hands, then what would we do to him?". Franciszek Karpiński explained it in a similar way in the *Historia mego wieku* (*The History of My Era*), quoting the words of someone who was standing in front of the church - "he can grab the Eucharist into his hands - how you will be able to assault him in a church". A bishop with the monstrance in his hands would obviously become untouchable - it would not be possible to snatch it from him, because it would risk a struggle with the Blessed Sacrament; you couldn't hang him with it, because anyone who would dare to do something like that would hang Jesus Christ. Kiliński took the credit for preventing such a troublesome, even fatal situation - "when I struck both of them with the flat side of my sword, they had to close the church right away".

Under the gallows, the hangman's henchmen were undressing the bishop from the banyan and purple stockings or (if Trębicki was right about how he was dressed) from the vest and trousers. Wyssogota Zakrzewski later informed Kościuszko, quite cautiously (this can be explained by the discretion of the president, who was a gentle and well-raised man) that Kossakowski was hanged "in only a shirt and trousers". Father Kitowicz, who was neither gentle nor well-raised, and in addition liked extreme situations (and also liked to describe them in a dramatic way), claimed in *Historia Polska* (*Polish Histo-*

ry) that the bishop was hanging in dirty underwear - "only in a shirt and linen trunk hose, and both were dirty". Kitowicz explained the poor condition of the underwear of the Bishop of Livonia by the fact that he was "a philosopher, a man of great intellect as a matter of fact", and therefore all gallantry was foreign to him, "he was not a gallant" - he therefore wore "one shirt for a long time, until it was well dirtied, so as not to pay the laundress for nothing". Who, when the henchmen undressed the bishop, came into possession of his banyan, purple stockings, or the bishop's vest – the reports are silent on this subject. The hangman (Stefan Böhm) pulled up Kossakowski on a harness and lowered him on a noose. It was four in the afternoon. "I looked - wrote Antoni Trębicki - how the half-dead man was lifted up and it was not until then that the master did the final deed". Karol Wojda, the future president of Warsaw, recognized (and rightly so) that he had witnessed a great historical event. "Nothing of the sort - he wrote in the book *On the Polish Revolution* - can be found in the history of Poland; it was not practiced to do likewise to chiefs, a bishop, and a marshal". As various accounts say, when Böhm was finishing his work and Kossakowski was riding up and then descended, a great burst of joy took place on Wide Krakowskie Przedmieście. People shot into the air, laughed, applauded, shouted: Vivat! - Long live the revolution! - Strangers fell into each other's arms and kissed on the lips. The ladies beneath the gallows sang Kokiel's song from "Henry VI on a Hunting Excursion" by Wojciech Bogusławski: - The intrigue goes up, the merit falls. – Who were these ladies, it is not known; maybe they were Warsaw whores.

Chapter 16.
FIELDS OF DEATH

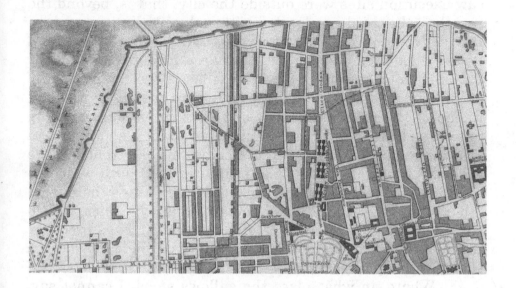

There were three execution sites in insurrectionary Warsaw. Almost nothing is known about two of them - they are really only known by name, and it is very difficult to establish exactly where they were. A little more is known about the third one, but not too much. I have in mind such execution sites, to which a certain tradition was attached, which were, if you can put it that way, traditional places – such places, where murderers, rapists, thieves, and all kinds of robbers were hanged, beheaded, and broken on the wheel immemorial, and, even if not immemorial, then for many decades, and during the insurrection, and before it, and after it. The insurrection used these places (quite cautiously) for its own purposes, but this does not mean that common criminals were not executed there at that time – criminals, whom we would now call political ones, began to appear next to them under the gallows. The fact that so little is known about these execution sites in Warsaw probably indicates that the people (as this certainly applies to all of humanity) did not like to talk about how they got rid of their supposed or real enemies. This is a bit reminiscent of a cat or dog burying or covering its stinking droppings with sand - why should someone else (some other cat or dog) know where they are and how they stink. Two of the three Warsaw execution sites were outside the city, that is, beyond the trenches, the third was located within the city limits and even relatively close to its contemporary center - to get there from Podwale or Miodowa you had to take a longer walk, but for example from Fawory (where the villas of the financial elite of that time were located) one could reach this place in about fifteen or twenty minutes. It was therefore enough, wanting to take a closer look at the hangings, to go for a short walk in that direction. As for the two places beyond the trenches, the least is known about the one located in the south-west, between the Jerozolimska and Mokotów tollhouses - there were other tollhouses there, near the Jerozolimska ones, which were called the Szubieniczne tollhouses, and it was precisely through them that ladder wagons full of convicts moved in a south-westerly direction.

Where, in what place the gallows stood, I cannot say. The line of trenches that surrounded the city from 1770 then ran in the area where now Raszyńska Street runs from Zawisza Square and further Koszykowa to the place where it joins Piękna (the territory now occupied by the Warsaw Water Works was already outside the city, i.e. beyond the trenches), so I would locate the fields of death and its gallows somewhere on the extension of Filtrowa, maybe next to Narutowicz Square or a bit further south - where Mianowski and Mochnacki Streets are now. Though maybe I'm wrong - that's just my guess. On the first day of the insurrection, April 17, it was precisely in this field that Russian units (Siberian Grenadiers, Akhtyrsky Chevau-légers, and Yamburg Carabiniers) regrouped around the gallows around three in the afternoon, they were commanded by a General named Novitsky and retreated from the city on his orders through the Szubieniczne and Jerozolimska tollhouses. The positions of Russian units during the April fights are well described (also on city maps) and on this basis the place where the gallows stood can be more precisely defined. I have not found any account stating that executions were carried out between April and November outside the Szubieniczne tollhouses and that someone was hanged there. This does not have to mean that the place was not used at the time - it may have been that some thieves were hanged there, though no one was hanged who would be known or valued for some reason - someone who would be remembered as a condemned person worth noticing. The second place of execution located beyond the trenches (i.e. outside the city) was in Piaski, and because Piaski was located past Powązki, in order to get there, one had to walk out or rather ride out of the city through the Powązki tollhouses, which were located at the exit of Dzika Street. The road beyond the tollhouses led north, then, in order to get close to the gallows, one had to turn a little west after passing Powązki. Now there are multi-story blocks made of large slabs in Piaski, at that time there was of course nothing standing there and that is why this place of execution was called The Field in Piaski. Sometimes, apart from the proper name, only 'Field' was mentioned. Perhaps there was some farmland around, belonging to the squire of a village called Piaski. Cereal and wheat, also beetroots, and in the wheat and beetroots, gallows.

Since the execution site, which was located within the city limits, was also similarly at that time sometimes called The Field, these two fields, if not further specified, may be mistaken by us - and when the reports refer to an execution field, we often need some additional information to find out which one it is. This is exactly the case in Father Kitowicz's *Historia Polska (Polish History)*. He added the following comment to *Sumariusz znaczniejszych powieszonych 1794 (The Summary of the Most Significant Hanged 1794)* which he himself composed (though it is a bit misleading). "Apart from these fourteen, they also hanged on a gallows in a field on July 3, Tepper's nephew, accused of belonging to a dissenters' conspiracy against the municipality of Warsaw during the siege of Warsaw. There, on the days of the 24th and 26th of this month of July various spies, rebels, Jews, and Catholics were hanged, unknown to the public by name, therefore also not known to the person writing this history". Reading sentences composed by Father Kitowicz is a real delight - especially for someone who knows how difficult it is arrange Polish sentences in such a way that they have their own good sound. As for "Tepper's nephew", his name was Karol Fergusson and he was somehow connected to, maybe even related to both bankers - but he was not the nephew of either of them, neither of the elder Piotr Tepper, nor of the younger Piotr Tepper Fergusson. Karol Fergusson was hanged on July 3 in Piaski, quite legally, as it was on the basis of a verdict of the Supreme Criminal Court, but for a reason other than what Father Kitowicz thought - he was one of the spies of General Karl Baur, head of Russian intelligence in Warsaw, and it was for this espionage service for the Russians that he was sentenced to death. When it comes to the "various spies, rebels, Jews, and Catholics" hanged "there" according to Father Kitowicz, it is not clear who the author of *Polish History* meant, or where these condemned (as can be seen, of various categories) were hanged. Wolfgang Heyman, who was the factor of the Prussian envoy in Warsaw, Ludwig Buchholtz, was hanged in Piaski (apart from Fergusson; and only these two incidents are well proven) at the end of July. This Heyman, of the Mosaic faith, was accused (as the Saxon *chargé d'affaires*, Johann Jakob Patz wrote) "on the basis of intercepted letters that he indicated ways of taking Warsaw and that he sent a code to the Prussian minister for further correspondence".

We also learn from Patz that the property of factor Heyman "was confiscated for the benefit of the treasury, after securing the rights of his wife and the claims of the creditors". The only other thing that is known about Piaski is that this place was also called The Square of Death as well as The Square of Punishment - I have not managed to get any other information on this subject, which does not mean, of course, that such information does not exist. Gallows, ladders, ropes, the executioner and his henchmen, some house, maybe just a shack where the bodies of those hanged were stored, another shack where the executioners' tools were stored, some clergymen (a pastor in the case of Fergusson, a rabbi in the case of Heyman), a platoon of little drummers as well as the beating of drums (this seems unlikely), the crack of a spine breaking when the hangman pulls the condemned man by the legs, and somewhere in the south the trees of Powązki, poplars and birches (there was already, from 1790, a cemetery, though it was still small) – one has to imagine this all. One could of course say that it is better not to imagine this, that it is better to be silent about these things, and it is best not to know anything about them - it's best not to know that something like this is happening. I believe that no side of human activity on this monstrous planet, in this monstrous cycle of nonsensical evolution, should escape our imagination. The species we belong to will one day disappear for the benefit of the wholeness of the planet - sooner or later something like this will surely happen, and I think about it with real pleasure. Then everything will return to its original order - the wheel of nonsense will stop nonsensically spinning and life on earth will gain (maybe regain) its deep meaning. Though it would be good to leave behind some testimony - one that would testify to the monstrosity and horror of our nonsensical existence. Some book that would talk about our existential monstrosity and existential horror. Such a book should probably be intended for slightly different readers - different inhabitants of the planet. I hope they will like this book of mine as well. Perhaps some educated hedgehog or educated mole will read it someday. Or some educated birch, some wise pine. I also think about this with pleasure. Thanks to the plans and tariffs of Warsaw at that time, it is possible to quite accurately determine - with an accuracy within several dozen meters - where the third execution site was located, precisely the one that could have been the destination of walks of the wealthy residents of Fawory Street - if they wanted to see hangings.

At that time, this place was most often called The Field behind Nalewki Street or simply The Field, it was also called The Public Gallows and The General Gallows. Ignacy Zakrzewski's letter to Tadeusz Kościuszko (of May 17) mentions a secluded place. In this letter, the President of Warsaw reported to the Chief that "the criminal court, having heard and obtained all the evidence and pleadings, announced its decree to Rogoziński, under which he will receive today the death penalty by the gallows in a secluded place". That Rogoziński, as the *Gazeta Powstania Polski (Polish Uprising Gazette)* informed its readers at that time (in an addition to Issue 13 of May 17), "the police intendant during the Muscovite government", became famous (apart from his villainy) also for the fact that beneath the gallows, when the harness and noose was put on, he was supposed to brazenly declare: "If I am to hang, then half of Warsaw must hang". This information comes from Father Kitowicz, and from the *Polish Uprising Gazette* we learn that Rogoziński "was hanged in the morning, near the Cuchtauz". This was yet another term used at that time in Warsaw to describe the place where the gallows stood. In order to walk to or ride to the gallows and Cuchtauz, or rather Cuchthauz - the Cuchthauz, also known as the House of Corrections, was in fact a prison and probably, as can be concluded from various accounts, a severe one, that is, one in which the correction of the residents was also cared for with the help of severe corporal punishments - so in order to get to the vicinity of this place of execution, one had to go from Nalewki Street, which, unlike today, was then a long street and ended near Pokorna (I am thinking about its northern end), previously crossing Miła, precisely to Pokorna Street, and after crossing Niska Street, reach the crossroads of Pokorna and Stawki. Currently, Pokorna is a small and meaningless street that disappears between Stawki and Inflancka Streets between plot gardens and construction sites. Soon, where there are gardens and construction sites now, new apartment buildings will be erected and this remnant of Pokorna will also disappear from the map of Warsaw. Back then, just as Nalewki Street, Pokorna was a long street, in the north almost reaching the outskirts of the city and connecting there with a road through which one could go beyond the trenches.

Stawki also ran differently than it does today, it broke off from Pokorna at an angle a little towards the west, and then turned a little to the north. Crossing Stawki (from the left) and the then Inflancka (from the right), one almost reached the end of the buildings on Pokorna Street. At number 2218 there was the Tobacco Factory of the City of Old Warsaw, at number 2220 the Jewish Warehouse (used by Jewish merchants), and between them, at number 2219, there were the buildings of the Cuchthauz. Further (towards the trenches there was an empty field, and this is precisely where the gallows probably stood. Then, in the nineteenth century, when the Russians built the Citadel in Warsaw and radically changed the street layout in this part of the city, the Tobacco Factory, the Jewish Warehouse, and Cuchthauz were torn down, and the Mikołajewski Barracks were erected in their place. The front building of the Mikołajewski Barracks, clearly visible on the plans of Warsaw from the mid-nineteenth century, can be considered the site of the Cuchthauz, and the then intersection of Pokorna Street with Kłopot Street located opposite the front building - as the field of gallows. The front building of the Mikołajewski barracks, clearly visible on the plans of Warsaw from the mid-nineteenth century, can be considered the site of Cuchthauz, while the then intersection of Pokorna Street with Kłopot Street located opposite the front building - as the field of gallows. Now, more or less at the point where Pokorna once joined Kłopot, there are plot gardens between the Arkadia Shopping Center and the Warszawa Gdańska railway station. If we stand near the metra exit on Słomiński Street and look towards the station and the tracks, then on the left side, near the station buildings, on the edge of the plot gardens, we will see an automatic car wash - and probably somewhere behind this automatic car wash and the cars being washed in it stood the gallows two hundred years ago. What the field of death near the Cuchthauz looked like, I cannot say. From the *History* by Father Kitowicz it could be concluded that the gallows "in the field behind Nalewki" were made of brick. Perhaps it was one gallows (one, but one that could serve or accommodate a few sentenced to be hanged), as Kitowicz wrote about a "general [...] though brick gallows". Though this very opinion of the author of *Polish History* is somewhat vague, and such a conclusion does not seem entirely legitimate. In addition to intendant Rogoziński, a certain Kobylański was hanged behind Nalewki (a little later, on June 4), a convert, the owner of taverns and brothels, who traded with Russian soldiers - the subject of trade (that is, what that Kobylański was selling) were teenage girls.

Later, on July 26, in the field behind Nalewki (probably right there), seven people sentenced for hanging were hanged - that is, those who on June 28 hanged others and were executed by a verdict of the Supreme Criminal Court of July 21. The fact that the hanging would take place behind Nalewki was decided by the Supreme National Council in a resolution of June 28 - it informed the "citizens of the free city of Warsaw" that the villain's place of execution "is designated by the Council to be Nalewki Square, where crimes against the Fatherland had been punished for centuries". One can imagine that the hanging on July 26 was quite a spectacle - all those who also hanged in June but did not get caught by Kościuszko's soldiers sent from Gołków to Warsaw probably came there to marvel at their colleagues being hanged. If that was the case, then a large crowd must have gathered near Nalewki and Pokorna. However, Jan Duklan Ochocki claimed in his *Pamiętniki* (*Memoirs*) that "the execution took place unexpectedly peacefully, as if in a time of peace and regular laws being in effect". It should also be added that in the field behind Nalewki Street, somewhere near the gallows, there was also a kind of cemetery - something like it, because there were probably no crosses and tombstones, and the ground was immediately trampled so that no trace would remain after the burial. The *History* by Father Kitowicz shows that something similar, a kind of cemetery, was also located in Piaski - all those "spies, rebels, Jews, and Catholics" who were hanged at the end of July were buried there near the gallows in the field. "All those, guilty and innocent, buried in the field by the gallows". At the execution site near the Cuchthauz, as Kitowicz claimed, the four hanged in the streets of Warsaw on May 9 were buried - "the bodies of those hanged [...] were buried by the gallows in the field behind Nalewki Street". This is confirmed by Jan Kiliński, who, talking about the events of May 9, wrote in the *Drugi Pamiętnik* (*Second Diary*) that in the evening the executioner "took down those hanging gentlemen", and then, "having put them on a ladder cart, ordered them to be taken out into the field". Such burials, a bit secret, are quickly forgotten, but it is quite certain that Kossakowski, Zabiełło, Ankwicz, and Ożarowski, probably also those who were sentenced and hanged in May and June, the intendant Rogoziński as well as the convert Kobylański, and perhaps also those who hanged in June and were later hanged for it, Officer Cadet Piotrowski, the mason Delgiert, the henhouse owner and poultry trader Dziekoński, the hay trader Jasiński, and the laborer Klonowski are still laying there and will lay forever. Mute, cut off from the noose, buried witnesses of our history – there, where among plot gardens between the Gdańsk Railway Station and the Arkadia hopping Center, Pokorna Street used to connect with Kłopot Street.

Chapter 17.
RUSSIAN MONEY

Russian Ruble 1793, (Author's Collection)

I re-read the Poznań edition (from 1865) of *Drugi rozbiór Polski z Pamiętników Sieversa* (*The Second Partition of Poland from The Memoirs of Sievers*; these are not so much the memoirs of Johann Jakob Sievers, but a collection of various materials, letters, as well as reports from the Sievers family archive that were published in the mid-nineteenth century by the German historian Karl Ludwig Blum) and it now seems to me that Tadeusz Korzon, describing Stanisław August's Grodno income - that is, what the king got from the Russian tsarina for participating in the Second Partition - might have been a bit wrong. It seems that the author of *Wewnętrzne dzieje Polski za Stanisława Augusta* (*The Internal History of Poland under Stanisław August*), when assessing the king's income, precisely those from 1793, based on documents preserved in the Sievers' archives, made calculations that could be made in a different way. In other words, that which was absolutely certain for Korzon is (if we look at the information Sievers provided and express it in a different way) very uncertain - this information can be understood as Korzon understood it, but it can also be understood differently. This does not mean that the king received less from the tsarina for his participation in the Grodno Sejm (and for the friendly cooperation there with the Russian ambassador) than Korzon believed. Maybe he even got more - except that this probably cannot be ultimately explained. Here are two examples which show that the calculations based on the information from *The Second Partition of Poland* could have produced a different result. According to Korzon, at the beginning of 1793, Stanisław August fell into "a complete recidivism of vileness". On his journey from Warsaw to Białystok and then to Grodno - in the first days of April 1793 - he first took 20,000 ducats from the Russian ambassador, and then another 10,000 ducats.

This travel money, which in fact was the payment for consenting to the Second Partition of Poland (let's say the first installment of such a payment), was taken then not only by the king - various high-ranking officials of the Republic were also encouraged to take this trip in this way. However, the Russian ambassador paid the royal dignitaries much worse – at that time they received ten, twenty, or even thirty times less for the costs of traveling from Warsaw to Grodno. "So, I think - wrote Sievers to Platon Zubov - that in order to gain Grand Chancellor Małachowski, Deputy Chancellor Chreptowicz, and Court Marshal Raczyński, it would be good to offer each of them one thousand to two and three thousand ducats for the journey as a secret gift". Though was the then "secret gift" for the king really 30,000 ducats? Let's see what it looks like in the documents from *The Second Partition of Poland*. The first information on this subject concerns Prussian money but paid to the king through the hands of the Russian ambassador. "The Prussian envoy said that one hundred thousand ducats were allocated, he had already collected ten, which he had given him [Sievers] for the king's trip to Grodno [...] as the Poles would not want to accept anything from the Prussians". The next piece of information comes from a letter by Sievers to one of his daughters. "I also give him [the king] all the comfort I can, and 20,000 ducats for the journey. He is going against his will". Thus, we already have 30,000 - with 10,000 from Ludwig Buchholtz (Prussian envoy) and 20,000 from Sievers. Though soon after, Sievers, enraged by the king's whims (because the king, although he took the money, did not want to go and excuses himself with illness, even with the illness of his doctor), informs Igelström (at that time commanding the Tsarina's troops stationed in Poland) that if things will continue to go on in this way, then the Polish monarch will be punished by him. "He will not receive the 20,000 ducats, granted by the empress, and he will not be able to count on any further support, indeed, I will sequestrate his income". Is this about the first 20,000 ducats? Maybe but not necessarily. This letter to Igelström also mentions 10,000. "I attach a promissory note to the banker Meissner, for which he will pay out to the king 10,000 ducats". Again, it is not known - does this sentence refer to the 10,000 Prussian ducats from Buchholtz or some other, next payout?

It was probably a different one, because Meissner (or Meysner) was then the banker of the Russian embassy. Sievers' documents mention the money for the trip to Grodno three more times. Following the information about Meysner, who is to pay out 10,000, we have - in Igelström's letter to Sievers on March 27 - information regarding 5,000 that have already been paid out. "I could not refuse him the 5,000 ducats that he got from me today, and which he absolutely needs for his primary travel expenses. I have the entire sum of 20,000 ducats here in my coffret". The next piece of information - from Sievers' letter to Platon Zubov - concerns Prince Józef Poniatowski. "They assure me that the king gave him an order to go to Italy and sent him on the road with some of the five thousand ducats that General Igelström credited to the account of the 20 thousand ducats he is to receive for this purpose". The last piece of information on this subject - probably from the first days of May - is in Sievers' letter to the tsarina. "I foresee - we read there - that the king, who is dragging a great wagon train with him, will soon not be able to pay for bread, for wine, and meat for himself. After the universals have been issued and the elections held, could I make him hopeful for ten thousand ducats, it is understood at the common cost [with Prussia] and for the same amount during the Sejm, if it turns out that the king is not getting involved in anything". As you can see, it would be very difficult to sensibly reconcile all of this and count it. It could be that these letters only inform us (as Korzon thought) about 30,000 ducats - that is, about two payments at the time for travel expenses, one from the Prussian envoy Buchholtz (10,000) and the other from Sievers or Igelström (20,000). Though it could be recognized that there were more payments, even five or six - and the 10,000 paid out by Meysner, 20,000 allocated by the tsarina, and also the 10,000 and the other 10,000 that Sievers asked the tsarina for, were some extra money which the king himself begged for (or, rather, he cried for - because when he asked for money, he was in the habit of wiping tears and sobbing, pitying his misery) from his Russian masters. The question of the money that Sievers paid out to the king during the sessions of the Grodno Sejm between September and October is also unclear. This autumn money (at least such a conclusion could be drawn from *The Internal History of Poland*) consisted of two payments of 14,000 ducats and a payment of 6,000 ducats in mid-November.

Sievers paid out 28,000 ducats to the king between September 1 and November 1, 6,000 were paid, at Sievers' orders, by Meysner's bank. To this, if one may say so, certain money, one should eventually add the uncertain money, that is, money where it is not certain that it was paid out - according to Korzon, in November, Sievers promised Stanisław August 3,000 ducats (again for travel expenses, but this time for the return trip), while earlier, between September and November, he could have added to the then 28,000 (but it is not known whether he added - Marshal Moszyński demanded this) two more payouts of 3,000 ducats each. Let's see what this looks like in the materials from *The Second Partition of Poland*. "From the 1st of September - we read there (this is a summary of Sievers' letter to the tsarina, probably written in mid-November) - he gave him [Sievers to the king] 150,000 francs, or 14,000 ducats, a month for his entire subsistence, and the king accepted this without complaint. Though this sum was not enough. After a careful calculation made together with Count Moszyński, he [Sievers] became convinced that another three thousand ducats every month was needed". This summary could indicate that between September 1 and mid-November 1793, Stanisław August took 42,000 ducats from the Russian embassy coffers (14,000 three times) and, as a result of a later calculation by Moszyński and Sievers, an additional 9,000 ducats (three times 3,000). Together, this would give - in the three autumn months - something along the lines of a quarterly salary of 51,000 ducats. This, however, is contradicted by the continuation of Sievers' account. This time it is no longer a summary, but a letter from the ambassador to the tsarina. "Therefore, after two months, September and October, I promised the king this amount from the common [Prussian and Russian] coffers or, if it was empty, to deduct it in a different way. When it was mentioned to pay out to him 14,000 ducats on November 1, eight days elapsed, and that much was not collected [...]. So at the urgent request of the king, I decided to have 6,000 ducats paid out to him by the banker Meissner this morning, before I went to him, for which he thanked me in the highest words at the end of our conversation". If we only considered the latter information, we would have to conclude that between September 1 and mid-November, the king received not 51,000, but much less - in September and October he might not even gotten anything (because Sievers only promised him something – to "deduct it in a different way"), and in the first days of November he was paid some (unknown) portion of the 14,000, and then the 6,000 that the ambassador had ordered Meysner to payout.

So, this would be only a few, maybe a dozen or so thousand ducats. To these few or a dozen or so thousand one could possibly add another 6,000 ducats, which are mentioned later in this letter from Sievers to Catherine. This information is particularly interesting, because it shows how the Saint Petersburg tsarina treated the Polish king at the time - without any at all reservations (because it finally was a delicate matter - money), she made him financial promises, promising some (in addition small) payments. "Let this serve him [the king] - wrote Sievers to the tsarina - as even stronger proof of what I precisely told him about the disposition of Y[our] Imp[erial] Majesty, and about what Y[our] Imp[erial] Majesty wrote herself, that I would provide him with three thousand ducats for the current month of November and that I would provide him with the same amount for the costs of the trip; he must stop at this, I cannot do more". The author of *The Internal History of Poland* probably considered these 6,000 ducats to be real income - that is, he believed that they were paid out - but there is no certainty in this case either, because Sievers could have not fulfilled his promise - if there was no money in the embassy's coffer. As all these examples show, nothing here is certain - and the Polish king, in 1793, could have cost the Petersburg tsarina even twice, even three times more than Korzon's calculations would suggest - but he could have also cost her much less. All of this could probably be explained quite easily if we knew the bills that Sievers presented to his monarch on his return to St. Petersburg. The fact that such accounts existed was mentioned in the Tsarina's rescript, ordering Sievers to leave Warsaw. This rescript (it implies that Sievers was not only dismissed, but also fell into disgrace, which can be explained by his bad relations with the tsarina's lover, Platon Zubov) was handed over to the ambassador up until that time, in December 1793, by the new ambassador, General Igelström. "Meanwhile, to the said general *en chef* - we read there - You will hand over the archives of Your predecessors [...] along with a detailed description and bills of expenses that you have made in our matters. We demand all the more that these bills be sent in as, due to Your abandonment of the old customs and example of Your predecessors, we have not received any such bills during the entire time which you were fulfilling your office, and apart from the sums that were sent to You from here, you were filling out thick promissory notes from our treasury, without at all explaining their real use".

It is not known how Sievers explained himself of these "thick promissory notes" in St. Petersburg. Some advice on this matter is a bit late now, but he could have been advised to explain the financial mess at the embassy on Miodowa Street (Sievers' office was not located where Igelström's was later, but across the street, at the Borch Palace, which is now the residence of the Primate of Poland) – by blaming the Polish king – on his unbridled greed and equally unrestrained extravagance. Knowing the bills that Sievers prepared in St. Petersburg at the request of the tsarina (as well as the earlier bills of subsequent Russian ambassadors in Warsaw - Repnin, Saldern, Stackelberg, and Bulgakov), we would know exactly how much the Russians paid for Stanisław August Poniatowski - how much this king cost them. Someone may say that it does not matter whether the Russians then paid this Polish king a million ducats or only half a million. Maybe it doesn't matter - from some moral point of view. Though in this particular case, I would be interested not so much in the moral as in the financial (or financial-political) point of view. Knowing the price of the Polish king, we could compare it with other similar prices - the price that Tsarina Catherine was prepared to pay for the king from Tiflis or the king from Stockholm. Was the Polish king cheaper or more expensive than the Georgian king? Did the Russian ambassador in Stockholm - before he was expelled from there by Gustav III, who could not be bought - have less or more money at his disposal (for the purchase of the Swedish king) than his colleague in Warsaw? This is precisely what I find very interesting.

Chapter 18.
THE EXECUTIONER

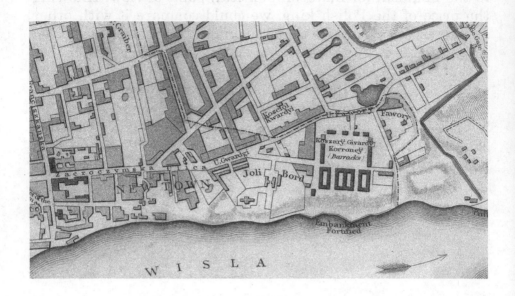

When the insurrection began, Stefan Böhm (his surname also appears in other forms - Beym and Bem) was a man in his prime - he was fifty-three years old. The family he came from was not rich, and in addition, Stefanek (as he was later fondly called in Warsaw) was the eleventh consecutive son in a row. From Chełm, where he studied, he was sent to study medicine in Królewiec in the hope that he would obtain a lucrative profession. Böhm did not complete his studies for unknown reasons, but the surgical specialization he chose could later be of use to him in his professional work. After leaving Królewiec, Böhm found a job with the Radziwiłł's from Niasviž - he was an official in the estate of Prince Karol Radziwiłł, My Beloved Sir, and then, in 1768, he joined the army of the Bar Confederation. His adventures in the Confederation are poorly known, it is only known that he fought in the vicinity of Kraków and was badly wounded in the Battle of Tyniec, as Kazimierz Władysław Wójcicki wrote in the second volume of *Cmentarz Powązkowski* (*The Powązki Cemetery*), "he was thrown from his horse and left in the field as if he was killed". The biography in Wójcicki's work is almost the only source from which one can draw a handful of somewhat credible information about Böhm's youth. The next day after the Battle of Tyniec, the courtiers of prince My Beloved Sir, found their colleague on the battlefield, and although the wound he received was not fatal, it must have had a considerable impact on his life - maybe it even somehow decided, that after many years, that he chose this profession and not another one. It was, as Wójcicki wrote, "a saber cut through the face and head", and the result of this slanted cut was a terrible scar that marked and even mangled Böhm's face. Something that the condemned, in their last moment, might have recognized - and even certainly did - as Stefanek's crooked smile, perhaps as a mocking smile, a diabolical smile, was thus in fact an inevitable and unfortunate grimace caused by a scar that ran diagonally from the forehead to the chin. The executioner's face - this was the last sight they took with them from here; and in this way the world bid them farewell with a crooked smile.

Please, let those who see me smile as I write this book take this into account. When the terrible wound finally healed, Böhm found himself – it is unknown how - in Heilsberg, the town in which, in Warmia (now called Lidzbark Warmiński), resided the bishop and poet Ignacy Krasicki. Their conversations, between the bishop and the executioner, in the episcopal garden, in the dizzying scent of red roses climbing over the pergolas - what a wonderful topic this is. Though, unfortunately, nothing is known about them, we would have to make them up entirely - and I don't like that. In 1778, *Monachomachia* (*War of the Monks*) appeared in print; it was precisely during this time that Böhm was living in Heilsberg. Perhaps Böhm played in Krasicki's court theater - his face, horribly cut and disgustingly twisted, predestined him to be an actor, of course, one who plays comic roles. Though these are just my guesses. In Heilsberg, Böhm became friends with someone named Müller or Miller who worked at Krasicki's court. This Müller was the bishop's surgeon, he was also known to conduct in Heilsberg some scientific experiments in the field of physics and chemistry - although he lived in the best age of enlightenment, it could also be that he distilled in Heilsberg some liquids (sulfuric acid?), wishing to make the elixir of life out of them. Müller, conducting his scientific research and cutting his patients, earned some extra money in Heilsberg as an executioner, and Böhm, befriending him, began to assist in the executions. In this way, he learned the technical secrets of the profession, which he probably began to like. Böhm's technique - the one he used during executions in Warsaw - was quite ingenious, but the question of whether he got acquainted with it in Heilsberg or invented it himself cannot be answered. It could also have come from some other source - if, which I don't know, there were German or French textbooks from which one could learn this profession. Around 1780, having abandoned Heilsberg and Krasicki's court theater, Böhm (again, it is not known how) found a job somewhere on the Bug - in a town called Pratulin. Wójcicki wrote that he "supervised the bridges on the Bug". In this Pratulin he married Marianna née Gliszczyńska in 1782, and two years later Marianna gave birth to a son who was given the name Kacper at the christening. The stay in Pratulin ended a bit unhappily as after the Second Partition in 1793, in was precisely in this place that Russian troops crossed the Bug and Böhm was recognized by someone as a Bar Confederate. "Since he was pointed out at being a former partisan - wrote Wójcicki – the only time he had was what he needed to save himself, his wife, and son". However, this unfortunate accident ended happily, because Böhm, with his wife and child, fled to Warsaw, where he was successful.

The Böhm's lived near Fawory Street, probably on Zielona Street at number 2075 - conclusions that can be drawn from contemporary Warsaw tariffs, however, are somewhat uncertain. Anyway, it was the best district in Warsaw - at that time the richest Warsaw residents lived in manor houses on Fawory and Zielona Streets. As nothing is known about the first months of the Böhm's stay in the capital, it is impossible to explain how they ended up in such a good place. Wójcicki explained this by saying that Böhm "received glorious graces from great leaders" as an "experienced soldier", but such an explanation does not seem sufficient - after all, many old soldiers were begging on the streets of Warsaw at that time. Writing about great leaders, Wójcicki had in mind General

Henryk Dąbrowski, who was the Böhm's neighbor, and Prince Józef Poniatowski, who supported them financially when the Böhm's were building their manor house on Zielona Street. Probably shortly after arriving in Warsaw, Böhm found the brother of his Heilsberg friend living here, the Müller or Miller, who was a surgeon and executioner under Bishop Krasicki. The brother in Warsaw, also Müller or Miller, was named Jan and he was the executioner of Warsaw. He was not young anymore and could not cope with the work that required a certain physical strength, so the city authorities were looking for his successor. Böhm, who had gained some experience in Heilsberg, was a good candidate. As the job (considering various extras) paid well, Müller managed to persuade him and thus Warsaw gained a new executioner. Since the essence of the executioner's profession consisted of keeping order and cleanliness (people then more often talked about cleaning the city or its tidiness), the executioner, as a city official, was employed full-time in the Street Commission, and his earnings were more or less the same as those of other officials who were responsible for the external appearance of Warsaw. It can of course be said that the executioner had more serious tasks - he was also responsible for the spiritual appearance. Though he, it seems, was paid no more than those who took care of the condition of the cobblestones, street gutters, or waste wagons. The place of work of the executioner and his assistants was the Kara Warehouse on Nalewki Street. It was quite a distance from Zielona or Fawory to Nalewki (behind the Krasiński Garden), I do not know how Böhm got to work - he must have ridden a horse.

The pay of the full-time job was 92 Polish złotys a month, i.e. (in 1793) less than 5 red złotys. It seems that it was not much, but we will see in a moment that the executioner actually earned much more. The duties of the executioner, apart from beheading or hanging, included, firstly, transporting out of town and burying the bodies of those who had been beheaded or hanged. As for this duty, it was obviously not the case that the executioner was personally fulfilling the role of the gravedigger; he only had to order and organize the burial of the condemned, and the removal was carried out by his journeymen. Secondly, the executioner had the responsibility of taking away the dead animals, that had died on the streets of the city; this responsibility also included taking them out of town and (as we would say disgustingly today) the utilization of animals that had not died yet but were sick and it was expected that they would die. It was the executioner's responsibility to utilize animals collected from the streets, but the contract with him stipulated that he would also take away dead horses and cattle at the request of the townspeople. As throwing dead animals onto the street was absolutely forbidden (this also applied to dogs and cats - animal corpses were terribly feared), any animal that died in the city, and there were plenty of them, had to pass through the hands of the executioner or his assistants. Third and finally, the executioner also had the responsibility to execute sentences that did not concern people, but various kinds of works - those that were considered by the criminal courts to be harmful or inflammatory. To put it another way, the duties of the executioner included the public burning of books, newspapers, advertisements, and any other papers in which was found something that could threaten the Republic. As one can see, some of the executioner's duties were very profitable, others were not. The greatest additional income was undoubtedly brought - though not always - by beheading and hanging. Burial could also be profitable, but it depended on the wealth of the families of the condemned. Dead animals were undoubtedly extremely profitable - because the transport, at the request of the town's inhabitants, was carried out for an additional, agreed upon fee, each such animal meant additional earnings. On the other hand, the executioner certainly did not earn a grosz by burning papers.

Böhm's additional earnings are well illustrated by reports of the four executions that took place on May 9. The earnings, of course, came from the fact that those who were going to be hanged had a vested interest in being hanged quickly and efficiently. It is worth recalling an accident that was much talked about at that time - the decapitation of King Louis XVI, who was beheaded by guillotine in Paris on January 21, 1793. The Parisian executioner reportedly then lowered the guillotine blade so badly that, instead of falling on the king's nape and cutting the king's neck, it struck a little from the side, slitting the skull and face diagonally. At least this is what the outraged monarchists later claimed; the Jacobin version of Louis XVI's death said that the king screamed and tried to break out until the last moment, and that was supposed to be the cause of the awkward cut. The highest gratification for the quick and professional execution of his executioner work was received by Böhm on May 9 from the Lithuanian Field Hetman Józef Zabiełło. Jan Kiliński's story says that Zabiełło, already in suspenders, gave Böhm a pouch with ducats, in which "there were more than a hundred". The second of the three condemned who were hanged in the Old Warsaw Market Square, Marshal Ankwicz, also turned out to be generous, who, as Karol Wojda wrote in his book *O rewolucji polskiej w roku 1794* (*On the Polish Revolution in 1794*), "gave a golden snuff box to the executioner". According to Antoni Trębicki, the gratification that Böhm received from the Marshal of the Permanent Council for his good work was even more generous - Ankwicz added a golden watch to the snuff box. Böhm gives me the impression of a serious man (and a good professional), so I don't think that, after examining the golden snuff box, he could say to the marshal standing on the ladder: - You're a little light. - That wouldn't be in his style. To the awards that Böhm received on May 9, we can also add a "triple ducat" mentioned in Kiliński's *Drugi Pamiętnik* (*Second Diary*), which was given to Böhm by Bishop Kossakowski. If one compares this triple ducat (it was a gold coin minted in 1794, more often called a triple red złoty and having, as the name suggests, the value of three ducats, i.e. two red one-and-a-half złotys) with Zabiełło's pouch, then it must be said that Bishop Kossakowski, paying with this one coin his hanging in front of St. Anne's Church, turned out to be surprisingly frugal. The fact that Böhm was not just anybody, some money-hungry rascal, but a serious and honest professional, is confirmed by his behavior on June 28. It is not known for what reason he was close to the gallows that day, but it is known that he found the hangings that took place on that day illegal and refused to cooperate with those doing the hangings. "He was threatened in vain - says the text entitled *Obrona Stanisława Augusta* (*The Defense of Stanisław August*; perhaps authored by the king) - [...] he made it known to them that he shudders with such acts, that he is an executor of court sentences, not of assaults and murders".

On June 28, people hung haphazardly, on whatever was there and whoever was there - and that's probably what Böhm precisely didn't like, who (at least it seems so) liked solid work. It arises from the *Historia Polska* (*Polish History*) by Father Kitowicz that Böhm, as he did not want to hang, was close to being among the hanged. This ended with the executioner's escape, and maybe a chase after him, which Kitowicz described in his wonderful, even a bit wild Polish. "He was already in danger of the noose of the enraged mob, he barely escaped with his students from among the heaps leading him to such an execution, pretending to be obedient, and then he quickly took things into his own hands in the turns of the streets". After the fall of the Uprising and the Russians entering Warsaw, Böhm continued to work as an executioner. He continued his profession until 1813, and thus also in the era of the Duchy of Warsaw and the Napoleonic Wars. A man of admirable diligence - when he died in 1813, he was seventy-two years old, and only then his son Kacper, previously a hussar officer in the army of Prince Józef Poniatowski, took over the duties of executioner. The condemned of that time were probably not happy with the fact that an old man was hanging them, because it must have taken an extremely long time. One can imagine old Böhm climbing with difficulty, rung by rung (his spine hurts, and he has sciatica), up the ladder and resting in the middle of this climb - the executioner's ladders, leaning against the crossbeam of the gallows, were very high, being at least six or seven meters tall. Nothing at all is known about this last period of Stefan Böhm's activity. From the biography posted in *The Powązki Cemetery* by Wójcicki, it can be concluded that Böhm remained a traditionalist until the end of his life, an executioner attached to the centuries-old executioner's tradition.

Wójcicki wrote that both he and later his son "kept the old custom, that after the punishment completed on the convicted felon, in their ceremonial dress, each stood before the president of Warsaw, and, drawing the sword from its scabbard, announced: that he had punished the criminal by virtue of the sentence of the criminal court". This ceremonial dress of the executioner of Warsaw was probably described by someone - it would be good to check what it looked like. Even more interesting would be a description, and it probably does not exist, of the outfit that Böhm put on when he left for work - we don't even know if he put on gloves for the hangings. Or whether they were thin silk gloves (black, shiny silk) or thick, quilted gloves, the kind I put on to work in my garden in Milanówek. Describing the graves of two executioners, of a father and a son, in *The Powązki Cemetery*, Wójcicki quoted a proverb which the people of Warsaw connected with the name of the first of them. Whether it was a proverb from 1794 or from later years, we do not find out from Wójcicki. Whoever wanted to frighten someone said: - You will go to Stefanek's for breakfast. - Wójcicki believed that it was a threatening proverb ("the name was known as a threatening proverb among the people of Warsaw"), but he was probably wrong, because the diminutive indicates that the executioner, although dangerous, also had something nice or funny in his aura. Perhaps Stefanek Böhm was a nice man - standing on a ladder and smiling spasmodically with his lips gashed on a slant, he strokes the condemned on the cheek. This amusing element could be further emphasized a bit, an idea of the people of Warsaw closing it in rhyming form. A proverb, reworked in this way, would then capture another, poorly recognized side of death – that which is funny about it. There's breakfast food under Stefanek's roof.

Chapter 19
THE THIRD FORM OF TRAVEL

François Blanchard took off from the Foksal Garden on May 10, 1789, at one o'clock in the afternoon. His aerial journey was supposed to take place the day before, but there were some obstacles - maybe the aerostatic machine (*la machine aérostatique*) could not be prepared in time or maybe the weather was unfavorable on May 9, stormy or rainy - and the Warsaw newspapers published a notice of the flight's delay by one day ("in a company of a certain Lady", as was mentioned in the *Gazeta Warszawska* [*The Warsaw Gazette*]).

The main avenue of the Foksal Garden - also known as Vauxhall or the Vauxhall Garden - ran exactly as the roadway of Foksal Street now runs - from Nowy Świat Street towards the Vistula escarpment and a narrow passage, through which one can currently get to Smolna Street. This passage did not exist at that time because, as the plans show, there were no buildings on the southern and northern sides of the Foksal Garden. Then there were structures on the land separating

Vauxhall from Nowy Świat - there was a wooden house under number 1297 that belonged to the banker Cabrit (or Kabrit). One could probably get on Foksal (I do not know if they spoke then, as we say now - on Foksal, or rather - to Vauxhall) through the gate of this house, surely also through one of the streets located at the back of Nowy Świat - through Wróbla or Szczygla. The carriage carrying the king, the pock faced Miss Grabowska, and the poet Trembecki to the show, thus went from the Castle - this is how I imagine it - through Krakowskie Przedmieście, past the Dominican Observant Church, turned left and through Aleksandria, and then Wróbla (just like Kopernik Street now runs), and that reached Vauxhall. Or it drove along Nowy Świat to Ordynacka Street and turned from Ordynacka Street onto Wróbla. Trembecki, although not young (he was fifty at the time), must have been quite excited. He wrote the first half of the ode *Balon* (*Balloon*) the day before (this is also my guess, of course) and was jumping in his seat in anticipation of what would happen next - whether the balloon would catch fire in the air and Blanchard and his lady would go up in flames over Warsaw (a spectacular eventuality), or whether the balloon would burst and Blanchard and the lady, having descended on two parachutes, would land in the Foksal Garden (also a spectacular eventuality, but a little less). - Trębuś - says the king - do not be nervous, don't jump around, if you write your ode *Balloon*, you will get de ma cassette 50 ducats, as I promised you. They will go to pay off your debts. Though if you go with Blanchard and jump with a parachute, you will get them into your hand, and I, Trębuś, will add 20 de surplus to your pension mensuelle. - It is a pity that the jump that I imagined here did not take place, because it would have been an unforgettable sight - the author of *Powązki* descending slowly on a parachute above Foksal Street.

A parachute, a poet, his skewed *tricorne* and the tails of his patched and dirty Chinese banyan flying over Foksal. During this descent, one of the poet's morning slippers, also of Chinese production, falls from his left foot. As the *Pamiętnik historyczno-polityczno-ekonomiczny* (*The Historical-Political-Economic Memoir*) published at that time in Warsaw (by Father Piotr Świtkowski) explained to its readers, "a *parachute* is like a large kitajka umbrella". Kitajka, that is silk, made of Chinese silk. I am including here a fragment of an article in which *The Historical-Political Memoir* (in its May issue of 1789), probably by the pen of Father Świtkowski, described Blanchard's flight in Warsaw. The balloon size given in this article is worthy of attention - 90 ells, this is almost the same as 55 meters. A balloon with such a circumference would be about twice the size of my house in Milanówek, and if it were now placed in the middle of Foksal Street, it would probably hardly fit there. "The Frenchman Blanchard, who had perfected and put into use the art of floating in the air invented by the Montgolfier brothers, having shown this unusual for centuries spectacle to various nations, also came to Warsaw to amaze and delight Polish eyes with boldness and dexterity. This was already the 34th aerial journey of this brave man. He set off on the 10th of May, in a Balloon made of rubbered kitajka and with a circumference of 90 ells, from the Foksal Garden on Nowy Świat, at one in the afternoon. The ropes suspended from the net that covered the top of the Balloon held the flimsy boat to which the aforementioned Navigator along with one female companion of this aerial voyage entrusted their lives. The East-South wind made the Balloon which was soaring to an immense height almost always travel along the Vistula and it could be seen from almost any place in the Capital, at the end after 45 minutes the aerial sailors descended without the slightest damage in Białołęka past the Vistula. A few days later this famous sailor conducted a test of a Parachute invented by himself, the last resort of saving oneself from a deadly fall, should the Balloon burst by any means. This Parachute was raised to an immense height by one small Balloon, to which it was attached with a rope. Above this, when this Balloon caught fire, the rope was burned through, and the Parachute itself began to unravel and come down along with a basket hanging underneath it, in which there was a large dog. For 6 minutes it descended and slowly planted the basket and the dog in it on the sand near the Palace of the Corps of Cadets".

Information about Blanchard's first flight in Warsaw, given in the *Memoir* of Father Świtkowski, can also be supplemented with those found in Antoni Magier's *Estetyki miasta stołecznego Warszawy* (*The Aesthetics of the Capital City of Warsaw*). The author of *The Aesthetics* mixed up a little the two Warsaw flights of the French, as it was then said, aeronaut - the first flight in 1789 and the next one in 1790. For this second flight, Blanchard took off from a garden on Senatorska Street in a balloon, which was made at the expense of Jan Potocki. As Magier wrote, "13,000 ells of kitajka of different smooth and shimmering colors" were used for the balloon, which Potocki had brought in "from foreign factories", and which was sewed together in Warsaw by eighteen tailor apprentices. The French aeronaut, now without a lady, the author of *The Saragossa Manuscript*, Potocki's famous Turk, as well as his equally famous poodle then flew from Senatorska Street to Wola and landed near Górce. As for the first flight, the one from 1789, we learn from Magier that Blanchard's balloon was then filled with "water-bearing gas" in the morning before the flight, cannons placed on the castle terrace were fired in honor of the Frenchman and his wife (the lady with whom he was flying was supposed to be his wife), and the "immense height", about which *The Historical-Political-Economic Memoir* wrote, amounted to, "as it was perceived and calculated by the Royal Observatory, 3975 ells". Thus, in May 1789 the Blanchard's soared to - if we convert it in the decimal system - a height of 2,365 meters. This seems a bit unlikely - that the kitajka balloon, in a flight from the Foksal Garden to Białołęka (Magier referred to it as the Białołęka Forest), would reach an altitude of almost two and a half kilometers, where it is terribly cold and there is almost no air. Perhaps Magier made a mistake in this point, or perhaps the Royal Observatory made a mistake in its calculations. In *The Aesthetics of the Capital City* we also have some interesting information regarding the material Blanchard used to fill his *machine aérostatique*. It was white and green vitriol, that is, zinc sulfate and iron sulfate.

"After this aerial experiment, 6,000 pounds of white vitriol and 2,000 green vitriol were left for sale on Foksal, the amount of iron used for this experiment can be used to judge the enormity of the balloon floating two people in the air". Although Blanchard's show was extremely popular in Warsaw, and, as Magier wrote, he was received with the "applause of all", there were also those who watched the first successes of aerostatic machines with suspicion. It seems that worry among thinking people was awakened (and indeed it must

have awakened) because balloons disturbed and even questioned the obvious order of the world, something that could
be called the natural and immemorial division of functions
- a person flying at the height of two and a half kilometers
was taking on some functions that had never been his, and
that was what was disturbing, even threatening - though it
threatened with something that was not well realized at the
time. If the natural order of the world can be questioned, if
one can ask whether it should be like this or differently - this
is how one could describe the doubts that after all arise for us
now on various occasions - then there is probably no order in
which one can believe and in which one can trust. Trembecki
saw in the ode *Balloon* the triumph of modern reason, which
evades or even nullifies "natural law" ("human reason passes
everywhere", "it taught boulders how to jump"), and he liked
this jumping very much, because he was lighthearted and had
a liberal mind, thus favoring various modernization projects.
This admiration for risky endeavors, visible in the ode *Balloon*, certainly had something to do with Trembecki's love of
playing cards, which the poet devoted most of his time to - he
even excused himself from going to Thursday Dinners at the
king's, because it meant getting up from the table. Let's take
a risk and then we'll see what comes of it - this is the attitude
of a card player who bids everything with a weak hand. People who were not at all stupider than the author of *Balloon*,
and certainly more prudent, did, however, make reservations,
although, as I say, they did not quite know yet (not quite exactly) what they did not like and what they were protesting
against. One of those with reservations was Canon Franciszek
Salezy Jezierski, a writer now completely forgotten, but then
very influential.

This incident is particularly interesting, because Father Jezierski was a friend of Hugo Kołłątaj's, one of the pil-
lars of Kołłątaj's Forge, a political radical, even more radical
than Kołłątaj himself. It can even be said that Jezierski was a
furious radical - one who would have eagerly turned the whole
of Poland upside down at that time and on the occasion would
have hanged on lanterns (if there were lanterns suitable for
this in Warsaw - such as in Paris) the king and all his people,
starting with Trembecki. While balloons, thought also radical,

and undoubtedly admirable from the point of view of an enlightened mind, were very much disliked by him. Interesting. As one can see, (spiritual) life is not easy at all. Father Jezierski expressed his dislike of balloons for the first time due to Blanchard's first flight. In a brochure published anonymously in February 1790, entitled *Ktoś piszący z Warszawy (Someone Writing from Warsaw)*, he asked a crafty question about the purpose of such flights. "The invented - he wrote there - and abandoned in past centuries way of rising into the air, has been returned to human use. All the periodicals heralded to the general public such a magnificent work of physics in our enlightened age. [...] I saw a Frenchman flying over Warsaw. What after that? When on this journey he did not know where he would go and how he would get out after his aerial pilgrimage. [...] In all of this I see more confusion than enlightenment". To this question, directed as much to the French aeronaut as to the liberal mind - where are you going and how will you get off? - Father Jezierski gave an answer in his most important work, which under the title *Niektóre wyrazy porządkiem abecadła zebrane i stosownymi do rzeczy uwagami objaśnione (Some Words Collected in the Order of the Alphabet and Explained with Appropriate Comments to the Topics)* was published after his death by Hugo Kołłątaj in 1791. In *Some Words* - this is a very interesting graphic lexicon, not a dictionary, and not a small encyclopedia - there is an entry entitled "Podróż" ("Journey"), in which Jezierski once again expressed his aversion to Blanchard and his balloons. "A journey takes place on the ground, and when it is done on the water it is called sailing, the third form of travel in the air is flying, by nature this belongs to the birds. Mr. Blanchard, of the French nation, showed ascension into the air in many places in Europe, he once showed his flying in Warsaw, promised to show it again, on the third time, instead of flying in the air over the city, he left Warsaw on the ground".

Now we can see why Father Jezierski disliked Blanchard - by wanting to be "flying in the air", the French aeronaut violated the order established by Providence, because he practiced "the third form of travel", which by nature "belongs to the birds". In other words, he was doing something that was inconsistent with human nature. That is also why he ended badly - "instead of flying in the air", he left "on the ground". Father Jezierski did not know, because he could not have known, that Blanchard would have an even worse end - in 1808 he would be hit by apoplexy in his balloon (then floating over The Hague). The answer to the question posed in the brochure *Someone Writing from Warsaw* was thus this - flying in the air and any other "confusion" into which enlightened reason falls, will ultimately end in violating the order of existence. However, it is necessary to add (so that Father Jezierski from Kołłątaj's Forge would not turn out to be an admirer of the old order, perhaps even an admirer of the St. Petersburg tsarina, the monster who, as we know, was the guarantor of all natural order), that even though flying with balloons was, according to the author of *Some Words*, inconsistent with human nature and also with the providential order of the world, according to him, something else was completely in line with this order - namely hangings. Father Jezierski also expressed this conviction in *Some Words Collected in the Order of the Alphabet*. Hanging - somewhat allusively - is mentioned in the entry "Latarnia" ("Lantern"). Jezierski started with a joke - "Lanterns as a dwelling of light provide an opportunity to show sights". The joke was a bit ambiguous, because the views that the Canon had in mind were the views in Paris in 1789. "A more peculiar thing in Paris in 1789. Lanterns without their own light, only by the surface light of the sun, showed the most horrible events that Providence prepares as a lesson to those into whose hands it has entrusted justice for the people". Some clarification is needed regarding the usefulness of lanterns - the Parisian ones, from 1789, standing in the streets and equipped with ropes, which were used to light them, were greatly, together with their ropes, suitable for hanging and this is precisely how they were used; it was different with the street lamps then in Warsaw, which were few in number in the 1790's and which did not stand in the streets, but were attached to the walls of houses and over gates.

It can be said that by presenting the Parisian lantern views as something that, although horrible, even the most horrible, is made by Providence, Father Jezierski offered us in his entry "Lantern" something akin to the beginnings of the theory of hangings. It is a pity that they were undeveloped beginnings - because we would have not a French, but our own, Polish, Enlightenment theory of hangings. If Jezierski had taken his thought a little further, he would have had to write that hanging, if it is - unlike flying with balloons - arranged and ordered by Providence, is also something that Providence likes and is under its care. Being a thoughtful and full of goodness work of Providence (caring for "justice for the people"), it is - to put it a bit differently - a prudent, saving idea of God the Father or (at least) the Holy Spirit. If, on the other hand, Providence, watching over mankind (the fate of its nations), invented just such a kind of moral lesson - it means, of course, that it wants something like that. Providence, which desires the hangings, seeing in it a "lesson", and even "causes" something like that, that is, personally participates in hangings – it is curious whether it was Father Jezierski who had this wonderful idea, or if something like that was suggested by his patron, Father Kołłątaj or perhaps both Jezierski and Kołłątaj found this providential idea in some French revolutionary lexicon. Since I will no longer have the opportunity to deal with Father Jezierski, at least in this book, I am including one more of his thoughts from *Some Words*, not having anything to do with balloons, nor with lanterns, nor with hanging - but showing well what was talked about in Kołłątaj's Forge at Czerniakowska Street under number 3007, and what were the topics of the philosophical discussions held there. This sentence comes from the entry "Aktorowie" ("Actors"). "The whole world is a worthy sight for itself [...] some are actors for others".

Chapter 20.
THE SEQUENCE OF EVENTS

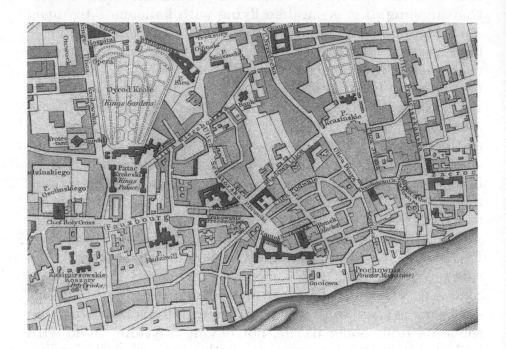

First, at the intersection of Krakowskie Przedmieście and Królewska Streets, the head of Prince Gagarin falls on the roadway, then Bishop Kossakowski is hanged beneath St. Anne's Church, even later by the Sophie Lhullier Apartment house some thug, unknown to anyone, cuts the throat of Stanisław August and cuts off his head, even later, in front of the neighboring tenement house, this king, but now with his head and even in a hat with a feather, is hanged and hangs until eight o'clock in the evening on the corner of Bednarska and Krakowskie Przedmieście, and even later (or maybe much earlier) in the crypt of the Capuchin Church *vis-à-vis* the Russian embassy, someone, a butcher armed with a spit rod, pierces General Igelström lying in a coffin. Even later - or even earlier - in the Castle's dining room, the corpse of Chancellor Sułkowski is placed on the table, and right next to the body, a young lady fastens her garter with a blue bow, and before or after (or even at the same time) Blanchard's balloon with the poet Trembecki and his poodle soars above Vauxhall and departs towards Białołęka. All of these events - and even others that are discussed in this book - can be dated (with sure or doubtful ones; established or guessed; real or fictitious) and probably could be arranged (if someone had made the effort to do so - but not me, it would have to be someone else) in the order in which they appeared in time or could have appeared in time - that is, in the order we call chronological.

In my book this is arranged (or was arranged by itself) somewhat differently, in some other order, but if I wanted to explain why there is this order - or disorder - of events and not another, and on what exactly this order (or disorder) is based on, then I would have trouble with this. That which was before and which was after, various scattered pieces of history, its broken fragments fell here side by side and began to exist differently - not as they once existed, before and after, but at the same time. Though that's not all this is about - that what was before and after found itself at the same time and the chronological became synchronous. My book (like all my books) is fragmentary, which means that it is stuck together from something that has fallen apart, disconnected, split apart, dispersed - of smaller and larger pieces that fit a bit, and do not fit a bit, that connect with each other a bit, and that don't connect a bit, maybe they would like to connect, but they can't connect.

In addition, it is not known why it is like this - at least I do not know. It can be said that this is precisely what it is like in life because life in its lively essence is fragmentary, made up of fragments, pieces that connect and don't connect, fit together and don't fit - but does that explain something? It would be good to know why life is fragmented and falls into pieces, and in addition it does not allow these pieces to be put together into a somewhat coherent whole, but it is obvious that this cannot be known - life does not want us to know why it is this way, why it is as it is, in pieces and shattering into pieces, and not different. Different - that is, as a whole, given to us to live as a complete whole. Life as a coherent and orderly whole, where everything fits exactly and matches itself perfectly - something like this cannot at all be imagined. If someone understands life, the verb "to understand" is not used well here, because one does not understand life, it cannot even be understood, because it is something completely incomprehensible, and therefore one should rather talk about something that is an unreasonable and incomprehensible (like life itself) experience of life - so if someone experiences life as something that constantly (throughout their life) breaks down into pieces that maybe would like to connect, but do not fit together or barely fit, and in addition, not letting themselves be put together into a meaningful whole, fall apart somewhere and disappear, it is unknown why and it is unknown where, probably in that which we call nothingness (which should therefore consist of such pieces which do not match each other and match nothing, but as it is known, is not made of nothing), so whoever, I repeat, experiences their life as something given to them in random, mismatched, falling apart pieces, recognizes them in the same way (although they do not have to know about it - recognition does not have to be conscious) as a kind of big bang - the falling apart pieces fell apart for some reason, let's say a mysterious one (because we know nothing about it), and such a mysterious reason could only be a catastrophe.

In other words, it is precisely such a way of living of life which presupposes that it is a mysterious catastrophe or the result of a mysterious catastrophe - a catastrophe occurred, about which we do not know anything, and as a result of it something has fallen to pieces. Either life is therefore such a catastrophic bang, or life happens because there has been a catastrophic bang - something (which we know nothing about) exploded. These two things are not identical, these are rather two possibilities, but the effect is similar. This huge, mysterious bang tears our lives apart, divides them into non-matching or poorly matching pieces which do not let themselves be connected, that fall apart somewhere - each piece separately. Somewhere - but even this indefinite pronoun is something too explicit and something naming something too clearly, because such a pronoun, so used, indicates some space, some place - and after all this is not about something that could be conceptualized as a space - cosmic space, time space, metaphysical space, or some other. It seems acceptable to think that those non-matching pieces that fall apart after a bang are not something that disappears, but something that revolves. I cannot see this place of revolving clearly enough (that is - I cannot name it), but the reason for this idea is that I see some pieces that are revolving - they are, it seems, mysterious parts of the world that do not necessarily belong to my life; rather, passing through it or passing right by it. I draw one more conclusion from this - it says that if my life is something like a bang, then everything that exists must have come into existence and must exist the same way - everything has to be constantly falling apart, so it has to be a kind of big bang.

Everything that exists - by its very existence - is, from the moment it comes into being, torn to pieces - and falling apart, piece by piece, it revolves, fragmented, beside me. We fall apart somewhere - into pieces – and the world, together with us, falls apart somewhere, but it is not known, firstly, why, secondly, in what way (is there any order, some purpose in this falling apart of pieces), thirdly, how to express and name this place-not a-place where one could find (in which it was found) that which fell apart and flew there. In addition, there cannot be any mention of any "there". Only those pieces that are falling apart can be comprehended - and this is precisely what I am doing. Then, when they are comprehended - precisely as pieces – they can be described. I know that the smaller and bigger pieces fit together poorly - or don't fit at all - but this does not have any greater meaning to me. The important thing is that they revolve around.

Chapter 21
MAY 9 – THE THREE GALLOWS ACCORDING TO NORBLIN

The gallows set up in Warsaw by Noblin

Both drawings by Jean Pierre Norblin, in which we can see the three gallows set up on May 9 in front of the Old Warsaw City Hall, a dozen or so executioners and three condemned (precisely - two already hanged and one being hanged) as well as a huge crowd assisting with the hangings, and also two frontages of the Market Square, the western and the southern side, that is (as it is now called) the Hugo Kołłątaj side (the one where Fukier's winery is, or perhaps was) and the Ignacy Zakrzewski side (the one with the Bazyliszek Restaurant) – thus both of these drawings (made in ink) show the same scene, and in both cases, together with the artist, we see it from almost the same, but not entirely from the same, place. Norblin chose some unbelievable place to observe from, he even invented for himself (because this is how it should be said) such a place, a precisely unbelievable one, and captured the hanging scene from some unusual, surprising perspective - he saw what was happening in front of the City Hall (between the City Hall and the western frontage, Kołłątaj's side), from above and at an angle, directing the gaze of the beholder (the one who is looking at the drawings) not at the gallows and the condemned, but beside them and above them, towards the compact crowd, a swirl of people, some gray, grayish mass that rests against the tenement houses of the western, Kołłątaj frontage - or, like gray lava, overflows from this frontage. Or, in a different way, it spills from under this frontage and over-flows. One of these drawings is now in the collection of the National Museum in Kraków, the other in the collection of the Library of the Polish Academy of Sciences in Kórnik. There is no doubt that Norblin was on the Market Square on May 9 and watched the hangings. Though he surely must have seen them from some different place. The one who watches the hangings in his drawings (and thus also the one who drew them) is placed in such a place which he could not get to - somewhere above the Market, above the roofs of the tenement houses (those on Dekert's side, the northern one), more or less at the opening of Nowomiejska Street or near this opening.

The drawing in Kraków places the viewer a little lower, somewhere on the second or third floor of apartment houses on the northern side, and also a little closer to the invisible open-ing of Nowomiejska to the Market Square – he has all three gallows on the left-hand side as well as under his feet. The drawing also clearly shows the City Hall, its front wall facing the tenement houses on Kołłątaj's side, as well as its tower, and the stalls surrounding it. As for the drawing from Kórnik, the viewer is situated much higher, maybe not so much above the roofs as above the Market Square - it can be said that the viewer rises, flies somewhere near the tenement houses on De-kert's side and near the Nowomiejska opening. They fly, rising over the gallows. While having them on the right-hand side and looking at them from above and at an angle, the viewer no longer sees the City Hall, but only the northern corner of the stalls and a small piece of space, a kind of passage separating the stalls from the City Hall. As I said, on two gallows - the one that stands in front of the entrance to the City Hall, and the one that stands on its southern edge, near the Bazyliszek Restaurant - two condemned are already hanging, while at the gallows that is closest to the opening of Nowomiejska and the viewer (that he has beneath his feet), the executioner and (probably) his henchmen are bustling about, as can be clearly seen. We can also see, in both drawings, a ladder placed against these gallows, and also, in the Kraków drawing, the condemned standing under the gallows, right next to the ladder. The human figures are very small, but from the arrangement of the body it can be concluded that the condemned, who stands with his head down, has his hands tied behind his back. Someone, probably one of the henchmen, bends down in front of him, almost squats, and probably ties or unties his legs. He's probably tying them. In the Kórnik drawing, the condemned seems to already be on the ladder, and someone standing next to the ladder, certainly someone from the crowd, raises a pałasz and with it drives up the condemned. It follows that the Kórnik drawing (the one which situates the viewer as someone who flew onto the Market Square from the Nowomiejska outlet and flies over the gallows) presents the situation as it took place a few or even several minutes later.

If we look closely at both drawings (there is no reason to suspect Norblin of fantasizing), we will see some details that are not mentioned at all in the written accounts of the events of May 9. Stefan Böhm, as evidenced by both drawings, had only one ladder, which was moved from gallows to gallows. The ladder, placed on the cross beam of the gallows, was very tall - comparing its height with the height of the human figures standing next to it or on it, it can be concluded that it was over 7 meters tall (assuming 1 meter 80 centimeters as the average height of a human being, I multiplied it by four). Since the top of the ladder was almost exactly at the height of the cross beam on which the hanging was done — it was only slightly above it - all three gallows also had a height of 7 meters (or a little more). It can be concluded that the hangings required from Böhm, who had to operate at a height of 7 meters (he was either standing at the top of the ladder or sitting on the cross-beam - but this is not shown in Norblin's drawings), not just any, but almost acrobatic dexterity. The Master of Justice (as Böhm was called) had at his disposal, as can be clearly seen in the Kraków drawing, only two henchmen. Though he was helped by some people from the crowd - this is evidenced by the pałasz that someone is waving right next to the ladder; the executioner's henchmen probably did not come to work armed with pałasz's. Both drawings also show that the hangings - if the gallows standing at the northern edge of the stalls was used as the last one (that is, the one that was located closest to the opening of Nowomiejska Street) - started (if one can put it in this way) in the south and moved to the north, towards Dekert's side. It is enough to compare this with the order of the hangings, which can be easily recreated based on written accounts (according to them, Hetman Ożarowski was hanged first, then Marshal Ankwicz, and finally Hetman Zabiełło) to exactly establish who was hanged where. The central gallows, the one facing the gate leading to the City Hall, was intended for Ożarowski, for Ankwicz, the one that was placed closest to the southern frontage of the Market Square and the opening of Zapiecek, while for Zabiełło, the one that was closest to the northern frontage and the opening of Nowomiejska.

This figure, standing with a bowed head in the Kraków drawing, and whose legs are being tied (or being untied) by one of the executioner's henchmen, is therefore Zabiełło. In Norblin's drawings, however, there is (this seems quite important - as far as the artist's artistic idea is concerned) complete anonymity - all his tiny figures are almost identical, and if they are distinguished by something, it is only by hats and pałasz's, because some of them have pałasz's (which are only small lines) as well as hats (which are little circles) and some do not. Zabiełło, the executioner, the executioner's helpers, people from the crowd - all of them are basically the same, all this creates (for Norblin or according to Norblin) a grayish, blackening mass, darkening and brightening lava that flows or cools down between the stalls and the western frontage of the Market Square. Is there anything else we can learn from Norblin? In the Kraków drawing, more or less under the feet of the one who is looking at this scene (under the feet of the flying artist), we see someone sitting on a horse in the crowd – this implies that someone came to the hangings on a horse and watched them from horseback. This single horse and the person sitting on it, though less visible, emerge from the lava also in the Kórnik drawing. Between the gallows on which Hetman Ożarowski hangs, and the one at which a henchman ties the legs of Hetman Zabiełło, something is happening - it is probably a small tumult, a small row, because several figures, having separated from the crowd, are swinging their pałasz's there. Maybe it is a duel, maybe a pałasz fight. In the Kraków drawing it looks more like a fight, in the Kórnik drawing (which shows this scene a bit more clearly) it looks more like a duel. A very interesting matter, but we will not learn anything about it from anyone anymore - in the Market Square, during the hangings, someone fought with someone or dueled with pałasz's - but who, why? This is now everything that I can say about Norblin's drawings. If I had looked at them through a magnifying glass, maybe I would have seen something more, but I'm sure Norblin did not anticipate such a possibility - that is, the artificial enlargement of his scenes. Still, without a magnifying glass, there is something worth paying attention to - the fronts of the tenement houses on Zakrzewski's side, the southern one, are partially in the light (in the Kraków drawing), while the fronts on Kołłątaj's side, the western side, are in the shade. The day was therefore sunny, and the rays of the sun, which passed over Warsaw on May 9, illuminated the Market Square from the south during the time of the hangings, or perhaps falling at an angle, from the south-west.

Thus, the gallows stood in the sun, the crowd, in front of the Apartment houses on the west side, stood in the shade - it was darkness gathered there. To what we learned from Norblin, we can add some details taken from those who were at the Market Square at that time, and then wrote about what they saw there. I will present these details in sequence, that is, in the order in which the hangings took place. As we already know, Hetman Ożarowski was hanged first. As Ożarowski could not - either because of his age or because of some disease - walk, he was brought to the gallows in a chair. "First - wrote Karol Wojda (*O rewolucji polskiej w roku 1794* [*On the Polish Revolution in 1794*]) - Ożarowski was brought in a chair, giving little signs of life, he barely seemed to know what was happening to him". According to the staff-doctor of the Działyński Regiment, Jan Drozdowski, who came to the Market Square just before ten o'clock (and claimed that the hangings had started precisely at that time), Ożarowski was hanged along with his chair. This would, if it were so, testify to Böhm's great ingenuity and skill. "We waited - wrote Drozdowski in his *Pamiętniki sztabslekarza* (*Memoirs of a Staff Doctor*) - until at 10 o'clock in the morning the general of the Polish army was led out first, and the Master of Justice hangs him on the middle gallows very skillfully and comfortably, because he himself chose a chair made of a raw material thong to which two ropes on blocks were attached, which were pulled by the helpers following a given sign by the master, while he, standing on the ladder in the back, threw the noose around the neck, and with the letting go of the chair the victim's life was ended". The hanging of Hetman Ożarowski could be presented a bit differently on the basis of what we learn from Kiliński's *Drugi Pamiętnik* (*Second Diary*). It does not mention a chair, but a harness. "The master immediately fastened his harness, and the scoundrels slowly began to pull him onto the gallows, and all the people shouted: 'Let Ożarowski hang!' Then they started to make a great clatter with their weapons, and in this the master put the noose around his neck and lowered it a little bit, unbuckled his harness and in this way Ożarowski, hetman, was hanged".

Kiliński undoubtedly very faithfully presented the contemporary technique of hanging in this fragment of the *Second Diary* - the harness, which was put on the condemned, made it easier for them to be pulled up, and then was unfastened so that they dropped down, were then used in all professionally carried out executions - but in the case of Ożarowski, considering the chair, Böhm must have used the method described by Drozdowski. So Kiliński seems to have confused different hangings here. In the *Second Diary*, we have two more interesting pieces of information from the sphere of customs. The first tells about how the hetman was dressed: "he was not wearing a uniform then, only a banyan, vest, and rather coarse pants, stockings, and yellow slippers on his feet". The second piece of information, from the field of dentistry, concerns Ożarowski's artificial teeth (or artificial jaw): "when he suffocated, his lips rolled over and his teeth were set in his lips". As one can see, this sentence sounds a bit vague - it may mean that Ożarowski, while choking, spat out (not fully) his false teeth, but it may also mean that he stuck his teeth (not necessarily artificial ones) into his lips. This matter is explained by the *Pamiętniki sztabslekarza pułku Działyńskich* (*Memoirs of a Staff Doctor of the Działyński Regiment*), where Drozdowski, telling how "with the letting go of the chair the victim's life was ended", added: "when it happened, it was an unpleasant sight, when the condemned man, having fake teeth, pushed them forward, as if he were laughing at his misery". Ankwicz, Marshal of the Permanent Council, was hanged on the gallows which stood near the southern frontage of the Market Square and near the Zapiecek opening. Józef Ignacy Kraszewski, who, describing the May executions, based them on an account unknown to me (without mentioning its author), stated that Ankwicz, a beautiful and elegant man, walked from the City Hall to the gallows "with his impressive figure, imposing, and very much unabashed". The face of Ankwicz, who was using blanc, was covered with a thick layer of this powder (or rather this goo), which gave the impression that the Marshal of the Permanent Council was heading towards the gallows in a white mask. Having climbed the ladder Ankwicz, according to Kraszewski, gave a speech to the crowd, and ended his speech with the words: "Noble nation, will I not find mercy in you?" We have a different version of the marshal's last words in Kiliński's *Second Diary*, where Ankwicz, walking down the stairs of the City Hall and heading towards the gallows, says, spreading his hands (or perhaps raising them to heaven): "Mighty God, how dear it is for me to go to this shameful death when my dear fatherland rises".

This sounds a little unlikely, but of course it is impossible to establish which of these two versions may be true - and there is no reason to establish it either. The differences between Kraszewski's and Kiliński's version also concern the outfit in which Ankwicz went from the City Hall to the gallows. From the third volume of *Polska w czasie trzech rozbiorów* (*Poland during the Three Partitions*) we learn that the marshal was "in a green quilted kaftanik", the description in the *Second Diary*, is much more detailed, it says that he was wearing a tailcoat, black pants as well as (perhaps a little unsuitable for the tailcoat) "a crimson satin kaftan". There is a significant difference between a crimson satin kaftan and a green quilted kaftanik – in addition difficult (even impossible) to explain. We are here, as you can see, very close to the very essence of historical research, the methodological knot, that everyone who deals with such research has to cut (or unravel) every now and then - but what I think about it, I may say in another place. All reports known to me agree on two points. Firstly, the condemned Ankwicz behaved with great dignity (a thing rare for traitors), secondly Böhm, when they both climbed the ladder, received a golden snuffbox from him. "Having opened it [Ankwicz] - we read in the *Second Diary* - took some snuff and immediately reaching his hand out to the master, gave him this golden snuffbox, saying to him: 'Here I am giving you my snuffbox in remembrance that you had the Crown Marshal in your hands'". The golden snuffbox is also mentioned in Wojda's diary *O rewolucji polskiej*, where we read that "the Marshal of the Permanent Council behaved with courage and indifference to death, stretched out, put on his noose and gifted a golden snuffbox to the executioner". What it could mean that Ankwicz "stretched out" is difficult to understand - maybe the point is that he himself pulled up on the harness (which would not be easy). The version in Antoni Trębicki's diary *O rewolucji roku 1794 (On the Revolution of 1794)* mentions, apart from the snuffbox, a watch - "he was to give the executioner who was putting the noose on his neck a watch and a snuffbox, so that he would dispatch him quickly and deftly". The third condemned, Field Hetman Zabiełło, did not match Ankwicz. "One of them - wrote Trębicki, and undoubtedly these words apply precisely to Zabiełło - went so far as to grab the enraged, or rather, the made audacious by spirits townspeople by their feet, begging for their mercy".

According to Kiliński's *Second Diary*, Zabiełło behaved even worse, because under the gallows, when he was tied - this is precisely the scene we see in Norblin's drawings - he tried to convince the executioners that he was innocent and that, instead of him, they should hang his wife: "that he is leaving this world as an innocent man, because he is not guilty of anything, only his wife, that she took the money for him". Perhaps this was even true, but the author of the *Second Diary* was very angered by such marital disloyalty - "hearing this, that he absolutely wanted to make his wife suffer, I ordered the master to hang him as quickly as possible". Zabiełło's hanging - as one can deduce from the pałasz fight, which took place then between two gallows - did not arouse much interest. It could be that - when Zabiełło was being hanged - Bishop Kossakowski was already standing in the gate of the City Hall and the crowd, agitated by the thought of the attractions awaiting him at St. Anne's Church, set off through Piwna and Zapiecek towards the Castle and the Kraków Gate. Ożarowski, Ankwicz, and Zabiełło hung in the Market Square until six in the evening. Around six, the bodies were removed from the gallows and taken to the execution field behind Nalewki Street, where - as Kiliński wrote - they were buried "in fresh aria", that is in the fresh air. Immediately after the hanged were transported out, the gallows - as President Wyssogota Zakrzewski informed Kościuszko in a letter written on the night of May 9-10 - "were taken out". Norblin's name - "Jean Pierre Norblin, peintre français" - is (at number 1331) on the 25th page of the *Akces obywatelów i mieszkańców Księstwa Mazowieckiego do Aktu Powstania Narodowego pod naczelnictwem Tadeusza Kościuszki [...] uczynionego w Warszawie dnia 19 miesiąca kwietnia 1794 roku* (Accession of Citizens and Residents of the Duchy of Mazovia to the Act of the National Uprising under the leadership of Tadeusz Kościuszko [...] made in Warsaw on the 19 Day Month of April Year 1794).

Chapter 22.
VESUVIUS

Vesuvius 1794 (British Museum)

The *Korrespondent Narodowy i Zagraniczny (The National and Foreign Correspondent)* appeared in 1794 from the last days of April to the end of December. The publisher and editor of this newspaper (earlier, before the outbreak of the insurrection, it was published under the titles *Korrespondent Warszawski [The Warsaw Correspondent]* and *Pismo Periodyczne Korrespondenta [The Correspondents Periodic Journal]*) was Father Karol Malinowski. In an addition to Issue 65, which was published on August 16, Father Malinowski published in *The Correspondent* a very interesting article, though having little to do with the situation in which the inhabitants of Warsaw found themselves at that time, describing the spectacular eruption of Vesuvius. The article was a bit late, even, you could say, out of date, because it was written in Naples (or maybe sent from Naples) six weeks earlier, on July 1, (which the editor of *The Correspondent* loyally informed about) and told about an event that took place even earlier, in mid-June - from the 15 to the 16 of June, that is twelve days before the great June hangings in Warsaw. It seems reasonable to suppose that the story about the eruption of Vesuvius had been previously printed in some Berlin or Viennese newspaper and that *The National Correspondent* took it from this source. It must have taken some time for this newspaper to reach Warsaw - and that would explain the significant delay. Anyway, the Warsovians were informed about the terrible eruption of the Italian volcano exactly two months after this event, and it is in connection to this that the question arises about the intentions that guided the editor of *The Correspondent* - did he really mean to inform someone about what happened near Naples, or rather about something else. Here one has to realize what the situation in Warsaw looked like in mid-August - just when *The Correspondent* and Father Malinowski were dealing with Vesuvius. On July 9, Russian troops (from the direction of Gołków) and Prussian troops (from the direction of Błonie) were approaching the Vistula, and four days later, on July 13, the siege of the city began. Polish units were deployed on the line Powązki, Marymont, Wawrzyszew, Bielany (where Prince Józef Poniatowski and General Mokronowski were in command), further on the line Czyste and Rakowiec (commanded by General Zajączek) and on the line Królikarnia and Czerniaków (there the units were initially led by Henryk Dąbrowski, and then by Kościuszko). It is not far to Krakowskie Przedmieście from Marymont and Czyste, not to mention Królikarnia, and the advantage of the besiegers was enormous - they had around 38,000 soldiers in total, Kościuszko had around 22,000 in Warsaw. If King Frederick William or General Fersen (the first commanded the Prussian troops, the second the Russian troops) decided to launch a great assault - a merciless assault combined with slaughter, something like the later November assault by Suvorov from the east - if even only one of them had decided to do this, then Warsaw would probably have been captured in one day, maybe two days.

In the last days of July, the Prussians conquered (the battle began on the 27th of that month) Wola, and at about the same time the Russians (Denisov's troops) drove the Poles out of Wilanów. Particularly fierce battles took place at the end of August, when the Prussians seized Wawrzyszew, and then attacked Marymont and Powązki. Almost throughout the whole of August, Prussian artillery also shelled the city from the direction of Wola, where the Prussian king set up his heavy batteries. So, what thought did the editor of *The National and Foreign Correspondent* have in mind when he informed his readers about the eruption of Vesuvius in mid-August; what was his reason? It is not at all easy to answer this question. I have two ideas about this. Perhaps Father Malinowski, having read an article about the terrible volcanic explosion in some Berlin or Viennese newspaper, thought to himself - and he was surprised by this unexpected thought - that nature has nothing to do with human history, history happens separately and nature separately, in isolation, the history of people by itself and the history of nature by itself (the cannonade on Wola separately and Vesuvius separately), and they are not connected by anything, they have nothing in common, they do not meet anywhere, and even if they occur or happen in parallel, even if they suddenly become a bit similar to each other, comparable, then the reason for this momentary similarity and this momentary parallelism is some cosmic coincidence, it is, this parallelism, cosmically random and cosmically nonsensical - and he decided to inform the readers of *The Correspondent* about this thought of his, he wanted to show them precisely this (this cosmic nonsensical parallelism) by printing the story about Vesuvius. Though the editor of *The Correspondent* could also have been provoked by a thought that was against the former, contradicting it, even excluding it - and also (for the person hearing the Prussian cannons from Wola and Wawrzyszew) unexpected. It would be a thought that human history is connected through a secret bond with nature and its natural ahistorical history, moreover, that human history belongs to nature, comes out of it, is its emanation, its explosion, its accidental and nonsensical eruption, something which resembles the eruption of Vesuvius, something like the flow of lava, which seethes and hisses, but soon cools down, will soon cool down, and after this eruption and cooling down, there will be another eruption, equally accidental and equally nonsensical, but all these are (and will be) eruptions of something that is in the depths of nature, its incomprehensible, not understandable (and not needed by anyone) emanations, something that it expels from itself - and because it is not known what the essence of this is, and even more so - what it is (what is hidden under the invented by us word "nature"), then it is also unknown why the something that is human history is expelled by it - it is expelled by something about which it is not known what it is. Like lava pouring out of unknown depths when a hole opens.

I rewrote the article from *The National and Foreign Correspondent*, modernizing a little the spelling and punctuation, as much as is necessary. I kept capital letters at the beginnings of words - where the author of the article wanted them. Twenty Old Polish ells is about 12 meters; 30 ells is almost 18 meters There was no such thing as an Italian mile, in Italy there were miles of different lengths - Lombardian, Piedmontese, Roman, Sicilian. A Neapolitan mile and a half is just over 2,780 meters; a quarter mile is approximately 460 meters. It should also be added here that the eruption of Vesuvius in 1794 is considered to be one of the six largest (observed and remembered by people) eruptions of this volcano. The previous great eruptions took place in 79, 472, and 1631, the next ones in 1872 and 1906. The most famous eruption, that interfered with human history and buried Herculaneum and Pompeii was, of course, the one in 79.

From Naples on July 1. On the night of June 15/16, here in Naples, an enormous rumble resembling a continuous cannonade was first heard. Vesuvius appeared in fire. Then the terrible Volcano, not from the top of the mountain as before, but from the very middle on the left side, having itself made a huge opening ½ an Italian mile in circumference, exploded so violently that all of Naples and its surroundings shook as if its foundations had been moved. The continuously growing smoke rising up formed the shape of a pine, but of an enormous size. This smoke was partly brighter due the emerging flames, partly dirty, as if dimmed from the ashes and the rising Lava. It widened at its peak, until at the end, it laid against the ground due to the weight of the mass on all sides. The flowing lava took two directions, the faster and more abundant stream went towards Torre del Greco, and the smaller one towards

Resina near Portici, dividing still into various other streams. Most of the inhabitants of Torre del Greco having escaped with their lives, had to leave all their property for the plunder of the fire. This stream poured out all the way to the sea, where the lava rose a quarter mile to 20 ells above the water. The second stream of thinned Lava, flowing towards Resina, split near this place into 3 streams: one rushed at the gate and the Franciscan Monastery, the second at the square, and the third to the Carmelite Monastery. Few of the houses in Resina remained in their place, and flames soon also engulfed them. The Lava made mountains 20 to 30 ells high everywhere. The spilled fire reflecting around shed a terrible light on all of Naples and its surroundings. The atmosphere was darkened again on the day of June 16 and so much ash exploded that it was impossible to see the fire that evening. The following day on the 17, the Lava made new openings again. At the end the flames stopped, but in the lowland of the mountain streams appeared like swift rivers of boiling and salty water, which flooded the surrounding fields and houses. This new defeat took away the lives and property of many inhabitants.

Chapter 23.
PRIMATE ON A CATAFALQUE

Kazimierz Poniatowski (left) Prince Primate Michael Jerzy Poniatowski (right) (Marcello Bacciarelli)

The idea of hanging the king's brother, Prince Primate Michał Poniatowski, appeared soon after the outbreak of the insurrection. It seems that the first - in chronological order - information on this subject comes from the Prussian envoy, Ludwig Buchholtz, a man undoubtedly very well informed and impeccably fulfilling his diplomatic duties. In a letter of May 12, Buchholtz informed his ruler, Frederick William II, that Stanisław August "is playing for very high stakes" and that "some misfortune" may happen to him, because everything indicates that the tsarina's agents "will fall victim to their attachment to Russia".

The rest of the letter says that the same "applies to the primate and a few other people from the royal family". It is interesting that of all members of the Poniatowski family, only the king and his brother the primate were then at risk. Whereas no one wanted the life of the eldest of the three Poniatowski brothers, the ex-Chamberlain of the Crown Kazimierz, and there are also no testimonies that would say that it was wanted to hang the king's sister, Elżbieta Branicka, known as the Lady of Kraków, or the king's mistress, mother of four or five children of Stanisław August, the pock faced Elżbieta Grabowska. As for the ex-Chamberlain Kazimierz, maybe his life was saved because he was considered to be the dumbest of the three brothers; the primate, Prince Michał, however, was considered to be the smartest of the Poniatowski brothers. While women, such was the noble Polish custom, were not yet hanged then - even the most terrible Warsaw mob was not so terrible as to come up with such an idea that the Parisian Jacobins came up with, who with complete calmness decapitated their countesses and princesses on guillotines; as is known, they even beheaded Queen Marie Antoinette and the king's sister, Princess Élisabeth. Admittedly, it may be argued that Stanisław August's lover (and, as it was later claimed, secret wife) was hanged, in a sense, *in effigy*, when Count Grabowski, who was her stepson, was hanged on June 28 - the son of her first husband by his first wife. There could have been something of a threat in this hanging of the stepson: look out pock faced Elżbieta, king's lover, for we will also hang you. Since the primate was considered the smartest of the Poniatowski brothers (he was also undoubtedly the most skillful politician of the three brothers; although, as we shall see in a moment, it did not help him much), it was believed that he stands behind the decisions of his slightly dumber brother Stanisław; maybe even making them for him. In Karol Wojda's book *O rewolucji polskiej* (*On the Polish Revolution*), we read that it was Prince Michał who "forced the king to sign the Targowica Confederation". If it was he who made this decision (if the king had not decided to join the Confederation, the fate of Poland would have undoubtedly been different; this does not mean that it would have been happier), then of course his responsibility (for all the Polish misfortunes at that time) would be equal to the king's; maybe even bigger. Wojda also wrote that after the death of the primate, "the Russian party lost its strongest supporter".

It can also be understood that the primate was a pillar of Russian power, even more important than the monarch. It was probably not like that, but Wojda confirms that this was precisely how it was understood. It is hardly surprising that in the then famous song, which was sung on the streets of the City of Old Warsaw around June 28 (maybe a little before the 28), the primate and the king were joined - the threat said that the people of Warsaw would deal with one and the other. The song is known from a letter that Stanisław August wrote on July 1, after the great June hangings, to Tadeusz Kościuszko. The letter begins with a sentence in which one can hear a plea for help, even the scream of a frightened man. "There is a need for you sir to know *exacte* to what extent things were occurring here". In the next sentence the king quoted just that song, which was heard "in the market square and in taverns" - "the end will be this: we Cracovians carry a knob at the waist, we will hang the king and the primate". The song of the people of Warsaw (whoever wants to, may recognize it as the Warsaw mob), although quite clear, was also, as one can see, a bit wild, a bit over realistic - it is not very clear what this Cracovian "knob at the waist" would mean, and why the Warsowians, threatening the king and the primate with the gallows, presented themselves as Krakowians. Perhaps there was an allusion in this (difficult for us today to grasp) to the Battle of Racławice and Kościuszko's oath on Kraków's Market Square. Later on in the letter, Stanisław August informed the Chief that "on Saturday evening after the hangings by gallows" one could "in other company's" (i.e. in some other pubs?) also hear the sentence - "we intended one thing, and another happened". The meaning, which the king did not say, is also completely clear here - we were to hang the Poniatowski brothers, but we hanged someone else, from which the conclusion was that it did not turn out right and someone deceived us. It seems to me that the king, in great fear (we read elsewhere in the letter: "there are someone's intentions [...] *directe* against me"), exaggerated a bit however - those who did the hanging on June 28 (and those who accepted this hanging; maybe provoked it), probably did not intend to hang the king and the primate for now. The song was a threat; a serious one, but only a threat. Such a threat (maybe I am also over-interpreting this all a bit; these were spontaneous actions, one caught on the other, one provoked the other, one attracted the other, and it was not known, no one knew, even could not know then, how it could end), such a threat, at least it seems, was also the gallows that was erected on Senatorska Street on the night of June 27-28 in front of the Primate's Palace.

Father Kitowicz, talking about the hangings on June 28, claimed that the gallows for the primate had been erected "next to the annexes" of the Primate's Palace and that it became the cause of Prince Michał's death - the sight of it "caused this gentleman to become panicked and die". This is not completely correct, especially these annexes raise some doubts. Other sources indicate that an attempt was made to erect the gallows right in the courtyard of the Primate's Palace, right beneath the windows from which the primate could clearly see it, so maybe it was "next to the annexes", but it did not work out - it is not known why; Friedrich Schultz, describing Senatorska Street in *Podróże Inflantczyka z Rygi do Warszawy* (*Travels of a Livonian from Riga to Warsaw*), claimed that the Primate's Palace "is separated from the street by bars, and in its center [there is] an entrance gate"; so maybe the amateurs of hanging did not manage to get through this gate - and ultimately the gallows was raised somewhere further, rather (I imagine it this way) near the intersection of Senatorska and Daniłowiczowska Streets. On the other hand, Father Kitowicz was right in the sense that the gallows on Senatorska Street was something of a sentence; postponed, suspended, but a sentence. It can therefore be said that on the day it was raised, the Primate was condemned to death and had no good way out of the situation of a condemned man, though he still lived for almost two more months. During those two months, it was considered how to remove him from life - or he himself pondered how to do this, that is in which way would he be able to most skillfully remove himself. The primate's situation after the events of June is well illustrated by what we learn from *Historia Polska* (*Polish History*). Father Kitowicz claimed that after the gallows was raised, the primate "fell into a severe melancholy" and moved out of his apartments. "He began to hide in the basements of his palace". This does not have to be true (and certainly is not), but it is worth paying attention to the certain symbolic value of Kitowicz's idea - the primate, hiding in the basements of his residence, was already underground, so he was in a way already gone. If he had decided, descending into the basements on Senatorska Street, to write down his thoughts and experiences there (after all, he did not have many things to do at that time; it could fill up his free time), and left us a diary or memoir telling about the two months of the insurrection that he lived in the basements of rebellious Warsaw, he would have ensured for himself long fame and would go on to posterity - not as a Muscovite or Prussian collaborator, but as the author of a great work.

Though such an idea did not occur to the smartest of the Poniatowski brothers. From other accounts it appears that the primate chose not this place, as in Kitowicz's work, but another, more comfortable hiding place - he stayed not at Senatorska, but at the Castle, where he could count on his brother's protection; this one, though dumber, was in a slightly better position, for he still had a few or a dozen or so aides on whom he could rely on. The death of the primate was preceded (this is not certain, but so it was said) by some consultations concerning his future fate; perhaps also the way in which - effectively and elegantly - he could be removed from Warsaw. President Wyssogota Zakrzewski was to consult on this matter with the royal family, the family and Zakrzewski were to consult with Kościuszko, while Kościuszko (according to Father Kitowicz) was advised by "the leaders of the people". The meetings were secret, so of course nothing is known about them. On this occasion it is worth recalling that the Primate's Palace on Senatorska Street was then considered to be one of the most beautiful or even the most beautiful building in Warsaw, and Prince Michał lived in it very sumptuously - his picky culinary tastes were known; people also marveled (to put it delicately) at the beauty of the young ladies with whom he surrounded himself. From Ludwik Cieszkowski, the author of the *Pamiętnik anegdotyczny z czasów Stanisława Augusta* (*An Anecdotal Memoir from the Times of Stanisław August*), we learn that one of Prince Michał's predecessors, Primate Antoni Ostrowski, who was also a collaborator and also liked to surround himself with young ladies, made Senatorska a wonderful residence. "The palace [...] formerly inhabited only by Jews, dirty, old, unworthy of its name, was almost completely remade by him, he transformed it with the most perfect architecture and now turned it into the most beautiful palace in Warsaw". As Prince Michał was eagerly visited in his beautiful palace, for various reasons, it can be imagined that the Poniatowski family was conducting the consultations on the fate of the brother precisely at Senatorska Street - and if so, then maybe even in his presence. "Well, what are we to do with you, mon frère - the king says, looking at Michał through his diabolical binoculars. - If we possessed Mr. Blanchard's aerostatic machine, then you could fly off, but we don't. Come up with something mon frère, me or you, someone must be sacrificed. - Michasiu! - says the Lady of Kraków. - You've always been a good boy. I expect to see you in that world".

The Primate died on the night of August 11-12. The story of his death is known in two versions, and while neither of them are entirely true, there may be some truth to each of them. According to the first version, poison was bought and administered by the king. It is precisely this version that is found in Father Kitowicz's *Polish History*. It said that Kościuszko and Zakrzewski had arranged a meeting with "the entire royal family" and convinced them that - in face of the threat of death by the gallows, that is, a shameful death - "they devise a different kind of death for the prince primate, a more honest one". The royal family agreed to this proposal - a family council was convened, and Prince Michał was informed about his situation; the king, in the course of these meetings, offered his brother snuff. "After which the primate - we read in Kitowicz's work - returning to his quarters from this council, fell sleep, and falling into an ever-deeper sleep [...] died a few days later". The rest is clear - the poison, combined with a sleeping agent, was in the king's snuff. It seems that in Warsaw at that time, it was precisely this version (which is somehow connected with the second version, about which we will talk about it in a moment) that was believed. This is confirmed by Kiliński's *Drugi Pamiętnik (Second Diary)*, where the king is also the poisoner, but instead of snuff and some powder poured into the snuff, we have an ominous goblet given to the primate in the Castle - "the king ordered the poison to be brought and the king himself also added poison to the goblet and said these words to the primate". Kiliński further informed that the whole scene took place in the presence of Kościuszko, and the words with which the king addressed the primate were as follows: "Here you have this goblet from my hand, drink it, because it is better that you die by my hand, than at the hands of the nation". From a historical point of view, this is obvious nonsense, but it must be admitted that Kiliński's imagination worked here in a way worthy of admiration - the Polish king putting poison in a goblet is a wonderful idea; the goblet, passing from hand to hand, is great too; we see how the king, reaching out the hand with the goblet, raises the other up and pointing to heaven, calls it to be a witness, at the same time ordering his brother to be silent. Be silent and drink. I see an interesting topic here for literary historians - what influence did the performances given by Wojciech Bogusławski at the National Theater have on the imagination of the people of Warsaw.

We have two more interesting pieces of information in the *Second Diary*. The first says that the primate drank the poison immediately ("taking the goblet in his hands, he drank it"), the second relates to the terrible power of the poisonous drink - "in half an hour the [primate's] head burst". One can also add here (mentioned years later in a letter written in 1859 to Karol Sienkiewicz by Joachim Lelewel, whose historical imagination worked, as you can see, a bit like Kiliński's imagination) that the poison used by the king was bought in Wasilewski's tenement house on Krakowskie Przedmieście. This apartment building, at number 372, was located at the corner of Krakowskie and Bednarska Streets. There was a pharmacy on the ground floor, whose owner was this Wasilewski. As it can be assumed, a footman or a pantry boy was sent from the Castle for the poison, which was later mixed into the snuff (or poured into the goblet); or someone trusted, perhaps General Mokronowski, went for it. We can also (under the influence of Kiliński as well as Lelewel) imagine Stanisław August who himself goes to the corner of Krakowskie and Bednarska Streets. The pharmacist Wasilewski puts his goods in front of him and encourages him to make a choice: - I would urge His Majesty to choose this yellow powder, which will work unfailingly. - The King looks a little suspiciously (through his binoculars, of course) at the colorful powders, then at Wasilewski (the pharmacist was known to sell dung sinapisms as a reliable cure for syphilis) and says: - This black one, please. Just make sure that it is not aired out. - According to the second version of these events, the decision regarding the death of the primate was made not by the Poniatowski family, but by Kościuszko. The Chief was to personally go to Senatorska Street from the camp near Królikarnia and present Prince Michał with proof of treason and poison. Black or yellow powder. We learn that Kościuszko was somehow mixed up in (let's say more carefully - joined) the matter of the death of the primate, from the *Wspomnienie* (*Recollections*) of Karol Kaczkowski, a Vilnius and Kremenets' doctor, published in 1876. That Kaczkowski, who lived in the first half of the next century, obviously did not know any of the heroes of these events, but he repeated, in the introduction to *Recollections*, the story of his father, who in 1794 was a young officer in General Madaliński's brigade.

This story tells that in mid-August, having then found himself in Warsaw or near Warsaw, Kaczkowski-father was sent with some official order to the Primate's Palace and met Kosciuszko there, who was waiting in the anteroom for a conversation with Prince Michał. The Chief, who had arrived unannounced, was immediately received by the primate and had a short conversation with him: "in maybe a quarter of an hour he came out at a quick pace". Of course, Kościuszko did not tell Madaliński's young officer why he had appeared at Senatorska Street, but this became clear to Kaczkowski when he heard that immediately after this visit "the primate suddenly fell ill". From the rest of Kaczkowski's story - or of both Kaczkowski's - we learn that the evidence of betrayal that Kościuszko then brought to Senatorska Street was a "packet of papers" sent by the primate, through some fisherman, to the "Prussian camp". The fisherman, although bribed (he was supposed to transport the papers "for a generous reward"), instead of handing the packet over to the Prussians (the packet contained information about the Polish military plans), delivered this "clear evidence of treason" to Kościuszko's headquarters. "A few hours later - wrote Kaczkowski - the violent illness of the primate was talked about all over Warsaw. The palace courtyard was full of carriages, various equipment, and horses; the king also visited his sick brother with the Lady of Kraków, and in the evening the news of the death of the primate [...] was circulating around the city". The primate was buried on

August 18, but before that he was shown to the people for a week in the Primate's Palace. It was, of course, about the burst head Kiliński wrote about. The people wanted to check, firstly, what the state of the primate's body is, and secondly, whether it really is the primate's body. This desire to establish the facts came from rumors that the primate did not poison himself and was not poisoned, but hid somewhere, either with the help of the king or with the help of Kościuszko - maybe he escaped from the city, or maybe lives (this would be in line with the version we have from Kitowicz) in his basements on Senatorska Street. The people who wanted to know the truth could not be refused, so a wonderful funeral hall was arranged in the Primate's Palace. As Lelewel's description in the letter to Sienkiewicz says, the body was shown on the ground floor, "down on the right, in the salon dressed for a funeral, on high, folded biers".

There were "black and red curtains" hanging there, the catafalque was surrounded by "a few prelates", and "high candle holders, six or eight" stood "near the bier, that is the catafalque". The windows were curtained, "the daylight [...] muffled," and the salon was lit only by the large candles that burned in these six or eight candle holders. "I saw this - wrote Lelewel, who was an eight-year-old boy in 1794 - with my own eyes". The catafalque was very tall and the primate was lying almost to the ceiling, but there were steps which one could climb up to see the body - and this was precisely what it was about. As can be seen from several accounts in which the appearance of the deceased was described, the condition of the body could raise serious doubts. The head of the primate was swollen and distorted, the face, also strangely swollen, was a bluish or black color. As there were clear signs of rapid decomposition – however this concerned only the head - the face of the deceased was covered with a green Chinese silk kerchief. Anyone who wanted to, however, could climb the steps, pick up the handkerchief and see the decomposing head up close. This was something completely unheard of - never before, and also never later had something like this happened in Poland, nothing like this, never before and never later was ever allowed, nothing of the sort even occurred to anyone - that anyone who wanted could pick up the kitajka kerchief and take a close look at the rotting face of the Primate of Poland; so that everyone could check if it was really him lying there or someone else. I repeat, so that everyone who reads this will be well aware of what we are talking about here - the rotting face of Primate Poniatowski could be seen by every watchman from Krakowskie Przedmieście, every chicken trader from Grzybowo, every Jew from Nalewki, every trader selling pierogi beneath the Kraków Gate, every beggar from beneath the Bernardine Church, every butcher from Leszno. Every whore from behind the Iron Gate could do this. Every coachman, every valet, every officer cadet. Between August 11 and 18, the insurrection reached its peak. This can even put it differently - then the Polish revolution achieved its definitive and final victory. The insurrection was victorious. Everyone was equal. Complete anarchy. If there is anything else to love in Poland, this is it - its miraculous insurrection. According to the story of Father Kitowicz, one could also touch, by picking up the green kitajka, the rotting face. "Due this swelling - we read in *Polish History* – making this face a terrifying sight, the head was covered with a kitajka, everyone visiting the body was free to reveal it and use their hands to check the body itself".

All these efforts - I don't know who they were invented by; whether by Kościuszko, or by Ignacy Potocki, or by Hugo Kołłątaj, or by the royal family - did not help much, because the death of the primate and his posthumous stay in the funeral salon on Senatorska Street was not really believed - or not believed at all. The doubts raised by the body on the catafalque were of two kinds. First of all, suspicions were raised because only the head was swollen or puffy ("the head and face became immensely swollen after death", wrote Franciszek Karpiński in *Historia mego wieku* [*The History of My Era*]), while the rest of the body looked completely healthy and not subject to decomposition. The conclusion that was drawn from this was that there was an ingeniously made wax figure on the catafalque - as Father Kitowicz put it, "the family placed a wax person on the catafalque". Secondly, it was even more suspicious that the source of the terrible stench that filled the funeral salon seemed to be the primate's head - and only it. "Unbearable fetor", as Kitowicz wrote, was coming out of the head, which in turn led to the conclusion that it was an artificial stench, which was coming from some vessel placed in the swollen head - "a fetor from a mixture of pharmacy potions was placed in the wax person". All these doubts were never cleared up; maybe because the time of the insurrection's defeats was approaching, and no one was eager to inquire about the source of the mysterious fetor. Besides, it was not difficult to check. It was enough to ask the pharmacist Wasilewski from the apartment house on Krakowskie Przedmieście at number 372 - whether he has vessels with fetor in stock and who, (between the second and third week) in the second decade of August, bought one of such vessels from him.

Chapter 24
MARYSIA IN A GREEN CORSET

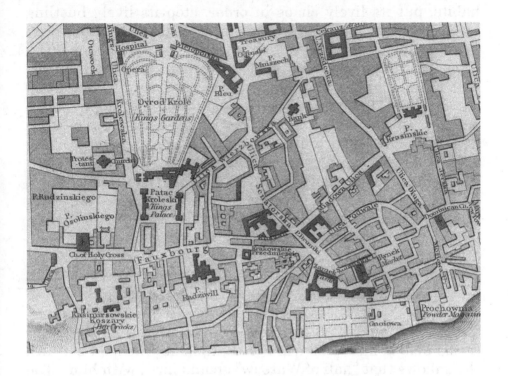

The *Gazeta Wolna Warszawska* (*The Free Warsaw Gazette*) published and edited by Antoni Lesznowolski, was published from April 24 to November 1, 1794. Among the few other news-papers that appeared in insurrectionist Warsaw, it stood out because it had a section called "Doniesienia" ("Reports"), and in this section Lesznowolski placed various types of announce-ments - most often they were announcements encouraging readers to either buy something or to use someone's services.

These announcements, interesting now mainly because of what one can learn from them about the customs of con-temporary Poles, have a certain additional value - they say that death, although it ruled in Warsaw at that time, did not interfere with life, which was still doing what it wanted to do in this city. There was probably nothing extraordinary about it anyway, because death and life match each other greatly, complement each other greatly, and life, always and everywhere, even when death desires to take over it (desires to impose something on it), still does what it wants, and nothing can prevent it from doing so, nothing can change its lively habits, put its lively chaos in order, stop its lively bustling and interrupt it in its lively madness. This is precisely why death adjusts and does not interfere, it only complements - someone was hanged and that was important, but someone had Turkish camlet for sale, someone had a gold watch and a golden key stolen, someone wanted to rent out a flat, someone got lost and was searched for, someone was eating lunch in the Latourowska tenement house, someone was walking from Senatorska Street to Daniłowiczowska Street and staggered a little, because they drank too much, and this was also important, even much more important - than that hangings were carried out. Wanting to show how life in insurrectionary Warsaw positioned itself against death (and coped with death), I made a small selection from the announcements that Lesznowolski printed in the section "Reports". I start with an announcement that appeared in Issue 15 and was related to a hanging - there was something about a rental left behind by the police intendant Rogoziński, who was hanged on May 17 in the field behind Nalewki Street, the one who said beneath the gallows that "half of Warsaw" should hang with him. "The undersigned deputies with the task of writing down the inventory of the estate left behind by Rogoziński report that two small manors, one on Chłodna Street, the other in Praga with gardens and orangeries, and apartments in Rogoziński's former tenement house on Krzywe Koło Street, are available for rent. The bidding to rent the above-mentioned standing goods remaining after Rogoziński will be held on the 16th of the current month and year at ten o'clock in the morning in the Deputation to secure the property of the arrested and sentenced at the Raczyński Palace on the second floor. Executed in Warsaw on the seventh day of the month of June 1794. Andrzej Kalinowski. Andrzej Masłowski Deputies".

Announcements from Issues 7, 11, 31, 34, and 36 concern lost as well as stolen goods:

"On Monday, May 12, a promissory note
for 900 Du[tch] fl[orins] was stolen; this promis-

sory note was issued, that is routed, by Mr. David van Lennep in Smirna on 10 Feb. Anni cur. to Mr. Hubese and Comp. in Rotterdam, to be paid in Amsterdam, with a deadline of 31 days after the visit. Whoever finds such a promissory note or knows about it, let them return it to the Tepper Office, and they will receive a reward, as well as make sure that this promissory note is of no use to anyone, because such instructions have already been made that it will not be paid there".

"On May 30, 1794, a certain citizen from the Nur Land, returning from the Małachowski tenement house on Senatorska Street, lost his wallet with papers needed by him while walking to Daniłowiczowska Street, this wallet is old, the leather is red, whoever finds it will have a reward, let them return it to the office of The Free Warsaw Gazette in the Palace of HE Chreptowicz".

"On the day of August 6, at 8 o'clock in the evening, a chestnut horse was stolen, with white feet, a korbonos, a big mark on the back thigh from mounting, lines in a cross and a letter like A. On the front like the letter E, with an elk saddle, navy blue shabrack, two stripes of white baize at the bottom, a black curb bit with a snaffle and bridle, a pair of pistols in holsters. Who would know something or find the horse, let them go to Grzybów at number 1101 to the manor of Captain Dobrowolski, and they will collect a reward". "If it should happen that someone would be selling a smooth gold watch with a gold chain, navy blue enamel inside between the chain, alongside this chain a gold stamp with a blue stone having gold strands, also a gold key with a navy blue stone and enamel in the center, it was stolen yesterday in the afternoon, that it be kept and brought to Grynert's manor on Pańska Street behind the Grzybów City Hall to citizen Bronicki, rittmeis-

ter of the 4th Regiment, and there they will receive a respectable reward". "On August 24, at
seven o'clock in the evening, a small, spiczek dog
was stolen, completely black, it has a small white
streak only under the belly, if it had been found
somewhere, please being information to the
home of citizen Gaszyński in Suchy Las on Długa
Street and a respectable reward will be given".

Announcements in Issues 7 and 9 inform about what
can be bought, eaten, as well as rented.

"In the apartment house of Mister Luciń-
ski, Deputy cup-bearer of HRH, no. 509 on Podwale
Street, there is the first floor entirely or partially
available for rent at any time with all comforts,
furniture, a stable for six horses, and a coach
house".

"Ludwik Fietta has the honor to inform
the Public that the English Coppersmiths' Warehouse, which until now was in the Minkenbek
tenement house opposite the Kraków Gate, is now
moved to the Cader tenement house on Krakowskie Przedmieście at No. 437, to the first floor".

"Poltz Traktier, known for his service to the
Public, where one could have a table at a moderate price with the greatest cleanliness, once
living on Podwale opposite Jgielstrom, after he
was robbed, has now moved to the Latourowska
tenement house next to the Theater and wants to
serve this Public as before".

"With the cancellation of Adam Sheyda
Jankowski's trade in the tenement house of Mister Berneaux opposite Marywil, at No. 469, various goods will be sold at the lowest possible price,
such as: single colored and striped nankeen cloth,
solid white and colored dyma, white striped muslin, colored muslin, white piqué, Turkish camlet,
single colored and striped Chinese bast, Chinese
and Turkish fabrics, Chinese and Turkish belts,

English and muslin shawls, various vests, white and black ties, silk and Ost Indian front handkerchiefs for the nose, musselbas, silk and thread stockings, yellow, black and red Turkish leathers, white Chinese kartun, tablecloths, balsam de mecca, Turkish tobacco pouches, real Chinese teas and other things, also in this trade are used horse harnesses, with brass, and lesser ones, with a collar and a saddle".

In addition to Issue 25, also in the "Reports" section, there is also talk of a loss, but a much more serious one than a small black dog, a wallet with papers, or a white-legged korbonos horse. "A tiny 14-year-old girl, Marysia, has gotten lost, recently brought from Lithuania, does not know Warsaw. Her head is trimmed, her face is long, her eyes are black, she is dressed in a Dutch shirt with a male collar, in a green leather corset, in a navy-blue baize skirt, in a Dutch apron, she speaks more Russian than Polish. Whoever would find her, it is asked that she be sent to the tenement house of Martyn, the royal jeweler, on Leszno, they will receive a reward".

Why the jeweler Martin, at whose place in the tenement house at number 653, at the corner of Leszno and Przejazd, there was a Russian guardhouse before the outbreak of the Uprising, and who, as is known from elsewhere, was also involved in the production and sale of beer, brought a fourteen-year-old girl from Lithuania, we do not know (maybe there were children working in Martin's brewery - it was a common practice at the time), but this last announcement looks a bit worrying and when one reads it now, after more than two hundred years, it's hard to get rid of the suspicion that something bad happened then. Various terrible things happened in Warsaw, not because there were hangings, but because what always happens was happening, and fourteen-year-old Marysia, who did not know Warsaw, could have encountered, even for sure had encountered some very unpleasant adventure - she could have even fallen into the hands of contemporary live goods traders and been sold to one of the wooden huts behind the Iron Gate, where what was done with such little girls in green corsets, it is better not to say. She was walking along Senatorska Street towards Marywil, marveling at the magnificent palaces of the capital and at the same time humming a cheerful song in Russian, and precisely then, at the intersection of Senatorska and Miodowa Streets, when she was reaching the Primate's Palace, and there, with her head tilted up, she stopped, so as to look at the great gallows standing in front of this palace - why was something like that set up here and what would it be used for? - oh naive child, do not raise your trimmed head and do not ask about anything, you better look around, maybe there is someone somewhere nearby who looks like a good person and will escort you to Leszno to the beer factory, and if not, quickly, as fast as your little legs can carry you, run away - and it was precisely there on Senatorska Street, when she was standing beneath this gallows, that a one-horse covered coach pulled up and two young men in black masks and in black triangular hats with feathers jumped out of it, and when later, in a wooden shack behind the Iron Gate (right in this room, where Marysia in a green leather corset was led in, next to the wooden bunk there was a cesspit dug in the ground, and from the ceiling there were two leather loops hanging on hemp ropes), so when there, in this shack, the two young men took off their black triangular hats and wigs with black bows, it turned out that they were two bald – oh poor Marysia.

Chapter 25
ROBESPIERRE, BUT IN A CASSOCK

Who caused the great hangings that took place in Warsaw on June 28? This question can also be formulated a little differently, somewhat more generally: what first caused these hangings, what was at the very beginning, and what did they begin with? The longer I think about it - and I have been thinking about it since I started writing this book; what I am writing right now is the last part left for me to write, and it is precisely on this part that this book ends – so the longer I think about it, the more confusion (in my head) this question causes - and no clear answer emerges from this confusion.

Hugo Kołłątaj (Jozef Peszka)

Though there are - in this confusion - many uncertain and partial answers. Maybe it is so that for such a question - what did they begin with? - there is not and cannot be any clear answer, because this is precisely what the phenomenon of hanging by the people is all about, this is where we touch on its essence - it does not have and cannot have any reason, and therefore it is as it is: dark, closed in on itself, impenetrable, and incomprehensible. People go out into the streets and, overwhelmed with terrible rage, overturn and burn cars, capture and demolish schools and kindergartens, break into large warehouses, destroy or rob everything that can be destroyed and robbed, and if this robbery and burning does not quench their incomprehensible rage, they begin to hang. All of this happens (most often, but not always) in darkness and rage, that rules it, is like that darkness in the streets – this is rage-darkness. Then, when it's all over and the water cannons and tear gas have done their job, this inconceivable rage becomes something that can be explained, even something that must be explained - various reasons are made for it and matched to it, because the better (enlightened) part of humanity desires to understand (explain to itself) why the inferior (dark) part of humanity fell into rage. In this way - one can also understand it - the enlightened part of humanity wants to prevent that which could happen in the future (destruction, burning, and hanging) and to ensure some kind of safety for itself.

Rage understood and thus tamed is something which, with the help of police and pedagogical means, prisons as well as television, one can somehow manage. Though I don't know if rage-darkness can be tamed. Mine (I belong to the dark, inferior part of humanity) - certainly cannot be. Right after the June hangings - during the hangings, and even earlier, when the hangings were just beginning, and even before they started - Father Hugo Kołłątaj was recognized as the one who caused them. The ex-Deputy Chancellor of the Crown – and now a counselor of the Treasury Department of the Supreme National Council (to put it in other words, the insurrectionary minister of finance) - was then seen in Warsaw as a sort of Polish Robespierre. So as someone who desired to transform the national insurrection into a French-style revolution and who, moreover, intended to use some Polish version of the Great Terror for this purpose. "He prepared - wrote the author of *Pamiętnik anegdotyczny z czasów Stanisława Augusta* (*An Anecdotal Memoir from the Times of Stanisław August*) - the people devoted to him to further ideas, preparing to imitate the French Revolution and to become in Poland a second Robespierre [...] for his exaltation and bringing to fruition his intended plans, he was ready to destroy those patriots standing in his way, and apparently also Kościuszko himself". When we read that Father Kołłątaj was the "second Robespierre" or the "Polish Robespierre" (it was also often formulated in this way), then an obvious question arises, on what basis were such opinions formulated, or - in other words - what did those who claimed something similar know about the ex-Deputy Chancellor and his Robespierre-style ideas? Antoni Trębicki wrote, for example, that Kołłątaj "was [...] always an admirer of all the severities of the French Jacobins and always maintained, that having them as an example, crowned with the most successful result, one should follow it in everything". It would be good to know (but one cannot know, of course) what the phrase "always maintained, that" in this sentence means. Does it mean that Trębicki, while working for Kołłątaj and his Forge during the times of the Great Sejm, heard precisely something like that from his patron (whom he later hated) at that time? It could also be that Kołłątaj had never said anything like that - that he was a fan of "all the severities of the...Jacobins" - and Trębicki, in his diary *O rewolucji roku 1794 (On the Revolution of 1794)*, was only expressing the common conviction that the deputy chancellor was the "second Robespierre".

An interesting insight into this matter – from where this opinion about Kołłątaj could have come - is given in *Życie Moje (My Life)* by Józef Wybicki. "People began to perceive - we read in this work - too much trust placed by him [Kościuszko] in Deputy-Chancellor Kołłątaj, whom everyone called Robespierre". In another fragment of *My Life*, Wybicki described Kazimierz Konopka (revealing and hiding it in the subtext in this place the surname of his patron): "the first hideous tool of this secret leader was a certain Konopka, a young man, apparently from the city of Poznań, a man of no importance, a copyist in the office of Fr. Kołłątaj". Further on, there is also a mention that Konopka "surely inspired by some Polish Robespierre, stood at the head of the drunken commune, [...] encouraged, incited to murder, plunder, and anarchy, the people whom he blinded, seduced, and bloodied, or rather made them drunk". When the insurrectionary adventures came to an end and Wybicki found himself in Paris - this happened quite late, not until November or December 1795 - he was struck by the fact that some traces of Jacobin activity could still be found there. "I still found [...] in offices the remains of these bloody, dirty, and dark demagogues, the fruits of the unheard-of monster of the human race, Robespierre". It follows that for enlightened Poles at the end of the 18th century - Wybicki was undoubt-

edly the perfect realization of the contemporary model of an
enlightened Pole - Maximilian Robespierre was a symbol not
only of the monstrosity of the revolution, but also of the monstrosity of human nature. The fact that Kołłątaj was the Polish
Robespierre would thus mean that such a monster appeared
among Poles as well, a terrible embodiment of the wildness
and wickedness of human nature. Wybicki (like many enlightened Poles of that time, perhaps even like all enlightened
Poles) believed that the nation to which he belongs is in its
essence noble and good, and that these features of Polish national character, goodness and nobility, have something eternal in them, that is, they exist beyond time, and therefore are
(or at least should be) indestructible. "As a Pole I will mention
only this - we read in *My Life* - as boasting of flawless national
humanity until now, that the day of 28 *Juni* cast the first blot
on the immemorial purity of the national character".

Seeing an unheard-of revolutionary monster among
Poles, Father Kołłątaj, must have been a very hard, even trau-
matic experience for the author of the song *Poland Has Not
Yet Perished*. The question for which it would be worth looking for an answer could be as follows: did Wybicki know from
his own experience (he knew because he knew Kołłątaj well)
that the ex-deputy chancellor was a monster "of the human
race", or did Kołłątaj's monstrosity stem for him from a commonly known fact, that he was the "Polish Robespierre"? Or
– phrasing this more generally – was it believed that Kołłątaj
is a monster because that is just how he is, he has such a vile
character, he is a monster by his monstrous nature, or was it
rather considered that his monstrosity has an incidental character - it appeared because the ex-deputy chancellor chose to
emulate a monstrous French example? Unfortunately, *My Life*
does not give us any answer in this matter. The conviction that
the responsibility for the events of June 28 rests with the Polish Robespierre turned out to be extremely lasting. Kołłątaj,
after his release from the Austrian prison in Olomouc (he was
imprisoned by the Austrians, in Olomouc and Josefstadt, for
over eight years, longer than any other of the leaders of the
insurrection, much longer than Kościuszko, Potocki, Kiliński, and Wawrzecki, who were imprisoned by the Russians),
had trouble with this matter for the rest of his life. Despite

his great sufferings, imprisonment and illness (he suffered from the disease of age, podagra), he was still regarded as a revolutionary monster and when he came to Warsaw during the times of the Duchy of Warsaw, he was refused hospitality in an inn. When he settled in the flat of Franciszek Ksawery Dmochowski, a crowd gathered in front of the house and all of Dmochowski's windows were broken. As I said, the accusations that the hangings were "inspired" by Kołłątaj and that he was a "secret leader" who let the hangmen out onto the streets and ordered them to be hung appeared even before the June hangings, even before a noose was put on anyone. There is no doubt that Kołłątaj, as we would say in our present language, was framed for the hangings by King Stanisław August, who hated the Deputy Chancellor of the Crown terribly. Probably with reciprocity.

One must say a sad thing here. Stanisław August, when he was trying to frame Kołłątaj for the hangings, was probably led by quite malicious motives - Kołłątaj humiliated and disregarded him (as the only one of the insurrection's leaders, he never appeared at the Castle, despite many invitations), and therefore the king wanted to take revenge. Though that's not all this is about. For the King, and this is precisely the very sad thing (a sad guess - because it is of course only a guess, there is no clear evidence for this), the hangings were probably fortuitus - they could have accelerated the entry of the Russians and Prussians into Warsaw, and such an entry (from a certain point of view) would be completely justified in this case, because it would mean the pacification of the rampaging Jacobins. It was precisely this - to be under the care of the generals of the St. Petersburg Tsarina as soon as possible - that could have been most important for the king at that time. On the night of June 27-28 - it is not known at what time, but probably people with torches were already putting up gallows on the streets of Warsaw at that time, hewing beams and nailing ladders together, adapting everything to the needs of the morning hangings - Stanisław August sent a note to Kołłątaj, which later, by a twisted road, found its way, somewhere in the early 20th century, into the collection of Professor Józef Kallenbach. I am quoting it here in its entirety. "I received news just now that Mr. Konopka encouraged the people to again put-up gallows and to hang a few persons, among whom the bishop is to be included. For all reasons, both as a king, and as a Pole, and as a human being, and most of all as a Christian, I demand most seriously that this cruel scene should not restart here. I would harm your reputation Sir if I were to expand here, about how much such an act would be oppositional and harmful not only to the greatest considerations, but also to our politics, so I am making only the strongest appeal to you Sir to turn the people's minds away from this harmful event by your authority. King Stanisław August". A very beautiful and even noble note. Though Kołłątaj was an intelligent and experienced politician, so he certainly did not fall for the king's moralizations as well as the king's talk about some kind of "our politics", that is, the common politics of the king and the leaders of the uprising - such politics, of course, never existed. It was also obvious from the note that the king - pointing to Kazimierz Konopka, Kołłątaj's man, as the one who animates the people to put up gallows, in fact points not to Konopka, but precisely to Kołłątaj - and tells him that it is precisely he who will be responsible for the hangings – if they occur.

This Kołłątaj could not fail to notice - he could not fail to see that he was being (let's use that ugly word here again) framed. From behind the note the king could be seen who, smiling crookedly, looks through his famous binoculars at the Polish Robespierre, Kołłątaj, and the Polish Saint-Just, Konopka, and turning to Robespierre, he says something like this: - So you see, my dear priest, they are already hanging, and it is you who are responsible for it; now do something about it, get out of this somehow; but you won't get out now! - Kołłątaj, realizing that he is being framed – this was also indicated by the obvious fact that the note was directed to the wrong addressee; the king should address his request that the "harmful event" be ended to someone who had real police power in Warsaw: either to the president of the city, Wyssogota Zakrzewski, or to the head of the Security Department of the Supreme National Council, Michał Kochanowski – so Kołłątaj, having understood what was happening, tried to get out of it somehow. He sent the king's note to Kochanowski, instructing him to get in contact with Wyssogota Zakrzewski and to, together with him, bring order to the streets - and this was undoubtedly a reasonable move, though a bit late – while to the king he sent a note with the later famous words "This people is good" as well as ensuring that there will not be any hangings. This note was an unwise move (if you look at it from some political point of view) – the hangings (and Kołłątaj late at night on June 27-28 should have known this) could no longer be avoided, and the king had proof in his hands that the one who had sent him the note with the assurance of the goodness of the people support- ed the hangmen, even protected them, even praised them - so he wanted the hangings. Perhaps Kołłątaj really believed that Kochanowski and Zakrzewski were sufficiently determined and that they would convince the people with torches to give up the hangings, take their ladders and axes and disperse to their homes - I do not know how it was, but this - such a belief of Kołłątaj's – would testify to strange naivety, and he was certainly not a naive man. Kołłątaj's note to the king, the one with the words "The people is good", in its entirety looked like this.

"I was looking at the people gathered in front of my house, who were looking for Kochanowski, who sits in the Se- curity Department, and he went with them and probably dis- suaded them from this idea. Your Majesty, be calm. This peo- ple is good, they are offended by the delays and sluggishness of the courts, yet I trust, that they will not tear authority from the hands of the courts; they will be calmed by the speeches of Kochanowski, and above all, of a president who is beloved by them. I certify with the respect due to Your Majesty - Fa- ther Kołłątaj". As can be seen, Kołłątaj was again disregarding towards the king (with a disregarding gesture he dismissed his fears), but he also admitted in this note that the good peo- ple had gathered before his house that night - and so it was precisely he, Kołłątaj, that they considered their leader. This was also probably not very (from the point of view of Kołłątaj's future interests) astute. For the rest of his life - until 1812, when he died - Kołłątaj tried to understand the reason for the June hangings, why they happened, and who was responsi- ble for them. If he knew this, he could have somehow protect- ed himself from the accusations that pursued him and which said that it was precisely him, sending Konopka or some of his other agents to the city, that caused the hangings, and in addition caused them completely deliberately, having in mind his terrible goal, that is, the introduction of something like the Great Terror in Warsaw. The fact that such accusations were made by the king and his supporters - we find them in the brochure *Obrona Stanisława Augusta* (*The Defense of Stanisław August*), signed by the royal chamberlain Mikołaj Wolski, but which was corrected and probably partly written by the king - so there was nothing strange about it, because something like this was to be expected - the king, with a background of his noble deeds, wanted to make wicked the deeds of the Polish Robespierre. It is also not surprising that Kołłątaj was later accused by people who were openly hostile to him - such as Antoni Trębicki, who allegedly denounced him in November 1794 (this matter has never been fully resolved) and turned him over to the Austrians. "This daily concentration of the people - wrote Trębicki (we are talking about work on strengthening the Warsaw fortifications) – was seen by Kołłątaj's ambition, aiming at absolute tyranny, as an opportunity to carry out his hideous intention, to consolidate his rule on blood and the noose.

Openly and conscientiously, I ascribe and everyone else ascribes this crime to no one else, but Kołłątaj. [...] [Kołłątaj] needed any kind of blood so as to fund terrorism. [...] So many reasons, so important and necessary for someone greedy of tyranny, led Kołłątaj and his supporters to incite a mob of the populace, so that in a way he carried out this justice to himself". Later on, Trębicki mentions what the "daring young man", Kazimierz Konopka, "a trusted home dweller and Kołłątaj's secretary", was doing on the night of June 27-28, who - inciting the mob to hang - gave vodka to the workmen and raftsmen "in the pubs on Szulc, Tamka, and along the Vistula River". If, as I say, Kołłątaj was then accused only by people like Trębicki or Wolski, it would not be surprising - but the belief that it was he who caused the June hangings spread then also among those who were, or at least should be, his allies. Pretty much everyone was convinced that Kołłątaj had blood on his hands. Father Kitowicz, who, when it comes to the assessment of Stanisław August, certainly fully agreed with the ex-deputy chancellor (the king was, according to Kitowicz, a "shameless stinker"), in the matter of the cause of the June hangings, he was precisely of the same opinion as Stanisław August, that is he believed that it was Kołłątaj who had caused them. "On June 28 at night - we read in *Historia Polska (Polish History)* - the frantic populace revolted under the leadership of a certain Konopka, the writer under Father Kołłątaj, deputy chancellor, at his instigation [...]. Kołłątaj was able to disentangle himself from this accusation". It has to be said that Kołłątaj, trying to figure out what the real cause of what happened on June 28 was, did not distinguish himself with any particular ingenuity - he even probably did not distinguish himself with any particular intelligence. Although he was, after all, a man of great intelligence. In 1808, the ex-deputy chancellor published a small book entitled *Uwagi nad teraźniejszym położeniem tej części ziemi polskiej, którą od czasu traktatu tylżyckiego zaczęto zwać Księstwem Warszawskim (Remarks on the Present Location of this part of the Polish Land, which from the time of the Treaty of Tilsit began to be called the Duchy of Warsaw).* The book (this says a lot about the author's situation at that time) was published anonymously, and although it was published in Warsaw, Leipzig was given as the place of publication on the title page. Between 1808 and 1810, *Remarks on the Present Location* had three publications (all supposedly in Leipzig), so there must have been something in them that interested readers.

That something was a penetrating analysis of the situation of Poles whom the French emperor had endowed with a strange state entity - the Duchy of Warsaw. Kołłątaj was very well aware of the fact that the Duchy is something terrible, because such a patch of land cannot be enough for the Poles, but being something terrible, it is also something blessed for the Poles, because the fact that they can live again in their own country (small state), restores hope and on the most important issue - that the nation will exist and will have a place to exist. "Let us show first on this small piece of earth that we are worthy to be a great nation; let us strive to earn this: and only then will we be allowed to inquire about the goals of this Great Man and judge about his whole work. We are not the only ones, to whom his care extends: the good of all of Europe depends on him today; so let us wait patiently for our turn". This Great Man is of course Napoleon. In *Remarks on the Pres-*

ent Location, he also appears as the "Great Lawmaker of Nations", the "Savior of France" and the "Resurrector of Poland". When Kołłątaj recognized Napoleon as the man who resurrected Poland ("the resurrection of her [Polish] name we owe to the wisdom of Napoleon and the bravery of his forces"), and earlier saved France, he was faced with two difficult questions about the past. The first was: if Napoleon saved France, what to think about the French Revolution? The second resulted logically from the first - the judgment of the French Revolution had to entail the judgment of the Polish Revolution. Kołłątaj dealt with the first problem very well. In 1808 he acknowledged the French Revolution as a great but necessary evil from which a great good was born. This great good was Great Napoleon. "This was - say the *Remarks* about the French Revolution - a necessary evil from which such a great good would result". The good that Napoleon brought with him (or who was Napoleon) was based on the fact that the French emperor had brought order - Napoleon "having healed the dangerous convulsions of his people, at the same time changed the old form of Europe". Revolution is therefore only "dangerous convulsions". A noteworthy judgement, given that it was the judgement of a Polish Robespierre (admittedly a Robespierre in a cassock). What these "dangerous convulsions" were, Kołłątaj accurately described, and just as we might have expected.

The "dangerous convulsions" are anarchy, and it is precisely this anarchy that Great Napoleon put an end to. The "Savior of France" - as we learn from *Remarks* - was a man who thwarted hopes for "the return of this great people to anarchy". If the French Revolution was dangerous convulsions and anarchy, then what was the Polish insurrection? Kołłątaj had more trouble with this, because it was ultimately about his own past. Of the few passages that are devoted in *Remarks on the Present Location* to the Insurrection of 1794, the most interesting is the one that talks about the events of June 28. "Throughout this revolution, there were two sad instances of a popular tumult, which made a disturbance for this reason alone, that there was no desire to judge criminals or suspects of crimes. These two instances could have been suppressed and not allowed to occur if the commandant of Warsaw had been in good communication with the president of the city; the hatred between the two and their awkwardness was a reason why the bad effects were not remedied in advance; nevertheless, a court against the rebels was appointed which punished them". Thus, according to Kołłątaj, the June hangings were caused by those, and only those, who allowed it to happen - first, by those who did not sentence the "criminals" in time, and then those who should have acted efficiently but acted awkwardly. That is, President Wyssogota Zakrzewski and the then commandant of the Warsaw garrison, General Józef Orłowski. Such an assessment of the causes that triggered the hangings was consistent with the overall assessment of the insurrection in *Regards*. Kołłątaj simply concluded that it was not a revolution - and at any rate it was not something that could resemble the French Revolution, because there was no one in Poland at the time who wanted to introduce a Great Terror - there were no followers of Robespierre and his methods. "Whoever takes a good look at the history of that time will find out: that in Poland, not only did Jacobinism never exist and expand; but even in such a sad and dangerous time, it was known how to prevent it". This is how (by becoming a Bonapartist) the Polish Robespierre in a cassock renounced his past. About the same time when *Remarks on the Present Location* were published, Kołłątaj received a letter (probably unknown to him up until that point), which Stanisław August wrote to Mikołaj Wolski on December 15, 1794 (after the entry of Russian troops into Warsaw).

This letter was later found in the papers left by Bishop Jan Chrzciciel Albertrandi, who died in 1808, and it was from there that it was retrieved for Kołłątaj. In it, the king accused his former deputy chancellor of wanting to murder him three times: first on May 9, then on June 28, and finally, when he was unsuccessful that time, again in November - "the day for this was to be chosen in November". In this way the terrible accusation was recalled again - that it was he, Kołłątaj, who caused what happened on May 9 and June 28. The deputy chancellor, having read the king's letter, wrote a reply entitled *Krótkie objaśnienie dla lepszego zrozumienia listu pana Wolskiego pisanego do Stanisława Augusta 9/Xbris 1794 i odpowiedzi, którą mu dał król pod datą 15 tegoż miesiąca* (*A Brief Explanation for a better understanding of Mr. Wolski's letter to*

Stanisław August 9/Xbris 1794 and the answer that the king gave him on the 15th of that month). In one of the fragments of this answer (it was probably disseminated in Warsaw at the time, but was never published in its entirety), he returned to the events of June 28. "Though having allowed - he wrote - any reason for this rebellion, wishing to accuse whomever he liked of it, it is hard to deny that it could have been prevented, because there was little of the gathered rabble. A small number of the rabble raged, fueled and predisposed by someone, and no one resisted them in the slightest, although several dozen soldiers with bayonets or loaded weapons were enough to do this". So, the rabble, which was – by some secret leader - fueled and predisposed, was carrying out hangings. Something like this - of course with Kołłątaj or his secretary Konopka in mind - could have been written by Stanisław August (for example in his letter to Wolski), Józef Wybicki could also have written this. Or even one of Kołłątaj's most terrible enemies, someone like Trębicki. It is curious if Kołłątaj, claiming in 1808 that the hangings were carried out "by rabble predisposed by someone", remembered that note from fourteen years ago, which he wrote to the king on the night of June 27-28, and about the sentence that was in the note: "This people, is good". In *A Brief Explanation for a better understanding*, the thought about the several dozen soldiers which needed to be sent (someone should have sent) to suppress the rebellion and restore order in Warsaw is also noteworthy. Soldiers "with bayonets or loaded weapons" - this was precisely what, according to Bonapartists (of all epochs), was the best way to deal with good people or a drunken rabble. This is where the spiritual adventures of the Polish Robespierre (in a cassock) end.

Chapter 26
HISTORY AS AN IMAGINED IMAGE

What is the study of history focused on? Generally speaking, such study deals with facts that took place in the past. One might also say that the study of history deals not only with facts, but also with various events, various ideas, and finally with various objects that existed in the past. Events, ideas, and objects can, however, be named (with some difficulty) – most generally speaking and wanting to achieve the highest possible degree of generalization - facts. Let us then acknowledge (we shall see in a moment what this leads us to) that the object of historical study are facts -

Józef Ankwicz

those which existed in the past. The capture of the Russian embassy on Miodowa Street on April 18, 1794, is a fact; an event that actually took place and which, because of its factuality, can be investigated and assessed - and only a mentally ill person could claim that the event did not actually take place and that the embassy was never captured.

Someone who studies history, who is a professional historian, a professional researcher of a piece of the past - writes books on this subject, and then, by presenting these books to his older colleagues for evaluation, obtains further academic degrees on this basis - such a person is therefore a research-

er of facts, a specialist of facts who is professionally involved
in revealing facts and confirming their (past or present) existence. Such a professional, a professional historian, having
discovered the existence of many facts, having revealed that
these facts existed in the past, must then (wanting to construct
a certain whole from them) somehow sort them out, put them
in some order. The matter of putting in order and the whole
is extremely complicated - every order by which the historian
arranges facts probably exists only in his head; every whole,
the puzzle that arises as a result of arranging facts, can also
be considered (if only someone, some critical mind, dares to
do something like that) as a completely fictional creation, existing only in the mind of the compiler. There are also, as we
know, completely different, opposite opinions on this matter,
according to which the whole and the order can be included in
the realm of facts - and such an operation, which is obvious,
also requires not just any courage.

Taking into account the high degree of complexity of the
problematic aspects of order and the whole, it would be better
to omit these matters, at least for now - so that they do not
complicate for us the simple and obvious problematic aspects
of the factuality of historical facts. So, let's stick to the facts -
the past is made of facts and professional historians deal with
facts, this is precisely what their profession is based on - that
they know how to handle them; how to reveal them (to extract
from the past) and how to state their factuality. This cannot be
said more generally - it is said as generally as possible, in the
most general way. In deciding to take such a general, even the
most general approach − in accepting that the past consists
of facts that happened in the past, and that the calling of historical study is to deal with precisely such a thing, such facts,
that actually happened - have we not committed any mistake?
Oh, I think so - we must have made a mistake somewhere.
What will we do - if we formulate the subject of the study of
history in such a way - with the two kaftans (or kaftaniks) in
which Józef Ankwicz, Marshal of the Permanent Council, was
hanged on May 9 (on the one of the three gallows that stood
closest to the southern frontage of the Market Square and not
far from Zapiecek's opening) in front of the City Hall in the
Old Warsaw Market Square? The gallows, clearly visible from

Zapiecek, is an undoubtable fact. The ladder leaning against the crossbeam of the gallows is also factual, even the hat which Ankwicz used to bow to the people while walking through the Market Square is factual, the harness on which the executioner pulled him up to a height of 7 meters is factual. This height is also factual. It is different with the two kaftans or kaftaniks – their accuracy (if someone wanted to insist on it) is very easy to question. Jan Kiliński (in the *Drugi Pamiętnik* [*Second Diary*]) claimed that the kaftan that Marshal Ankwicz took off beneath the gallows was made of satin fabric, while the fabric was crimson in color. "He pulled up his black pants and pulled down the crimson satin kaftan". Whereas in the third volume of Józef Ignacy Kraszewski's work, *Polska w czasie trzech rozbiorów* (*Poland during the Three Partitions*), we learn (Kraszewski, while describing the events that took place on May 9, used an account the author of which he did not mention and whom I have not been able to find) that Ankwicz was wearing not a kaftan, but a kaftanik, and that the kaftanik was quilted and green. "He walked to the gallows in a green quilted kaftanik".

It is obvious that these two kaftans cannot be reconciled - the crimson kaftan could be quilted, and it could even be a kaftanik, but in no way could it be green; the green kaftanik could be satin, and it could be a kaftan, but in no way could it be crimson. What can a historian who deals with facts (what factually happened) do with two such kaftans? It is immediately apparent that there is nothing he can do - he can only acknowledge (and must acknowledge) the factual existence of both kaftans. The other possibilities are such. If he chooses one of the kaftans and acknowledges (for example) that Ankwicz was wearing a green quilted kaftan, then he will have no basis to do so. If he states that Ankwicz was not wearing any kaftan, he will also make a baseless decision. If, on the other hand, he decides that this difference - green or crimson - is irrelevant, because a kaftan, or even more a kaftanik (in addition, of a condemned man), is not an important matter, then he will hear a question: what if it were not about two kaftaniks, but about ten batteries of six-pound cannons during the Battle of Maciejowice? The matter of Ankwicz's kaftaniks becomes even more complicated (and must get more complicated) when to the two kaftaniks we add a third one. For if we assume (which, of course, should be done – this is immediately implied) that one of the authors of the account of the hangings (Kiliński or the unknown author) did not remember what kaftan Ankwicz was wearing, and therefore this kaftan (crimson or green) was mistakenly or half-mistakenly imagined by him, then we can equally (and with equal probability) assume that this applies to both accounts - both authors forgot what kind of kaftan it was, and therefore both kaftans, crimson and green, are imagined - Ankwicz had some other kaftan on. What kind - this is very easy to imagine, and I am already doing it, my imagination is already starting to work. The caftan was yellow, satin on the outside, smooth, and the lining was also yellow, but with tiny flowers, made of kitajka. Should I keep talking - what kind of buttons and loops did it have? This is how we turn the subject of historical research - if we seriously deal with the problem of Ankwicz's kaftans-kaftaniks (a topic as good as any other; like the topic of six-pound cannons at Maciejowice) - into an imagined image. Not a fact, not a factual state, but an imagined image – that which we imagine when we look back at the past and reflect on the past.

History - and this results, this probably cannot be expressed otherwise, because of some core inclinations of ours, genetic conditions - is the object of imagination. Whoever looks deep into their head - their mind - will find their imagined images about the past there. Various - wise and stupid imagined images, imaginary imagined images and factual imagined images (or semi-factual, quarter-factual). The matter with the hat which Ankwicz used to bow to the people is a bit similar to the kaftans. We know about the hat (from the only account that mentions it) only that it was a hat and that when Ankwicz was walking through the Market Square, bowing, he took it off and put it on. Though anyone who is not an idiot and who reads a sentence that talks about bowing with a hat will soon (and rightly so) imagine something - an eighties-style hat or a nineties-style hat, a tricorne or just a bicorne, a hat with a feather or without one, or with a swan feather, a hat with a ribbon or without a ribbon, with or without a bow, and, if one desires, with a band and a loop. Then we have - immediately, as soon as we see Ankwicz with his hat near the gallows - a multitude of hats hidden under one hat, covered with that one. All of this in a clear way belongs to history, and so it can belong to studies and be a subject of study: a feather, one kind or another, a swan or geese feather, a loop, a ribbon, a tricorne or just a bicorne. It should also be taken into account that the account mentioned here (of Karol Wojda) mentions Ankwicz, who bows when entering the City Hall or crossing the Market Square, and it seems very probable, and to me it seems almost certain (I see it clearly) that Ankwicz bowed to the people of Warsaw also later, when he was climbing the ladder. Then, having finished bowing, he tossed his beautiful hat with a frayed feather into the crowd as far as possible – with the thought that his hat would still be useful to someone, someone will wear it. The hat, in a great arc, glided towards Zapiecek and Piwna Street.

Does the further fate of this hat, which was thrown into the crowd, also belong to history and the study of it? A professional, specialist historian, employee of the Institute of History of the Polish Academy of Sciences (the one located on Kołłątaj's side, not far from the hat gliding towards Piwna), will say no, that in no circumstance does it belong, it cannot belong, because nothing about this matter (further fate of the hat) is known. What is not known, does not exist. Hey! Though after all it did, it happened, came into existence (this flight of the hat over the crowd), and even if it came into existence only as an eventuality, one of many possibilities, hypothetically, not for certain, if it could have happened and may have happened – then can it be thrown out of history? Can the study of it - such a hypothetical existence – be ignored? In my opinion - it cannot. The hypothetical flight of the hat, Ankwicz's hypothetical (with a hypothetical yellow kitajka lining) kaftanik, the hypothetical loop - all these exist half-way, have only a half-existence, even a quarter-existence. It exists a little, and it does not exist a little. It is a bit factual, a bit imagined. One has to put some effort in to imagine it - the triumphant flight of the hat, which is thrown up by the condemned man. Though this is precisely what history is made of, these are the pieces that one can use to make it.

Chapter 27.
JUNE 28 – EIGHT HANGED ON TEN GALLOWS

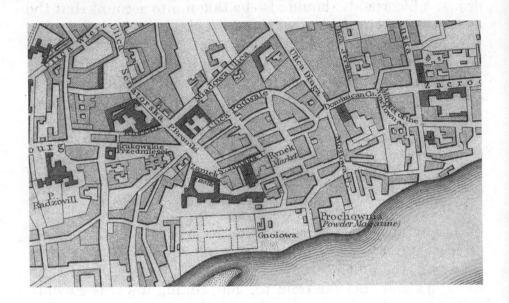

If there were eight hanged on June 28, and they were hanged, as has already been mentioned, on ten gallows (three in the Old Warsaw Market Square; two in front of the Krasiński Palace; one in front of the Brühl Palace; one on Nowy Świat between the Branicki Palace and the Dominican Observant Church; one on Krakowskie Przedmieście in front of St. Anne's Church; one somewhere on Senatorska Street, or near the Primate's Palace, or opposite the Reformist Church; and the last one on Miodowa near the Załuski Palace - ten in total) - so if eight were hanged on ten gallows, then two gallows remained unused - no one was hanged on them. Throughout the entire day, the two gallows (if one can imagine them as living beings) waited that someone would approach them and take advantage of their kindness.

There are, as can be easily seen, two other possibilities which come into play. I am talking about certain possibilities, which result from the fact that the accounts of the incidents that took place on June 28 are unclear, complicated, and in pieces - on their basis (even when carefully analyzing them) it is impossible to gain absolute certainty about how the events transpired. There are therefore, as you can see, two more possibilities which come into play. The first, very likely, is this. Some gallows – lets say two or three - could have been used several times, two or even three times. In this case, there would be many more gallows that were not used – the number of such gallows, which had been raised just in case (in the morning hanging frenzy that overwhelmed the hangmen) and which later turned out to be unnecessary, could be even five or six. I will try to determine if this could be the case. The second option, which is also quite probable, would be this. We know the surnames of eight hanged, which does not necessarily mean that there were just eight hanged.

There could have been eight of them, but there could have been a dozen or so, or even over twenty of them. Among the hanged there could be (as shown by the incident of instigator Majewski) completely random passers-by who, having stopped near the gallows, watched the hangings and for some reason were not liked by the hangmen - they did not like them to such an extent that they hanged them. It could also be that no one asked about such additional or extra hanged people, and their subsequent absence was not noticed by anyone - and therefore they were omitted in the accounts. In this situation, one would have to accept even such an assumption, that out of the ten Warsaw gallows, all of them were used that day - maybe even several times each. This is not at all impossible, because the accounts, as I said, are partial and on June 28 there could also have been other events that no one remembered or wrote about. It must also be kept in mind that later, when the repressions began and the hanging of those who hanged others began, no one bragged about or told about that fact that they had hanged someone - those who were accused rather denied that they had taken participation in this procedure.

As far as the latter is concerned, it is immediately evident that after the 212 years which have passed since 1794, nothing can be established in this regard. If someone was hanged at that time, who was not (if one can put it this way) noticed and was lost somewhere, then there is no hope that we would be able to find them now - to state that they were hanged somewhere. Now let's see what the accounts of the time and later say. It should also be added that among the eight known incidents that took place on June 28 on the streets of Warsaw, there are those that are known quite well, those that are somewhat known, as well as those that are almost unknown - that is, they are known only in the sense that the surname of the hanged person and the place where they were hanged are known - but almost nothing else. The eight hanged are, in alphabetical order (for now): Karol Boscamp-Lasopolski, partially an agent of the Russian police operating in Warsaw, and partially an agent of the Tsarina's subsequent ambassadors, also an agent of Stanisław August, so not only an ordinary Russian spy, but also an agent of a higher level, though he is best known not for his spying, but for the fact that he brought from Constantinople to Poland and sold here Zofia Glavani, known as the beautiful Greek woman or the beautiful Bithynian; Prince Antoni Czetwertyński, advisor of the Targowica Confederation; Count Stefan Grabowski, the royal chamberlain and the stepson of the king's secret wife, Elżbieta Grabowska; Józef Majewski, the Crown Instigator (i.e. someone like a prosecutor); Ignacy Massalski, the Bishop of Vilnius; Marceli Piętka, an agent of the Russian police (possibly also an agent of the Russian spy network, whose boss in Warsaw was the mysterious Dr. Schwartz); Mateusz Roguski, police intendant, Crown Instigator (and surely also an agent of Dr. Schwartz's network); Michał Wulfers, deputy councilor in the Provisional Council, Warsaw attorney (as it was said at the time - patron). These are the hanged eight - those who were for sure hanged that day, thought I am convinced that others were also hanged, such people that our native history (a capricious lady) has thrown out (for reasons known to her) from her memory. I start with the Brühl Palace - what happened there has been remembered relatively best (also for some unclear reason - but this is what happens in history). I just bring attention (your attention, my pretty young reader who is reading right now - with flushed cheeks, I hope) to the fact that my order is not chronological – everything indicates that the events at the Brühl Palace took place a little later than the events on the Old Warsaw Market Square as well as those at Saint Anne's.

The Brühl Palace had several names at that time - it was called the Brühlowski Palace or, more often, Brylowski Palace, but it was also called the Palace of the Republic (because, like the Krasiński Palace, it was owned by the Crown Treasury) or the Stackelberg Palace (because, during his reign in Warsaw, for almost twenty years, until 1792, this ambassador resided there). The populace (this word, the meaning of which I will try to describe later, was most commonly then used when referring to the inhabitants of Warsaw who were involved in the incidents of May 9 and June 28, so I will use it here too, although there is no doubt that it does not define it sufficiently clearly - both those doing the hangings and those supporting it) - the populace, some group of it of an unable to be determined number, appeared in front of the Brühlowski Palace only around 11 a.m., maybe even half an hour later. The circumstances of the capture of the Palace - that is, the removal of the guards - are unknown. It can be assumed that the guards, having understood what was happening and what was going to happen, simply fled at the sight of the populace, not wanting to be the first ones hanged. There was a large number of guards, there could have been even several dozen of them in front of the Brühlowski Palace, because the Supreme National Council (which results from the documents it produced) was very diligently (though completely ineffectively) caring for the prisoners' safety at that time, especially those who could be called political ones. As for the number of people in these groups that appeared on the streets of Warsaw before dawn or even late in the evening of the previous day, that is on June 27, and then took part in the hangings (probably moving from place to place, from one gallows to another), this number is assessed quite variously - accounts speak about several hundred executioners, but also of a thousand, even several thousand. "For it is certain - wrote Antoni Trębicki in his memoir *O rewolucji roku 1794 (On the Revolution of 1794)* - that the mob, which carried out the hangings, was not larger than three thousand".

As a result of the fighting that took place around Wierzbowa Street and Saxon Square on April 17 and 18, the Brühl Palace was terribly ruined, and it really is not known how such a ruin could even be used as a prison. This is stated

in a description of Warsaw at that time, which was left by
Jan Duklan Ochocki in his *Pamiętniki* (*Memoirs*). "In most
of the houses, the windows were shot out, there were chips
and gaps in the walls, or deep marks from cannonballs, some
of the walls, due to canister shot, looked like faces freshly
recovered from smallpox. The Brylowski Palace, close to the
Saxon Palace, suffered the worst: no window in it, no doors, no
furniture, everything shattered, broken, damaged, shattered
remains of expensive porcelain dishes, mirrors, and marble
were scattered on the floors".

Among these porcelain shells, in rooms without doors
and windows - this is how one might imagine it - the unfortunate
prisoners wandered, paid agents of the Petersburg Tsarina,
waiting (they knew what awaited them) for those who would
come to hang them. The prisoners, at least those kept in the
Brühlowski Palace, were not (as follows from a letter in which
President Wyssogota Zakrzewski informed Kościuszko about
the arrest of Bishops Massalski and Skarszewski as well as
of Count Moszyński) in shackles. "Their guard is just as strict
as it was with the earlier prisoners, that in prisons without
shackles they are safe". This is a circumstance important
enough because the hangmen did not have to waste time
unshackling those they were going to hang. The first one, who
was found in the palace chambers (or cellars) and dragged to
the gallows - there was probably one gallows in front of the
Brühlowski Palace gate – and so, the first candidate for the
gallows was, or actually was supposed to be, the Bishop of
Chełm Wojciech Skarszewski, the later (from 1824) Primate
of Poland. Skarszewski managed to be saved, which was
undoubtedly something of a miracle. There are two versions
of this event. According to one of them, recorded by General
Józef Zajączek in his *Pamiętnik albo Historia rewolucji czyli
powstania roku 1794* (*Memoir or the History of the Revolution,
i.e. The Uprising of 1794*), the bishop, when he was "being
dragged to the gallows", was saved by some person, one of those
who was watching the spectacle. "One person from the crowd
called out: 'Do not hang this gentleman, because he was very
merciful'. These words stopped the anger of the people, who
handed him over to justice. Skarszewski himself often later
recounted this incident and attributed his rescue to the alms

that he had once bestowed upon this man. A ragged nobleman came to him for support, and he gave him a ducat".

According to the second version, which is found in *Historia Polska* (*Polish History*) by Father Kitowicz and looks more probable (the populace would have probably not believed such a ragged nobleman who was referring to the fact that he had once received alms), the miracle was that the Bishop of Chełm had change in his pants (or banyan) pocket and managed to buy off the one who was dragging him to the execution - or perhaps those who were dragging him. "He survived in custody only because of a paltry two złoty which he put in the hand of one of these torturers, a footman, who was quite significant in this band, who exclaimed: 'Ho! Let us give this one peace, because he is a good gentleman'". Either way (whether Skarszewski saved himself for a ducat or for two Polish złotys), this is very instructive information - that life in revolutionary Warsaw then cost between two silver złotys (two złoty coins were silver) and one red złoty. By buying off those that were going to hang him, Bishop Skarszewski - at least according to Father Kitowicz's version - contributed to the death of Bishop Massalski. The footman, who took the two złotys, was supposed to shout, pointing to the other bishop: "Though let us lead out this scoundrel [...], who orders that the people who serve him be given one hundred rods". One can have certain doubts whether it was like this - although Kitowicz's colorful account is surprisingly accurate in many places (this comes to light when one analyzes it and puts it against the background of everything that is known about the events of that day), the Bishop of Vilnius, the most hated of all the Muscovites jurgieltniks would most likely have been executed even if the footman had not pointed to him. The hanging of Bishop Ignacy Massalski in front of the Brühlowski Palace is the best-known event of that day. Above all the surnames and even the names of those who carried out the execution are known. They were Stefan Klonowski, called in the reports and documents of the investigation, a laborer or herdsman, i.e. a shepherd, Lorenc (probably Laurenty) Burzyński, who was a bricklayer, as well as Tadeusz Dalgiert (also known as Delgiert or Dolgiert), also a bricklayer by profession.

Two bricklayers and a shepherd. It can be assumed that - although the accounts do not clearly say it - Józef Piotrowski, an officer cadet in the Royal Foot Guards, also took part in the hanging of Massalski. He was the only one of the hangmen to wear a uniform and ride a horse, which allowed him to move from place to place and take part in several, maybe even all, of the executions. Piotrowski most likely did not hang personally (there is nothing that indicates this anyway), one can rather imagine him as someone who - from a horse - gave orders and watched over the course of events - so that the hangmen (just simple people) would not get lost and not do something foolish. We will talk about officer cadet Piotrowski later. According to Stanisław August's opinion, one of Massalski's hangmen - certainly not Piotrowski, instead perhaps, if it is even true, one of the three previously mentioned - took money for this execution.

The king was not sure about this, but his reference was someone who had informed him about it. This is mentioned in a letter in which, on July 5, Stanisław August told Prince Józef Poniatowski about what was happening in Warsaw after June 28, that is, about the repressions against the hangmen. "*Dicitur*, that Konopka and Dębowski [Dembowski] brought themselves to be arrested, and that the one who with his own hand hanged the Bishop of Vilnius admitted that he had been given four złotys for this by someone whom he did not know". Massalski was led out of the Brühlowski Palace by the herdsman Klonowski. The bishop did not want to go, so he was beaten - urging him to move livelier – on his head with fists. There was no ladder or ropes outside the Brühl Palace, but a peasant wagon appeared nearby, which was just then passing through the Saxon Square. The reins were taken from the peasant, or perhaps some cart driver, who was sitting on the cart and thrown, lifted with pikes, over the crossbeam of the gallows. The bricklayer Dalgiert climbed these pikes to get to the top the gallows and tied the knot. Was he the one who took four złotys for tightening the knot? I do not know. The Bishop of Vilnius was seated on a stool under the gallows and was pulled up on the reins. This was perhaps a technique somewhat similar to that used by Stefan Böhm when he hung Hetman Ożarowski in the Market Square on May 9, but it is not clear whether Massalski was pulled up from the stool or together with the stool - and then the stool was thrown out from under the condemned so that he would hang well.

The differences in accounts are limited to the type of reins taken from the cart driver passing by. "It was the populace itself - wrote Father Kitowicz - [...] that hanged Prince Massalski, the Bishop of Vilnius, on hemp reins, taken from a peasant that was passing by"; in other accounts we have reins, or rather, since this noun was used then (perhaps even exclusively) in the singular, a leather rein. Massalski was hanged, as the Saxon *chargé d'affaires* Johann Jakob Patz wrote, "at noon". The next prisoner who was pulled out from the Brühlowski Palace - probably immediately after the hanging of the Bishop of Vilnius - was the Grand Marshal of the Crown (granted by the Targowica Confederation) Count Fryderyk Moszyński. The marshal, which was of course well known then, was a child of a royal family - grandson of Augustus II the Strong and Countess Cosel. If he was hanged, it could mean that the Polish Revolution, like the French one, would have no mercy for kings and their descendants - the next one could be Stanisław August or someone from the Poniatowski family (maybe some lady). According to the story of Father Kitowicz, Moszyński was to be hanged on the same gallows on which Massalski was hanged. Whether the Bishop of Vilnius was cut down beforehand, or whether the Marshal of the Crown was to hang next to him, it is not known. Anyway, Moszyński, when he found himself under the gallows, "defended himself and struggled with the populace as much as he could, not allowing the noose to be put around his neck" and this was probably what saved his life. Thanks to this struggle at the gallows, the hanging was delayed by a few minutes, and the carriage in which President Wyssogota Zakrzewski was riding was just then approaching the Brühlowski Palace. "When he was thrown down - Kitowicz said - and a noose was being put on the one lying down, Zakrzewski, the president of Warsaw, came by a more peculiar fortune, and having lied down on him, he cried out: 'Kill me and free the innocent one'. He soothed the furious mob in this way". This beautiful scene was presented somewhat differently in the first volume of *Pamiętniki o Polsce i Polakach* (*Memoirs about Poland and Poles*) by Michał Kleofas Ogiński

- according to him, Wyssogota Zakrzewski fell to his knees beneath the gallows and begged for mercy for Moszyński. "He spoke to the people until his voice was exhausted; he threw himself onto his knees, wringing his hands, so as to plead to the villains to cease their shameful actions, which cover the Polish nation with disgrace and jeopardize the fate of the Fatherland. His dedication saved several prisoners, calmed the people, and restored public peace".

Jan Kiliński described this event in an even different way later in the *Drugi Pamiętnik* (*Second Memoir*), who claimed that he was present there and that the Marshal of the Crown had survived thanks to his intervention. "Information came to the Council, so Zakrzewski took me to the vehicle with him and we barely got through such a large crowd of people, and if it were not for me, Zakrzewski would never have squeezed through. Though the people loved me and let me go everywhere". This is of course very likely - although Kiliński's boasts in many places make his story a bit unreliable. In order to appreciate the beauty of this extraordinary scene, it should be remembered that Zakrzewski was handicapped from birth (he had a great hump, or actually two humps, at the front and at the back) and he spoke in a very unpleasant, screeching (as Niemcewicz put it in *Pamiętniki czasów moich* [*Memoirs of My Times*] – duck like) voice. Only when one knows about this can one see this all well - as in some *image d'Épinal*. Moszyński lies under the gallows with a noose around his neck, on top of him lies the humped Wyssogota and in a duck like voice he calls: - Kill me!, and Massalski sways over them on a hemp rein; or Wyssogota kneels over Moszyński and, folding his hands, begs the hangmen for mercy; over Moszyński and Wyssogota, and under Massalski, Kiliński stands and raises his saber, threatening the populace with it. The account from the events of June 28, which was published (in Issue 20 of July 1) in Antoni Lesznowolski's *Gazeta Wolna Warszawska* (*The Free Warsaw Gazette*), says that the intervention of the President of Warsaw at the Brühlowski Palace on Wierzbowa Street ended the hangings. Wyssogota Zakrzewski - it was written - "went to the prison in the Palace of the Republic, called the Brühlowski Palace, from which more prisoners were to be taken, there raised above the citizens surrounding him, he spoke to the people. [...] he made such a scene that he stopped the further steps of the people [...]. During the return, partly carried by the people, partly in a carriage pulled by the citizens, he was led home amid shouts and various examples of endearment, and the returning calmed down people brought down the gallows which were not occupied. The bodies of the hanged were taken down, they were buried in cemeteries". We also find a similar opinion in Kiliński's *Second Memoir*: "immediately after our [that is, Kiliński's and Zakrzewski's] persuasion, this hanging stopped, which cost us a lot of our health, because we became hoarse from talking a great deal". This is not true - from Wierzbowa the populace went to another place with the goal of hanging further. It also took attorney Michał Wulfers and Prince Antoni Czetwertyński, two prisoners taken from the Brühlowski Palace.

Before the hanging beneath the Brühlowski Palace, about an hour, maybe even an hour and a half earlier, somewhere around ten in the morning or a little before ten, armed groups of the populace appeared in the Old Warsaw Market Square. From the Market Square to the intersection of Boleść, Rybaki, and Mostowa Streets, that is to the Gunpowder Depot on the Vistula River - then also known as the Gunpowder Tower – a slow walk takes eight, no more than ten minutes. I checked this out by taking such a walk. Ten minutes is not long, but the populace could have, by giving up this unnecessary walk, found someone suitable to hang - even many who would be suitable - much closer. It was enough to go down to the basements of the City Hall, in front of which stood three gallows, and to choose from among the prisoners held there. This would take not sixteen or twenty minutes (back and forth from the Market Square to Mostowa), but a few. Why, in search of victims, they went to the corner of Mostowa and Rybaki cannot be sensibly explained. "The angry mob - wrote Jan Duklan Ochocki in his *Memoirs* - bringing to fruition its earlier threats, broke into the Gunpowder Depot, where some of the accused were kept, captured the prison and led the unfortunate ones out". From this sentence one could conclude that arms were used at the Gunpowder Depot (or in it) - if "the mob [...] captured the prison", then it might have clashed with the guards from the marshal's police defending the prisoners. More details about this event - if anything like this happened there at all - are however unknown. The prison in the Gunpowder Depot was considered extremely severe. Whoever ended up on Rybaki was treated as a criminal, and there, criminals were kept in basements, damp and smelly ones - anyway, the whole neighborhood smelled, because Boleść Street ended (we've already talked about this) with a wooden pier going down to the Vistula, from which waste was poured into the river, brought by waste wagons from Warsaw cesspits. When, in mid-May, delegates appointed by the Prisoner Supervision Department appeared at Rybaki to inspect the conditions in the prison, they saw terrible things there. Presenting the state in which they found those arrested in the Gunpowder Depot, they later wrote in their report: "We saw some beating their heads against walls, others crawling on the ground, others calling out for justice with a terrifying voice and crying".

It can be assumed that on June 28, when the populace conquered the Gunpowder Depot, similar scenes were taking place there - that is, crawling on the ground and hitting one's head against a wall. Three or four prisoners were led out of the Gunpowder Depot - Karol Boscamp, Marceli Piętka, Mateusz Roguski as well as, probably, Stefan Grabowski. As for the latter, the matter is not clear, because there are reports that could suggest that he was not imprisoned at Mostowa Street, but in some other place - so he could have been taken with, a little later, by those who were at the Brühl Palace and took Czetwertyński and Wulfers from there. The road of Boscamp, Piętka, and Roguski (and possibly Grabowski) from Mostowa Street to the Market Square is unknown, as none of the accounts mention this walk to the gallows. Though it can be assumed that it must have been something of a great and cheerful, also noisy, even screaming procession - with standards, the beating of drums, with cries of drunk men, the sobbing of women, and the crying of babies; something like those Paris parades in which the French commoners carried in the streets the heads of the victims of the Reign of Terror stuck on pikes. One such procession was described by Chateaubriand in *Mémoires d'Outre-Tombe* (*Memoirs from Beyond the Grave*). "Nous entendons crier: 'Fermez les portes! fermez les portes!'

Un groupe de déguenillés arrive par un des bouts de la rue; du milieu de ce groupe s'élevaient deux étendards que nous ne voyions pas bien de loin. Lorsqu'ils s'avancèrent, nous distinguâmes deux têtes échevelées et défigurées, que les devanciers de Marat portaient chacune au bout d'une pique; s'étaient les têtes de MM. Foulon et Berthier. Tout le monde se retira des fenêtres; j'y restai. Les assasins s'arrêtèrent devant moi, me tendirent les piques en chantant, en faisant des gambades, en sautant pour approcher de mon visage les pâles effigies. L'oeil d'une de ces têtes, sorti de son orbite, descendait sur le visage obscur du mort; la pique traversait la bouche ouverte dont le dents mordaient le fer: 'Brigands!' m'écriai-je, plein d'une indignation que je ne pus contenir, 'est-ce comme cela que vous entendez la liberté?'"[1]

That which was happening near the Gunpowder Depot - though there were no decapitated heads or eyes gouged out - might have looked a little similar. As we do not know anything about the march through Mostowa and Nowomiejska - or another way, through Brzozowa and Kamienne Schodki - due to a lack of testimonies, it would be good to quote one more small fragment from Jan Duklan Ochocki's *Memoirs*, who described groups of the populace walking in the streets of Warsaw in June - it was "a rabble clustered as if in rows under the standards of its guilds, armed with all kinds of weapons, in variegated, festive, and patched clothes, with capon's, goose's, chicken's, duck's feathers, with tufts of horse hair on their caps, to add face and a martial attitude". Guild standards, hats with duck feathers, horsehair tufts, pikes or axes, we can imagine all of this on the streets leading from the Gunpowder Depot to the Market Square. Poor people lived around Freta and Mostowa, so the retinue to the gallows was surely joined by some ragged

---

[1]"We heard shouts: 'Close the doors! Close the doors!'. A group of ruffians appeared at the end of the street; in the center, two banners were raised above it, which from a distance we could not see well. When they were a little closer, we distinguished two disfigured heads with loose hair that these men, Marat's predecessors, carried on pikes; these were the heads of Foulon and Berthier. Everyone backed away from the windows; I stayed in place. The murderers stopped by the window and held out their pikes towards me, singing, bouncing, and jumping, bringing them closer to my face so that I could see the pale images better. An eye, pushed out of the socket, was sliding down the gray face of the deceased; the pike passed through the open mouth and the teeth clenched on the blade: 'Scoundrels!' I cried out in indignation, which I could not control, 'this is what freedom is for you?'".

paupers, cripples jumping on crutches, beggars wearing sacks with holes, local bandits with knives hidden in their shoes, and local prostitutes in torn stockings, drunk, and with shaggy hair. Somewhere along the way, maybe where Nowomiejska meets Podwale - but this is only my guess - the procession probably split up. Chamberlain Grabowski, if he was taken from the Gunpowder Depot at all, could have been led to St. Anne's Church in Bernadine Square (or, if someone prefers, on Wide Krakowskie Przedmieście); instigator Roguski, who was certainly imprisoned in the Gunpowder Depot, could have been taken by those who went to Senatorska Street. Piętka and Boscamp were, undoubtedly, brought to the Market Square. As we know, three gallows stood there. They were probably placed in the same way as on May 9, that is, in the way we see them in Norblin's drawing - that is, along the western front wall of the City Hall. Who of those who were led in the parade to the gallows from the Gunpowder Depot was hanged in front of the City Hall, and who elsewhere cannot be determined, because there is a great mess in the accounts with regards to this matter. If one is to believe what Kiliński wrote in his *Second Memoir*, Boscamp and Piętka were hanged in front of the City Hall, and earlier, sometime before ten o'clock, that is even before the Gunpowder Depot was captured, instigator Majewski was hanged there as well.

"Then they went to the Gunpowder Depot, brought Boskamp and the one called Piętka [...] and these two were hanged in the Market Square". According to the information provided to Dresden by Johann Jakob Patz (in the report of July 2), things transpired completely differently. Writing about the three gallows in the Market Square, Patz claimed that "Boscamp was hanged on one, Chamberlain Grabowski and Instigator Roguski were hanged on the second one, while on the third Instigator Majewski and Piętka". So, we would have five hanged on three gallows. This version seems to be confirmed by the story in *Polish History*, where - when counting the gallows one by one, maybe only those in the Market Square, but not necessarily - Father Kitowicz established this order of those hanged. "On these gallows were hanged: Boskamp, that is Lassopolski [...]; on the second, Grabowski [...]; on the third Piętka, a Muscovite spy [...]. On the fourth Mateusz Rogowski".

Rogowski is, of course, Roguski. Other accounts present this in an even different way. Józef Ignacy Kraszewski, in the third volume of his *Polska w czasie trzech rozbiorów* (*Poland during the Three Partitions*), claimed - on the basis of some testimonies that he possessed - that Grabowski was hanged "in front of the Bernardines", that is, in beneath St. Anne's Church on Wide Krakowskie Przedmieście, and Roguski was hanged "in front of the Reformists", that is, on Senatorska Street. This is of course very likely, as Kraszewski certainly did not make things up, that is, he saw the testimonies on the basis of which he composed his story - he just did not have the habit of quoting or giving exactly what source he was using. It was similar with Bronisław Szwarce, the author of the book *Warszawa w 1794r.* (*Warsaw in 1794*), published in 1894 – he also, while providing various interesting pieces of information, did not worry about informing the reader where he had obtained them. While he did have - as is shown by his story about the money paid out by the Russian embassy to Stanisław August and his people – documents, which later got lost somewhere. Well, Szwarce - talking about the pock-marked Mrs. Grabowska, who was "given to the king by his brother Kazimierz the chamberlain" - maintained, similarly like Kraszewski, that the stepson of the pock-marked lady, Chamberlain Grabowski, was hanged "beneath the Bernardines".

As for Roguski, then - unlike Kraszewski - the author of *Warsaw in 1794* was of the opinion that he was hanged together with Grabowski, that is also on Wide Krakowskie Przedmieście. "In the lawsuits given to Kościuszko he called the Kraków Uprising a revolt against the Fatherland, hated for this, he was hanged in front of the Bernardine church". Now let's look at what was happening in front of the City Hall. It may seem strange, but the accounts are not about those who were hanged, but about those who participated in the hangings or assisted with them. It looks as if the fate of Boscamp, Roguski, Grabowski, and Piętka did not really interest anyone - let them hang there, but we will not look at them. Perhaps this is what the fate of traitors should precisely be. On the other hand, those who were carrying out the hangings, and those who watched, aroused interest, and therefore perhaps not too much, but a little is known about them. Above all, a few names of those who carried out with hangings in the Market Square are known. There were two leaders there - the already mentioned officer cadet of the Royal Foot Guards Józef Piotrowski and the quack Tomasz Stawicki. A quack is the same as a vet; that was also the name used for a person who castrates horses. Piotrowski, also referred to as a loose man, was either expelled from the army for some crimes unknown to us, or released, like many other soldiers, during the great reduction of the Polish army that preceded the insurrection. Aleksander Linowski, Kościuszko's first insurrectionary secretary, later stated in his propaganda pamphlet aimed at Kołłątaj (*List do przyjaciela odkrywający wszystkie czynności Kołłątaja w ciągu Insurekcji* [*A Letter to a Friend Discovering All of Kołłątaj's Activities during the Insurrection*]) that Piotrowski had a suspicious past - "this one had been known for a long time as a miscreant" - but it is not known on what the officer cadet's pre-insurrectionary mischief would be based on. Piotrowski, as I said, probably did not personally participate in the hangings, but rather directed them. Stawicki - who, apart from the fact that he castrated horses, was also a professional thief – did take an active part in the hangings. According to the term used later in the sentence issued by the Supreme Criminal Court, the hangmen were assisted by Jakub Roman, who was in some sense an official person - a setnik in one of Warsaw's districts[2]. Of course, there had to be a few or a dozen or so hangmen, but later those accused of specific acts committed in the Market Square were only these three - Piotrowski, Stawicki, and Roman.

As for the others, those whose names are also known, it is impossible to say whether they personally participated in the hangings or only, assisting the leaders of the hangmen, bustled around the gallows – so perhaps they should not be rashly accused here. Besides, I am not accusing anyone - the purpose of this book is not to accuse, condemn, or induce moral indignation. This book – which can probably be well seen now - does not deal with morality, but with life. Someone might say that with regards to this it is amoral - I would not take this as an accusation, I would only add that it just so happens to be like life and exactly like it. Among those who were then

---

[2] Setnik: A government or military official in charge of 100 people.

bustling around the gallows in the Market Square (and maybe participated in the hangings, but maybe not), there were also: the later famous philosopher and logician, Kalasanty Szaniawski, as well as the known lexicographer - but in this case to say known is not enough it must be said: the great and famous lexicographer - the author of the fundamental dictionary of the Polish language, Samuel Linde. Linde's dictionary serves us to today - even if its author took part in the hangings, it is good that he was not hanged for it, because it allowed him to later successfully carry out his memorable work. There were also two priests there, Józef Meier as well as Florian Jelski. As for Father Józef Meier, it was later claimed that he was near the gallows with a stole around his neck and a pistol in his hand; maybe (according to some accounts) even with two pistols and a saber. This could indicate that Meier took on the duties of confessor on June 28, but it does not seem - at least no account says anything about this - that any of the prisoners of the Gunpowder Depot, Piętka, or Roguski, or Boskamp (they were certainly unbelievers, maybe even Voltaireans), confessed before being hanged. It is true, however, that Father Meier had his printing house and the office of his paper exactly *vis-à-vis* the City Hall (and therefore also *vis-à-vis* the gallows). They were located, the printing house and office, in the tenement house of the record holder Rogalski at number 43 - then it was (and now is) the fourth apartment house from Zapiecek; I am talking about the western frontage of the Market Square, that is, the side that is now called Kołłątaj's side. Even before the insurrection, in January 1794, Father Meier printed and sold his *Dziennik Uniwersalny* (*The Universal Journal*) there, while later, during the insurrection, he had his apartment in this place, the apartment house of the record holder Rogalski.

On June 28, when the hangings began, Father Meier stood in the window of his apartment (or in the window of the office) and applauded - as the condemned was being pulled up. He was later interrogated in this matter, even imprisoned, but the fact that "he applauded and clapped" (as the testimony of witnesses said) proved insufficient for conviction - and he was released. This is all we know for sure, the saber, stole, and pistols, while probable, seem a bit questionable to me. The other priest, Florian Jelski, also probably did not take part in the hangings - that is, he did not personally participate in the hangings and only watched, perhaps because what was happening was interesting. Jelski was also interrogated, and it was then discovered that during the hangings (it seems that when instigator Józef Majewski was being hanged) he lost his nerves - he could not stand it and started to cry. This Jesuit sobbing (Father Jelski was, before the dissolution of the order, a novitiate with the Jesuits) was not liked by someone who was there (maybe the philosopher Szaniawski or the lexicographer Linde did not like it), and that someone, Szaniawski or Linde, approached Jelski, looked at him sternly and asked, but not only did he ask, he even shouted: - What is this! Being a patriot, you are crying? - Then Father Jelski, who was a patriot, got scared that he would be punished (by the gallows) - and stopped crying. Apart from those who were brought from the Gunpowder Depot, two (Boskamp and Piętka) or four (also Grabowski and Roguski), another fifth person was hanged in front of the City Hall, the very instigator over whose fate, when he was being hanged, Father Jelski cried. As I said, on June 28 there may have been more who were hanged somewhat by chance, only because they were near the gallows and were not liked by the hangmen. However, only one such case is known - and that case is precisely about Majewski. When the hangings were underway (or when they were just beginning), he was walking from the Raczyński Palace, where the Supreme National Council had its headquarters, to the City Hall in the Market Square. In other words, he was walking from the intersection of Długa Street with a small street, which at that time had no name, but is now called Kiliński Street - he was walking along this street and then turned, as he could not turn otherwise, onto Podwale and then onto Dunaj. Or perhaps he was walking somewhat at an angle, along a shorter path, between the houses and the walls of the Old Town, through that part of Dunaj which is now called Wide Dunaj.

At the City Hall, the prosecutor was probably supposed to take care of something - give some papers, which the Supreme National Council decided to give to the municipal authorities. The content of these papers is unknown. Kiliński, in the *Second Memoir*, maintained that Majewski was carrying a resolution of the Supreme Council to the magistrate, the resolution contained a response to a note calling on the authorities to quickly sentence the traitors. "The Council responded to the note it received, persuading the people to wait three more days until permission would come from Kościuszko". The fact that there was just such a resolution in the documents carried by Majewski seems unlikely, however. In the Market Square, where the hangings were taking place, the hangmen, according to Kiliński, asked the instigator to let them read the resolution, but he, "stupid, not only did he not let them read it, but also, holding it in his hands, tore the resolution into small pieces". It was for this "audacity" that he was immediately hanged "on a peasant's whip" and "in the very Market Square". Another version of Majewski's hanging - or rather: a different and more probable version concerning the contents of the papers carried by the instigator - can be found in *Polish History* by Father Kitowicz. He mainly claimed that Majewski did not want to hand over to the people "the papers he was carrying under his arm (these were a registry of those incarcerated)". It was also precisely because this was a prisoner registry, which could be the basis for further hangings, that the instigator was "grabbed and hanged as though he was a friend of the culprits". It is not ruled out that Majewski exposed himself to the hangmen due to something else - not so much that he did not want to release the papers he was carrying under his arm and he audaciously tore them, and even ate or at least tried to eat (because something like this was also claimed), but because he did not like the hangings, and when he saw the gallows standing in front of the City Hall, he expressed his indignation. Perhaps even, having left Dunaj onto the Market Square, when Piętka was precisely on his way up, the instigator tried to interrupt the hangmen - and that is precisely why he was hanged next to Piętka. The fact that Majewski protested was mentioned in a letter of July 2 - it is a pity that in only one short sentence — by Johann Jakob Patz: "he was not even arrested but tried to protest against these atrocities and with this he outraged the people". General Józef Zajączek probably also had Majewski in mind while reporting on the June events in his *Memoir or the History of the Revolution* - he wrote (without mentioning the surname) that "one of the court officials, preventing the people from entering the prison and using insulting words, also fell to the same fate as the culprits".

Zajączek - or his informants - could have of course made a mistake, but it could also be so, that the instigator, having left the Raczyński Palace on Długa Street and finding out that the populace was fighting with the marshal's police beneath the Gunpowder Depot, went there and seeing what was happening, used "insulting words" - for which he was hanged, and so that the shame would be greater, next to the spy Piętka. These are, of course, only guesses. Majewski's case is connected with a somewhat unclear case of a little drummer who appeared in front of the City Hall while the hangings were taking place. It is not known where he came from, for what purpose he came, and who he was. Perhaps this was a drummer from one of the Warsaw regiments, well-uniformed, even in a uniform triangular hat, or perhaps a Warsaw rascal, a little tatterdemalion, a thief from Piwna or Dunaj, who had through thievery acquired a military drum. The little drummer - seeing that hangings were being done; and Majewski was being hanged just then - wanted to escape, but he was grabbed by the collar and ordered to drum. He was probably drumming miserably - maybe he lost the drumming rhythm because of fear - because the one who was hanging the instigator, Tomasz Stawicki, a specialist in horse castration, interrupted his work, grabbed the little drummer's drum, broke a stick or a cane in two, and started drumming himself, singing a song, a thief's or a drinking song. The words of the quack's gallows song were not remembered, or perhaps they were just not articulated clearly enough. From Father Franciszek Ksawery Dmochowski's *Gazeta Rządowa* (*Government Gazette*), which mentioned this scene, only four or really two words of the song are known: "Onward, faithful! Onward! Onward!". Władysław Smoleński, when talking about Stawicki in his *Kuźnica Kołłątajowska* (*Kołłątaj's Forge*; a book from 1885), expressed his belief that the thief-quack "encouraged murder" with this song, but I would be careful with drawing such (it can be said rational, and therefore even somewhat justified) conclusions. This wild, inarticulate song from the Warsaw gallows, a song accompanied by the beating of a drum – this was rather something completely irrational, something in which the irrational reveals itself and lets one know about its existence.

The meaning of such an ecstatic song - whether it encourages murder or something else, and whether it encourages something at all - cannot be understood and verbalized. One can only say that in such ecstatic songs, songs of ecstasy, in such a beating of the drum and the screams accompanying it, that which is irrational and incomprehensible is precisely heard - the voice of life coming out of its deepest depth, the voice of this monstrosity that hides in the depths of life; the voice of that foreignness, the voice of that stranger who is somewhere out there; that monstrosity from which life springs, which is at its beginning and which is - life.

Those who took the lawyer Wulfers and Prince Czetwertyński from the Brühlowski Palace (perhaps also Chamberlain Grabowski) split, as one can assume, on Krakowskie Przedmieście, probably somewhere near the opening of Trębacka Street. Wulfers (perhaps with Grabowski) were led to the Bernardine Church, Czetwertyński had a much longer journey to travel - his gallows stood behind the Dominican Observant Church, almost at the intersection of Nowy Świat and Świętokrzyska Streets. There was of course no logic, no order, no sense, and also no rational intention in this movement of the populace - those going north and those going south, those towards the Bernardines, and those towards the Dominicans. As it is with human things. It also cannot be explained sensibly - for there was no sense in this at all - why the gallows for Wulfers was erected precisely outside the Bernardine Church, and not elsewhere. It could have been the other way around after all - Wulfers could have been hanged in Czetwertyński's place, and Czetwertyński in Wulfers' place. This would also not have any meaning - and could not be explained. The information of what happened at the Bernardine Church is very sparse. It is not even known why it was Wulfers who was taken from the Brühlowski Palace, as there is no indication that the Warsaw populace felt a particular aversion towards him. Johann Jakob Patz claimed (in a letter to Dresden of April 21) that Wulfers was arrested because "without the [Supreme National] Council's knowledge, he held night meetings with some prisoners of the state". Among these prisoners, Mateusz Roguski was mentioned - the one who was hanged either on the Market Square or on Senatorska Street opposite the Reformists - a figure that was ultimately not very important and did not play any political role.

The lawyer was to visit (although it was forbidden) Roguski, as well as Boscamp, in the Gunpowder Depot and enter there with these two, as Father Kitowicz described it in *Polish History*, into a "secret agreement". Wulfers was also accused, although it is not known how justified it was - but this particular accusation could have provoked the anger of the populace - that, having access to the papers from Igelström's archive (as a councilor in the Provisional Council), he removed everything that was incriminating to Stanisław August from them. That is, all these (as we would say today) receipts on the basis of which the king could be condemned to death and hanged. It seems that several of those who had previously hanged Bishop Massalski at the Brühl Palace were involved in the hanging of Wulfers. The main role at the Bernardine Church was played not by the herdsman Stefan Klonowski, who went with Prince Czetwertyński towards the Dominican Observants, not even by the officer cadet Piotrowski, who also appeared there, but by the bricklayer Lorenc Burzyński. Burzyński made some money on this hanging, because when Wulfers was already hanging, he took the cloak off of the hanged man and quickly sold it to someone right next to the church. As for the cloak, it is not certain whether it was a cloak - it was also written later that the bricklayer took an undefined coat from Wulfers. Burzyński reportedly received a few złotys for his cloak or coat, but the details of the transaction (how many złotys) are unknown. A cloak or a coat, the bricklayer Burzyński, this is almost everything that is remembered from the hanging on Wide Krakowskie Przedmieście. It can also be added that the gallows at the Bernardines stood a bit uncertainly or a little crookedly and Wulfers - as Father Kitowicz wrote - was hanged by the populace "on a gallows badly dug in, wobbling, therefore supported by pikes and sabers". There was no rope, so the noose was twisted together from strings.

The last of those hanged that day - the last one in my story, but that does not mean the last one in chronological order; such an order cannot be established in any way, there is no such possibility – so the last of those hanged, Prince Antoni Czetwertyński, was brought to the Branicki Palace on Nowy Świat. Father Kitowicz later claimed in *Polish History* that Czetwertyński was imprisoned precisely in the Branicki Palace ("but half of this gang, having gone to the Branicki Palace, kidnapped and dragged Prince Czetwertyński, the castellan, onto the street"), but he was certainly wrong - first, from several other testimonies it turns out that Czetwertyński (who, by the way, himself reported to prison; as Wyssogota Zakrzewski wrote to Kościuszko on May 4, "today he voluntarily put himself into custody") was kept in the Brühl Palace; secondly, there is no indication that anyone was imprisoned in the Branicki Palace at the time, as it was, after the battle at the junction of Nowy Świat and Krakowskie Przedmieście on April 17, almost completely ruined. The gallows at the Branicki Palace was - of all the gallows in Warsaw, which were erected on the night of June 27-28 - the farthest placed south. It can therefore be said that it was there, at the junction of Krakowskie Przedmieście and Nowy Świat, and close to the opening of Świętokrzyska Street to Nowy Świat, that the southern border of the gallows ran. Southern Warsaw did not hang anyone - maybe because it was much less populated, or maybe because it was elite; inhabited mainly by people who we would now count among the salon elite. Czetwertyński was hung directly *vis-à-vis* the windows of the Library of the Institute of Literary Research (also an elite place), that is, to put it a bit differently, *vis-à-vis* the Dominican Observant Church which was standing in this place at that time. On June 28, around noon, the shoemaker Kiliński was sitting there - that is, not in the church, but in the tavern of the Dominican Observants next to the church - and drinking vodka. As we remember, Kiliński (according to his own story) appeared a little earlier, together with Wyssogota Zakrzewski, at the Brühl Palace. So it seems that the leader of the people of Warsaw - like those who did the hangings – was moving from place to place at the time; maybe he changed taverns, wanting to see all the executions up close. As Antoni Trębicki said in his memoir *On the Revolution of 1794*, it was then as Kiliński was feasting in the Observants' tavern, that a deputation of the Supreme National Council came to him (that is, it sought him out in that tavern) with a request that he try to stop the hangings - "so that he would calm the people". Kiliński looked at the deputies of the Council, then at the gallows on which Prince Czetwertyński was hanging (maybe he was already hanging), staggered on his stool and declared that he could do nothing, because he does not mean anything in Warsaw anymore.

"Tell the Council that as befits a shoemaker - I am drinking". The hanging prince, when Kiliński looked at him, was half-naked, because his clothes had been torn off during the hanging. As there are several accounts of the hanging of Prince Czetwertyński, even small details of this event are known quite precisely. Those that took part were (these three surnames were remembered, but there were certainly many taking part) Jędrzej Dziekoński, who was a chicken farmer by profession, i.e. a poultry breeder and seller, Dominik Jasiński, who was a hay trader, and the already known to us Stefan Klonowski, a herdsman or laborer. A person who traded hay was called a sianiarz (hayer) or szeniarz (strawer). Dziekoński kept his hens in a henhouse, which was located near these gallows, somewhere near the Holy Cross Church - and there, beneath the Holy Cross, he had his poultry stall. Father Kitowicz's story says that Prince Czetwertyński, when the noose was being put on him, "went humbly, fell down at his executioners' feet", but this obviously did not help - "he barely managed to have them give him a few minutes to confess to a Dominican who came quickly". During the hangings, according to the documents of the Investigation Department, there was a certain controversy, maybe even a quarrel between the hangmen - it was probably caused by the fact that the rope turned out to be too short and it had to be lengthened. It also seemed to be about priority in hanging, that is, who was to do the hanging and who was to help. The chicken farmer Dziekoński, standing on the ladder, was to snatch the rope from the szeniarz Jasiński (also standing on the ladder), shouting at the same time: "Run off, I will hang him myself". Jasiński, however (as he himself insisted later), did not want to lengthen the rope and was forced to do so, not by Dziekoński, but by some people he did not know, as he put it nicely, by "unknown people" who threatened to slash him with sabers. Generalizing the words of the szeniarz a little, it can be said that everything that happened on June 28 was done by "unknown people" - one could even say that on that very day it showed, this people, that they were "unknown".

As for this row on the ladders (resting on the gallows), its real and most important cause may have been (and probably was) not so much the length of the rope, but the dispute over who will take what and what is owed to whom. It seems that they began to undress Prince Czetwertyński before he was hanged, and the activity was completed when it was over. Ultimately, it ended on chicken farmer Dziekoński taking the vest and trousers of the hanged prince, herdsman Klonowski came into possession of his underwear, and szeniarz Jasiński his banyan[3]. Once again, I draw attention to the extraordinary role that banyans played in the events I am talking about. Czetwertyński's banyan, Hetman Kossakowski's banyan (the yellow nankeen banyan, the one in which he was transported to the Vilnius gallows), the fur-lined banyan in which his brother the bishop was arrested, and finally the banyan in which General Ożarowski was hanged. Let us add to this the banyan in which the king showed himself in the Castle to his guests (delegations of the people of Warsaw), as well as Tadeusz Kościuszko's banyan, a Chinese banyan, and in addition mysteriously stolen - it will still be discussed (a little later). It seems that no other garment was talked about as often at the time as banyans. I do not know how to explain this intense presence of banyans (their intense existence at that time, even their over existence). Maybe banyans were then considered something impossible to do without, and that is why they attracted such attention. Or maybe it was that every better-off man (one who belonged to the elite from the south - from the villas in Mokotów and Ujazdów) had a banyan, and therefore banyans were the subject of a great, even wild desire of those who did not have them, the poor from the Old Town district - and that is precisely why so much was said about them, especially Chinese banyans, the most beautiful ones; special attention was especially paid to the nankeen ones and those lined with lambskin. Though I now return to Prince Czetwertyński, though only for a moment. When he was

---

[3] A robe or coat

hanged and undressed, something extraordinary happened. It turned out that the szeniarz Jasiński, chicken farmer Dziekoński, herdsman Klonowski, and other hangmen were convinced that they were hanging someone else - not Prince Czetwertyński, whom they might not have wanted to hang at all, but a Milanese troublemaker, the owner of Królikarnia in Mokotów, a card shark and a pimp who appeared in Poland under the name of Tomatis.

The procuring of Count Tomatis' (title bought, of course) were not just of any kind, on the street or in a brothel - he was the king's procurer, serving the king (even with his wife). This mistake - fatal for Czetwertyński, but certainly very fortunate for Tomatis - could not be corrected, because when it was realized, Czetwertyński-Tomatis or Tomatis-Czetwertyński was already hanging. This is mentioned in Antoni Trębicki's memoir. He said that the hangmen, having done what they wanted to do, were jumping around the gallows on which the prince was hanging, while jumping they were shouting - "Vivat the Italian Tomatis!". Someone (from Trębicki's memoir it appears that it was not someone who was taking part in the hanging, but someone who was walking along the street), however, realized that something was not right, and pointed out to those jumping that Prince Czetwertyński was hanging on the gallows, not the Italian Tomatis. This did not stop the jumping at all, "even better", was replied to the one who corrected the mistake, and "the shouts continued" - except that they shouted out: "Vivat Czetwertyński!" "The people were jumping around the gallows shouting". It is worth stopping at this jumping people. If this jumping is recognized as a kind of dance, we would have here probably the only evidence that in May and June, around the Warsaw gallows, maybe a bit ineptly, people danced or at least attempted to dance. The problem - whether there was dancing - also concerned French scholars, who wanted to know if their people danced around scaffolds on which people were decapitated during the Reign of Terror. I am not an expert on this subject, but I did manage to find that there are several accounts, three or four, which may suggest that something like this happened - and the people of Paris, indeed, danced around the guillotine. This happened at least once, on January 21, 1793 (i.e. *le 1er Pluviôse, An 1er de la République* [*the 1ˢᵗ of Pluviôse, 1ˢᵗ year of the Republic*]), when the French king, Louis XVI, was beheaded on the Place de la Révolution. This execution delighted (and also stunned - because a divine king was killed) numerous spectators. Its description, in the work *Le Magicien Républicain* (*The Republican Magician*), published in 1794 (its author was called *Rouy l'aîné*), contains the following sentence: „Les citoyens chantèrent des hymnes à la liberté en formant des ronds de danse autour du l'échafaud et sur toute la Place de la Révolution".

"Citizens sang hymns to freedom, also creating dance circles around the scaffold and on the entirety of Revolution Square". These French dances around the scaffold were certainly light and graceful jumps, somebody could have even been playing for the dance circles on a small flute called a *flûte à bec*, our jumping, as I say, must have been a bit inept - it was probably, as it is with the peoples of the north and the north-east, some kind of bear or wolf jumping. *Hymnes à la liberté* - some wolf howling. Though we danced, as I proved - and he who claims that in this way we were imitating the French is a fool. The jumping people, about whom Trębicki wrote about, probably did not even know, may not have known that there is a France and some French people dancing gracefully "sur toute la Place de la Révolution".

This is more or less all I can say about the events that took place in Warsaw on June 28. As can be seen, a few questions arise here for which there is no good answer, or even an answer at all. Why did the populace that broke into the Brühl Palace only pull out from there Bishop Massalski, Bishop Skarszewski, Prince Czetwertyński, Count Moszyński and the lawyer Wulfers, and only them, and did not take interest (it seems that they did not even show the slightest interest) in other Russian agents imprisoned in the palace? The same question applies to other prisons and other inmates. More than a month earlier, *The Free Warsaw Gazette* (in addition to Issue 8 of May 20) presented in such a way the manner in which detainees were distributed in Warsaw prisons, who were then called prisoners of the state - that is, those who were accused of crimes of a political nature (everything indicates are that the place of imprisonment was not decided by the Investigation Department, nor by the Prisoner Supervision Department, or the Security Department of the Supreme National Council - decisions in this matter were personally made by the President of Warsaw Wyssogota Zakrzewski). "Number of state detainees. In the Krasiński Palace of the Republic, persons 3. In the Brühlowski, 11. In the Gunpowder Depot, 37. In the City Hall of the C[ity] of O[ld] W[arsaw], 83. In the Post-Jesuit Schools, 1. In the Marszałkowska Guardhouse, 7. In the monastery of the Reformist Fr. 2. At the Carmelites, 1. At the Dominicans 1. In the Cekauz, 5. Summa of heads 151".

As one can see, out of the eleven prisoners who were in the Brühlowski Palace, only five were hanged or it was attempted to hang them (or six, if we add the miraculously rescued card shark Tomatis), but even more interesting here is the matter of the Old Warsaw City Hall, into which - although three gallows stood before it - the populace (as everything indicates) did not try to get in at all. It was similar with the Krasiński Palace, which was not captured, although two gallows had previously been erected in front of it, as well as with the Reformist Monastery, which was also bypassed, although there was also a gallows in front of it, probably on the other side of Senatorska Street. It seems to me that we are dealing here with the strongest argument in favor of the thesis (otherwise completely impossible to prove) that the hangings were directed by someone - at least in its initial phase - and that this person, acting in a deliberate manner, pointed out to the hangmen the prisons they were to go to as well as the people they were to bring out. Was this Hugo Kołłątaj's secretary, Kazimierz Konopka? Or the secretary of Ignacy Potocki, Jan Dembowski? Or Father Józef Meier? Or officer cadet Józef Piotrowski? Perhaps someone else, someone, about whom we know nothing - for his existence, along with his surname, have been concealed by history, although it is not known for what purpose. There is also the question about the fate of the Russian officers imprisoned on April 17 and 18 (and then kept mainly in the Krasiński Palace, but also in the Arsenal, i.e. the Cekauz, as well as in the basements of the City Hall) - at least the fate of one of them, namely Brigadier Karl Baur, head of the Russian military police and Russian intelligence in Russian-occupied Warsaw. This Baur, of Swedish nationality, also of Swedish beauty, was especially hated by the populace of Warsaw, and at the same time his appearance was very well known, because he had a habit of personally carrying out arrests. Thus, on the way to arrest someone, he would often appear on the streets of the city in the company of his Polish and Russian entourage. So on June 28 he was, if one can put it in this way, easy to hang for two reasons - firstly, he was easy to recognize, and because of his Swedish beauty, one couldn't make a mistake about if it is him or not; secondly, he was very close by, because he was held, wounded and beaten (as the Prussian envoy Ludwig Buchholtz stated in one of his reports), in the City Hall, in one of its basements.

So why did Stawicki, Linde, or Szaniawski (each of them would certainly be happy to do this, and the public would not spare applause and cheers of encouragement) not pull out Baur from the basement and hang him on one of the three gallows that were standing in front of the City Hall? A beautiful Swede, a favorite of the Warsaw ladies (maybe that's why he showed up in the city on horseback, so that our ladies could admire him), he would certainly look great there in the white parade uniform of an officer of the Akhtyrsky Chevau-léger Regiment - right next to his subordinate, ragged prisoner, Marceli Piętka. Someone may accuse me (in connection with this uniform) of being an esthete - but it's hard not to notice that hanging, like every human activity, also has its esthetic side. The sparing of Baur, even explicit omission of him, could also be an argument for the thesis that there was someone in the crowd of hangmen who supervised the hangings - he said who to take and who to leave. The fact that the hangmen did not enter the City Hall and search the basements where the Russian officers were kept, could, moreover, indicate that this someone (an unknown leader of the hangmen) was acting on the orders of some authorities, was following someone's clear and firm orders - do not touch the Muscovites! - maybe orders from military authorities, maybe civil authorities, maybe Kościuszko, maybe Kołłątaj, maybe Potocki, or maybe someone else. We will of course never find this out. The great Warsaw hangings ended at three in the afternoon. We know this hour thanks to Antoni Trębicki, because it was he (as far as I know he was the only one) who noticed and remembered at what time a great storm broke out over Warsaw and a terrible rain poured down - washing away everything that happened, the gallows and those who hanged on them, and those who hanged those who were hanging, and those who indicated those who should be hanged. "Suddenly around three o'clock - wrote Trębicki - it grew gloomy and the most beautiful day turned into a storm the likes of which I have never encountered". Where the storm came from - from Marymont or Ujazdów, or from another direction – it is not known, as no source (from that era) clearly specifies this. This was however, and this is worth considering, the third great historical storm of this epoch.

The first one broke out over Warsaw two or three hours after the adoption of the May 3rd Constitution, the second one a year later, on the first anniversary of this event, when the king and the primate blessed the cornerstone beneath the Temple of Providence in Łazienki. In both of these May storms, the one in 1791 and the one in 1792, sinister and ominous signs were seen (which is easy to understand) - they told Poles that a catastrophe is approaching. If, on the other hand, to the two historical May storms we add a third one, also a historical one, the one in June, it could even be concluded (although somehow no one came up with such an idea - at least I did not come across anything like that during my reading) that the great historical events had at that time something in common with great atmospheric events, these and those were falling in a common order - and maybe, in this common order, they somehow intertwined, and even conditioned each other, atmospheric events triggered historical events or, conversely, historical events were an obscure (secret) reason for atmospheric events. "A torrential rain - Trębicki continued – began to pour, which turned into a downpour so powerful that it seemed that it would flood the streets. It was accompanied by thunder, thunderbolts, and lightning, which increased the horribleness of this extraordinary storm". In Trębicki's opinion, it was precisely this terrible storm (and not the pacification speeches of Wyssogota Zakrzewski, i.e. "the voice of reason") that prevented further executions, because "it forced the people to disperse and look for shelter wherever they could". So maybe the head of Russian intelligence, the contemporary Warsaw Smersh, a beautiful white-haired Swede in a white *bicorne* hat and the white uniform of an Akhtyrsky hussar with golden epaulettes (the angelic beauty of an albino, at least this is how I imagine it), would have hung in front of the City Hall on the Market Square - had it not been for this storm, which saved his life. The belief that it was the storm that interrupted the hangings, which under different circumstances would otherwise probably have continued, seems to have been widespread at the time. "Then followed - wrote Józef Krasiński in his *Pamiętniki* (*Memoirs*; he was then a teenage boy) - the hanging of the victims sentenced to death. The execution was interrupted by a storm with lightning bolts from which the terrified people fled. God only knows how many innocent people could have lost their lives". It was even believed - such an opinion is found in the letter sent to Dresden on June 28 by Johann Jakob Patz - that when the storm passed, the populace would return to the streets and the hanging would begin anew.

"The storm which unexpectedly arrived dispersed the crowd, but we fear that there will be more unfortunate victims". There were no further victims, because when the populace dispersed and hid somewhere (probably in the gates on Krakowskie Przedmieście - we see how the more courageous ones, between two lightning bolts, jump out on the road for a moment and raise their wet heads - or somewhere in the south or in the north a patch of blue can already be seen), so when the populace disappeared from the streets, Major-General Jan August Cichocki (a man of Stanisław August's, commander of the Warsaw garrison before the outbreak of the insurrection), taking advantage of the cover of the heavy rain, set up cannons on Krakowskie Przedmieście, Miodowa, and Senatorska, and about half an hour, maybe an hour later, the 2nd Małopolska National Cavalry Brigade, commanded by Brigadier Piotr Jaźwiński, sent from Kościuszko's camp near Gołków, reached the city. Jaźwiński's squadrons, which appeared, as Trębicki wrote, "with the end of the downpour", began to disperse those who were still on the streets - "they dispersed the insolent ones with pennants, chased the stubborn ones to shackles and prisons". The report by Johann Jakob Patz sent to Dresden (a bit unclear in this spot) says that probably a bit later, but

still on the same day, Kościuszko's infantry entered the city
from the direction of Mokotów and surrounded the prisons.
"General Kościuszko sent several infantry regiments here [...].
An infantry company with 2 cannons and 3 squadrons of the
national cavalry were sent to the Saxon Palace to guard the
Brühl Palace against a possible attack on the state prisoners
by the people. The remaining national troops took up position
near the prison in the Gunpowder Depot". As can be concluded
from this, it was most probably feared that the riots would
have some continuation. This is how June 28 ended. Behind
Major-General Cichocki's batteries, behind a curtain of rain,
in the post-storm half-darkness, half-light, we can only see,
somewhere far away on Wide Krakowskie Przedmieście, a few
hundred meters from us, maybe on the corner of Bednarska,
maybe at Trębacka Street, officer cadet Józef Piotrowski
prancing on his horse - in a red Foot Guard jacket, and in a
triangular hat of the same red color, on a black horse, with his
arm raised, and in his hand he has a torn up black scarf - the
one he was tearing into shreds beneath the gallows and giving
the shreds, as a sign of brotherhood, to those who were doing
the hanging.

Chapter 28.
THE POPULACE

Królewska Street horse market (Jan Norblin)

The anonymous crowd that went onto the streets of Warsaw on April 17 and 18 to fight Igelström's troops (the Polish regiments would not have won this battle, the participation of the crowd was decisive), and then, when the insurrection was victorious, did not disappear from the streets and demanded some kind of continuation, above all, to punish the traitors, and when it was not heard out, it decided, without delay, to punish them and erected gallows - this crowd was called (trying in this way to recognize it) various things: people, commune, nation, and also rabble, band, as well as mob. Most often it was called the populace, sometimes with an epithet attached to it that would limit its meaning or at least explain its (obvious at first glance) ambiguity. This word, present in the Polish language since the early Middle Ages, made an extraordinary career in 1794. It can be assumed that this career began a little earlier, but its effects appeared precisely in 1794, right after the outbreak of the insurrection. It was that this, that which was happening in Warsaw – above all in Warsaw, and probably only in Warsaw, because, for example, this completely did not apply to Kraków - so what was happening in Warsaw at that time could not be described at all without the use of this word, and therefore it could not be well understand without it.

We are in a somewhat similar situation as the people of that epoch - to understand what happened then, what the insurrection was, we need to know who carried it out. It was, of course, carried out by politicians and soldiers - Kołłątaj, Potocki, Kościuszko, Zajączek, Jasiński, Madaliński. Though they would not have carried it out without the populace - if they had not used it, and if it had not used them. The populace (pospólstwo) - what is this? I will start with what I learned from a very good entry in Andrzej Bańkowski's *Etymologiczny słownik języka polskiego* (*Etymological Dictionary of the Polish Language*; published in 2000). As Bańkowski asserts, between the 14th and 15th centuries the word had a legal meaning and meant a community property. It was also used to translate certain phrases in religious texts – it was talked about the Communion of Saints (pospólstwo świętych; *communio sanctorum*), the populace could also mean the church (*ecclesia*). Later, between the 15th and 18th centuries, the meaning changed - the definition given by Bańkowski says that populace then began to mean "the community, society, the general population of a city, country", and because this general population was "with time more clearly" contrasted against authority and the elite, populace gained an additional meaning - "communes, plebs, rabble". In other words (Bańkowski does not say this), it meant the whole society, but also its slightly worse part, one that either has some worse attributes or is in a worse situation. I will return to Bańkowski's entry, now let's see what was happening with the populace around 1794 - how it was attempted to explain, in various ways, the vague meaning of this word. Since everyone who spoke at the time had something to say about the populace (simply because the populace was impossible to ignore - it was in large numbers, right alongside, on the streets), the examples could be endless. I tried to choose those that clearly show the situation of the populace at that time - in society and in history. According to Karol Wojda, the author of the book *O rewolucji polskiej w roku 1794* (*On the Polish Revolution in 1794*), the inhabitants of the city were divided into two parts - the populace and the citizens. The populace "was especially active during the attack on Igelström's Palace. It was not the citizens of Warsaw who did this, because they closed themselves in their homes for both days [...]. The groups of the fighting people consisted of craftsmen, their journeymen, servants, caretakers, farm hands, and Jews".

Wojda also wrote that "the populace turned out to be the most active there, where there was something to rob". We have a comparison which is a bit similar, but also a bit different, in Aleksander Linowski's pamphlet (written in 1795), *List do przyjaciela odkrywający wszystkie czynności Kołłątaja w ciągu Insurekcji* (*A Letter to a Friend Discovering All of Kołłątaj's Activities during the Insurrection*). Wojda contrasted the populace against the citizens, Linowski against the people - in both cases the populace was something worse. Kołłątaj, in Linowski's opinion, after the defeat at Maciejowice "strove to [...] seize all the authority in the nation, to surround himself not with the people, but with the populace, only in this way to supposedly save the Fatherland". Linowski went on to explain that "the people and the populace are not one, because the former is the general population, while the latter, if incorrectly called the people, will become the assaulter and illegitimate usurper of the sacred laws of the nation". Linowski therefore identified (probably) the people with the nation, and he refused the populace the right to be a nation. Ludwik Cieszkowski, the (alleged) author of *Pamiętnik anegdotyczny z czasów Stanisława Augusta* (*An Anecdotal Memoir from the Times of Stanisław August*; published in 1867 by Józef Ignacy Kraszewski), similarly to Linowski, connected the populace and Kołłątaj's name. The *Anecdotal Memoir* says that those who hanged on June 28 were under Kołłątaj's care: "the culprits [...] escaped a just punishment due to his protection". So the culprits belonged to the populace - "the Warsaw populace was especially proud of Father Kołłątaj's great care over the nation (that was the common name of the mob and the public band)". We learn about the fact that the populace is a rabble and a band also from Antoni Trębicki's memoir, *O rewolucji roku 1794* (*On the Revolution of 1794*). Trębicki, who - like Wojda - divided the inhabitants of Warsaw into two parts ("the townspeople and the rabble"), gave a kind of psychological theory of the populace. "The populace - he wrote – is everywhere a populace, that is, a commune without character, audacious and murderous in happiness, mean and slavish in adversity". Further on in Trębicki's memoir it is talked about that the populace cannot be counted on in matters of national life ("everyone is mistaken, who thinks that the fate of countries depends on it"), because it is subject to elementary and uncontrolled emotions - it is "passionate so long as drink, booty, or blood warms it up, but is sluggish and groveling when it returns to its natural state".

However, Trębicki's convictions regarding the psychology of the populace were not consequential - he wrote elsewhere in his memoir that "the populace, and especially those from Warsaw, are gentle, hardworking and calm, until a bad man stirs them up and incites them". In the memoir, *On the Revolution*, we can also find an interesting distinction between a higher and a lower populace. The lower one would be a rabble, the higher one - it is not sure what. "Nowy Świat, slowly from Crosses, began to be so filled with the rabble, and slowly even with the higher populace, that I could not get through on a horse". Crosses is the name of the place we call Three Crosses Square. This division of the populace into its various segments or layers - higher, lower, and even the lowest - must have probably explained something, at least to those who came into contact with the populace, because we meet it quite often at the time. The lowest populace is spoken about in Michał Ogiński's *Pamiętniki o Polsce i Polakach* (*Memoirs of Poland and the Poles*) - "the attack committed on the 28th" was performed, according to the composer of polonaises, by "a crowd of people from the lowest populace". The division of the populace into higher and lower ones was also done with the help of epithets assigned to them. It could therefore be a normal populace, that is, a populace without an epithet defining it, and it could also be one that, thanks to the epithets, was presented as a rabble, a mob, or some other wild and monstrous force. "The enraged populace – wrote Father Kitowicz in *Historia Polska* (*Polish History*; clearly favorable to the enraged populace) – slaughtered all those sutler houses, from which shots was given, to the last, not even sparing children". The enraged populace appears in *Polish History* also in connection with the description of the murder of the young Igelström, who was "torn to small pieces by the enraged populace". In Julian Ursyn Niemcewicz's *Pamiętniki czasów moich* (*Memoirs of My Times*), we have (in his description of the events of June 28) – synonymous with the populace and appearing right next to it – an enraged people, as well as a fired-up and dark rabble. "The fired-up rabble attacked various prisons, captured them and dragged out those locked there, [...] and immediately hanged them on gallows"; "Dembowski, by birth a Jew [...] became the commander of the dark rabble"; "because the enraged people does not know what attention and reflection are"; "when fearless Zakrzewski barges in among those shouting [...] the populace begins to ease at the sound of his voice".

All this did not prevent Niemcewicz from recognizing, in this excerpt from *Memoirs*, that the dark and fired-up rabble is a gentle people - "by nature our people is gentle". A sequence of synonyms similar to Niemcewicz's work is also found in Józef Wybicki's *Życie moje* (*My Life*) - the "dark populace" (in the description of the events on May 9) is identified there with a dark mob, and the dark mob placed next to the commune. "In every work, into which the dark mob and the commune enters, a sound of turbulent confusion, plunder, and atrocities is borne in its conception". Franciszek Karpiński spoke in a much more restrained way - than Wybicki or Niemcewicz – on this matter. In his memoir, *Historia mego wieku i ludzi, z którymi żyłem* (*The History of my Era and the People with Whom I Lived*), the synonym of the populace is the people – but not angry, dark or some other, but simply the people. "The court room was filled by a crowd of people, and as many hands there were, so many pałasz's hung over the heads of the judges, and the entire City Hall was surrounded by a multitude of the armed populace". This at all does not mean that Karpiński knew well what this was, that which was the people and the populace at the same time. For him it was probably something indefinite, varied, composed of various elements. This is well illustrated by the sentence from *The History of my Era* about the first day of the Warsaw Insurrection, in which Karpiński added the adjective "varied" to the populace - and he did this, as it seems to me, completely spontaneously, without thinking, expressing some deep conviction that the populace is something that is varied, composed of various segments, and is constituted by its variedness. "The guilds and varied populace were thrown various weapons through doors and windows from the arsenal". Another synonym - interesting in that it did not connect the populace with any segment of society at all - was used by the President of Warsaw Wyssogota Zakrzewski in his letters to Kościuszko. For him the populace meant not the people or the rabble, but only the presence - that is, of those who were present in this very place. If this is how (I am not sure) it can be understood, then the populace would be synonymous with all those present, and all those present would be synonymous with the populace.

"They were taken - we read in Zakrzewski's letter from May 5 - into detention for their own safety in the first moments of the general uproar, they were kept from then on to please the public". Zakrzewski used his identification (populace = public) consistently and also those who did the hanging were not a rabble or mob, but the public. This is evidenced by a letter to Kościuszko of May 9, which says that "between 10 and 12 at night the public was engaged in the erection of four gallows [...]". It is not until a little further in this letter we have the people synonymous with the public - "there, from countless people filling the streets and the market, I was greeted here with a shout, there with insistence that the traitors of the Fatherland be punished". My last example occurs a bit earlier, it comes from *Niektóre wyrazy porządkiem abecadła zebrane* (*Some Words Collected in the Order of the Alphabet*) by Franciszek Salezy Jezierski, published in 1791. The entry "Nags" in *Some Words* says that nags are "the horse populace, because as there are the nobility and populace among people, so are horses and nags among herds in Poland". This would imply that the populace is something worse, because nags are worse, but this comparison was conceived as a joke - aimed, of course, not at nags, but at the nobility who torments the nags. We learn more about this in the entry "Populace". According to Father Jezierski, the nag populace was what Poland had which was the best – as it was its nation. "We call the greatest part of the poor and hardworking people the populace; with the French the populace is the third estate, in my opinion the populace should be called the first estate of the nation or, more clearly, the complete nation. The wealth and power of states are made up by the populace and the populace upholds the character of nations". Jezierski had interesting views on the place and role of the nobility in the Polish community - he was namely of the opinion that the nobility, being a European formation, could not pretend to be a nation, even more so, it is incapable of being a nation even if it wanted to. Through its noble, European essence, it is an elite, and being an elite, it is thus similar and must inevitably be similar to other European elites - thus being similar to European elites, living like them, in the same way, it loses at the same time, it even has to lose its Polish uniqueness, and therefore also its identity.

"The nobility throughout Europe, in all nations, is similar to each other and forms as if one generation of people; they speak to each other in languages which they learn in their youth, they have teachings and politeness, hypocrisy and pride. Whereas the populace makes nations individual, maintains the nativeness of their mother tongue, keeps the customs, and follows a uniform way of life". The examples could be multiplied even more, but we probably wouldn't learn much more. Anyway, one can already see what the problem was with regards to the populace around 1794 - there was complete confusion with regards to this matter and nothing was explained or, perhaps it is better to say, agreed upon. The language only shows this - but this was not (only) a linguistic problem. The populace was a people and was not a people, it was a nation, and it was not a nation, it was dark and furious, but also calm and gentle. The only thing that was clear was that this was some terrible force whose place - in society and in history - remains unrecognized. Andrzej Bańkowski's entry in the *Etymological Dictionary of the Polish Language* ends with an attempt to establish where the noun "populace" (pospólstwo) in the Polish language came from. Bańkowski (in agreement with what was commonly believed) believes that this is a word that probably comes from "pospołu" (meaning "together"). However, he is puzzled by, as he writes, the variants "postpólstwo" and "postwólstwo" which are repeated in fourteenth and fifteenth century Old Polish sources - according to this lexicographer, they testify that apart from "pospólstwo" from "po społu" there was also "postwólstwo" from "po stwołu".

Bańkowski's entry proposes to us to compare this "postwólst-wo" with old Polish local names - Stwolna and Stwolno - and also with the Russian "stvol", meaning "trunk". Bańkowski, in accordance with the customs prevailing in lexicography, does not comment on the source he found, but I (not being a lexicographer) can allow myself to do it. Whoever likes to observe the mysterious life of plants knows well that it is never possible to predict what will grow out of a trunk – in which place this something (that fragment from the depths of life emerging on its surface) will suddenly appear and in which direction it will grow; whether this something will grow slowly or quickly, straight or crooked, what it will look like and what it will be similar to. Will it someday be a big new trunk, a great new tree, or a small branch? Nobody could know this. What grows out of a trunk does not even have to be named – either way it grows; just simply - it grows.

Chapter 29.
KOŁŁĄTAJ'S PLOT

Did Father Hugo Kołłątaj and the poet Jakub Jasiński form a plot somewhere at the end of October - or maybe a little earlier, even some two or three months earlier - to kill the king and his large family? I haven't counted the royal family yet - it's not that easy - but it seems that there were three or four of the king's children in the Castle in the last weeks of

Jakub Jasiński (unknown)

the insurrection. Together with the king's two sisters and his secret wife, this amounts to about eight people - wanting to kill them all, one would have to erect at least eight gallows. It was also stated - various wild rumors were circulating in Warsaw about the October or August or September plot of Kołłątaj's - that the ex-Deputy Chancellor with the general-poet (according to rumors, several priests were also supposed to belong to the plot) also planned to hang Tadeusz Kościuszko and Ignacy Potocki.

In other words, they planned the total destruction of the insurrectionary authorities. The one who took the news about the plot the most seriously - which is hardly surprising – was the king himself. In a letter to his chamberlain, Mikołaj Wolski, written at the Castle "on Xbris 15, 1794", and so after the occupation of Warsaw by Suvorov's army, he informed his dear Wolski (he was his favorite, then residing in Białystok) - and through him the next generations because the letter was directed to posterity and the king clearly wanted posterity to find out what kind of monster Father Kołłątaj was - so the letter informed dear Wolski and posterity that there were even some documents that could be evidence in this matter - that is, they testify that a plot had been formed. It is true that the king did not see these documents personally, though there were people who did. "These documents - we read in the king's letter – were not read by me with my eyes, but there are those who say that they have read them, and such an opinion is common in Warsaw". As emerges from this letter, Kołłątaj decided to kill the king (and also, additionally, some other people), because he believed - at least this is how the king explained it to his chamberlain - that this was precisely how he would be able to convince the French Jacobins to support (financially and militarily) the Polish insurrection.

Stanisław August (I don't quite understand why) called those who, on behalf of the insurrection, tried to gain some help for Poland from Robespierre in Paris ("they went to the French Government") schemers. "These, I say, schemers were answered in Paris: we will not give you money or troops as long as you have a king". Hearing such an answer, the monarch explained to his dear Wolski, that the schemers decided to remove the king. This reasoning presented by Stanisław August was true to some extent - Robespierre did actually say in one of the talks to Franciszek Barss, who was seeking French help on behalf of the insurrection authorities, that France could not help the Polish revolution because it was a revolution of the nobility, not of the people. "This answer [of Robespierre's] - Stanisław August wrote further in his December letter - was to be the reason that Father Kołłątaj destined a violent death for me, as well as for many other people, whom he did not manage to kill on May 9 and June 28, and the day for this was to be chosen in November". It would be good to know where the information the king shared with Wolski came from, but it seems that there is no way to establish this. "There are those who say" as well as "such an opinion is common in Warsaw" - could indicate that Stanisław August received (perhaps it was even not until after Kołłątaj had escaped from Warsaw and Russian troops had entered) some rumors that spoke of the ex-Deputy Chancellor's sinister intentions. One could draw a completely different conclusion from the mention of documents and those who "say that they have read them" - that the king's informants were some spies of his or (let's say more carefully) paid agents who might have been somewhere near

Kołłątaj. Especially the date of the intended action - "the day [...] chosen in November" - could testify that this was information that came (could have come) from sources that were somewhat credible. Though there is nothing else that can be said about this matter. Some information about the October plot, which also - for various reasons - could (just barely) be called primary sources, can be found in two more places.

One of them is the second volume of *Pamiętniki o Polsce i Polakach* (*Memoirs of Poland and the Poles*) by Michał Kleofas Ogiński, the other is *Żywot Juliana Ursyna Niemcewicza* (*The Life of Julian Ursyn Niemcewicz*) by Prince Adam Czartoryski. *Memoirs of Poland and the Poles* was first published in 1827 in Paris. This was a publication in French, and in Polish, in a very sloppy translation by an anonymous translator, *Memoirs* were not published until 1870. In the second volume of *Memoirs*, Ogiński told about his meetings with General Jasiński, which probably took place sometime in mid-October. The composer of polonaises was completely devoid of literary talent, so his story, quite factual, does not recommend itself with anything except this dry matter-of-factness - we do not see any of the interlocutors or the place where they talk, we also do not learn anything that would allow us to establish whether any particulars were discussed, or if only - as generally as possible – it was theorized about the topic of the eventual hangings. The passage about the October plot says the following. "General Jasiński, a good patriot and combative as his saber, but passionate about luxury, came several times to dine with me one on one. On one occasion he offered me to join the Jacobin club, adding that if I did not accept the offer, I was putting myself in danger of being hanged, which he would worry about". Ogiński, faced with such a choice - either participation in the Jacobin plot, or the gallows - behaved bravely and replied to the general that such threats did not "make any impression" on him. Jasiński, however, did not give up. "He came back - we read in *Memoirs of Poland* - a second time, trying to convince me that if the entire nobility is not slaughtered, Poland cannot be saved". The talks between the poet and the composer of polonaises ended in nothing and Jasiński, perhaps discouraged by the fact that he had failed to persuade Ogiński to participate in the Jacobin plot, or by some other failures, decided, as we learn from *Memoirs*, to leave Warsaw and go to Paris - "he suggested to me to go with him on foot to Paris, because, as he said, in Poland there are only traitors or people who are weak and without energy". However, Ogiński did not agree to this proposal either (he was much wealthier than the poet-general, so maybe he did not want to walk to Paris; he preferred to go there in one of his carriages) and explained to Jasiński that it would be better "to die with a weapon in hand rather than leave the country".

As we know, this is also what happened - the poet was killed with a weapon in his hand, as Ogiński wrote - "a week later he fell [...] near Praga". If the author of *Memoirs* did not make a mistake in this place and he actually talked to Jasiński only a few or a dozen or so days before his death in Praga, then these talks on the slaughtering of the "entire nobility" (as well as Ogiński's possible participation in this event) must have taken place even in last days of October. Praga was conquered by the Russians on November 4 and Jasiński fell there, firing from behind the Zwierzyniec palisade on that very day. I don't know why the well-known lithograph depicting the lone Jasiński, defending the Praga rampart, has neither a palisade nor animals wandering among the trenches, and the general's rifle was replaced there with a saber. Jasiński was killed, hit by a stray bullet or a piece of canister shot when, among his soldiers, he tried to stop the attack of Russian infantry with rifle fire – this is certain. In *Memoirs of Poland and the Poles*, we also have - as far as I know, this is the only testimony of its kind - a specific day on which Kołłątaj and Jasiński decided to cause a popular tumult (or perhaps a military revolt), and then kidnap the king and seize power in in Warsaw. "On the other hand - Ogiński wrote - several people close to the king came to secretly warn me that on October 28, the Jacobin party would try to incite the people, to kidnap the king and murder all who would be suspected of belonging to his party". Those supporters of the king who appeared at Ogiński's also had some conspiratorial ideas, because they also intended to appear armed. "I was urged to join with a small number of armed men, which were around me [...] with the goal of defending the king and to prevent bloodshed". As one can see, both the Jacobins and the king's men counted on Ogiński. If Stanisław August had been kidnapped in October and his supporters had acted in his defense with arms (the information saying that Stanisław August was to be kidnapped and taken away somewhere is nowhere else; it is only found in *Memoirs of Poland*), then in the streets of Warsaw, just before the Massacre of Praga, we would probably have had something along the lines of a civil war.

Maybe it was a small one, but still a war. More about Kołłątaj's and Jasiński's plot was learned, but much later, probably only somewhere in the 1830s, by Prince Adam Czartoryski - while what he found out was revealed even later, as it was not until 1860. It was precisely then that the prince's last literary work, *The Life of Julian Ursyn Niemcewicz*, was published in Berlin. Prince Adam was then ninety years old. "At the end it came to mind - says his story about the events of 1794 - among some plotting incessant turmoil, that the king, at that time removed from all acts and guilt, and all the higher, richer, and more respected people, be killed in one night". Czartoryski, very sensibly as well, explained the intentions of the conspirators in that they wanted, through their "disgusting, rogue deed", to extract from Poland the strength hidden in it and absolutely needed by it (at that desperate moment, when the insurrection was dying). "The implementation of the crazy idea was to create in Poland the strength which it did not have". "It was expected [...] to give the nation some imagined power of ruthless, mindless, ferocious, desperate, ready for anything despair". Further on in Czartoryski's work, we have the accusation of Kołłątaj - an explicit, but also very cautious accusation, because Prince Adam did not mention any surname at first, only suggesting that some "eminent persons" had participated in the plot. "Some eminent persons, even in their position and former friendship close to the Chief, were not, it was said, completely alien to the councils of this conspiracy". Only at the end of his story, and still very carefully, did the prince decide to point to Kołłątaj. "However, the public voice long after the revolution blamed, I do not know if it was justified, especially Kołłątaj for the knowledge of this plot". Czartoryski's story moves the establishment of the plot to a period a little earlier, preceding the defeat at Maciejowice. The conspirators, according to the information Prince Adam possessed, wanted to carry out their "crazy idea" (or maybe they just discussed it) more or less when Warsaw was besieged by the Prussians and by the Russians - "this thing was plotted during the ongoing siege of Warsaw" - so in July or August.

As this was before the Battle of Maciejowice, Kołłątaj also included the Chief (Kosciuszko) on the list of those who were to be murdered "in one night". "Even Kościuszko was not to be spared, because like Aristides, he was too virtuous, cordial, and without guilt". It could, of course, be that Kołłątaj and Jasiński wanted to carry out a coup earlier, even in July or August, but something prevented them from doing so - and that is why they postponed the execution of their intention until the end of October. As one can see, Czartoryski's story (I have extracted all the most important elements from it here) is somewhat general, although his informant - Julian Ursyn Niemcewicz was undoubtedly him - must have known the whole matter very thoroughly and in detail. Prince Adam explained his restraint and the generalness of his story with the fact that Niemcewicz, although he knew a lot (this knowledge was ensured by his position at the time - he was Kościuszko's adjutant and secretary), "shuddered" before uncovering the whole truth, and he did so for two reasons. First, "the uncovering of a similar kind of truth" would burden "those still alive, already enough and even overly unhappy". Here, too, Czartoryski, although he did not mention any surnames, undoubtedly meant Kołłątaj and his later fate. Secondly, revealing the whole truth about the plot would, according to Niemcewicz (and certainly also according to Czartoryski), be tantamount to penetrating into some "hideous secrets" of Polish life, and this would "surely cast a derogatory and heavy shadow over the whole of Poland". It was precisely this, the prince explained, that forced Niemcewicz to "remain completely silent about the sad and dark secrets of the end of the uprising". Silence - to a certain extent - was also maintained by Czartoryski, who could have known, and certainly knew much more. While if he knew, then perhaps he promised Niemcewicz that he would be silent - he would only say as much as is proper to do so, bearing in mind the national interest of the Poles. This is now all my knowledge of Kołłątaj's plot. Since there was no continuation of these events, which Kołłątaj and Jasiński designed, and what was

supposed to happen never happened, there is no other way to
go about this continuation, we must somehow imagine it. So
first we have some October, maybe even September evening.

An unpleasant, cold, foreshadowing early autumn (and
the impending defeat of the insurrection) rain falls over Warsaw and to the residence of Father Kołłątaj, where there is also
Father Józef Meier and Father Florian Jelski - it is accepted
that Kołłątaj lived in the so-called Pasztets (or in one of the
Pasztets), two rotundas (or in one of these rotundas), which
were located in a large garden at Czerniakowska Street at
number 3007, right on the bank of the Vistula, where Czerniakowska then joined the coastal Solec, but this, the residence
we are talking about now should not be confused with the
Pasztets or Pasztet, because at the beginning of the summer
of 1794 Kołłątaj found himself a residence in the very center
of contemporary Warsaw, at the corner of Wide Krakowskie
Przedmieście and Bednarska Street, in the tenement house
where Wasilewski's pharmacy was - so General Jakub Jasiński as well as someone Jasiński brings with him under his elegant Parisian umbrella, who does not introduce himself and
remains unrecognized, arrive at Wasilewski's tenement house
on a late October evening, maybe even after midnight. This
someone takes a roll with golden ducats out of his wet hat (it is
a black *tricorne*) or from the folds of a long black cape or from
a wet shoe (or a pouch in which there are triple red złotys) but
does not participate in the meeting and having placed the roll
in front of Kołłątaj, leaves without saying a word. Jasiński
vouches for this someone but cannot say what this person's
name is. The supposition that the stranger with the roll is a
troublemaker and an agent of several intelligence services
(Russian, French, as well as Prussian) named Chaćkiewicz
vel Chodźkiewicz does not seem far from the truth. The money, gold ducats or triple red złotys, will be distributed in the
streets two or three days later, in the evening, on the eve of
the October events. They will be handed out by boys from the
printing house of Father Franciszek Ksawery Dmochowski,
little print shop boys, and those who receive them in exchange
will put up a dozen or so or even several dozen gallows on
Krakowskie Przedmieście, Nowy Świat, Podwale, and Długa
Streets. The subject of the conference, which takes place after

the stranger in a triangular hat has left, is the proscription list, previously prepared by Kołłątaj. General Jasiński adds a few surnames to it, among them Michał Kleofas Ogiński, Father Meier asked if Stanisław August's mistresses will also be hanged.

General Jasiński's answer - we do not hang women – does not please Father Meier, as he believes that the era of brotherhood and equality has come, and therefore women should be treated as brothers, that is, exactly the same as men - a different way of treating them would offend their human dignity and would make them different persons, half-animal. - Disgusting animals - Father Meier shouts. - Disgusting hairy vessels serving to satisfy men's desires. - Father Kołłątaj, made impatient, says that the hanging of women will begin only after the philosophical foundations of feminism have been worked out, when it has been decided whether feminists are our brothers or sisters. If they are brothers, we will hang them. - But what do you mean, Kubuś – he asks Jasiński. - I do not understand you. What do you have against Kleofas? As I like his polonaise *Pożegnanie Ojczyzny* (*Farewell to the Fatherland*) very much. - The meeting in Wasilewski's tenement house ends before the morning, and the next day Kołłątaj and Jasiński and their helpers (Father Meier and Father Jelski) begin their work. The proscription list - King Stanisław August is the first, Ignacy Potocki is the second, Kościuszko is third, Bishop Skarszewski is the fourth, and the fifth (to satisfy Father Meier) Skarszewski's two lovers, one female and the other male - is copied in the printing house of the *Gazeta Rządowa* (*Government* Gazette; its editor-in-chief, Father Dmochowski, is one of the conspirators) and can be read, nailed by little boys, on the doors of all insurrectionary institutions – it hangs on Długa Street, on the doors of the Raczyński Palace, where the Supreme National Council has its headquarters, and on Senatorska Street, on the doors of the Primate's Palace, where the Supreme Criminal Court holds its meetings, and on the doors of the insurrectional post office on the corner Kozia and Trębacka.

Someone tears the list off the guard booth in front of the Castle (some Old Town ragged man hung it there) and brings it to the king. Stanisław August holds out his hand with the proscription list and gives it to someone who is standing in the dark (it is a woman, but we cannot see her face), at the same time repeating (with tears in his eyes) the last famous sentence of the French king, Louis XVI, which he uttered on the steps of the scaffold: - Je n'ai jamais désiré que le bonheur de mon peuple. (I have never wanted anything but the happiness of my people) - On Wola, Ujazdów, and Mokotów, where Warsaw ladies from Krakowskie Przedmieście, together with Warsaw whores from Trębacka Street (ladies and whores alike in blue stockings and straw hats with a small brim), are working to strengthen the embankments and deepen the trenches, young men show up - they say that someone was caught who was carrying an encrypted letter, which Stanisław August wrote to his old friend, a general of the Petersburg Tsarina, Nikolai Repnin - in this letter he was revealing to the Russian commander the secret plan for the defense of Warsaw developed by Kościuszko. Everything is ready and soon the great October hangings will begin, which will make something incredible out of the Polish insurrection; something which we are truly incapable of imagining. The gallows on which the king will be hanged will be built right at the spot where Wasilewski's tenement house stands and Wide Krakowskie Przedmieście becomes Narrow Krakowskie Przedmieście - so that Father Kołłątaj could watch the hated condemned man, as much as he wants to, from his balcony. The condemned man in a waistcoat with thin pink stripes, a shirt (dirtied) with lace cuffs and white trousers made of Brussels camlet; and at the foot of the gallows lays his summer hat made of black straw; and separately a white, frayed feather. Though there will be hundreds of gallows, and there will be thousands, thousands of victims - because this will be the Polish Reign of Terror, the Polish *Grande Terreur*, which will only end (also unimaginably) by some Polish Thermidor. It also seems obvious that the gallows, machines that work very slowly, are not enough and that guillotines as well as specialists who know how to operate them will be brought in from Paris. The first of these fast machines will be set up in the place called Three Crosses or Golden Crosses - a bit far from the center, but the square there is big enough that all those desiring to come and watch will be able to fit. There where the street that runs to Miejska Kawa (Rural Coffee) begins - a quietly falling blade and a faint thud, one, when the head, before it falls into the basket of sawdust, hits a plank while jumping up. This whole fragment, from the October rain and the arrival of General Jasiński to the residence of Father Kołłątaj, of course consists of fabrications - Chaćkiewicz did not bring a roll of money, it is not even certain whether he was working for the French or Prussian intelligence at that time, Kołłątaj did not prepare a proscription list, Father Meier did not think (with pleasure) about hanging women, Bishop Skarszewski did have two lovers, but both were female, and General Jasiński did not plot against Kościuszko, and even if he did plot a little bit, nothing came of it, because he was killed in Zwierzyniec in Praga, thus becoming a Polish hero.

Ladies and whores, who were at that time voluntarily working on the expansion of the Warsaw fortifications, wore blue stockings and straw hats - only this is true. Though everything I had made up could have happened, and it would even certainly have happened (that or something similar), because everything was ready. Not in the sense that Kołłątaj with Zajączek or Jasiński with Dmochowski were preparing an excellent project and ordered fast guillotines in Paris. Everything was prepared in the sense that there was such a mood, such a conviction prevailed - among those who wanted it and among those who did not want it. Everyone was convinced that there had to be a way out - out of this hopeless, no way-out insurrectionary situation - and that the only way out is the death of the king. I will quote here one more small fragment from the king's letter, of December 15, to Chamberlain Wolski - this fragment just so happens to show well the conviction that there is no other way out and that the king must die. Stanisław August — now completely safe, because he was under the care of Russian generals - told Wolski (one can admire the king's insight and intelligence, as well as the king's sense of humor) such an anecdote. "Here I cannot pass one anecdote, showing how far and with what effort Father Kołłątaj and his dependents poisoned the minds of people who by their nature are the best. Lady Sołtan, leaving this place after our fall, said these words: The King is at fault for everything; He should have been - and pointed a finger at the neck". He should have been. Everyone knew it, and everything that I made up above would have happened, the king's throat would have been cut (cut by the history of Poland) if at least one of these conditions had been met - if the Petersburg Tsarina had delayed military intervention for some reasons (difficult to imagine, by the way) if the Prussian king had decided that some small remnant of free Poland, some buffer state on the Vistula with its capital in Warsaw, would be more beneficial for him than a border with Russia, if the French Jacobins had come to the aid of the Polish insurrection, if Kościuszko's army was much larger and much better armed.

In other words, something like this (not necessarily what I imagined here, but something like it) could have, and even would have to happen, if only this single condition were met - if the Polish insurrection, which ended in November with the Massacre of Praga, had continued a little longer, another year or two or three. Then what Ignacy Potocki and Hugo Kołłątaj come up with in Dresden as our national uprising would have happened - without anyone's will or desire; by the sheer force of historical necessity; by the sheer force of its volcanic historical momentum - something along the lines of a terrible revolution - similar to the one that was raging in Paris at that time. I am kidding a bit (bloodily), but the matter was and is serious - the national benefits that result (would result) from such a solution, that is, in the transformation of the national insurrection into a national revolution that would transform the nation (and therefore, even if it were defeated, it would be a victorious revolution), seem obvious to me - and these benefits, although we will never take advantage of them, must be appreciated. Of all the benefits that can be imagined here, the most important benefit would be the hanging of Stanisław August Poniatowski. His death on the gallows would be a great event in the history of Poland, an event which, in all its abomination, monstrosity and greatness, would radically and forever change our history - we would now have a completely different image of it in our heads. The nation would have found itself on this murder - it would have become a dangerous and savage nation of regicides through this act - and this wild and terrible act would make Poles (perhaps prematurely, or perhaps just in time) a modern nation - going through blood towards their new destinies. It should also be noted here that the hanging of the king would have been extremely beneficial for him himself (even if he would be of a different opinion on this matter). Stanisław August was and remains a somewhat indistinct king - it is not really known whether he was prudent or merely cowardly, whether he was a lazy sybarite, or a diligent and cunning politician, whether he cared for his nation, or only for his lovers and his money. It is not even known whether he wanted to be loved and respected by the Poles, or if he only wanted us to leave him alone - so that he could look at Italian drawings in peace in the evenings as well as play in bed with countless ballerinas. If he had been hanged, he would have immediately and for centuries been terribly singled out - he would have become a hanged king. A condemned man from beneath Wasilewski's apartment house and his pink-striped waistcoat - what a magnificent sight! Also Father Kołłątaj, looking at this from the balcony, lost in thought (beautiful in this reflection - he was a beautiful man). Such a king would also be much more visible and easier to remember, also for those who are not interested in their native history, because he would have risen, even literally, to a certain height, and such an image is not forgotten. This event - putting on the harness and pulling the king up on the gallows (and also the wooden artificial teeth then falling out of the king's jaw) - would be something that children would learn about in our schools - this would be something along the lines (an event of similar importance) of the *Battle of Grunwald*, *Batory at Pskov*, maybe even something like the *Baptism of Poland*. Poland then baptized with this hanging, Poland baptized in front of Wasilewski's tenement house on Krakowskie Przedmieście would be a completely different Poland even today - I cannot quite imagine it, but it would certainly be a radical Poland, radicalized for centuries. To those whom she does not like, saying, - Get out of our sight, or you'll be hanged. Oh, right there, on Krakowskie Przedmieście - beneath Wasilewski's apartment house.

Chapter 30
ON PIASKI

The arrests began on the evening of June 28, immediately after Brigadier Jaźwiński's squadrons, sent from Kościuszko's camp near Gołków, entered the city, and continued for the next several days. The first detainees were taken to prisons and guard posts during the huge storm that ended the June hangings. The exact number of those arrested is difficult to establish and historical works contain different opinions on this matter. It is usually accepted that about 1,000 people were then arrested,

Tadeusz Kościuszko (Karl Schweikart)

but there are also more specific numbers - 947 or 987 people. The thing is that this cannot be calculated well, because apart from those who participated in the hangings and who a little later stood trial (and were or were not sentenced), after June 28, many people called loose, beggars, vagabonds, homeless, whom the army had gathered from the streets and who might not have had anything to do with hangings were also sent to various prisons for a longer or shorter period of time, or for a really short time.

This is also from where the contemporary differences in the assessment of the number of arrested comes from. Johann Jakob Patz, in a letter sent to Dresden on July 5th, wrote that military patrols "were seizing all the vagabonds found on the streets, and searches are also being carried out in many homes to arrest the authors of the criminal acts [...]. Their number has now reached 700 or 800 people". In the next letter, of July 7, Patz informed Dresden that the number of detained vagabonds "has already exceeded 1,500" and that "they had been sent to Kościuszko's army". In Kiliński's *Drugi Pamięt-nik* (*Second Memoir*), we have a number somewhat similar to that from Patz's first letter - "generally speaking there were over 800 people arrested" - while in *Historia Polska* (*Polish History*) by Father Kitowicz it is a little lower, but it includes only those conscripted into the army: "Kościuszko divided another 600 more livelier of the populace among the regiments". Whereas from a letter that Stanisław August (probably well informed) wrote to Prince Józef Poniatowski on 5 July, it can be concluded that those arrested, guilty or innocent, were kept in Warsaw prisons for at least a dozen or so days, gradually sending them to the camp in Gołków. "Last night more than a thousand people were caught, either suspected of deeds juni 28 or loose, of no certain condition or profession, the latter are to be sent at 50 a day to the Chief's camp as recruits. Kiliński has the title of colonel of this new recruitment". To make it stranger - or perhaps scarier - those accused of hanging were kept in the same prisons from which they extracted their victims on June 28. This happened to Father Meier, who, not arrested until July 6, was imprisoned for three weeks in the Brühlowski Palace. It is also difficult to determine the final number of those who it was decided to bring before the Supreme Criminal Court. The first list of those accused of participating in the events of June 28, announced on July 13, contained 97 surnames, later, probably due to the progress of the investigation, the number increased a little, and then it decreased a little.

Kościuszko insisted on the quickest possible sentencing of the perpetrators of the riots, and even demanded that the Supreme National Council end this case as soon as possible - as can be assumed, for two reasons. First, he was terribly outraged by what had happened in Warsaw, and he probably wanted to convince himself and others that the hangmen were acting against the insurrection and were being paid off by its enemies, that is, by foreign powers. A similar position was also taken, perhaps following Kościuszko's example, by the Supreme National Council, which in the *Odezwa do Narodu względem zdarzenia na dniu 28 czerwca* (*Proclamation to the Nation regarding the event of June 28*), issued on July 11, placed the responsibility for the hangings on "foreign anger". "It is sure that foreign anger attempted to harm the work of the revolution by purchasing a few rogues and traitors, but your prudence can track them down".

Kościuszko's impatience had its cause, secondly, also in the fact that the matter of the hangings had to be dealt with as soon as possible for military reasons - Russian and Prussian troops were approaching Warsaw, a great battle for the city was beginning, a great siege, and in this situation Kościuszko could not have against himself (and against his army) the populace of Warsaw. He couldn't fall into its disfavor too much, he couldn't treat it too harshly, and he also couldn't just forgive it. He was really in a very difficult position. Kościuszko's appeals, then addressed to the Supreme National Council, are something between orders and lamentations. "From the fatal - he wrote on July 12 from the camp in Mokotów - and hopefully never resumed day of June 28, there was hardly a dispatch in which I would not remind the Council of the need to examine and punish the leaders who incited the people to commit assaults and misdeeds; so far I see, instead of urgency, reprehensible sluggishness [...] the accused should be sentenced; let it turn out that they are innocent or criminals, but let it be over". We also have a similar lament in a letter addressed to the Supreme Council of July 21. "Far from endangering anyone's life, I want simple and pure justice, that is, punishment for those who incite the people to arms [...] and also those who incited this people to hang and gave them money". The Supreme National Council, urged in this way by Kościuszko, in turn directed its non-orders and non-pleas to the Supreme Criminal Court, which was instructed to settle this matter.

On July 6, the Supreme Council ordered the Supreme Court that "all those charged with actions committed on June 28" be sentenced "immediately"; a week later, on July 13, it called on the Court to "proceed as bravely as possible to finish the matter in question" and to "soon complete" its activities, "punish the guilty"; and another week later, on July 20, referring to the "repeated orders from the Supreme Chief," it demanded that the Court sentence the accused "as quickly as possible" - and close the case as soon as possible, "and even, if possible, in three days". This repeated urging and persuasion of the Court to hurry up may indicate the impatience of Kościuszko or even the impatience of the Supreme National Council, but it may also indicate something completely different - that there were people in the Council or in the Court (or perhaps somewhere in the vicinity of these institutions) who, for some reason, wanted the crime committed by the "schemers and instigators" (as they were called in the proclamations of the Supreme Council) not to be judged or that it be judged as late as possible. It would be easiest to accuse Hugo Kołłątaj, and eventually also Ignacy Potocki of delaying this matter and putting pressure on the Supreme Council and the Criminal Court not to rush (which prompted calls for them to hurry) - because their people were among the imprisoned "schemers and instigators" and only they could have had any interest in delaying the handing down and execution of the sentences. Kołłątaj might have wanted to save Kazimierz Konopka, Potocki might have wanted to save Jan Dembowski. However, nothing concrete is known about such pressures (if there were any, then after all they were secret) and there is not any sort of clear evidence that would allow us to say something more about this.

The fact that there was someone who sought that Konopka be released from prison could only be properly evidenced by two (very unclear) sentences from two letters which Kościuszko, addressing the Supreme National Council on July 21 ("I want simple and pure justice"), attached to them. In one of these letters (written to Kościuszko by his former secretary Aleksander Linowski) we read: "there is more effort to glorify and acquit some Konopka than to bring justice to an offended community". In the second letter, written to Linowski by Joachim Moszyński (he was the chairman of the Investigation Department at the time), we have the following sentence: "before noon we must talk to the Chief, and there are many people saying that if Konopka is freed, the scene will repeat itself".

The scene that would repeat itself is obviously the hangings. The first sentence in the case of the most heavily accused (those who did the hangings and those who persuaded them to do so) was issued by the Supreme Criminal Court on July 24. The *Gazeta Wolna Warszawska* (*The Free Warsaw Gazette*) published it (in short) only two days later - in issue 27 of July 26. We have a certain strange ambiguity here, which could also indicate that the issue of the announcement of the sentence was the subject of some mysterious negotiations - maybe someone, at the last minute, tried to influence how this sentence should sound and who it should concern, and the judges of the Supreme Court were being pressured or threatened by someone in this matter. On July 25, between the giving of the verdict and its public announcement, the Supreme National Council demanded that the Supreme Court inform it of its decision. This piece of writing is worth quoting in its entirety. "The Supreme National Council submits a requisition to the Supreme Criminal Court, that the decree in relation to those charged for offenses committed on June 28, issued yesterday, be immediately communicated to it *in originali*".

This sounds completely nonsensical - the Council should know the decree on the day of its issuance, the Supreme Court should convey it to the Council and Kościuszko and publicly announce it on that day, and the Council should have no reason to call for it in this tone - "immediately"! *"in originali"*!. On July 25, probably also in the previous days, something must have been going on around this decree - someone tried to do something then, as if we would say now, act - but who acted and what they did, we will never know. The "final decree" encompassed 12 accused. One of them, Jan Regulski (or Rogulski), who was an engraver at the Warsaw Mint, was found innocent, as one may guess, simply because he was needed - even before the sentence was passed, he was released from prison at the request of the Treasury Department of the Supreme National Council because he had to complete work on the stamps that were to be used to mint the insurrection money. Seven of the accused were sentenced to "death by the gallows, and this was for the disgracefully done action of June 27 and 28".

The deadline for the execution of the sentence was also set immediately - "with the date of execution set for the 26th of the current month". The following were sentenced to death: Józef Piotrowski, Tadeusz Delgiert (Dolgiert), Jędrzej Dziekoński, Dominik Jasiński, Stefan Klonowski, Tomasz Stawicki, Lorenc Burzyński. In turn: an officer cadet of the foot guard, bricklayer, henhouse owner, hay seller, herdsman, quack, bricklayer. Sebastian Nankiewicz, a blacksmith as well as a dziesiętnik from the Old Town district, and Jakub Roman, a setnik from that district, were each sentenced to "three years in public prison with using them for work and denying them from holding all offices"[1]. The decree also included two leaders of the hangings, using Kościuszko's language, "leaders who incited the people to commit assaults and misdeeds" - Kazimierz Konopka and Jan Dembowski. Konopka, the man of Hugo Kołłątaj's, was, "as a destroyer of public peace, decreed for eternal exile from the country, but only after the calming down of the Fatherland, and in the meantime sent to public prison". Dembowski, Ignacy Potocki's secretary, for "taking part in this action around putting up the gallows and not dissuading the people from this crime" was sentenced "to prison for six-months with a declaration only for him, that this still does not harm his citizenship". A rumor, repeated in Warsaw at the time, said that these two sentences were subject of negotiation and the votes of the judges of the Supreme Criminal Court were divided. "I was clearly told - wrote Aleksander Linowski in his poisonous pamphlet about Kołłątaj - that it is absolutely necessary that Konopka hang [...] and all his efforts were devoted to this, to save Konopka from the death penalty".

The next two sentences, which - for unknown reasons - were not published in newspapers, were issued by the Supreme Criminal Court on July 28 and 30. By the sentence of July 28, Jędrzej Wasilewski, about whom nothing is known (even his profession is unknown), was sentenced to death by hanging, by the sentence of July 30, Father Józef Meier and Father Florian Jelski were acquitted, as well as dozens of other accused, even those who were proven to have taken part in the hangings. The Supreme Criminal Court - perhaps because the city was under siege, the Russians and Prussians were nearby, and falling into disfavor with the people of Warsaw would be something highly inadvisable in this situation - suddenly turned out to be extremely forgiving, and all those who were proved something were deemed "more [...] mad rather than criminal".

---

[1]Dziesiętnik: A low ranking police official or commander of ten people.

All the "mad" people were thus instructed to "obey governmental authorities" and were immediately drafted into the army. At least a few sentences should be devoted to the further fate of the convicted and acquitted. The fate of Sebastian Nankiewicz, a blacksmith from Mostowa Street, is relatively best known, and actually not so much his fate as the fate of the entire Nankiewicz family. The wife of the blacksmith, Franciszka Nankiewicz, turned to the Supreme National Council with a request to release her brave husband, recalling that on April 17 and 18, during the battle for Warsaw, "he captured seven Muscovite soldiers, handed them over to be imprisoned, while the weapons taken from them he gave out to his neighbors and his journeymen", while later, when the insurrection was victorious, "he gave as a gift shirts, coats, shoes, copper kettles, tin, and an expensive pałasz", which Kościuszko himself, the Supreme Chief, "noted in his wallet". There is no doubt - the blacksmith Nankiewicz, even if he hanged someone, was a good Pole. "Everything is expensive - wrote Franciszka Nankiewicz to the Supreme National Council – and there is no one to provide for me, a poor, helpless, weak wife with children, and for him a prisoner; taxes are required, soldiers are quartered, winter is coming, I, almost standing over the grave, cannot cope with the children anymore, and my husband, a poor prisoner is just looking at this through the bars". Father Józef Meier, released by a sentence of July 30, was given a post in the Investigation Department, which interrogated and indicted the enemies of the insurrection. After the fall of the Uprising Meier found himself in Paris - his signature appears on the act of establishing the so-called Deputation (August 22, 1795), which was to maintain relations with the French Committee for Public Safety and to manage Polish agents operating (at the request of the Committee) in Constantinople, Venice, Stockholm, and Copenhagen. The further fate of the priest editor is not clear - in later years there were several Father Meier's, and it is not known which of them should be identified with Father Józef. Kazimierz Konopka was reportedly - but this is uncertain information - released from prison by Hugo Kołłątaj. This was supposed to happen just before the capture of Praga by the Russian army, on the same day that Kołłątaj escaped from Warsaw.

Another version, also quite probable, given by Antoni Trębicki in his memoir *O rewolucji roku 1794 (On the Revolution of 1794)*, says that Konopka and Kołłątaj were in Warsaw even after Praga was taken by Suvorov. "When, after the capture of Praga, Konopka was seen walking freely around the city, when he was seen at Kołłątaj's home and disappearing with him from Warsaw, there could be no doubt that the hangings on the shameful day of the 28th were the work of Kołłątaj". Konopka, like Father Meier, reached - using, as was said, the name Lisowski - Paris, joined the French army and fought against bandits in Corsica, and two years later, at the beginning of 1797, he reported to the Legions in Italy. "Konopka, that terrorist", wrote the leader of the Legions, General Henryk Dąbrowski, in one of his letters (in February 1797). Though he did not have anything against Konopka and made him a captain in his army.

In the middle of 1805, Konopka died of a heart attack in Bari. Of those who carried out the hangings or persuaded others to do it, Jan Dembowski had the most beautiful career - and rightly so, because he was the most intelligent of them all. Like Father Meier, Dembowski signed the act of establishing the Paris Deputation, but then sided with Józef Wybicki, who was fighting the Deputation. "The lucky convert Dembowski - wrote Julian Ursyn Niemcewicz in *Pamiętniki czasów moich (Memoirs of My Times)* - got through to the French, where he rose to high military ranks with his insolence and Jacobin-style speeches". All of this - the "convert" and the Jacobin-style speeches - Niemcewicz thoughtlessly invented, only the high military ranks are true. In the Legions, General Henryk Dąbrowski took Dembowski to the command staff and made him a captain, and later, in 1799, after the battles of Cortona and Trebbia, he was promoted to major and battalion chief and made him his adjutant. It was not until Dembowski joined the Italian army that he made a truly great career - he became a brigadier general there, and in this rank, commanding one of the brigades in the corps of Viceroy Eugène, he took part in the Russian Campaign of 1812. He lived long and happily - life with a beautiful woman, and in addition a lover of a genius; there simply could be no greater happiness - valued as a soldier, mason, and lover. Though this has nothing to do with his insurrection achievements in Warsaw. His wife was Mathilde Viscontini, Stendhal's lover.

The eight sentenced to death - I will mention them here once again: an officer cadet of the guard, bricklayer, henhouse owner, hay seller, herdsman, quack, another bricklayer, and one with an unknown profession - were probably hanged in the execution site which was located in Piaski. Previously, when describing the Warsaw fields of death, I assumed that the execution took place in the square behind the Cuchthauz, i.e. the House of Corrections, also known as Nalewki square or field because it was this place ("the place for the execution of the sentenced") that was indicated by the Supreme National Council in an proclamation to residents of Warsaw, released after the events of June 28. Now it seems to me that in July Nalewki Field could have already been closed and not in use - and if it was so, then the execution had to be moved to Piaski. On June 30, the Supreme National Council changed its original order, according to which criminals were to be executed in Nalewki Square, "where crimes against the Fatherland had been punished for centuries" and indicated the area behind Powązki as the place of future executions. This decision was justified by the dense buildings and the lack of space in the vicinity of the Tabaco Factory, the Jewish Warehouse, and the Cuchthauz. "The Supreme National Council - said the new ordinance - by the name of the Magistrate of the Republic's free city of Warsaw, that the place for the execution of the sentenced, by the proclamation of the Council [...] declared to be Nalewki, as significantly built-up, cannot be convenient for this purpose, declares that the aforementioned executions should take place not in Nalewki but in Piaski in the place used until now". As the execution of the eight prisoners was not described by anyone and therefore nothing is known about it, it may even seem a little doubtful whether it happened at all. The only reference I have found about it says that the sentence was not carried out and the condemned to death were released. This version of the events can be found in *List do przyjaciela odkrywający wszystkie czynności Kołłątaja w ciągu Insurekcji* (*A Letter to a Friend Discovering All of Kołłątaj's Activities during the Insurrection*) by Aleksander Linowski. "Several dozen sinners were arrested on that day, four of whom were simple and deceived, the fifth Piotrowski (this one had already earlier been known as a rogue) was punished with death [...] then the rest, similarly to the five accused, whom I mentioned, not by a court decree, but by a declaration obtained from the Chief [Kościusz-ko] were released from everything".

This does not sound entirely clear, but it is probably about the fact that those who were sentenced to death ("punished with death") were ordered to be released by Kościuszko before the execution of the sentence. The fact that Linowski's pamphlet was a lampoon and that he had made a mistake about the number of those sentenced does not in any way prove that his statements are true or false. So it could have happened that, there were seven executions in Piaski on July 26, and then, at the beginning of August, another, eighth one (of the one who was sentenced to death at a later date); but it could have happened that on July 26, one of Kościuszko's adjutants came from the camp near Królikarnia to the gallows in Piaski, jumped off his foaming horse (the day was hot, and he was galloping) and delivered to an official of the magistrate an order signed by the Chief that the condemned be released. Stefan Böhm climbed down the ladder, took a checkered handkerchief from his frock pocket and wiped the sweat from his diagonally cut face. If he was carrying out the hangings in a frock - this is my idea. Officer Cadet Piotrowski came to down after him and replied with a crooked smile at the crooked smile caused by the diagonal saber cut. Then everyone, the executioner, officer cadet of the foot guard, henhouse owner, hay seller, bricklayer, quack, and another bricklayer, dispersed from Piaski, went somewhere, in an unknown direction, each in their own direction.

Chapter 31.
THE PLEDGE

In the letter dated "Warsaw Xbris 15, 1794", which Stanisław August sent to Mikołaj Wolski, his dear Wolski, who was staying in Białystok, along with the messages in an obvious way intended for posterity (such as the one about the plot that Kołłątaj started in November in order to inflict a "violent death" on the king and "many other people"), there were also various current piece of information, including the news about the fate of Tomasz Wawrzecki - the one who was appointed to the position of the Chief of the National Armed Forces by the Supreme National Council (moreover, against his will) after the Battle of Maciejowice and the imprisonment of Kościuszko.

Stanislaw Poniatowski (M. Bacciarelli)

The king (not without some satisfaction that the insurrection ended just as it should have ended, that is, in a total defeat, and that his royal sufferings had come to an end) told his chamberlain about how Wawrzecki, with the remnants of the army - "when at the end he did not even have a thousand people with him" - was surrounded near Radoszyce by the corps of General Denisov and taken prisoner, and then brought to Warsaw. "When brought here, he did not want to sign the pledge, he preferred to be led into captivity and became a victim. The remaining four generals with him signed the pledge". The pledge, which Stanisław August wrote about, was something like the papers that the communists, in the second half of the twentieth century, gave Poles to sign, and which, in our twentieth-century language, we called lojalkas (loyalty agreements) - between the eighteenth-century pledge and the twentieth-century lojalka there was almost no difference, except that the one who signed the pledge in the 18th century pledged not to harm Russia, and the one who signed the lojalka in the 20th century pledged not to harm the authorities of the People's Republic of Poland. A difference, as can be seen, which is very slight. I wonder if General Suvorov (now probably a field marshal) or General Buxhoeveden, paying the king a courtesy visit to the Castle after their troops entered Warsaw, gave him such a pledge to sign, the one Tomasz Wawrzecki did not want to sign. This is very probable. Though I don't know what it was like. Stanisław August, sending the letter to Wolski, attached to it several copied documents - among them copies of two of his letters to the Petersburg Tsarina, written in November and December, as well as a copy of this pledge. The letter to the Tsarina (of November 21) began with the words: „Madame ma Soeur! Le sort de la Pologne est entre Vos mains. Vôtre puissance et vôtre sagesse en decideront" (Madam my Sister! The fate of Poland is in Your hands. Your power and wisdom will decide). You could say that this was also a kind of pledge. Though perhaps Suvorov and Buxhoeveden had been instructed that some formal conditions be met, and that all pledges signed by all the people who were on the list prepared in St. Petersburg (there must have been countless such pledges) should be placed in St. Petersburg cabinets dedicated for this purpose. If so, then the king also signed it. However, we should be grateful to him, because thanks to him (that is, thanks to the annexes he attached to the letter of December 15) we know what such a pledge looked like at that time. It seems almost certain that the pledge was something like a form and that everyone who was required to sign was signing the same form. One can also guess that the text of the pledge was written in St. Petersburg and that it was the subject of high-level arrangements - perhaps even the tsarina was consulted on this matter.

The basis for the copy that Stanisław August sent to Chamberlain Wolski was a lojalka signed by the president of rebellious Warsaw, Ignacy Wyssogota Zakrzewski. "Ex-president Zakrzewski - the king wrote to his dear Wolski – was brought here all the way from Sandomierz and prompted to sign the pledge, as can be seen *sub* letter E". How such prompting took place, I have no idea - whether the Russian officer who asked for the signature would raise his voice at one point and start screaming, or whether other, less pleasant methods were used. The cunning of the Russians was that whoever signed the pledge also admitted that he had participated in the revolution and had acted "against Russia". So, despite his signature, he could not be sure what would happen next and how it would end for him - whether the St. Petersburg monster would forgive him or punish him. Wawrzecki did not sign and went to Petersburg, where he was imprisoned in the Peter and Paul Fortress, Wyssogota Zakrzewski signed and also found himself in the same place. The content of the copy sent by the king "*sub* letter E" (published by the Poznań researcher Leon Wegner in 1869, together with Stanisław August's letter to Wolski, as an annex to the article "Hugo Kołłątaj na posiedzeniu rady królewskiej z dnia 23 lipca 1792" ["Hugo Kołłątaj at the meeting of the King's Council on July 23, 1792"]) was this.

Copy of the pledge of his Lordship Zakrzewski, Chorąży of Poznań

Signed below, I make the most solemn Recess since the Revolution that took place in Poland, as well as from everything that can be associated with it, I oblige myself and I pledge most solemnly that I will peacefully live and behave and I will not get involved in anything, neither by myself or through someone else, that would be against Rossya, or that could oppose and harm the public peace. Though if I should not keep my pledge, I submit myself to the most severe punishment under the Laws, loss of property, honor and life; which, for greater weight, I affirm with my signature of my own hand. Dated in Warsaw on December 12, 1794. Signed: Ignacy W. Zakrzewski.

Chapter 32
BATTLEFIELD

Kościuszko in the battle of Maciejowice (Jan Plersz)

From the book by Franciszek Paszkowski, *Dzieje Tadeusza Kościuszki pierwszego naczelnika Polaków* (*The History of Tadeusz Kościuszko, the First Polish Chief*), we learn that Kościuszko, when he was beginning the Battle of Maciejowice, was absolutely sure of victory. "He did not have any - we read in *History* – doubt about defeating Fersen". Paszkowski also wrote about the victory, "in his mind there was no doubt". The fact that the Battle of Maciejowice could have and should have ended with the victory of the Poles and that the Polish commanders had anticipated such a turn of events was certainly learned by Paszkowski from Kościuszko. The material from which the author of *The History of the First Polish Chief* developed his book (not published until 1872, but written, in the first version, much earlier, already in 1819), came largely, maybe even almost entirely, from Kościuszko's accounts, his confessions which Paszkowski listened to in Berville in 1801. Kościuszko's conviction that he would be victorious at Maciejowice was even to some extent justified - first, it was he who forced the Russians to this battle, and not they him; secondly, it would be much more convenient for Fersen to fight a decisive battle somewhere closer to Warsaw, and not right after crossing the Vistula; finally thirdly, having taken Maciejowice, Kościuszko found himself in a much better position - Polish troops attacked - or at least could attack - from a dry plateau, while Russian troops were deployed on marshy meadows and, in order to attack the Polish positions between the Castle of Maciejowice and Oronne, they had to pass through marshland called Błoto Dużylas; and if they started to retreat, they would be pushed to the Vistula and suffer a terrible defeat. If the Russians had fewer cannons and the Poles more, Kościuszko could be quite sure of victory. It is no wonder then that after the first two or three hours of the battle - and even when the left flank of the Polish troops was retreating, unable to cope with the charges of Denisov's cavalry - Polish commanders were convinced that they were winning.

"The Chief is sure - wrote Paszkowski - that the longer the battle lasted, the closer Poniński and victory were, he instilled this certainty into his entire army". The course of the first hours of the battle was similarly assessed by Julian Ursyn Niemcewicz, who devoted a beautiful chapter to the Maciejowice battle in his memoir work entitled *Notes sur ma captivité à Saint-Pétersbourg* (*Notes on my captivity in Saint Petersburg*). Recalling the conversations of Polish officers that took place on the eve of the battle, on October 9, in the Maciejowice Palace ("*c'était la veille du plus malheureux jour de ma vie*" [it was the eve of the most unhappy day of my life]), Niemcewicz wrote (I translate from French): "We talked about how strong our position is, about the difficulties the enemy will have, almost about the impossibility (*de l'impossibilité presque*) of attacking us". The next day, October 10, began very promisingly, according to the adjutant-poet. "We were in a dry and elevated area, the Russians were moving through the marshes, where people were getting stuck and cannons getting stuck at every turn. For almost three hours we had a decisive advantage (*un avantage décidé*), to such an extent that General Sierakowski, whose troops were deployed exactly opposite of the enemy and in front of the house of bricks (*la maison de briques* - this was what Niemcewicz called the Maciejowice Castle), he came to tell us that in his opinion the Russians would give up on the attack and would withdraw". Sierakowski (according to one of the many accounts of the battle) was then supposed to tell Kościuszko: "It seems that the Muscovites are preparing to retreat". After about the next three hours it became clear that these were illusions - and everything turned around tragically. Around noon - *"vers midi"*, according to Niemcewicz - the Polish artillery ran out of ammunition and Kościuszko's cannons fell silent. It then turned out that the Russians have many more soldiers, and above all many more cannons. In addition, the Russian cannons were of a much larger caliber and could fire at the battlefield from a much greater distance. "Their enormous bombs - wrote Niemcewicz – were breaking through the undergrowth towards us, breaking tree branches and their tops with a monstrous thud and falling among our soldiers".

The result of the battle was ultimately decided by the artillery - the caliber of the cannons was decisive, as the Russians could wait for the effects of the fire from their heavy guns. Poniński's fatal delay (as was later believed and as Kościuszko believed until the end of his life - his treacherous procrastination and lingering) obviously had some influence on how the events unfolded, but if Poniński had come on time and his troops supported – as they were supposed to - the Polish left flank, then the right flank would still probably not withstand the fire of the Russian artillery. When the Russian cannons broke the ranks of the Polish infantry, Fersen's jägers attacked with bayonets and then - as Niemcewicz wrote - a chaotic retreat began, *"la déroute générale de notre armée"* (*the general rout of our army*), and during the retreat there was a terrible slaughter - *"la boucherie commença"* (*the butchery began*). Apparently, the Siberian grenadiers who captured the castle hill were finishing off the wounded Poles (these were soldiers from the regiment under the command of Działyński, those who, five months earlier, on April 17, went to the attack by the Holy Cross Church and the Saxon Forge) - so these grenadiers, when they captured the courtyard of the Maciejowice Castle, were finishing off the Działyńczyk's there, shouting: *Pomnitie Warszawu? Eto za Warszawu!* (*Remember Warsaw? This is for Warsaw!*) - As Tadeusz Korzon wrote years later, the Działyńczyk battalions "fell to the last man, and the line of their pink revers and yellow shoulder marks on the battlefield showed that they did not give way". Niemcewicz, wounded in his hand, could have escaped from the battlefield, but he was a little late and was surrounded by Cossacks who took him prisoner. Some Russian officer stripped him of his uniform, took his watch and money pouch, and dressed him in a uniform torn off a slain Polish soldier. Fortunately, somewhere nearby was another, higher-ranking officer, who realized that he was dealing with Kościuszko's adjutant, and led the poet through the battlefield to the brick Castle, *la maison de briques*, where the Russian command was already residing. We are provided this walk among the corpses by the unusual, though only a few sentences long, description of the battlefield in *Notes sur ma captivité*. As we will see in a moment, Niemcewicz's description is not very specific and there are few details, or actually there are no details at all - if the poet had given at least a little more of them, we would certainly be very grateful for them, because thanks to this we would see the battlefield at Maciejowice a bit better.

Though the description, conceived as vague, is exactly how it should be, and Niemcewicz, leaving out the details, knew exactly what he was doing. If there were a bit more of these details, if the poet's eyesight brought out from the Maciejowice battlefield what was clearly visible, picturesque, and detailed there, what smelled and stuck to shoes there, then these details would hide the wonderful pathos of this description, worthy of Greek or Roman historians. The deep meaning of the description that is, precisely what the author of *Notes sur ma captivité* wanted, would be deformed - by the details. Since Niemcewicz wanted to turn our gaze towards Greek and Roman battles, Greek and Roman warriors, he did not need details. This is just a few sentences - but these few sentences perfectly illustrate our eighteenth-century conviction that the Poles are something like the Greeks or Romans of Northeast Europe; that they fight like the Romans and remain Romans after death. One can therefore conclude from Niemcewicz's description (it will be entirely justified - even if something like this did not occur to the author of *Notes sur ma captivité*) that near Maciejowice, in the swamps there, in Błoto Dużylas, Poles - Romans fought with barbarians - on the edge, on the last patch of their falling Roman empire. I do not know if I will manage to capture in the Polish translation what Niemcewicz meant - this exalted Roman meaning of the Polish battlefield. "We traversed the entire battlefield once more. The ground was covered with naked corpses, which were already stripped of uniforms and underwear. There was something great about this excruciating spectacle - this greatness was even in its monstrosity. All those naked soldiers, most of whom were six feet tall, stretched out on the ground, with their breasts pierced with bayonets, those veiny limbs covered in blood that had long since congealed, that despair or horror that still showed on their faces bruised and frozen by death, all of this, but above all the thought that these brave people died for their Fatherland, defending it with their bodies, this all filled my soul with deep and painful feelings, ones that will never fade away". Perhaps instead of faces made still or frozen by death ("glacés par la mort") there should be faces covered with the ice of death, instead of veins covered with congealed blood (difficult to translate *"membres nerveux couverts d'un sang déjà figé"*) nerves and veins filled with curdled blood.

Niemcewicz learned about what happened to Kościuszko only when that Russian officer, who had taken pity on him, brought him to Fersen's headquarters. The Russians had already settled in the Maciejowice Castle - the portraits of the Zamoyski's (the last owners of Maciejowice) were cut with sabers and their eyes were pierced with bayonets. We learn from *Notes sur ma captivité* that the Chief was not brought there from the battlefield until evening, somewhere between four and five in the afternoon. Kościuszko was half-alive, *"à demi mort"*, and was lying on a stretcher hastily made of branches, *"sur un brancard fait à la hâte"*. "The blood - wrote Niemcewicz - which covered his body and head, contrasted in a terrible way with the bruised pallor of his face. He had a large wound resulting from a saber cut on the head and three pike strikes in the back, above the kidneys". Niemcewicz initially assessed these wounds, seeing that the Chief "is barely breathing", as very serious. The next morning, when Kościuszko regained consciousness, the poet acknowledged however, that his commander is not in the worst condition - much better, at any rate, than might have been expected from those horrible wounds. "I soon found out with joy that he was not as seriously injured as I had initially believed". The account from *Notes sur ma captivité* differs slightly from that in another memoirist work by Niemcewicz, namely, *Pamiętniki czasów moich* (*Memoirs of My Times*). In *Memoirs* there is mention of only two wounds inflicted with a Cossack pike (or pikes) - "he suffered a deep cut on the head and two wounds from a pike above his hips". Of these three or four wounds of Kościuszko's (probably three, because other accounts, like *Memoirs of My Times*, speak of two stabs with a pike), the most dangerous was the one caused by a saber cut on the head. According to the notes that the Russian command allowed, the next day after the battle on October 11, Kościuszko's adjutant Stanisław Fiszer (later Major General) to send to Warsaw (Fiszer's notes were found years later and published in 1911 by Szymon Askenazy), the wound was very deep, for the blade of the saber damaged the skull.

"The Chief - Fiszer wrote to General Zajączek – was severely cut in the head, such that the bone was weakened". According to some accounts - perhaps a little exaggerated - the saber cut was so deep that it exposed the brain. This wound caused not only unconsciousness but also a temporary loss of speech. Kościuszko fell into a kind of lethargy for the whole day, and it was not until the next day after the battle that he regained his speech. According to Niemcewicz, he was behaving that day like a man emerging from lethargy - *"comme un homme qui sorte d'une profonde létargie"*. "Just yesterday - as Fiszer reported to General Zajączek in the next note (of October 12) - he began to speak again". We can find some interesting information about the saber blow that damaged (or maybe even cut through) Kościuszko's skull in *The History of the First Polish Chief*. Paszkowski claimed there that the wound left by the saber strike, poorly treated, had permanent effects in the form of severe headaches. "The deep wound [...] in the head, barely treated in Maciejowice, neglected on the way, too carelessly treated in St. Petersburg, constantly caused him great pains, for which the only relief he found for himself was in squeezing his head tightly with a wide ribbon". This information seems to be confirmed by lithographs showing Kościuszko in the last years of his life. On some of them we see the Chief with his head tied (or rather wrapped) in a black or white scarf. Also on one of the numerous lithographs that show Tsar Paul, freeing Kościuszko from St. Petersburg captivity, the head of the Chief is wrapped in something - maybe a scarf, maybe a bandage, maybe (as it was then called) lint, or charpie. The second interesting information, given in Paszkowski's *History*, concerns this lethargy of Kościuszko's, *"une profonde létargie"*, which Niemcewicz mentioned in *Notes sur ma captivité*. Lethargy, but also something that undoubtedly must have been the result of damage to the skull - perhaps a temporary, or perhaps a permanent weakening or even loss of memory. "He himself - wrote Paszkowski - later could never tell when he was wounded and when he supposedly stopped living, but when he opened his eyes for the first time, it seemed to him as if he was waking up from a deep sleep, he did not recognize where he was and among what people; it was only an hour later that he realized that they were not Poles". It was not, of course, that Kościuszko completely did not remember what had happened on the battlefield at Maciejowice. That his memory, after the saber strike - memory cut by a saber - had completely and forever erased everything that had happened just before this blow. In reporting these events in *History*, Paszkowski was with all certainty basing this on what he had learned from Kościuszko in Berville, and thus - to put it differently - on what Kościuszko remembered.

However, it can be seen from this account that Kościuszko remembered a little inaccurately, only in some general outline and probably not in sequence. When the 2nd Wielkopolska National Cavalry Brigade, commanded by Brigadier Paweł Biernacki, could not withstand the impact of the Russian cavalry and began to flee towards Maciejowice, "trying - Paszkowski wrote - to immediately turn this cavalry and carry it to the enemy flank, the Chief goes by himself, and, jumping across a ditch he falls with the horse; Cossacks get him and wound him with pikes, a carabinier runs up after them and deprives him of his senses with a cut to the head. [...] The Muscovite general Tolstoy, who had known Kościuszko in Warsaw in the past, recognized him exposed and soaked with blood, when after the battle, walking across the field, he saw a crowd of soldiers staring at him to see if it really was him.

So various things were done to see if he was still alive, until he opened his mouth at the frightening screaming in his ear. Tolstoy ordered him to be covered and called a doctor". This is more or less precisely the order of events that all biographies of Kościuszko follow - the horse, jumping over the ditch, falls over, Kościuszko falls off his horse, and then Cossacks with pikes appear, and a little later a carabinier with a saber; the carabinier strikes a blow and at that moment Kościuszko loses consciousness - he cannot remember anything else. If we accept that this is the sequence remembered by Kościuszko, then it must be said that it is a sequence not well remembered - which is confirmed by the earlier information given by Paszkowski: "later could never tell when he was wounded and when he supposedly stopped living". Somewhere between these events one has to fit one more event (also remembered by Kościuszko) and it can be seen immediately that it cannot fit anywhere, because nowhere is there enough space for it - neither between the turning of the horse towards Biernacki's cavalry and jumping over the ditch, nor between jumping over the ditch and the fall, nor between the fall and the appearance of the carabinier with a saber. The sequence of events on the Maciejowice battlefield - when the fate of the Poles was being decided there in the last hour of the battle - had to thus be a bit different, maybe even completely different; however, there is no sensible possibility to somehow change this order, which is in Paszkowski's book, and arrange the events in a slightly different order.

This event which I am talking about - it is, in my opinion, the most important event of that fateful day at Maciejowice - it would be easiest to fit (if we had followed Paszkowski's order despite everything) between the fall of the horse and the appearance of the Cossacks and the carabinier; the Cossacks and the carabinier would, however, in this case have to be some distance from Kościuszko; at least at a distance of some 100 or 200, even 300 meters. So let's say that it was like that (or it could have been) - Kościuszko is lying in a ditch or next to a ditch after the fall from his horse, the carabinier and the Cossacks, seeing that someone has fallen off his horse and is lying (so now he can be robbed and killed), run towards his direction. Kościuszko told only one person about what happened then (maybe precisely then), and then to no one else - Julian Ursyn Niemcewicz. The account of this event - between the fall from the horse and the blow from a carabinier's saber - fits into one sentence. Perhaps Kościuszko's memory, slashed by the sword blow, had failed him, and he therefore remembered the event very vaguely, only in some general outline. Or perhaps Niemcewicz - having heard Kościuszko's account - became frightened (that he was learning something that he did not want to know about) and repeated what he heard as briefly and as quickly as possible, preferring not to deal with the matter any closer. Though he did, because he knew it was the memoirists duty to repeat such things. Niemcewicz learned about this event, which was later told in one sentence, on December 10, 1796. It was the day when Kościuszko and Niemcewicz, freed by Tsar Paul, left St. Petersburg. They were riding in a large carriage, which the Russian Tsar had gifted to Kościuszko. Immediately after leaving the city, when the carriage passed the St. Petersburg tollhouses, the Chief realized that his favorite Chinese banyan was missing - someone, before or at the time of departure, perhaps in the Peter and Paul Fortress or while packing the luggage into the carriage, had probably stolen it.

The Chinese banyan also appears in the Maciejowice notes from Fiszer to Zajączek from October 1794 - Kościuszko wanted to take it with him on his way to captivity, and it was delivered from Warsaw to Maciejowice. Perhaps it was because the Chinese banyan, stolen on the threshold of freedom, was associated with Maciejowice (but this is only my guess) that Kościuszko remembered the Maciejowice Battle in the carriage and told Niemcewicz about the event that took place on the battlefield. This was a confession, as Niemcewicz later put it - "he made two confessions to me, which I will put here". The memoir, or rather a fragment of the memoir in which Niemcewicz wrote down this confession, in just one sentence, was published by the *Przegląd Poznański* (*Poznań Overview*) in 1858 under the title "Podróż Juliana Ursyna Niemcewicza z Petersburga do Ameryki w r. 1796; z francuskiego oryginału na język polski przełożona" ("Julian Ursyn Niemcewicz's Journey from Petersburg to America in 1796; translated from the original French into Polish"). Later, this memoirist fragment was completely forgotten, and it was not until 1921 that it was reprinted by Józef Tretiak in his book *Finis Poloniae*. The carriage was going towards the border with Sweden, along the road leading from Petersburg to Vyborg, "we saw each other - wrote Niemcewicz - for the first time without witnesses". It was precisely then that, a bit desperate (or perhaps angry) because of the loss of his Chinese banyan, Kościuszko confessed to Niemcewicz that on the battlefield at Maciejowice, "when everything was lost", he decided to commit suicide - and he put his intention into action. Let's take a closer look at this scene - one of the most beautiful in our national history. Kościuszko's horse is trying to get up and get out of the ditch into which it fell. We see the horse on its knees on the edge of the ditch. Around, scattered, on the marshy meadow, lie the naked bodies of Polish soldiers, the ones that Niemcewicz saw there - bruised, stabbed with bayonets, stripped of uniforms and underwear. A little further, actually in the background, three ladies in pink cloaks walk across the battlefield towards *la maison de brique*, deftly jumping over the naked corpses - these are three Russian women, the wife and two daughters of General Khrushchov. The carabinier with the saber raised up and the two Cossacks with pikes are getting closer, their faces can already be seen. "When the Cossacks were about to, about to catch him, he put a pistol in his mouth and pulled the trigger, but the pistol did not fire".

Chapter 33.
THE AEROSTATIC MACHINE – HUMANITY WAS SLOWLY RISING UPWARDS

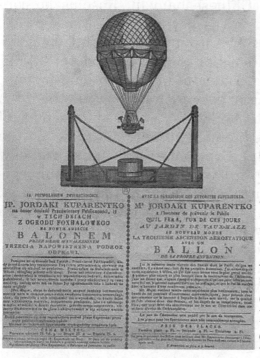

Stanisław Trembecki dealt with the problem of aerostatic machines - how to control them in order to rise up without problems, and then, also without problems, to move in the air from place to place - for the second time in 1795, when, after the fall of the Uprising, together with the entire court of Stanisław August (or rather - with some miserable remnants of that court), he found himself in Grodno. This can be called, to use our language, internment. An interned king, an interned poet - the Grodno castle was a place of internment. It is no wonder then that it was in the Grodno castle that Trembecki began to think about a way that would allow him to rise into the air and fly away, from the place of internment, into some other, undefined, air space. The flight of an aerostatic machine touched his imagination for the first time, as we know, several years earlier, in May 1789, when, soon after Blanchard's first flight in Warsaw, he wrote his famous ode entitled *Balon (Balloon)*, which was rightly considered the most beautiful Polish poem of that era. Stanisław Tomkowicz, to whom we owe the information about Trembecki's experiments in the field of aerostatics in Grodno and about his extraordinary Grodno invention, later claimed in his treatise on this invention that *Balloon* was written "under artificial inspiration" - and one can even agree to this; one only has to add, claiming something like this, that masterpieces also arise, or at least can be created from such strange inspiration - and precisely *Balloon* is completely sufficient proof of this. Later, attempts were made (in the 1960s) to take *Balloon* away from Trembecki and assign it to another poet, Adam Naruszewicz, but I do not accept this nonsensical (and completely unjustified) attribution. Naruszewicz is separated from Trembecki by a great abyss, which is called the lack of talent - Trembecki, it is not known why, had talent, and Naruszewicz, it is also not known why, did not.

That's the way it is with poetry - one can write *Balloon*, the other cannot, and there is no advice for this, no efforts of literary historians (if they wanted to change something in this matter) will help. Besides, there is no reason to deal with the matter of *Balloon's* authorship, as it has been settled long ago (by common sense), so it is better if we talk about Trembecki's Grodno invention. Thanks to this invention, on which the poet worked during the winter and spring of 1795, a great problem was to be solved, which plagued European scholars at that time - namely the problem of controlling aerostatic machines: how to make balloons, or aerostats, as well as other airborne vehicles invented at that time (ones which are a bit fantastic), to fly not where the wind wants, but where humans want; and if something like that - putting aerial vehicles under the will of man - is even possible. Blanchard, who flew over Warsaw and over the Vistula, pushed by the wind from the south (or from the south-west), did not know such a way, which would make it possible to control the flight of aerostatic machines, and the first air sailors, the Montgolfier brothers, did not know it either. What did Trembecki's invention entail? We learn about it from several letters the poet wrote in Grodno to Stanisław August. They have survived only in fragments (copied in 1882 by Stanisław Tomkowicz from the later lost portfolio *Litteraria*, which was in the Popiel's collection in Kraków) and are not dated, but they undoubtedly come from the first half of 1795, because the last one is the dated by the hand of the king "28 Juni 1795". So this was occurring (exactly) on the first anniversary of the great hangings - but of course that doesn't mean anything. "When there was a conversation about balloons yesterday - says the first of the preserved fragments (dated by the publishers of Trembecki's correspondence as January 1795) - I have thought about it and it seems to me that I could invent something that could give them direction". Further on in this fragment, Trembecki asked the king "to give orders to the local Dominicans to make a balloon as small as a playing ball, on which one could conduct experiments in YRH's room"[1]. While the next sentence goes like this: "later it will be easy to take a proportion from less to more".

It can be concluded from this that the poet, after conducting experiments in the royal study with a small balloon made by the Dominicans, intended to construct a larger balloon in Grodno, one in which one could fly somewhere. He may even have constructed such a balloon, with the help of the Dominicans, in the courtyard of the Grodno castle or in the meadows by the Neman near the royal residence - but there is not any information about this. The two remaining fragments, which were copied from this letter by Stanisław Tomkowicz (they are really only fragments of sentences), allow us to more or less understand what the invention, which was to enable one to control a balloon, looked like. "[...] This should not miss any measurement, as long as the proportion of the plate with the balloon and the magnet with iron was taken correctly as well as their mutual distance [...]". "[...] it would be even better if instead of with a pole the flyer, holding the magnet at the end of a rod, directed the balloon *per attractionem*, bringing it closer or farther away as needed [...]". Trembecki's magnet, placed on a pole protruding from the balloon or on a rod, was supposed to attract the plate or iron that would be connected to the balloon. While the pole or rod would be moved in the balloon boat by the flyer - that is, an aviator, pilot, navigator. To this first letter about the balloon, the poet attached a piece of paper with a drawing of his idea - a balloon, plate, pole, magnet, and ways of connecting these elements. The page was lost with the entire *Litteraria* portfolio and now we only have a description of the drawing, made in 1882 by Stanisław Tomkowicz. "The page added to the letter contains a balloon, hastily and unskillfully drawn by the author, with a large plate of iron attached to the front. Opposite it, at the

---

[1]YRH: Your Royal Highness

end of the rod, placed diagonally upwards and moving in the mount, there is a magnet. So as the flyer, that is the aeronaut sitting in the boat under the balloon, with the assistance of an appropriate mechanism to direct the pole to the right or to the left, the balloon will have to turn with the impulse given to the iron plate". Tomkowicz rightly noticed that our great poet, by placing on a pole attached to a balloon a magnet that moved the balloon, invented at the same time the *perpetuum mobile*. Perhaps this was the first Polish *perpetuum mobile*, perhaps Trembecki was the first Polish poet, even the first Pole to find himself at the source of perpetual motion.

"Having put a wagon with a magnet at the front on iron rails - wrote Tomkowicz - having the shape of a closed circle, one would only have to add grease to the wheels, so that the vehicle would never stop circling". With the balloon it would be similar - if the invention could be implemented, of course. The magnet on the pole would attract the iron plate connected to the balloon, this would pull the balloon with the boat and the navigator (flyer) holding the pole, and in this miraculous way the balloon would be constantly pushed or rather constantly pulled, pulled forward by the magnetic energy emanating from its devices – so it could go (together with Trembecki and his king) on a journey leading straight into infinity, and still further, through all infinity, somewhere on the other side, where there is nothing left. Stanisław Trembecki's endless journey - back and forth around nothingness. It seems that the author of *Balloon*, maybe a bit vaguely, but somehow, understood that what he invented was precisely something like a *perpetuum mobile* - and that by placing the magnet on a pole and the pole in the hands of a navigator-flyer, he arrived in this way to the source of eternal and ever-renewing movement. In the next letter (also in this case we only know a fragment of it), he assured the king once again that the experiment in the room with a balloon the size of a ball "should not miss", and it should not miss because the method invented by him of controlling balloons and other machines flying in the skies has the same basis, which could be called cosmic or even metaphysical. Of course Trembecki (a reckless man, libertine, card player, and profligate) did not believe in any metaphysical creations, but he was probably convinced that he had discovered (perhaps a little by chance) a spring or a lever that moves not only balloons or other flying machines - but the entire universe, at least our entire planetary system. "The entire *systhema planetarum* - we read in this letter, dated the beginning of February 1795 - is built on such a basis". The Grodno magnet on a rod would thus be an image of the divine cause of all movement, and from the libertine and profligate point of view - if not divine, then at least the first and eternal. This would be something like a model of such an age-old cosmic device. For Trembecki, and it seems for Stanisław August also, it was obvious that the magnetic invention, representing a higher order, perhaps some higher Force, cosmic or metaphysical, would also have some temporary significance, because it would influence, at least it would be able to when it is used, influence the history of Europe - if only the English understand its consequences and want to use it in the war they were waging then with the French.

In the same letter, which mentions the magnetic principle on which the *systhema planetarum* is based, we also read: "I have no doubt that in London an experiment would be conducted in 24 hours, and in a week, it could be used to the detriment or advantage of the human race". What, according to the poet, benefit the English would have from a magnet on a pole or a rod, and from balloons controlled in this way, is stated in the next letter (also known only in a small fragment). It is worth noting that Trembecki formulated a visual project of using zeppelins in combat operations - a project that was realized during the First World War, almost one hundred and twenty years later. "[...] My fast imagination is already presenting before me a fleet leaving Torbay, among which numerous balloons circulating in the air throw *les feux d'artifice* on invading ships, destroy and disperse them, and this great victory, cause by important consequences, England owes to YRH. [...] The fleets may fight in April, an experiment should be done as soon as possible, so that there would be time for improvement". Torbay is a bay in Devonshire County at the southern end of the English Channel. The English fleet would owe its victory over the French fleet to Stanisław August, because Trembecki wanted (renouncing copyright) that the king should come out as the inventor and present the magnet on the pole to the world as his own work. In this letter (dated February) we also have proof that the poet, although his thoughts circled around balloons and floating in the skies, was very well aware of the total consequences of his invention - that is, he understood that it could be used not only in air warfare and not only for controlling balloons (or other aerostatic machines), but also in other situations and environments, on the water, in naval warfare, maybe even everywhere.

"For speed, if there will be a balloon, by an order of YRH to make a wooden booth in the same proportions, which, if according to your will it will go on standing water in the study, then the balloon will follow the same law in the air". What does Stanisław August say to this? It is unknown whether he conducted an experiment with a magnet and a wooden booth on still water, but he decided to present his poet's invention to scholars from the Berlin Academy of Sciences. The magnetic source of movement project was sent from Grodno to Berlin as an anonymous work. According to Jan Kott, the publisher of Trembecki's correspondence, the Berlin academics probably figured out that the letter they had received was written by Stanisław August, and that is precisely why they answered it quickly and politely. However, there is no proof that the Polish king was recognized in Berlin as the inventor of the magnet on a pole. Only the answer that the Berlin academics sent to the anonymous inventor is known. It says that the invention was discussed at a session of the Berlin Academy of Sciences on March 9, 1795. "The gentlemen academics, having read the anonymous project of freely directing the forward motion of aerostatic balloons by means of a large magnet, judged that even if a slight oscillation about its own axis resulted (which is also very doubtful according to the device proposed by anonymous), then in any case the forward motion of the balloon, according to the direction of the wind, would not be affected in the slightest, since the device to be designed provides no gain of any secondary force at all capable of changing the direction of motion given by the wind". As one can see, our poet's invention was disqualified, but it is worth noting that the Berlin academics treated the anonymous person from Grodno quite understandably - they could have after all (and one should rather expect something like this) ridiculed or laughed at him. Or they could have ignored him, not replying to the letter at all. Perhaps there is something about the *perpetuum mobile* invention that tells to take it seriously. The one that knows how a planetary system works (where is the cause that sets it in motion) also deserves to be taken seriously - even if he is tragically or ridiculously wrong. Trembecki was quite outraged by this disqualification from Berlin, and he did not think to accept the sentence of the Prussian professors - he simply recognized that they were some scoundrels.

"The academic answer (which YRH has graciously let me know) is not *ad rem*. For this was not at all a question of what was stronger, a whirlwind, or a piece of magnet. [...] From this answer I only learn that either Those giving it do not know how to make a balloon, or They avoid the cost of making it without the immediate reward; since I know well that the northern academies are most often composed of misers and greedy people who are more interested in one certain coin than in the discovery of a new truth". After accusing the Berlin academics of greed, Trembecki continued to ask his fundamental questions - and urged the king to find some other more decent scholars to answer them. "Supposedly only two paths lead to wisdom: doubt and curiosity. Doubt tells you not to decide without first definitely convincing oneself, and curiosity advises you to look for this belief through experience. [...] The question is thus this, and not any other [...]: 1) Can direction be given to a balloon according to the marked figure? 2) What should be the proportion of the magnet to the weight of the balloon?" This story ends with these questions, and nothing else is known, because Trembecki's further letters on this matter (if he dealt with it later together with his king) are unknown. Although the Grodno *perpetuum mobile* did not gain the recognition of scholars and the author of *Balloon* probably did not manage to convince the king for further experiments - others, those with more luck, were more successful a little later and with various aerostatic machines, including aerostat-balloons, soon began to obey human will. Humanity was slowly rising upwards - the era of zeppelins and airplanes was approaching, followed by the era we are living in right now - the era of telecommunication sputniks, space probes, and moon shuttles. The description of the last seconds of the American space shuttle, which under the name Challenger took off from the coast of Florida in 1986 and exploded 15 kilometers above the Earth - its flight, from take-off to catastrophe, lasted exactly 73 seconds, and each of these seconds was then dismantled by NASA scientists into fragments and carefully analyzed – so the description of these 73 seconds says that the seven astronauts (five men and two women), who were to be torn to pieces after 73 seconds and rise, each piece separately, into space, realized that the something bad was happening only at the last second.

This was the last second of the flight and the last second of their lives. Perhaps not all of them realized, perhaps out of the seven only the pilot figured out, and the others did not even know that they were about to die - falling apart in cosmic space into small, smaller pieces. In the 73rd second. the machine was flying at Mach 1.5 (which is 1.5 times faster than sound would be transmitted under identical conditions), in these 73 seconds the fuel tanks broke apart, a burning chamber with liquid hydrogen stuck a chamber with oxygen and an explosion occurred. Then the pilot, still going up, realized what was happening and shouted, "Oh boy!"

ABOUT THE AUTHOR

Jarosław Marek Rymkiewicz (1935 – 2022) was a Polish poet, essayist, dramatist and literary critic who was born and raised in Warsaw, Poland.

As a poet, he was influenced by the traditions of classicism and the baroque. He has received multiple prizes for his novels, essays, and translations, including the Kościelski Prize (1967), S. Vincenz Prize (1985), and Polish PEN Club Prize. His volume of poetry *Zachód słońca w Milanówku* won the prestigious Nike Award in 2003.

Although Rymkiewicz was primarily a poet, he is better known as the author of two influential novels that contributed to the two most important debates of the 1980s: that involving martial law (1981) and Polish-Jewish relations. His novel *Rozmowy polskie latem, 1983* (Polish Conversations in Summer 1983) discusses the meaning of being Polish and the preoccupation with achieving independence. Rymkiewicz's second novel, entitled *Umschlagplatz* (1988), had a greater impact.

As an essayist, Rymkiewicz concentrated on Polish history (the partition period, World War II).

BOOKS, ESSAYS AND ARTICLES CITED

Akty powstania Kosciuszki T. 1-2. Wydali Szymon Askenazy i Wlodzimierz Dzwonkowski. Krakow 1918.

Akty powstania Kosciusz i. T. 3. Wydali Wlodzimierz Dzwonkowski, Emil Kipa, Rocb Morcinek. Wroclaw 1955.

Szymon Askenazy, *Glos z Maciejowic.* "Tygodnik Ilustro-wany" 1911, nr 25.

Andrzej Bankowski, *Etyniologiczny slownik języka polskiego.* T. 1-2. Warszawa 2000.

Ludwig Buchholtz, *Powstanie kosciuszkowskiew swietle korespondencji posla pruskiego w Warszawie. Listy Ludwiga Buchholtza do Fryderyka Wilhelma II (styczen-czerwiec 1794r.).* Z rękopisu przelozyl, wstępem i przypisami opatrzyl Henryk Kocoj. Warszawa 1883.

Chateaubriand, *Memoires d'Outre-Tombe.* Edition nouvelle etablie d'apres l'edition originale [...] par Maurice Levaillant et Georges Mouhmer. Paris 1958.

[Ludwik Cieszkowski], *Pamiętnik anegdotycznyz czasów Stanislawa Augusta.* Z rękopismu wydany przez Jozefa Ignacego Kraszewskiego. Poznan 1867.

Adam Czartoryski, *Zywot J.U. Niemcewicza.* Berlin 1860.

Diariusz króla Stanislawa Augusta podczas powstania w Warszawie 1794 roku. "Rocznik Towarzystwa HistorycznoLiterackiego w Paryzu. Rok 1866". Paryz 1867.

Jan Drozdowski, *Pamiętniki sztabslekarza pulku Dziatyńskich.* Ateneum" 1883, t. 3.

Wlodzimierz Dzwonkowski, *Przyjaciel ludzkosci. Warszawa wiosną 1794 r. Listy prezydenta Zakrzewskiego do Tadeusza Kosciuszki.* Warszawa 1912.

Lew Engelhardt, *Pamiętniki.* Poznan 1873.

Franciszek Giedroyc, *Warunki higieniczne Warszawy w wieku XVIII. Ulice i domy.* Warszawa 1912.

Zbigniew Goralski, *Stanislaw August w insurekcji kosciuszkowskiej.* Warszawa 1988.

Franciszek Salezy Jezierski, *Ktos piszący z Warszawy dnia 11 lutego 1790 r. [oraz] Niektore wyrazy porządkiem abecadla zebrane i stosownymi do rzeczy uwagami objasnione. W: Wybór pism.* Opracowal Zdzislaw Skwarczynski. Wstępem poprzedzil Jerzy Ziomek. Warszawa 1952.

Karol Kaczkowski, *Wspomnienia z papier6w pozostalych po [...] general sztablekarzu wojsk polskich.* Ulozyl Tadeusz Oksza Orzechowski. T. 1. Lwow 1876.

Walerian Kalinka, *Ostatnie lata panowania Stanislawa Augusta. Dokumenta do historii drugiego i trzeciego podzialu.* T. 1-2. Poznan 1868.

Franciszek Karpinski, *Historia mego wieku i ludzi, z którymi zylem*. Opracowal Roman Sobol. Warszawa 1987.

Jan Kilinski, *Pamiętniki*. Opracowal Stanislaw Herbst. Warszawa 1958.

Jędrzej Kitowicz, *Pamiętniki czyli Historia polska*. Tekst opracowala i wst pem poprzedzila Przemyslawa Matuszewska. Komentarz Zofii Lewinowny. Warszawa 1971.

Hugo Kollqtaj, *Memorial o przygotowaniach do powstania r. 1794, napisany dla Tomasza Wawrzeckiego*. W: Waclaw Tokarz, *Ostatnie lata Hugona Kollqtaja. (1794-1812)*. T. 2. Krakow 1905.

[Hugo Kollqtaj], *Uwagi nad terainiejszym polozeniem tej części ziemi polskiej, którą od czasu traktatu tylzyckiego zaczto zwac Księstwem Warszawskim*. Lipsk 1808.

Korespondencja Joachima Lelewela z Karolem Sienkiewiczem. "Rocznik Towarzystwa Historyczno-Literackiego w Paryzu. Rok 1870-1872". Poznan 1872.

Korespondencja Króla z Naczelnikiem podczas powstania 1794 r. Podal do druku Jan Riabinin. "Przeglqd Historyczny" 1914, z. 3.

Tadeusz Korzon, *Wewnętrzne dzieje Polski za Stanislawa Augusta (1764-1794)*. Badania historyczne ze stanowiska ekonomicznego i administracyjnego. Wyd. 2. T. 1-6. Krakow 1897-1898.

Nikolaj Kostomarow, *Posliednije gody Rieczi-Pospolitoj. Istoriczeskaja monografija*. Wtoroje izdanije. S.-Peterburg 1870.

Jozef Krasinski, *Pamiętniki*. Skrocone przez Franciszka Reuttowicza. Poznan 1877.'

Jozef Ignacy Kraszewski, *Polska w czasie trzech rozbiorów. 1772-1799. Studia do historii ducha i obyczaju. T. 3. 1791-1799.* Warszawa 1903.

Tadeusz Kupczynski, *Krakow w powstaniu kosciuszkowskim*. Krakow 1912.

La guillotine dans la Revolution. Texte de Daniel Arasse, documentation de Valerie Rousseau-Lagarde. Musee de la Revolution Frarnçaise. Chateau de Vizille 1987.

Boguslaw Lesnodorski, *Polscy jakobini. Karla z dziejów insurekcji 1794 roku*. Warszawa 1960.

Filip Lichocki, *Pamiętnik prezydenta miasta Krakowa z roku 1794*. Poznan 1862.

Xawery Liske, *Cudzoziemcy w Polsce*. Lwow 1876.

[Aleksander Linowski], *List do przyjaciela odkrywajqcy wszystkie czynnosci Kollqtaja w ciqgu Insurekcji. Pisany roku 1795*. Wyd. 3. Wroclaw 1846.

Antoni Magier, *Estetyka miasta stolecznego Warszawy*. Opracowanie tekstu, przedmowa, komentarz, indeksy Hanna Szwankowska. Komentarz teatralny Eugeniusz Szwankowski. Komentarz historyczno-literacki Juliusz Wiktor Gomulic-' ki. Wroclaw 1963.

Henryk Moscicki, *General Jasinski i powstanie kosciuszkowskie*. Warszawa 1917.

Julian Ursyn Niemcewicz, Dziennik mojej podrózy. W: Jozef Tretiak, Finis Poloniae! Historia legendy maciejowickiej ijej rozwiązanie. Krakow 1921.

Julien Ursin Niemcewicz, Notes sur ma captivite a SaintPetersbourg en 1794, 1795 et 1796. Paris 1843.

Julian Ursyn Niemcewicz, Pamiętniki czasów moich. Tekst opracowal i wstępem poprzedzil Jan Dihm. T. 1-2. Warszawa 1957.

Nurty lewicowe w dobie polskich powstan narodowych.1794-1849. Wybór zródel. OpracowaliJ. Kowecki, T. Lepkowski

Z. Mankowski, F. Paprocki, M. Zychowski. Pod redakcją Emanuela Halicza. Wstępem opatrzyl H. Jablonski. Wroclaw 1961.

Jan Duklan Ochocki, Pamiętniki z pozostalych po nim rękopism6w przepisane i wydane przez Józefa Ignacego Kraszewskiego. T. 2. Wilno 1857.

Michal Oginski, Pamiętniki o Polsce i Polakach od r. 1788 az do kofica r. 1815. Przelozone z j zyka francuskiego. T. 1-2. Poznan 1870.

Opis wszystkich palaców, domów, kosciolów, szpitalów i ich posesorów miasta Warszawy dla wygody publicznej wydany w roku 1797. W: Wladyslaw Smolenski, Mieszczafistwo warszawskie w koncu wieku XVIII. Warszawa 1917.

Jan Zb. Pachonski, haslo Dembowski Jan. Polski slownik biograficzny. T. 5. Krakow 1939.

Jan Pachonski i Helena Wereszycka, haslo Konopka Kazimierz. Polski slownik biograficzny. T. 13. Wroclaw 1967.

Franciszek Paszkowski, Dzieje Tadeusza Kosciuszki pierwszego naczelnika Polaków. Krakow 1872.

Jan Jakub Patz, Z okien ambasady saskiej. Warszawa 1794 roku w swietle relacji dyplomatycznych przedstawiciela Saksonii w Polsce. Z rękopisu wydali, przelozyli i przypisami opatrzyli Zofia Libiszowska i Henryk Kocoj. Warszawa 1969.

[Johann Jakob] Pistor, Pamiętniki o rewolucji polskiej z roku 1794. Tlumaczyl Boleslaw Prawdzic Chotomski. Poznan 1860.

Fryderyk Schulz, Podróze Inflantczyka z Rygi do Warszawy i po Polsce w latach 1791-1793. Przelozyl Jozef Ignacy Kraszewski. Z oryginalem sprawdzil, wstępem i przypisami opatrzyl Waclaw Zawadzki. Warszawa 1956.

Johann Gottfried Seume, Kilka wiadomosci o wypadkach w Polsce w roku 1794. W: Polska stanislawowska w oczach cudzoziemców. Opracowal i wstępem poprzedzil Waclaw Zawadzki. Warszawa 1963.

[Jakob Johann Sievers], Drugi rozbiór Polski z Pamiętników Sieversa. Poznan 1865.

Jakob Johann Sievers, Jak doprowadzilem do drugiego rozbioru Polski. Opracowali, wstępem i przypisami opatrzyli Barbara Grochulska i Piotr Ugniewski. Warszawa 1992.

Adam Skalkowski, Z dziejów insurekcji 1794 r. Warszawa 1926.

Wladyslaw Smolenski, Emigracja polska w latach 1795-97. Materialy historyczne. Warszawa 1911.

Wladyslaw Smolenski, *Konfederacja Targowicka*. Krakow 1903.

Wladyslaw Smolenski,. *Kuinica Kollątajowska*. *Studium historyczne*. Z przedmow Zanny Kormanowej. [Wyd. 2]. Warszawa 1949.

Wladyslaw Smolenski, *Mieszczanstwo warszawskie w koncu wieku XVIII*. Warszawa 1917.

Wladyslaw Smolenski, *Ostatni rok Sejmu Wielkiego*. Wyd.2. Krakow 1897.

Franciszek Maksymilian Sobieszczanski, *Rys historyczno-statystyczny wzrostu i stanu miasta Warszawy od najdawniejszych czasów az do 1847 roku*. Tekst opracowal, wstępem i komentarzem opatrzyl Konrad Zawadzki. Warszawa 1974.

Stanislaw August i książę Jozef Poniatowski w swietle wlasnej korespondencji. Wydal Bronislaw Dembinski. Lwow 1904.

Eugeniusz Szwankowski, *Ulice i place Warszawy*. Wyd. 2. Warszawa 1970.

Bronislaw Szwarce, *Warszawa w 1794* r. Krakow 1894.

Samuel Szymkiewicz, *Warszawa na przelomie XVIII i XIX wieku w swietle pomiarów i spisów*. Warszawa 1959.

Tajna korespondencja z Warszawy 1792-1794 do Ignacego Potockiego. *Jan Dembowski i inni*. Opracowali Maria Rymszyna i Andrzej Zahorski. Warszawa 1961.

Waclaw Tokarz, *Deputacja Indagacyjna*. *W: Rozprawy, i szkice*. T. 1. Przejrzal i wst pem opatrzyl Stanislaw Herbst. Warszawa 1959.

Waclaw Tokarz, *Insurekcja warszawska 17 i 18 kwietnia 1794 r.* Warszawa 1950.

Waclaw Tokarz, *Klub jakobinów w Warszawie*. *W: Rozpra wy i szkice*. T. 1. Przejrzal i wst pem opatrzyl Stanislaw Herbst. Warszawa 1959.

Waclaw Tokarz, *Ostatnie lata Hugona Kollątaja*. *(1794-1812)*. T. 1-2. Krakow 1905.

Waclaw Tokarz, *Papiery ambasady rosyjskiej*. *W: Rozpra wy i szkice*. T. 1. Przejrzal i wst pem opatrzyl Stanislaw Herbst. Warszawa 1959.

Waclaw Tokarz, *Warszawa przed wybuchem powstania 17 kwietnia 1794 roku*. Krakow 1911.

Waclaw Tokarz, *Warszawa za rządów Rady Zast pczej Tymczasowej (19/IV-27N 1794)*.*W: Rozprawy i szkice*. T. 1. Przejrzal i wstępem opatrzyl Stanislaw Herbst. Warszawa 1959.

Stanislaw Tomkowicz, *Trembecki i wynalazek balonu*. *W: Z wieku St. Augusta*. T. 1. Krakow 1882.

Stanislaw Trembecki, *Listy*. Opracowali Jan Kott i Roman Kaleta. T. 1-2. Wroclaw 1954.

Stanislaw Trembecki, *Pisma wszystkie*. Wydanie krytyczne. Opracowal Jan Kott. T. 1-2. Warszawa 1953.

Jozef Tretiak, *Finis Poloniae! Historia legendy maciejowickiej i jej rozwiązanie*. Krakow 1921.

Antoni Trębicki, *Opisanie sejmu ekstraordynaryjnego podzialowego roku 1793 w Grodnie. 0 rewolucji roku 1794*. Opracowal i wst(;!pem opatrzyl Jerzy Kowecki. Warszawa 1967.

Tomasz Ulanowski, *Challenger - wyzwanie zakonczone klęską.* "Gazeta Wyborcza" 2006, nr 24.

Leon Wegner, *Hugo Koltqtaj na posiedzeniu rady królew skiej z dnia 23 lipca 1792.* „Roczniki Towarzystwa Przyjaciol Nauk Pozna:6. skiego". T. V. Poznan 1869.

Stanislaw Wodzicki, *Wspomnienia z przeszlosci od roku 1768 do roku 1840.* Krakow 1873.

Karol Wojda, *0 rewolucjipolskiej w roku 1794. Poznan 1867. Mikolaj Wolski, Obrona Stanislawa Augusta.* „Rocznik Towarzystwa Historyczno-Literackiego w Paryzu. Rok 1867". Paryz 1868.

Kazimierz Wladyslaw Wojcicki, *Cmentarz Powqzkowski pod Warszawq.* T. 2. Warszawa 1856.

Jozef Wybicki, *Zycie moje oraz Wspomnienie o Andrzeju i Konstancji Zamoyskich.* Z rękopisow wydal i objasnil Adam Skalkowski. Krakow 1927.

Andrzej Zahorski, *Warszawa w powstaniu kosciuszkowskim.* Warszawa 1985.

Jozef Zajączek, *Pamiętnik albo historia rewolucji czyli powstania roku 1794.* Przekladu Hugona Kollataja. *Histoire de la revolution de Pologne en 1794 par un temoin oculaire.* Poznan 1862.

Jaroslaw Zielinski, *Atlas dawnej architektury ulic i placów Warszawy.* T. 7. Krakowskie Przedmiescie. Warszawa 2001.

Teodor Zychlinski, *Zlota ksi ga szlachty polskiej.* T. 4. Poznan 1882.

NEWSPAPERS QUOTED

"Dziennik Ekonomiczno-Handlowy Zajmuja,cy w Sobie Wiadomosci Ekonomiczne, Targowe, Fabryczne, Transportu Splawnego i Lądowego, Opisanie Miast i Ich Jarmarkow, Kontraktowe na Dobra, Summy i Rozne Produkta Krajowe, a za tym Zajmuja,cy Wiadomosci Calego Handl " 1791.

"Dziennik Handlowy Zawierający w Sobie Wszystkie Okolicznosci, Pisma, Uwagi i Mysli Patriotyczne, do Handlu Sciągające Się!" 1787.

„Gazeta Narodowa Wileńska" 1794.

„Gazeta Obywatelska z Wiadomosci Krajowych i Zagranicznych" („Gazeta Warszawska Patriotyczna") 1794.

„Gazeta Powstania Polski" 1794.

„Gazeta Rza,dowa" 1794.

„Gazeta Warszawska" 1789.

„Gazeta Wolna Warszawska" 1794.

„Korrespondent Narodowy i Zagraniczny" 1794.

„Pamiętnik Historyczno-Polityczno-Ekonomiczny" 1789.

„Pismo Periodyczne Korrespondenta" 1794.

More books from Winged Hussar in association with Poland translation Program

Look for more books from Winged Hussar Publishing, LLC –
E-books, paperbacks and Limited-Edition hardcovers.
The best in history, science fiction and fantasy at:
https://www. wingedhussarpublishing.com
or follow us on Facebook at:
Winged Hussar Publishing LLC
Or on twitter at:
WingHusPubLLC
For information and upcoming publications

Jozef Pilsudski
Hero of Poland

Antoni Lenkiewicz

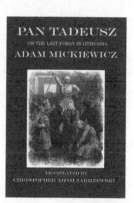

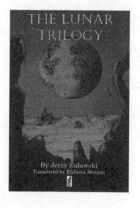

BOOK INSTITUTE

©**POLAND**

This publiction has been supported by the © POLAND translation Program